Dear Reader,

Last month I asked if you'd like to see more humour, romantic suspense or linked books on our list. Well this month I can offer you all three!

I'm thrilled to bring you the final part of Liz Fielding's critically acclaimed and very popular Beaumont Brides trilogy. But, if we're lucky, maybe Melanie's story won't be the end after all . . .

Two stories which can be classified as suspense, but which are very different in style and plot, are offered by Laura Bradley and Jill Sheldon. These authors have won plaudits from critics and readers alike for their earlier *Scarlet* novels.

And finally, those of you who've asked for more books by Natalie Fox will, we're sure, enjoy reading our exciting new author, Talia Lyon, who brings a delightfully humorous flavour to her story of three gals, three guys and the holiday of a lifetime.

As always, I hope you enjoy the books I've chosen for you this month. Let me have your comments and suggestions, won't you and I'll do all I can to bring you more of the kind of books *you* want to read.

Till next month,

Sally Cooper

SALLY COOPER,
Editor-in-Chief – *Scarlet*

About the Author

Jill Sheldon (aka Jill Shalvis) is a multi-published romantic/suspense author. *Summer of Fire* was her first novel for *Scarlet*, followed by *Time to Trust* and *Revenge is Sweet*. We are now delighted to bring you *Forgotten*. In 1995, Jill was a finalist in the prestigious North West region's Romance Writers of America's 'Lone Start Writing Competition'.

Jill majored in journalism and has written many short stories. She lives in Southern California, with her husband and three young children and is an active member of the Romance Writers of America organization, particularly in her local area.

Other *Scarlet* titles available this month:

GIRLS ON THE RUN – Talia Lyon
WILD FIRE – Liz Fielding
DEADLY ALLURE – Laura Bradley

JILL SHELDON

FORGOTTEN

Enquiries to:
Robinson Publishing Ltd
7 Kensington Church Court
London W8 4SP

First published in the UK by Scarlet, 1997

Copyright © Jill Shalvis 1997
Cover photography by J. Cat

The right of Jill Shalvis to be identified as author
of this work has been asserted by her in accordance
with the Copyright, Designs and Patents Act 1988.

All rights reserved. No part of this publication
may be reproduced in any form or by any means
without the prior written permission of the publisher.

This book is sold subject to the condition that it shall
not, by way of trade or otherwise, be lent, re-sold,
hired out or otherwise circulated in any form of binding
or cover other than that in which it is published and
without a similar condition including this condition being
imposed on the subsequent purchaser.

A copy of the British Library Cataloguing in
Publication data is available from the British Library

ISBN 1-85487-948-0

Printed and bound in the EC

10 9 8 7 6 5 4 3 2 1

PROLOGUE

He had to have her. It'd always been that way for him, ever since they were kids. Yet he couldn't say the same for her. She'd never taken him seriously, ignoring his advances with a sweet smile.

He didn't understand it.

No one ignored Trent Blockwell. Everyone loved him. And if they didn't, well then, they were persuaded differently. Discreetly, of course. After all, it wouldn't do to have any negative rumors following him around, not with such a brilliant political career ahead of him.

It was true, without his Hope, he'd never gain full control of her father, and Trent desperately needed to do that. But he still would have fought for the vivacious, lively woman of his dreams, Hope Broderick. Bottom line – he wanted her for himself, he always had.

Trent leaned back in his leather chair, eyed his perfectly neat office and sighed. She'd be rough on his personal life. She was stubborn as hell. What man wanted a woman who not only had strong opinions, but always wanted to do exactly as she pleased? Who wanted a woman like that?

He did.

Her outgoing personality attracted people, even with her strange sixth sense, the one that set her apart from the norm. More than half of their small town was in love with her; men, women and children alike, and while she cared about everyone in return, there remained an aura of mystery about her that set her slightly apart. It might have been the fact that she was the only doctor for several hundred miles. That tidbit would look good in his press kit. And she photographed well. When he ran this country, she'd be a huge asset.

Trent saw Hope as the key to his future, and if he had to force her hand, then so be it. She'd come around. No one could resist his charm for long. Besides, he'd already set the ball in motion, and by now she would know what he'd done.

She'd hate him for it, which made him grin as he stretched his legs out on his desk. Despite the good-boy, elegant image he'd carefully cultivated, secretly he liked his women feisty, liked them hot.

Especially hot.

Hope was one hot woman; inside and out. It was that Russian gypsy heritage, all that flowing dark hair, those flashing eyes. Oh, she tried to hide it, yet beneath the cool, calm exterior that made up Dr Hope Broderick, there lived a wild soul.

He had to have her.

She'd resist him, no doubt, but in the end, she'd have no choice. No choice at all. Not if she wanted to save her father's pathetic hide. And she would want to do that, desperately.

Yeah, Hope would marry him, kicking and screaming. It would make for an interesting honeymoon.

Trent laughed, picturing her dark fury, that feisty temper she had when riled. Make that a very interesting honeymoon.

CHAPTER 1

The jostling startled him back into consciousness, then he abruptly wished it hadn't.

He hurt like hell. Every last inch of him felt like it was on fire. Something trickled down the side of his face and he had a sickening feeling that it was probably blood. His.

Another sharp jerk made him moan, and he realized he'd been gagged. Cuffed as well, he thought with welling panic.

'Here,' a gruff voice barked. 'Dump him here.'

'He'll drown in the river.'

'Nah. He's already dead.'

Before he could fully assimilate that information, a door opened – a car door – and he was roughly yanked out. Cold rain hit him in the face, but the discomfort was nothing compared to the hard fall he took when someone abruptly dropped him.

Pain closed in on him . . . and he felt himself start to fade out.

But the rain came down persistently, jerking him awake a minute later. For a long time he just lay there in the mud in which he'd been unceremoniously dumped. His vision had faded, or maybe that was just fog. He didn't know, didn't care.

Because something had just occurred to him, something far more important than the fact that his every muscle quivered with aching agony.

He had no idea who he was. Or even where he was.

With the last of his draining energy and fading consciousness, he raised his head, squinting in the dark to see. Nothing but tall trees. He could hear nothing but the roar of water.

What the hell was his name? Why couldn't he remember that simple fact?

Something beeped annoyingly, and he realized it was the watch on his wrist. It continued to beep, until his pounding head echoed with the sound, torturing him.

Moaning a little with the effort, he lay back, plopping his head down into the mud. Rain continued to pelt him.

Beep. Beep. Beep.

'Dammit!' With precious energy, he fumbled for the watch, but his hands were tied. The best he could do was smother it in the mud. He sighed when the noise faded.

But his head still drummed with pain. And with the knowledge that he was hopelessly lost.

Because while he might have known who he was when he'd woken up that morning and dressed in the now torn and tattered clothes that covered him, he sure didn't know now.

About the only thing he did know was that he hurt more than he ever had. And that he was about to lose consciousness to the cold and rainy night.

* * *

The storm battered her windows, thrashed the trees in her yard. It darkened the night so that she could see nothing beyond the black, not even a glimmer of the dawn she knew couldn't be too far off.

Though Hope couldn't hear much of anything, she knew by the looks of things, this storm had to be noisy. Destructive. It matched her mood – a surprise, since she was usually cheerful and upbeat to a fault. Leaning her forehead against the cold glass of the sliding door, she could admit now what she'd been avoiding all week – she'd sunk low enough that she actually felt pity for herself.

It wasn't an easy thing to admit, but it was the truth. She justified it by telling herself that anyone in her situation would feel this way. Too much at once, she thought miserably. A wonderful, loving father who had suddenly become stubborn beyond belief, trying to force her to give up her medical practice to have grandbabies. The overbearing man who worked for her father, the one that insisted on giving her those babies. Insisted so strongly in fact, he was willing to blackmail her.

Willing, ha! Trent Blockwell had not only been willing, he'd done it. And unless she produced a baby – her own – she would lose everything she cared about; her clinic, her father's respect, everything.

Molly, her black Lab, lifted her big, dark head from her front paws and whined, indicating she'd heard, or sensed, something out of the ordinary. Hope tilted her head and concentrated, but could hear nothing.

Not that she put an ounce of stock in that, since she was medically deaf in one ear. Closing her eyes, which helped to heighten her sixth sense, she concentrated . . . and sucked in her breath just as Molly whined again.

She sensed it too. *Someone was out there*.

Her clinic was known for its extended hours, but that anyone would come in the middle of the night meant only one thing – an emergency.

Even she could hear what came next. The screeching of car tires might not be unusual in any city, but this was the country. The deep, back mountain country of Washington. She was hours from the closest big city, on a dead end road that led only to her house, and it was far past midnight. Not good.

Squinting through the thick, dripping window, she just made out the quick flash of lights before they disappeared.

Molly gave one sharp bark.

'You're right,' Hope murmured, patting Molly's head. 'Something's up.'

Bouncing with purpose, Molly leaped to the door, jumped up and pawed at the handle.

'Coming.' It was crazy to go out in that weather, crazier still since she was alone, yet she had to. It was a feeling, nothing more, but she never ignored them. Couldn't, since when one came this strong, she was never wrong.

A gift from her Russian gypsy mother, this strange ability. But someone, or something, needed her, and she wouldn't get any peace at all until she took care of it.

When she'd slipped into her parka and raised the hood over her head, she opened the door. Molly raced out into the night as Hope flipped on her flashlight. Following the dog proved difficult. The minute she stepped off the porch, she sank ankle deep into mud.

'Great!'

But she kept going, pushed now by an almost desperate urge to hurry. Her property was huge, surrounded by woods. In summer, a tiny creek ran a hundred yards off the back. Now, in the middle of spring, it had become a raging river. Molly bounced off toward it.

Hope followed, slipping twice. 'If you've found another animal for me,' she called out to the quickly disappearing Molly, 'just forget it. We've got all we can feed now.' But of course, she'd never turn down anyone in need, even an animal. *Especially* an animal. Didn't she have three cats, two parrots and a raccoon to prove that? She had no idea what she'd do with them all if her father did indeed go through with his threat to take his house back from her.

'Maybe you could find me a husband to keep Trent and my father off my back,' she suggested to Molly as she bounded over the wet terrain. 'A temporary one, of course.' She didn't want a permanent one, just desperately needed to buy some time so she didn't have to hurt or disappoint the father she loved so dearly.

Molly barked, a high short sound that might have been a laugh. Hope couldn't have agreed more as she forced her way against the billowing wind. The situation she'd found herself in *was* funny. And unbelievable. She would have loved to tell Trent what she thought of him and his blackmail that was close to ruining her life – but confrontation wasn't a strong suit of hers, even if she had known him nearly all her life.

She was sick and tired of people trying to run her life. Her personal life had always suited her just fine. And if it was just a teeny weenie bit boring, then it was her own business. She liked it. But both Trent and her father had interfered, and now nothing would ever be the same again.

The roar of the water told her the creek was only a few feet away. She took one more step and tripped over Molly, who was standing over something, growling low and deep.

Long legs stuck out from beneath the dog. *A man's legs*.

'Good Lord!' Dropping down to her knees, she immediately reached for the man's neck, checking for a pulse. *Please, please,* she prayed without hesitation. *Please let him be alive*.

It was instinctive, for Hope was a true believer in the human spirit. She hated things to hurt, people or animals, and ached badly when they did. When she felt the pulse in the man's neck, faint but there, she sagged in relief.

Then he moaned, and because her other hand was on his back, she felt it vibrate through her, clear to her toes. 'I'm here,' she said quickly, pushing Molly back when she would have licked the man's face clean.

Rapidly, she checked for broken bones. Finding none except the ribs she suspected were cracked, she carefully shifted him onto his back, then gasped. 'Oh – Here, hold on.' He was gagged, darn it. She hadn't seen it because of all the mud. His hands were cruelly and tightly tied. Fumbling with the knots on the gag, she freed his mouth and set to work on the tie at his wrists.

'Who?'

The voice came hoarse, barely there, but she read his lips. 'My name is Hope,' she told him. Knowing the importance of keeping him calm and conscious, she maintained contact by stroking his arm while she ran her gaze over him, trying to discern how badly injured he was.

A car accident? No. Not with him gagged and tied up. But he'd been worked over good.

He struggled to sit up.

She held him down, though it wasn't easy. He was determined, obviously tall, and very strong. 'It's all right, I'm a doctor,' she said, trying to reassure him.

'No.' He licked those bruised, cut lips and shook his head sharply, wincing as he did. 'Who am *I*?' he nearly yelled.

Her head whipped up and she stared down into his face. *He didn't know*? He'd definitely been beaten, she saw. One eye had swollen shut. A cut at the corner of his mouth bled wildly.

A beeping sounded, startling her until she realized it was the man's watch.

'That's a Timex,' he whispered slowly, his eyes closed as she fumbled with the small knob to turn the thing off. 'Takes a beating and keeps on ticking.' At the sudden silence, he sighed.

Now he turned his head toward where she knelt at his side. With great effort it seemed, he looked at her with his one good eye. His mouth opened, as if he was about to speak, but he hesitated.

So did Hope.

For in the man's gaze she saw something that had the storm around them fading into the background, the circumstances that had her drenched and hovering in the mud forgotten. In that flash in time she didn't feel the wet, or the driving, cold rain.

It disappeared until all that existed was the two of them. His one-eyed glassy gaze remained on hers, and she couldn't have looked away if she'd wanted to.

What she saw there startled her beyond belief.

She saw a heart that mirrored her own, one equally stranded and in trouble. She saw his loneliness as it matched hers. His desperation, identical to what she felt.

Molly whined and nudged her arm.

The man blinked and the moment was gone. She had to shove Molly back again, but she knew she'd never forget that moment when she'd looked into his soul and seen herself.

Molly barked sharply and the man winced, lifting a hand to his head. It came away bloody.

'Molly,' she reprimanded. 'Quiet. Stay.' What was she going to do with this man? She had to get him to the house, quickly.

'Who am I?' he repeated, closing his eye.

. *He was her destiny*.

The thought disappeared as quickly as it'd come, but it knocked the breath out of her just the same. It was the wind, she told herself. The storm. The strange whimsy of the night that brewed around them.

It had nothing to do with her special feelings. It just couldn't. Yet she knew deep down it did. It was her strongest one yet. *This man was hers*.

No, she told herself firmly. Too much. She was a doctor, for goodness' sake, well-respected and known. She lived in the twentieth century, in the States, where such things didn't happen. *Couldn't happen*.

Yet it just had.

'Who?'

He spoke quietly, and the storm whisked his words away from her ineffective ears, but she had no problem reading his lips. 'I don't know,' she whispered.

'Dammit,' he said hoarsely, taking her arm in a surprisingly steely grip. But he went white as a sheet immediately, lessening his grip. He gasped, holding his ribs, trying to curl up into a ball.

She reached for him, but he shook his head sharply, wincing at the movement.

'Just . . . tell me . . .' His voice faded away and she knew he was close to passing out.

Who was he? Molly barked again and Hope stared at her. *A husband*. Hadn't she just wished for one to prove Trent's rumor a lie? Had one just been dropped in her lap?

No . . . what she was thinking was wrong, very wrong. She couldn't.

The man moaned, and for the first time she saw the cut over his head. The lump her fingers discovered a minute later was huge, and as she touched it, he moaned again.

He would die out here if she didn't get him help immediately. Even with a helicopter, the hospital was too far. She was the only help he was going to get, but she could do it, she had all the equipment and the knowledge.

She could save his life.

It could be the last life she would save in this isolated community. If Trent got his way, soon she'd have to leave. Her father would close up the house she used as the only clinic with medical care for miles around.

And people would die.

Hope knew that with as much certainty as she knew she had to take her next breath. If she quit practising medicine here, the remote county population would suffer.

She couldn't stand the thought.

She'd have to make her father understand. The urgency to do so made her stomach clench. She stared down at the bloody man stretched out before her, the man who so badly needed her medical expertise.

She'd make her father understand. *She'd have to.*

The man, stiff and tense as he waited for her to speak, shivered. Beneath her fingers, his muscles flexed and remained taut.

Before she could consider the wisdom of what she was about to do, she blurted out the answer she knew he was waiting for. 'You're my . . . lover,' she said softly, tripping over the unaccustomed word as she touched his arm.

Oh, she had his interest now, that one-eyed gaze was sharp on her.

She took a second to suck in a deep breath, though she kept her hand on him. She knew the contact kept him conscious, knew how it could warm a chilled soul. She didn't question how she knew his soul needed the warmth.

It was the only apology she could give for now.

Then she sealed her fate, and his.

'You're my lover, and soon to be a daddy.'

CHAPTER 2

Thank God for the darkness. Without it, his head would have fallen right off. Warmth and safety prevailed there. But the voice that called him shoved that blessed blankness back, making him aware when he didn't want to be.

It hurt to be awake.

'Come on,' a female voice cajoled. 'Please, you've got to help me. I can't get you to the house by myself.'

He realized he was half draped around a female body, a *curvy* female body, and he was being dragged. Because he couldn't feel them, he flexed his fingers. Soft, warm flesh filled his hands and she squealed.

He hit his knees hard.

'Oh! I'm sorry.' That voice, now breathless, came in his ear. 'You . . . tickled me.' She helped him up and he couldn't stifle his groan of pain when she touched him. No doubt about it, his head was going to fall right off.

'Come on,' she begged. '*Please.*'

To keep his mind off the searing agony in his body, he concentrated on the woman supporting him. Given their positions, he estimated he'd gotten a nice handful of breast a moment ago.

Soft, giving, pleasantly curved.

A distinct twinge in his lower regions assured him that while he might not be able to breathe without pain, certain vital parts still worked.

Then he stilled. This woman. Had she said she was his lover?

That she carried his child?

A dog barked and he winced.

'Molly!' the soft voice admonished. 'Quiet.'

He shivered.

'I know, it's cold.' The voice was sweet, caring, sympathetic. He tried to open his eyes, but he couldn't. 'Almost there,' she told him, huffing. 'Just a little further now.'

For a minute, just a minute, the wonderful, all-consuming blackness took him again, but the woman shook him awake.

'Dammit,' he gasped, guarding his ribs with his arm. 'Don't!'

'I'm sorry,' she soothed, sounding genuinely apologetic. 'But you can't go to sleep. Not yet. Not until I see how badly you're hurt –' She grunted as she tried to push him.

He could see nothing. 'What – '

'Steps,' she gasped, managing another.

Why couldn't he see? Then he realized it was because he had his eyes closed. But to open them made his vision swim. Had he been beaten soundly? It seemed likely.

Why? What had he done? What had he gotten himself into?

He straightened away from the woman's arms, wanting to take a look at her. But he'd underestimated the support she'd been giving him. He teetered for one wild minute before falling to his knees again with a teeth-jarring impact that made him cry out.

'Oh!' she exclaimed, and he felt her land on her own knees beside him. But he just crumpled down. Had to. He lay on solid ground, probably a porch, his cheek flat against the wood. *Finally*. Rest.

'Please, get up.'

'No.' *Down was good*.

'Come on,' she entreated.

No way, babe, he wanted to say. Staying down felt good, damn good. The pain faded, replaced by a delicious numbness.

For the life of him he couldn't move, and no matter how she begged him, his vision grayed and went to black.

There was an angel hovering over him, a sweet, beautiful angel with wide, intriguing eyes and long, dark flowing hair. An angel with an unusual voice.

He wanted, badly, to reach out and touch her, but he couldn't.

His arms were lead weights.

Warmth, blessed warmth. He snuggled towards that heat and nearly yelped in pain.

Every part of him hurt.

'It's going to be all right now,' the angel murmured. He heard scissors, felt a cool draft that made him shiver. 'You're safe here.'

It was his rescuer, the one with that low, gentle voice.

Her soothing hands touched his bare chest, and he realized with shock that she was busy mollifying him with that seductive voice while she cut off his clothes.

Wait until the date's over, he wanted to quip, but then she touched his ribs and agony had his vision fading again.

When he next came to, his angel was helping him get more comfortable. He relaxed marginally. His one good eye remained closed, then jerked open. He remembered . . . she wasn't an angel, she was a doctor. *And his lover*.

But for the life of him, he couldn't remember if he'd known that, or if she'd told him. Dammit.

She tucked another blanket around him, which he burrowed under, finally starting to lose his chill. She murmured her approval and stroked his arm. At the sound and touch, something unaccustomed happened. He warmed, from deep inside. Though he still had no idea who he was, couldn't remember a thing about himself, he just knew . . . warmth wasn't something he experienced often. He rarely felt this strange sense of rightness. Comfort.

Or at least, he thought he rarely felt it. He could be sure of nothing, except that this woman had no reason to lie to him. She said they were together and that she carried his child.

And he didn't even know her name. 'What's –' He had to stop to lick his dry lips. 'What's your name?'

'What?'

She looked startled. Her dark hair had come loose of

its restraints, and covered most of her face, but what he could see was lovely. So were her even darker, deep eyes.

'What's your name?' he repeated.

She stared at his lips. 'Hope.'

Hope. She looked like a Hope, all sweet and full of promise. 'And . . . mine?'

Now she looked nervous. 'Clayton Slater.'

The way she said it sounded as though she were saying it for the first time, and for an instant, he doubted every word she'd said.

'Clay,' she said quietly. 'I call you Clay.'

It rang a bell. And he liked the way she said his name, soft and full of familiarity.

Was it all true? A child . . . he had no idea how he felt about that, except for another burst of that strange warmth.

He watched her, focusing on the part right in front of him. Her middle.

Her tiny, thin middle.

No bulge of a baby there, which meant she'd just gotten pregnant. Which meant they'd very recently had sex. Ridiculously, since he had no recollection of her, only that she had a low voice unlike anything he'd ever heard, the thought turned him on. But he wished he could remember having her.

'Are we . . . good?'

Again he startled her and she jerked back, then bent so she could see his face. 'Shhh,' she whispered. 'You shouldn't talk, not yet. You keep making your lip bleed more.'

She had a pair of dark brown eyes that were so huge

and wide, he could see nothing else but them. 'Are we good?' he repeated.

Again, she stared at his lips. 'Good?'

It hurt to talk. Hell, it hurt to breathe, but he had to know. 'Together.'

Her eyes filled with things he didn't understand; regret, sorrow, pain.

Had he been so awful then? 'Please. I want to remember,' he said weakly. *Had* to remember.

'You need to rest,' she insisted, rising. Patting his arm gently, she moved away. 'I'm going to have to X-ray you. With my tech gone, I need to set up. And I have to gather some things to treat you and clean you up a bit.'

'Am I in the hospital?'

'The closest thing to one,' she said. 'I run this clinic, which should meet your needs. The closest hospital is hours from here.'

He had a quick vision of tall, unforgiving mountain territory. Cold, wet climate, but nothing more. Thankful to be inside, he asked, 'How . . . did this happen to me?' He felt her come closer, but he couldn't open his eyes again to see her, he was simply too tired.

'Don't you remember that either?' she asked finally.

'No.'

He felt her hand on his arm. 'I think I should call the police. Tell them what happened.'

For some reason, that spurred panic such as he'd never known. 'No!' He managed to look at her as pain ricocheted through his head. 'No cops. Please.'

'I'm a doctor,' she whispered in that odd voice. 'I *have* to report this.'

'You're my lover, too,' he reminded her. 'Doesn't that count for something?'

Her eyes flickered as the emotions warred within her, and he wished he could have heard some of those obviously turbulent thoughts.

'Why can't I call?' she asked. 'Are you in trouble? Can you tell me that?'

Danger, was all he could think. If he brought anyone in on this, they would be in perilous jeopardy, including this beautiful, concerned woman staring at him with the most lovely eyes he'd ever seen. 'I can't,' he admitted.

'But why?'

'I can't remember.'

For a long moment, she just stared at him. 'Were you in a car accident? I saw lights from a car before I found you.'

It would be far easier if she thought so. And safer, though he had no idea how he knew this. 'Maybe.'

Those dark eyes saw right through him. 'You were gagged and tied up when I found you. I don't think you were in a wreck. I think someone hurt you, badly.'

Ego demanded he tell her that it was more than just one someone, but it hurt so badly to talk, he said nothing.

'What if they're still around?'

'They're gone,' he said flatly. 'I was obviously left for dead.' Or so he hoped, since he didn't want them coming back and finding someone else – like Hope.

'But why would someone do this to you?'

With his last bit of energy, he looked at her. 'Don't *you* know?'

Those eyes of hers widened slightly. Her face went red, and for the second time, he doubted everything she'd told him. Then she squeezed his arm gently and smiled. 'All I know is that no one deserves to be treated as you were. Please, let me call the police so we can find out what happened.'

He'd have to compromise, he saw. She'd expect that. 'Not yet.'

'Soon?'

'Yes,' he whispered, as pain consumed him. Panic, too. Why couldn't he remember? He *had* to remember. He closed his eye. 'Soon.'

'Okay,' she whispered back.

Just as he started to drift off, he could have sworn he felt her lips on his face. The unexpected sweetness of it, the softness of her mouth on him, the burst of comfort . . . all made him smile. She *was* familiar.

She was his.

'I'll be back with what I need,' she said. 'Sleep for a few minutes, okay?'

The cut on his mouth made it hard to talk. He held it closed. 'Why can't I remember?'

'What?'

He dropped his hand from his mouth and repeated his words.

'You will,' she promised in that low, almost rough voice that had begun to fascinate him. 'Don't push it. Sleep now.'

He didn't want to. But the pills she'd given him after she'd gotten him in the house had started to affect him. He was so groggy. And in such agony he didn't think he could move to save his life. But he didn't want to sleep. He wanted to know who he was, where he was.

And why he couldn't remember being with the lovely, brave woman who'd saved his life, who carried his child.

Hope would have been surprised, and relieved, to know Clay put such stock in what she'd told him, though she shouldn't have been.

Most amnesia patients have an almost desperate need to believe the first things they hear about themselves.

The man in her care was no exception.

Sitting in the rocker by the front window, she watched the sun come up. She'd cleaned up her 'lover' and now knew the full extent of his injuries.

Someone had roughed him up pretty good. It sickened her, what he'd gone through. What he was going to go through as he recovered.

Who could hate him so much to do this?

She'd stayed up all night, checking him often. His concussion warranted that, but she would have done it regardless. Hope tended to give all to any patient, even her animal ones, but she needed sleep. In just a few hours, more patients would start arriving, and it could be a very long day, made difficult by no sleep. Made all the more so since she'd just hired a new nurse after her last one had retired, and she'd have to be trained.

But still, she sat, agonizing over what she'd done last night. The truth meant everything to Hope. Always had.

So why had she lied?

Yes, she wanted to protect her clinic. She needed to be able to keep working here, because she believed her work was important. But there had to be another way to convince her beloved father to let her keep this place and do that. There had to be.

She couldn't afford another house or building. Even if she had a penny to her name, which she didn't, she certainly wouldn't be able to gather enough of them to get a place the size she needed.

And no one in Green County had the money to back her, with the possible exception of her father. But as loving as he'd been, he'd always been over-protective to the point of near obsession, and that hadn't changed over the years. He worried about her being a doctor. He worried about her refusing to marry. He didn't understand why she didn't want Trent, a man she'd known forever.

No, she couldn't – wouldn't – ask her father.

Trent Blockwell could help. Tall, dark and handsome . . . the most eligible bachelor for two hundred miles. As the closest and favorite right hand man to her father and his logging company, Trent seemed to have it all. He was charming, polished, intelligent . . . and supremely arrogant.

She was in a position to know, they'd grown up in this small town together, though they'd never truly been friends. She'd been far too shy for that. Even so, he'd spent the better part of the past two years trying to talk her into having a relationship, but she'd resisted.

Though he was the apple of the town's eye, something about Trent bothered her. Everyone she knew loved him, yet when she looked into his dark eyes, she saw nothing but an empty chill that scared her. She'd brushed him off, as politely as she could, even when he'd gotten more and more aggressive.

Now, thanks to him and the rumors he'd spread, the entire county believed she was pregnant – *with his child*. It was laughable, not only because she was probably the only twenty-eight-year-old virgin in the western hemisphere, but because she wouldn't have slept with her father's right hand man, no matter how young and attractive he was. Not even if he were the last man on earth.

Yet none of that mattered, not when whatever Trent said was repeated gleefully, then taken for gospel. Not when everyone was poised on the edge, waiting for the first signs of her pregnancy to show, to prove the rumors correct.

She truly didn't understand Trent's wide appeal. People loved him, especially women. It had to be his elegant, yet dangerous looks, but to Hope, he seemed just that – *dangerous*. He truly scared her, because she sensed his hidden agenda.

She just wished she knew exactly what it was.

Her medical clinic had never been so busy. Granted, she lived in the remote Green County, where she was the only doctor, as well as the only female to have ever become one for nearly two hundred square miles. But not even the fact that she'd done it all in eight years instead of twelve, after graduating high school at the age of fifteen, explained her sudden influx in business. Nor did her IQ. The people of Green County were used to that by now.

She'd like to think it was her special talent for healing,

but she wouldn't flatter herself that way. Not when she knew the truth. Knew that people came daily from all over, with all sorts of flimsy excuses, trying to figure out if the pregnancy rumors were true or not.

She'd love nothing more than to dispel those falsehoods, but to do that she'd have to hurt her father. If only she could bring herself to do that. If only he didn't want this so very much. If only he hadn't looked so old and vulnerable last time she saw him.

If only he hadn't lovingly but sternly threatened to pull the deed on the property she loved if she didn't get down to the serious business of giving him a grandchild.

If only . . .

He didn't do it to be mean. She knew that. He truly believed she wasn't living life to its fullest, and thought he could force the issue. Thought he could make her let others into her life.

Unfair as it was, the rumor that Trent had started was actually going to buy her some time. Time to get the money together she needed to buy this place from her father. She couldn't lose it, not when she loved it so. Personality and character shone from the nearly one-hundred-year-old house. The huge, rambling, old cabin-style place had been picked by her mother, though Hope couldn't remember much about those years. She'd been five when her mother had died.

But if Hope had to leave, it wasn't just that she'd miss this house. The entire county would go without medical care. Children, elderly people . . . all would have to make the long drive into Seattle. Few would, even if they could afford it. The thought killed her.

She wanted to stay. Her life's work was here, her hopes, her joy. Here she felt happy, needed, important.

That Trent had jeopardized everything for his own gain unnerved her. What kind of man did that? A very bad one, she decided. Granted, no one else felt that way about him, but Hope couldn't trust him. And now everyone she knew believed she'd slept with him, which infuriated her as nothing else could have.

Pregnant. By Trent, no less. Yuck!

Which brought her back to the man in the next room and what she'd done.

Luckily she'd found Clay's wallet, and though it'd been conspicuously empty, it had been monogrammed with his name. Thankfully.

Good grief, what was wrong with her? That man was badly hurt and she'd lied right to his face. Worse than that, she'd purposely fooled a patient, one who needed her help desperately.

It was wrong, despite the fact that he'd asked her not to call the police. It was probably illegal as well, which meant she'd just jeopardized the medical license that meant absolutely everything to her. And if Clay was half as tough and complex as she was beginning to think he was, then he would be more than furious when he found out the truth. Rightfully so.

She'd lied.

Her always vivid imagination had her picturing her mother turning over in her grave. Her mother had once given up her entire life for truth.

Now her daughter had forsaken it.

CHAPTER 3

Though it was not even six a.m., Hope placed a call to a private investigator friend in Seattle. With tense hands she'd waited while he'd joked about it being far too early for a friend to pull a favor. But they went back a long way, and he agreed to run Clay through his computer.

Hope held the special telephone to her one partially functioning ear. The receiver was equipped with a maximizer so she could hear the voice in the receiver, but she still had to concentrate closely. Taking a deep breath, she waited . . . then she wasn't waiting at all, but letting out her breath in relief.

Clayton Slater – not married. Self-employed. Resides in Seattle in a rented apartment. Parents living in Florida, currently on a two month cruise. Not listed as missing.

Hope hung up, leaned back and stared thoughtfully at nothing. Could she have found someone more perfect?

She had to stop this. She didn't really need a husband, she needed a shrink.

She'd tell Clay the truth, the minute he woke up. She would, regardless of what she faced with her father and Trent.

Gathering her resolve, she rose, then sighed in exhaustion. As the sun came the rest of the way up over the horizon, she washed her hands and prepared to see to her patient.

At her side, Molly nudged her. Hope didn't hear the whine so much as felt it vibrate against her leg. Looking down at the eager, hopeful face, she had to laugh. 'I don't care what you sense outside this time, girl. I've got my hands full now. No more strays.'

She kicked the back door open for the dog to go out and made her way down the hall to where Clay slept. She'd left him, not in one of her clinic rooms, but in a spare bedroom across the kitchen, where he'd be more comfortable. Still close, but not close enough to be accidentally seen.

He lay prone and still, just as she'd left him, and she sighed at the pain etched so eloquently in every line of his body. He hurt so badly, and she was about to make it far worse. What would she say?

Sorry, but you caught me off-guard, in the middle of a self-pity storm that rivaled the storm I found you in. That my well-meaning father is about to rip the ground from beneath my feet unless I produce a baby. That his trusted friend and best employee wants to give me that child, but he gives me the creeps, and I don't know what to do.

It all sounded so ridiculous now, in the light of day.

Clay lay so still, looked so positively awful. Someone had gotten to him good, had hurt him so thoroughly, it was a miracle he hadn't fallen down the embankment and drowned in the creek before she and Molly had found him.

Now, she thought. *Tell him the truth now.*

But her patient was sound asleep. He stayed that way even when she pulled the specially rigged stethoscope from around her neck to check his vitals. The one side for the ear in which she was completely deaf was useless, but the other side had been specially made with a hearing device that allowed her to accurately monitor her patients. In her clinic, she had all sorts of trick equipment, designed to allow a nearly deaf woman to be a doctor.

She'd never get past the thrill of that.

Her patient was normal, but still asleep. She gently roused him until he mumbled, but he didn't wake fully.

Nor did he for another twenty-four hours.

During that time she continuously checked him, just to be safe. That she hadn't kept him in the clinic made this more difficult, but she didn't regret the decision.

She didn't want him in the clinic. Didn't want to have to explain his presence to her staff or any curious patients. Not until she had told Clay the truth, then figured out how to get herself out of this mess she'd made of her life.

On the second morning, Hope woke up knowing she had to break the truth to Clay – no matter what. No matter how tired he looked, or how startling . . . cute.

He simply had to be told because she couldn't live with herself until she did.

There would be patients soon, and her animals needed to be fed. Clay needed to be faced. But there was one thing she had to do first, something she'd put off all week.

She reached for the phone and dialed her father.

'Hope,' he said immediately, warmly, obviously relieved to hear from her. A shaft of guilt sliced through her. 'I've been thinking of you,' he said.

'Me, too.' She smiled, because in spite of everything, it felt good to hear his voice. 'I miss you.'

'That's easy to fix. Come see me.'

'You know it's hard for me to get away. It's an all day trip, and the clinic – '

'– can wait.'

'Father – '

'Forget it,' he said kindly. 'I don't want to argue. Just come soon, or you'll force me all the way out in those woods you call a home.'

'It was your home before mine.' And if she didn't convince him otherwise, it would be his home again all too soon.

'I've been getting some interesting phone calls.' His voice raised slightly with anticipation. 'Are the rumors true?'

She inhaled deeply. How to tell him? He hadn't been himself since his business had run into serious resistance from the Department of Forestry and certain ecology groups who were suddenly protesting the use of the land he leased from the government. She knew how he loved his business, and she felt for him, but wished he'd worry more about his problems than her personal life.

'Hope? Are they? Are the rumors true?'

'You know better than to believe everything you hear,' she said, trying to gather courage to speak the truth, regardless of the pain she'd cause.

'But I didn't hear this from just anyone. I heard it from Trent.'

'And you believed him?'

'A man can dream. Honey, I'm getting old, and – '

'– And you want a grandchild.' She rubbed her temples and suppressed a tired laugh. 'We've been down this road, Father. Thousands of times. But it's not going to happen, at least not now. Trent is wrong.'

'Are you sure?'

'Very. I'm sorry you're disappointed.'

'Whatever happened to the good old days?' he demanded with a grudging good-naturedness. 'Daughters married and produced children dutifully.'

'Thank goodness the times have changed,' she said. 'They're even letting us women vote now.'

He laughed, but she knew he meant everything he'd said. And the slight shakiness to his voice terrified her. Was he sick? Or just aging? He'd never in her entire life asked her for a thing, which only amped the guilt factor. 'I've got to go get ready for my patients, but I'll call again soon.'

'You work yourself too hard. And now that you're going to settle down – '

'No one said anything about settling down,' she told him gently.

'Everyone has said so except you.'

So calm, so sure. She sighed and started again. 'I'm not getting married – '

'I just want the best for you. I just want you to live your life for *yourself*, not holed up in the clinic, living life through others.'

It hurt that he believed that was what she was doing, but deep down, a good portion of it was true. She *would* rather work twenty-four hours a day than face the empty, lonely life she'd made for herself. She *would* rather be with her animals than face the population of Green County that thought her Trent's little showcase.

'I'm not closing myself off to life,' she protested, thinking about what would happen if the gossip train got a glance at Clay.

'Then prove it. Marry Trent. He wants you badly enough.'

'I can't do it,' she whispered. 'Not even for you. I'm sorry.'

'Now, now,' he said quickly. 'Don't make that decision hastily. Just think about it. When are you going to come and see me? Sunday?'

She tried to get to Seattle every couple of weeks to visit him, but it took her a minute and a shaky breath to respond. 'I'll be there.'

She hung up, hating the disappointment she'd heard in his voice. But she wouldn't give in just to please him. She couldn't.

A minute later, Hope leaned over Clay, a hand to his chest. He was sleeping peacefully, thank goodness. She knew he'd had several nightmares already and it hurt to watch him suffer.

Under her palm she felt the rumble as Clay moaned softly in his sleep, reminding her of how close he'd come to death.

Many, many times, she'd reached for the phone,

intending to call the police, but each time, she'd stopped herself.

She'd promised him she wouldn't.

Since when had she made a promise she couldn't keep?

Since she'd lied. Oh, this just got worse and worse.

A second call to her private investigator friend had assured her that, still, no one was looking for Clayton Slater. That no one had been reported missing who fitted his description.

Why not?

She understood his parents not only lived across the country, but were away on a trip. Was there no one else? At least he wasn't a wanted man.

It didn't mean he was a good man.

He was, she assured herself. She knew that unquestionably. Now if only she could be so sure of Trent and what he was up to. Everyone thought her pregnant, with his child, and they thought it simply because he'd said so.

What would he do next?

In the warm, cozy room, Hope shivered. She stood resolutely and then, after making sure Clay still slept, made her way to the clinic.

Excitement pushed back some of her exhaustion from two nights with little to no sleep. She couldn't help it, but running the clinic always revved her up. So did the thought of Kelly, her new nurse, because it meant she'd have someone to share the thrill of practising medicine with, someone who would understand her dedication.

Without looking out the window, she knew Kelly had pulled up and was stepping up onto the porch. Unlocking the front door from the inside, Hope pulled it open with a smile of greeting on her lips.

'Oh!' said Kelly, clearly startled. She stood there, her keys dangling from her fingers. 'I – I didn't knock.'

No, she hadn't. But still, Hope had known she'd be there. Maybe a quick subject change would help? 'Beautiful morning, isn't it?'

'How did you know I'd be standing here – Oh!'

Some of Hope's excitement drained at that look. When, oh when, would she learn how uneasy Kelly felt when she got a 'feeling'? 'I didn't mean to scare you.'

'That's all right.' But it wasn't.

'Well . . .' *This was horribly awkward*, Hope thought. 'Good morning.'

'Good morning,' Kelly replied loudly, slowly.

So formal. So distant. Hope sighed, but didn't know what else she had expected when she'd hired the nurse last week. Kelly was tall, thin, blonde and model beautiful – and always perfectly made-up. Hope had some reservations about how a woman like that would hold up to the demands of clinical work, but her qualifications had been completely acceptable . . . and no one else in the entire county had been trained as a nurse. Getting an outsider in wasn't likely, not many people were interested in Washington State's backwoods.

Still, Hope loved it.

But as cheerful and happy as she naturally was, it had never been easy for her to make friends. Now she feared she'd given the impression to Kelly that she wanted this distance, this coolness between them. She didn't, she just didn't know how to casualize the relationship.

'Come in,' Hope said, careful as she always was in the company of others to enunciate her speech properly. 'Oh . . . I'll get it.'

'Get what?'

The phone rang, and above it was Hope's accompanying signal of the bright red light flashing in case she didn't hear the tone of the ring.

Kelly's eyes widened as she obviously realized that Hope had 'heard' the phone, before it had actually rung. 'You – I – ' She closed her mouth. 'Wow!'

Hope sighed and ran for the phone. The minute she picked it up, the red light clicked off. The entire time she answered Mrs Watson's questions on bringing down little Jimmy's fever, Hope felt the weight of Kelly's avid stare.

Her feelings were a way of life, she often didn't think twice about them. It was easy to forget that she wasn't normal.

'Pretty neat trick you've got there.'

Hope shrugged and tried to keep it light. 'Now if I could only figure out who the caller is ahead of time, I'd know which calls to avoid.'

She'd been joking, but Kelly didn't crack a smile. She backed away, clearly a little unnerved by her boss's special talent. 'I'll get the rooms ready,' Kelly said several decibels louder than necessary, exaggerating her every word.

Hope nodded, stifling her sigh as she watched the woman hurry from her presence. No matter how many times she told Kelly she could hear her just fine as long as Hope could see the nurse's lips, Kelly still spoke that way to her, as if she were slow-witted as well as hard of hearing.

That Hope had just scared the woman to death hadn't helped the situation either.

But nearly everyone spoke to her that way. No matter how kindly they did it, it still frustrated her. It disturbed her as well, for when she'd hired Kelly, she'd hoped – silly as it seemed now – that she could actually find a friend in the new nurse.

Didn't seem that would happen, not with Kelly being so uncomfortable around her.

But that wasn't Hope's concern, not today. Her concern lay with the semi-conscious man in her spare bedroom. She followed Kelly into the first patient room, watching as the nurse straightened things up.

'I must have forgotten to clean this room up yesterday after we finished,' Kelly said, sending Hope a look of apology.

Hope hesitated, knowing she'd made another mistake. After X-raying Clay for the second night in a row, she'd forgotten to check the room.

Why it was so critically important she keep Clay a secret, she had no idea, she just felt it was. But before she could say a word, Kelly frowned and looked up.

'Have you seen a patient already this morning, Dr Broderick?'

If things had been different between the two women, Hope might have confided in her about her midnight adventure the night before last, and her consequent visitor. As she opened her mouth to answer, Kelly repeated the question as if Hope hadn't heard her.

'I did hear you, Kelly,' Hope said quietly.

The nurse blushed. 'I'm sorry, Doctor. I just – I just assumed you didn't. I'm sorry,' she said again, turning away, making Hope take yet another deep breath.

Nope. Definitely not a friendship in the making. Not with this tension.

Hope watched Kelly toss the crinkled paper over the gurney away. The phone rang and with efficient, graceful movements that Hope envied, Kelly moved from the room to the small greeting area, where she also performed her receptionist duties.

'Dr Broderick?' she called a moment later, popping her head up through the receptionist window. 'Trent Blockwell, line one.'

Hope stood in the doorway, gripping it with tense, white knuckles. All she'd caught was the name, but it had rendered her paralyzed. She stared at the large phone. Not even her deafness could be an excuse here, not with her specially equipped phones.

'Doctor?' Kelly repeated, holding out the phone. 'Trent Blockwell.'

The man wouldn't let up, wouldn't take no for an answer. Any flattery she might have gotten from his attentions had faded long ago, and so had any residual feelings of friendship. She owed him nothing. 'Take a message, please.'

Her eyes curious, but voice pleasantly polite, Kelly said, 'Certainly.'

With no great surprise, Hope listened to the one-sided conversation, not missing how Trent obviously flirted and charmed her employee into smiling, even laughing.

'He said he'll call back later,' Kelly said when she'd hung up, her voice instantly back to the cool, respectful tone. 'He knows how busy you are.'

Hope resisted rolling her eyes. Kelly busied herself behind the desk, obviously waiting for her employer to leave.

Without understanding it, Hope experienced a yearning to see her latest patient, knowing somehow he'd never try to hurt her. 'I'll be back in a few minutes,' she said, and made her way out of the clinic.

Together with Molly, Hope tip-toed into the room where Clay slept.

He slept soundly, as he had for nearly two days. Stubble lined his cheeks, bruises marred his face, but didn't detract from the little jolt of pleasure she got just looking at him.

As she stared down at him, she remembered her conversation with her father. For the brief moment, when he'd asked her about Trent, he'd sounded so thrilled. She knew he hadn't believed she wasn't pregnant.

He'd sounded ecstatic, happier than she'd ever heard him. And proud. She'd never heard that in his voice before. Never. Not even when she'd become a doctor – especially not then.

It hadn't been what he wanted for her.

The thrill of having that pride now, even for a short time, had her swallowing her own, which demanded she again deny the things Trent had said. Her father liked Trent, trusted him, had high hopes for him within the logging company. It wasn't that Hope thought her father would believe Trent over her, so much as he would *want* to believe Trent.

Trent could charm the light right out of the moon.

Hope sighed and wondered how wrong it could be to let this work to her advantage, just for a short time. Her father wouldn't take this property away from her if she were carrying a baby, would he?

Trent had made sure that he'd spread the rumors well, hoping to force her hand in marriage. In a place as little populated as Green County, that wasn't too hard. One couldn't have PMS without the entire county discussing it. Now everyone thought her pregnant, and was waiting to see what would happen. Marriage was out of the question. The thought of being married to the sweet-talking, charming snake gave her the chills.

God forgive her, but it had been why, when she'd seen Clay, for one brief moment she'd thought her problem solved. If her father had to think her pregnant, she didn't want it to be by Trent.

The man stretched out and sleeping so peacefully before her didn't deserve the deception, and it made her sick to think she'd sunk so low as to contemplate it.

She wouldn't again, no matter how desperate she got.

Clay hadn't moved. The strong lines of his face were firm, but still discolored. His shoulders and chest, bare and revealed by the slipping blanket, softly rose and fell with his breathing. The bruises there broke her heart.

So wide, so powerful, she thought with a burst of fresh sympathy. Too strong to have been brought so low.

Her eyes remained on those well-defined arms, on the chest that felt as hard as it looked – she'd had to touch him plenty to get him in the bed – and despite the coolness of the room, she felt heat flood her face.

For a minute, she'd actually assessed him as if he were her lover. He wasn't, no matter what she'd told him, or herself. He was her patient and she'd do well to remember that.

Carefully, so as not to disturb him, she lifted a corner of the blanket, intending to check on the cracked ribs.

A strong hand clamped down on her wrist, surprising a gasp from her. 'Looking for something?' he rasped.

Molly immediately stepped forward, growling a warning deep in her throat, but Hope knew Clay posed no threat. With her free hand, Hope stroked the dog's head. 'Stay,' she murmured. To Clay, she said, 'I want to check your ribs.'

'You're too young . . . to be a doctor,' Clay managed, undeterred by the growling dog. His voice came low, gravely and husky from sleep. His eyes remained closed.

'What?'

He licked dry lips. 'You're . . . not really a doctor, are you?'

So he was starting to doubt. A good sign, actually. Soothing Molly, she sighed. 'Yes. And I'm not that young.'

'Yes you are,' he said persistently, and she sighed again, knowing she was going to have to discuss what always made her feel very uncomfortable.

'I'm . . . rather quick,' she said, trying to strive for lightness, while her insides clenched.

'Quick?' One eye opened, leveled on her.

She hated this, having to explain. It embarrassed her. 'I finished high school at fifteen.'

'Still,' he said. 'Too young.'

'I did my under grad work in two years.'

'Ah . . . a genius.'

She tensed. So did Molly.

But he wasn't making fun of her at all, she realized, when he flashed her an easy smile. 'I like that,' he said. 'Smart and looks. Killer combination, I think.'

But then he lifted a hand and rubbed at the bandage on his head, covering his mouth when he spoke again.

'I'm sorry,' she said, straining toward him. 'What?'

'Where am I?' he asked again, his eyes closed now, as if he were too tired to keep them open.

'I told you.'

'No.' With what seemed like a great effort, he lifted his head and slitted his one good eye open. 'You said we're lovers. That my name is Clay. You never said where we are.'

With her free hand, she settled his blanket back down around his bare chest, her fingers brushing against his warm skin. It sent a jolt through her body that electrified her into a tingling sense of awareness.

She'd had a wonderful life, but a sheltered one, partly because of her handicap, partly because of her overly-protective father. That Green County was so isolated didn't help. If there'd been a man in her life who had ever made her feel so . . . vibrantly alive, she couldn't remember it. It was wrong to be thinking this way, she knew that.

She was a doctor. Wide, sinewy male shoulders should not be a turn on.

But they were, and no matter what she told herself,

nothing seemed to lessen the impact of what she knew lay under that blanket. Over six feet of hard, corded muscle, without a spare ounce of fat anywhere. Long, toned, muscular limbs, spattered with light hair in all the right places. His hair was thick, blond, and slightly on the long side, as if he hadn't bothered with a cut.

And from what she'd seen when she'd checked under his eyelids, he had a set of the most amazing emerald green eyes she'd ever encountered.

One of those eyes stared at her now, waiting for an answer.

'We're in my house. I run a clinic from here.'

'Where did you find me?'

'The other night?'

He nodded, watching her carefully.

'In the woods, not too far from here. It was very late.'

'What were you doing in the woods in the middle of the night?'

'Molly found you, I just followed.'

Molly, obviously sensing Clay couldn't have harmed a fly if he'd wanted to, relaxed a bit at the mention of her name, then nosed Clay playfully in the arm.

Still holding Hope's wrist, Clay crooked his arm around the dog's neck, inviting her to move in close to lick his face. He stared at Molly with a wonder Hope didn't understand.

'You . . . never told me what I was doing outside in the middle of the night,' he said, whispering now, as if it hurt to talk.

'No,' she said, watching his lips carefully as he spoke in that quiet voice so she wouldn't miss a word. Hadn't she known? He would have a barrel of questions, most of which she couldn't answer.

Still watching her, his thumb traced over the sensitive underside of her wrist, which did all sorts of interesting things to her insides. 'You haven't said a lot of things,' he noted.

'You've been sleeping.'

His touch on her was simple, light as a feather, but it caused some not-so-simple feelings inside her. As his fingers continued to play over her skin, another shock of awareness shot through her, and their gazes met.

'You're . . . quite tense,' he said softly.

'A little,' she admitted.

'Because of me?'

Because of your touch, because of what it does to my insides. 'Not – Not really.'

'I don't mean to upset you.'

That voice . . . she'd never been affected by something as superficial as a voice before. Suddenly too warm, she used her free hand to tug at the neck of her blouse.

Clay watched, that one good eye flaring with an awareness that matched her own.

'I have a question,' he said.

'Okay.' She didn't need her sixth sense to know she wasn't going to like this.

He moistened his lips. 'Why in the world would I be out in that storm when I could have been in bed with you?'

CHAPTER 4

Clay still held Hope's hand. Molly sat on the floor, sandwiched between them. Clay closed his eye again, clearly exhausted. Hope leaned over him, watching his lips so she could catch his every word.

He wanted to know why they hadn't been in bed together. Just the words had a liquid heat stealing through her that she couldn't explain. And then the image of them doing just that, lying together entwined, had her insides fluttering.

'You . . . need to rest.'

He couldn't. 'I need answers.' Weak, he dropped her wrist. But the feel of her smooth skin remained forever imprinted in his mind, and her scent teased his nostrils. She seemed so *almost* familiar. Just like when he'd forgotten a name, or a place, and it was on the very tip of his tongue.

'You can have answers after you feel better,' she said.

'How bad is it?'

'Probably not as bad as it feels.' That she hesitated told him far more than her words. 'Concussion,' she said, watching him carefully. 'But no skull fractures or swelling. Two cracked ribs. You're bruised from head to toe, as I'm sure you can feel.'

'So I'll live.'

Her gaze fell from his eyes to his lips, something she did a lot. Did that mean she was wondering what hers would feel like on his, just as he was?

No, he thought bitterly. She hadn't lost her every last thought to a nasty bump on the head. He had. She'd remember what it felt like to be together.

'Yes,' she said finally. 'You'll live.'

'Why can't I remember?'

'You will. This isn't so uncommon for a head trauma. Give it some more time.'

'And if nothing happens?'

'I'll take you into Seattle for some more tests.'

'No!'

She smiled at him as if he were a child. 'You don't have much of a choice here. I'm the doctor, remember?'

Molly whined softly and nudged at him, as if sympathizing with his plight. He should have recognized this dog. Having her warm fur against him should mean something, but it didn't. Except for a vague sense of unease. Discomfort. 'I hate this.'

Hope's face softened, her eyes filled with compassion, understanding. Then nerves. 'Clay . . .'

When she trailed off unexpectedly, he slowly turned his head toward her, getting a shaft of pain through it for his efforts. 'What?'

'I'm not who you think I am.'

'No kidding?' he asked dryly. 'Sweetheart, I can't even

remember my own birthday. Just who the hell do you think I think you are?'

He grinned when she shot him a sheepish look . . . and split his lip again. 'Dammit!'

'Oh,' she whispered in a low voice, whirling for a washcloth. She came back to him and gently placed it to his mouth. 'I'm so sorry.'

'Why? Are you the one who beat me up?'

'No! Of course not.' Then she caught the humor and her mouth quirked. 'I wouldn't hurt you. Unless . . .'

'Unless what?' he pushed when she trailed off.

'Unless you do something really stupid. Like be late if I've actually cooked dinner.'

She smiled again, but this time he knew it was a token effort. Her eyes remained flat. She'd been about to say something else, something important.

But what? How else could she possibly hurt him?

It was hard to think straight or seriously when she leaned over him as she did. Up close he could see her smooth, pale skin. Her wonderfully expressive eyes. She fascinated him. 'Am I late often?' he asked.

Now her pretty smile faded. She took a deep breath.

What the hell was going on in that lovely head of hers?

'How did we meet, Hope?'

'I'll try to not be insulted you don't remember that momentous event.'

'Funny.' He rubbed his head. 'Do you realize I could run into myself while looking in a mirror and not recognize the face? Obviously someone tried to kill me, and I can't remember why. Am I a wanted man? A thief? Maybe . . . worse?' The thought made him sick.

'No!'

'Well, I don't know. It's frustrating as hell.'

She made a small disparaging sound and stroked his arm. 'You should be resting. The memory will come back, don't rush it. Not now.'

'When?'

'When you're better.'

They stared at each other, in mute passé. When his one good eye met hers, something strange happened. Hope, with her pretty face, the small, lush body . . . the outside of the woman didn't spark his memory. But beyond the shell that made up Hope, in her depthless eyes, he found something he thought he'd never find. *Home*.

And he wanted to stay there forever.

The small noise she made in the back of her throat as she stared back at him told him this revelation wasn't one-sided, that she was just as startled by the heat between them as he was.

'Clay . . .' she whispered, a little hoarsely, her voice full of surprise and wonder.

He knew just what she meant, and he wished he could reach out for her, but he couldn't because of his pain

Then she blinked and the moment was over. The genuine emotion and wonder vanished from her face, replaced by a cool professionalism he recognized as denial.

She didn't want to feel for him.

Why? he wondered. *Had he been that bad?*

'I need to take another look at your injuries.' She tried again to lift the covers, but a sudden ridiculous burst of modesty had him holding them down.

'I'm naked, Hope.'

'I couldn't bind your ribs over your clothes.' She spoke in that low voice, matter-of-factly, but he caught the faint red tinge to her cheeks.

He was struck by the absolute contrast of the sizzling heat between them and the sweet, very real innocence shimmering in her eyes. Then she lowered her lashes, stiffened her shoulders . . . and became a professional again – detached and cool.

She tugged at the sheet and again he stopped her.

He didn't think he was a shy man, but still . . . the image of her hands on him, taking off his clothes . . . Shock mixed with forbidden pleasure, and he found himself blushing too. 'I suppose it's nothing you haven't seen before.'

'Uh . . . right.' She lifted her gaze to his one-eyed one, and though she tried to remain composed, calm, he saw the wave of desire before she could control it.

She was attracted to him, something which should have stroked his suffering ego, but it didn't. Not when she wanted to hide it. He couldn't think of one healthy reason why she'd want to, if they were as close as she claimed. Yet another mystery, which only made his head ache all the more.

'Where's my underwear?'

Again, she flushed. 'You weren't wearing any.'

Hmmm. Maybe he'd been called away from something critically important – like making love to this beauty – since he assumed they'd been living together.

He slid a hand out from beneath the covers and spread his fingers wide, palming her flat stomach.

Beneath his hand, her muscles quivered. She made a sound, a half-choked, disbelieving sound, which told him a lot. She wasn't used to being touched this way. Curious, since he couldn't imagine being able to keep his hands off that nifty little body. 'Don't I do this?' he asked, squeezing gently and wondering if the man he'd been was crazy.

'Do . . . what?'

Her breath came quick now, giving him a surge of ego. So did the way her eyes had darkened to a deep, fathomless brown, the way she leaned towards him as if she couldn't get enough of his touch. 'Don't I touch you like this often?'

'You – ah, I . . . can't remember.'

'You can't remember.' He gave her a dry look. 'I'm the one with amnesia, and you can't remember?' Then he flexed his fingers on her lightly but possessively, loving the way his hand looked on her body.

Her voice, when she spoke again, sounded weak, another boost. 'I can't think when you do that.'

'Yeah?' Silly to puff and primp with male pride when he was flat on his back, but he couldn't help it. 'Good. Neither can I.'

She made another sound, and he wished he could rear up and kiss her. Unfortunately, his body refused to respond – except for a certain pesky part that didn't seem to realize his limitations at the moment.

'It's a crime if I don't touch you a lot,' he whispered, pulling his hand back from her, hoping his body behaved, hoping his sheet didn't turn into a tent. 'I'll have to change that.'

'You'll – we're fine.'

It confused him, the sudden influx of feelings that swamped him. He didn't know who he was, what he was. Knew only a deep seated fear for what had happened to him and how he could avoid it happening again.

Yet, he loved the feel of this woman he didn't remember, loved the thought of his baby inside her. Of their own will, his fingers moved back to her, tightened softly over her belly. 'Is it a boy or a girl, Hope?'

He heard her sharp intake of air. Molly divided an almost comical quizzical look between the two of them, tilting her head far to the side.

'Hope?'

She let out her breath, obviously flustered. But why? Because she couldn't control her response to him? It didn't make sense.

'I really can't think with your hands on me like that,' she whispered.

He liked the chemistry between them, the sparkling sexual tension. He just wished he could remember actually being with her. Wished too that she didn't struggle to hold back, that she liked what was happening between them as much as he did.

Then he asked the question foremost in his mind.

'Why aren't we married?'

'What?'

'Married,' he repeated patiently. 'Why aren't we?'

The way her eyes widened amused him. 'Um . . . married?'

Her voice squeaked, went to a much higher octave

than usual, making him want to smile. But this was serious, and it'd been bugging him.

He wasn't the type of man to get into anything lightly, much less a relationship with a woman. Or at least he didn't want to think he was that sort of man. If he'd been serious enough to get her pregnant, why hadn't he been serious enough to marry her?

'I . . . wasn't ready,' she said finally.

'But I was?'

For a minute, she just stared at him, and he found himself drowning in the most beautiful, expressive eyes. Everything she felt was there for him to see; embarrassment, awareness . . . tension. It was the last he didn't understand.

'Yes,' she whispered, just when he'd thought she wouldn't answer. 'You're ready for marriage.'

It was a relief to know he hadn't been a complete jerk, that he would have married her – if she'd have him. 'So why weren't you? Was I that bad?'

She licked her lips, let her gaze fall to his chest, revealed by the sheet which was bunched at his waist. Never in his life had he felt a look as if it were a touch, and never in his life could he remember wanting to be touched so very badly.

'It's nothing personal. I just don't want to be married.'

There were a million things he wanted, needed to know. What did he do for a living? Did he have family? What was his favorite color? Yet he couldn't get past this, couldn't understand what he had with Hope. He had to know why this sensuous, intelligent, beautiful woman wouldn't have him.

'What's the matter with marriage?'

'You're tired, Clay.'

Yes, he was. But he was also driven by an insatiable curiosity about her that outweighed his exhaustion and pain.

She shifted uncomfortably, and when she ducked her head, her luscious brown hair covered her face.

'Hope?' He wished for the energy to tuck that hair back behind her ears, to pull her down beside him so he could see her expression more clearly. He wished to see her soft smile, feel her gentle hands on him, hear that unusual voice of hers. But she didn't answer, and with effort, he lifted her chin. Immediately, her gaze shot to his lips, something she seemed to do a lot. He whispered her name, silently urging her to continue.

'I'm just not sure I believe in marriage,' she said quietly. 'My parents had a rough time, though they were deeply in love. They were so different, each so set in their ways. It destroyed them.'

'How?'

'My father is a wonderful man, but he's . . . rather rigid, unforgiving. It's the military in him. He met my mother when he was on leave in Russia. They were both young and passionate, but the very opposite of each other.' Her voice softened, went husky. Her eyes darkened with memories. 'My mother was a gypsy, a free spirit, a traveler . . . completely wild and free. Yet she gave up everything, just to be with him. Everything, her country, her heritage, her family.'

'She made that choice willingly. She must have loved him very much.'

'She did.' Her voice went dreamy, yet sad. 'But you can't take a woman like that and confine her. She was a beautiful, untethered vagabond. My father's life revolved around plans, strategies. My mother didn't know the meaning of organization. They were a time bomb.'

'What happened?'

'He brought her here, to this country, this house.'

'It's a beautiful place. Far from the city, surrounded by the wild. She must have felt at home.'

'No,' she whispered. 'She missed her world. People didn't understand her here. She . . . It killed her.'

'I'm sorry, Hope.' But the not knowing was killing him. And he couldn't remember one little thing. He hated that. 'Are we as different as they were? You and me?'

She'd looked away again, but now her head snapped up, and her startled eyes met his. 'What?'

The depth of his need to know surprised him. So did how badly he wanted to hear that they were suited. 'Are we so very different?'

'I'm not sure.'

How could she not be sure? 'Weren't we together very long?'

'It's not that.' Hope hesitated, remembering how he'd been missing for two days, yet no one had reported him as such. Was there someone else in his life?

She remembered too, how that first night, in the middle of the storm, when their gazes had met and she'd seen herself mirrored in his eyes. She'd felt his loneliness, his pain as if it'd been her own. 'No,' she said

55

finally. 'I don't think we're all that different.'

'So why didn't we try?' He raised his hand and took hers. His thumb ran over her knuckles. She could see the wobbly strength in his arm, roped with tendons. This was a powerfully built man, made weak by thugs, yet he could make her breath catch with just a look. His face still swollen, she had no idea what he really looked like.

It didn't matter, not with his fingers on her hand, making her tremble with a simple touch. She'd never met anyone so naturally romantic before, and it left her at a disadvantage.

His lips curved in a slight smile, made all the more sweet for the cuts and bruises marring his features. It melted her heart, tugging on an inner part of her she hadn't even been aware of.

She'd told him they were together. A lie, of course. But was this delicious sort of yearning what it would be like to have someone care deeply? Enough to pledge an entire lifetime together for real, not pretense? How wonderful that would be, if only it were true, not some fantasy she'd drummed up to solve her problems.

She'd have to remember that, she told herself ruthlessly. This was not real. She couldn't fall for her own lies.

'You're carrying my baby, Hope,' he said in a voice husky with emotion. 'Doesn't that count for something?'

He squeezed her hand gently, his dark emerald green gaze piercing hers. A yearning stole through her, catching her completely unaware. His fingers continued to skim lightly over hers. For a minute, no matter what she told herself, the fantasy became real – as if she'd really made love to this man. Goose bumps ran up and down her body and she had to open her mouth to breathe.

Then he lifted her hand to his own rough cheek and rubbed gently, holding her stare.

Her heart nearly leaped out of her chest at the contact and her insides sizzled, melting with lava hot emotion.

'You're all I've got,' he whispered. 'Don't clam up on me now, sweetheart. Please.'

He trusted her. He wanted her, and even more crazy, she wanted him – a perfect stranger. She would have doubted her sanity, but something nagged at her.

The absolute sense that this was right.

Right then and there, for the first time in her life, she ignored one of her 'feelings' and refused to think about it. It couldn't be. She wouldn't allow it.

'I can't do this,' she murmured, lifting her head. It wasn't right to go on deceiving him for the sake of her own needs. It was the worst thing she'd ever done. She took a deep breath. 'Clay, I'm not really – '

Clay winced. 'What the hell was that wail?'

She'd heard nothing, knew only she had to tell him the truth before she lost her nerve. 'What?'

'You mean you can't hear that?' he asked, incredulous. 'It sounded like a – '

It came again, and this time she had no trouble hearing it. The people in the Republic of China could have heard it. 'It's the cats,' she said with a laugh.

A frown crossed his face. 'Cats?'

He said *cats* like it was a bad word. 'There are three of them. They like to eat first thing and they don't think they should have to wait.'

'Three?' he asked, horrified. 'We have three cats?'

Another sound joined the first, a sort of screeching. She winced. 'And there are Fric and Frac, joining in the ruckus.'

'Fric and – Who the hell are Fric and Frac?'

'The . . . parrots.' At this rate, she'd never get to tell him what she needed to. And at the look of his frown, he wasn't much more fond of birds than he'd been of cats. 'They're hungry too.'

'A dog, three cats and two parrots. Where's the partridge in the pear tree?'

Humor sparkled in his one good eye. She'd never had to justify her strange group of pets before, and in truth, had never felt the need. Each had come to her hurt or in need, and she hadn't the heart to turn one away. 'No partridge,' she said carefully, a little defensively. 'Just . . . a raccoon.'

That dark green eye widened before a short bark of laughter escaped him. Flinching, he brought a hand to his swollen lip. 'Ouch.'

Still feeling ridiculously defensive, she again pressed the cloth to his lip as she spoke. 'He came down from the mountain last spring with a hurt leg and I fed him a couple of times. He never left. I think Homer believes he belongs here with me and the others – '

He lifted her hand from his mouth and fixed her with a laughing stare. 'Wait a minute. You named the poor raccoon Homer?'

Afraid that dangerous glitter in his one eye was more humor at her expense, she lifted her chin. With as much dignity as she could, she said, 'He has a bit of an attitude. The name seemed . . . to fit him.'

'Really? I can't imagine why you feel he belongs here,' he said blandly. 'You certainly don't have an attitude of any kind, do you?'

Yes, his eye lit with a touch of amusement, but also something much, much more. Affection, warmth and a hint of the hunger she'd glimpsed once before. It startled her into losing her words, even as some of her tension drained.

Until she remembered. *She still had to tell him the truth.* 'Clay, I need – '

She expelled her breath, muttering with frustration.

'What?' he asked.

'My nurse, Kelly, is about to call me – '

A bell rang.

She could feel the full weight of Clay's stare, which she ignored by studying the tips of her shoes.

'How did you know?'

'I uh, I knew what time my first patient was due.'

He accepted that with a slow nod, still studying her intently.

The bell rang again. But she didn't move, just looked at him, full of dismay. She'd be busy from now until nightfall. How could she let this go on that much longer? 'I might be a while. It's hard to get away once we get started.'

'You're the only doctor at the clinic?'

She nodded.

'That must be a lot of work.'

'Sometimes. But I love it.' The bell rang again and she winced. Kelly kept right on ringing it, probably certain that Hope couldn't hear the damn thing.

'The bell is loud enough to wake the dead,' Clay said.

Or to rouse the nearly deaf. But she had purposely installed a loud, clanging bell so she could hear it the first time. Kelly knew that. How was she going to break through to that woman?

'I'm fine,' Clay said, understanding. 'Go.'

He didn't look fine. His skin was pasty. She could see the light sheen of sweat on his brow, telling her he was hurting far more than she could even guess. Then the bell rang again and she let out her breath. 'You're not fine.'

'You have other patients,' he reminded her gently. 'I can wait.'

'But I need to talk to you.'

'And I need to talk to you. It can wait.'

Again, the bell rang and she closed her eyes briefly. 'My own fault,' she whispered. Her gaze then met his. 'I'll be back, Clay.'

'I'll be here,' he said wryly, closing his eyes. 'Oh . . . Hope?'

'Hmm?'

'What do I do for a living?'

Her stomach dropped to the floor. 'Don't push your memory so hard, Clay. It'll come.'

'It's driving me crazy not to know.'

'It'll come,' she repeated inanely.

'I could be anyone,' he mumbled. 'A mass murderer.'

'No,' she said firmly. 'But you will remember, Clay. I promise.'

'Okay,' he murmured, obviously exhausted past the

point of pressing her. He seemed to relax, and his eyes remained closed, as if it were too difficult to even open them.

The sheet hugged itself to him, the light cotton conforming to and outlining his body clearly. The hard planes of his chest, broken by the bandage around his ribs, caught her eyes. So did the rest of him.

Man, oh man. He was something.

And he needed clothes. She'd had to cut off his shirt, and his jeans were torn beyond repair. For now, he could make do with the scrubs she kept, for he wouldn't be needing anything more for a few days at least.

His body was simply too injured to wear anything other than the soft cotton. But all too soon he'd need something else. She couldn't have him strolling around half nude.

She'd have to go into town, buy men's clothing from the general store. That should stir everyone up, but she couldn't very well ask Kelly to do it.

She looked at him for one more second, then moved to the door. Molly, ever loyal, gave Clay one last lick and followed her.

'Sleep now, okay?' she called out softly.

'Okay.'

His voice was low, mumbled, and if she hadn't read his lips, she wouldn't have been able to hear him. She knew it wasn't rudeness, it was sheer exhaustion and pain. He was hurting so badly, trying to hide it from her, and she had to struggle with the urge to run back to him and give him a hug.

A hug. Where had that come from?

This strange thing between them had to stop, she told herself, horrified. He was a patient, nothing more. And even if he weren't her patient, he wouldn't really be interested. Not once he got to know her. Not once he found out who and what she was, and what she'd done.

But he thought himself her lover, the father of their child. What was she going to do?

CHAPTER 5

Trent left the board meeting the minute it was over. He didn't change his pleasant expression until he'd left the building and sank into his car.

Then he scowled.

Dammit. The old man wouldn't give up. He was far tougher than Trent had counted on. So was his daughter for that matter. Dammit!

Trent wanted so much his head was spinning with it.

He wanted fame, and more fortune. He wanted his political career. He wanted Broderick's business. But most of all, he wanted Hope.

Grimacing, he slammed a hand down on the steering wheel. Hope. It all came back to her. He'd wanted her for so long. But even he could admit that longing was making him lose his edge. Certainly he'd lost it when he could say he wanted her above all else, even his career.

It had to stop. She had to give in. Surely once he had her, he could concentrate on everything else. When he'd first come up with his plan, it had seemed like such a simple thing. Marry Hope to satisfy his life-long obsession. Then use the logging business to his advantage, to propel him into politics. This was the tricky part.

Although Trent was second in command at Broderick's business, he'd gotten there by bribing and bullying. And no amount of shoving could convince the old man to give him a full partnership.

Much as he didn't want to do it, he'd have to hurt the company to gain control. Once he had it, he'd fix whatever damage he'd created. He'd destroy the reputation of Broderick's business in order to weaken it – something he had in motion already by stirring up the Department of Forestry.

Broderick would cave then, rather than see his precious company go down. Yeah, he'd cave and Trent would jump in. He'd make the old man step down. Then, and only then, would Trent step in and save the day, conforming to the government's demands. By doing so, he'd come out a hero in the protesting groups' eyes – *and he'd gain control of the largest logging company this side of the Rockies*. Talk about a career! He'd be the talk of the country.

Easy enough.

Only he hadn't counted on such resistance from Hope. He should have, she'd been managing to brush him off for years, but it still stung.

They belonged together, dammit, and he'd make her see that if it was the last thing he did.

She'd been going non-stop for hours and, combined with her lack of sleep, exhaustion had long ago claimed her. But the patients couldn't be kept waiting. Taking a deep breath, Hope pushed open one of the patient rooms and planted on a smile.

The smile turned genuine at the sight of little Tommy Springer sitting on the bed, his short legs pumping wildly, a toothless grin splitting his face.

'Hey, Doc.'

'Hey, Tommy.' Hope turned to his mother, Betty, with a resigned smile. 'Don't tell me.'

'I'm sorry, Doctor,' the quiet, shy woman said, getting to her feet with a tired sigh. 'I don't know what to say, except I think he does it just to see you.'

Though that knowledge gave Hope a warm, fuzzy feeling she couldn't deny – she fell a bit in love with each and every one of her patients – it had to stop. Affecting a firm air she didn't necessarily feel, she sat beside the little boy with the laughing eyes. 'Tommy, honey, you know you can come see me any time. You don't have to do this.'

'Ma says we can't afford to come see you unless one of us is sick or hurt.'

Making a mental note to make sure Betty didn't get charged for this trip, Hope tipped the boy's head up to see into his nostrils. Yep, it was there all right. 'A blue crayon this time,' she remarked, standing to fetch a pair of tweezers.

'Blue's your favorite color,' Tommy announced happily in a slightly nasal voice. 'Isn't that right?'

'You remembered,' Hope said, flattered, giving Betty a helpless shrug.

'Yeah. And I remembered you like animals, too.' Tommy wiggled up to his knees and shoved a fist into his jeans pocket. 'I brought you a worm. I found it by our pond.'

His mother made a choked sound of disbelief.

He opened his hand, revealing a worm squished nearly beyond recognition. 'Like it?' he asked hopefully.

'Ah . . . thank you,' Hope managed. 'Now about the crayon, Tommy – '

'Oh that.' With a sly, cheeky five-year-old smile, he lifted his free hand and blew his nose noisily into it. While both Betty and Hope cringed, Tommy held out the crayon.

'Here you go, Doc.'

When the patient flow slowed briefly early afternoon, both Hope and Kelly sagged behind the reception desk and stared at each other.

'Busy,' Kelly said in her typically cool, one-worded manner.

'The day's not over,' Hope said glancing at her watch. 'We'd better grab lunch while we can.' And she wanted to check on Clay without drawing attention to herself, as she'd been doing every hour or so. 'I'll . . . be back in a few minutes.'

'You're not going to eat here in your office?' Kelly asked with surprise, shooting her yet another strange glance.

Hope could hardly blame her, she had a reputation for working non-stop. That she was actually going to leave the clinic, even to go to her own kitchen, was unusual. 'I just have to . . . check on something.' Or someone.

If Kelly thought that stranger yet, she didn't remark on it. But just the fact that she remained silent and serious told Hope her nurse thought her a little off, and nearly everything Hope had done these past few days had only confirmed that; her quick trips to check on Clay, how she'd refused all Trent's calls.

'Are you feeling all right?' Kelly asked quietly in her most professional nurse voice, her gaze dropping briefly to Hope's stomach.

It served as a vivid reminder that she'd been asked by each and every patient she'd seen today – with Kelly looking on in interest – if she was really pregnant, which had dashed her hopes that people wouldn't believe a word that Trent had said.

Obviously, they did.

More than a few speculative gazes had dropped to her belly, but she'd refused to fuel the fire in fear of making everything worse.

Let them think what they wanted, as long as they continued to come for medical care.

Kelly had given her a wide berth every chance she got, going to great lengths to avoid taking a break at the same time – not difficult when they'd hardly gotten a break at all. Hope could only sigh, and continue to be as friendly and professional as possible. And hope that Kelly would come around.

'I'm fine,' she said in answer to the nurse's obviously clinical concern.

With a brow raised, Kelly studied her silently.

'I am,' she said insistently, just resisting the urge to cover her stomach. And she had nothing to hide, darn it!

'Well, then. Here's the mail.' With that, Kelly slapped the stack of mail into Hope's hands and turned away, reaching into a lunch box for a sandwich.

Hope flipped through the mail as she left the room,

groaning at the bills. But she had to stop in the hallway to lean weakly against the wall at the last envelope.

It was a formal letter from her father's property management company, and it shook in her hands. They were giving her notice – she was to vacate by the end of the month.

He was going to sell the property.

Fine, she'd thought, shoving back her panic as she pushed away from the wall. She'd just find a way to buy it.

Right! Half of her patients couldn't pay her, the other half didn't pay on time. The noose closed in on her faster each day.

So did despair.

She wanted to see Clay now, far more than she wanted to understand. But first she had to call her father. She used the kitchen phone, hoping for some privacy. Not nearly as firmly or as confidently as she'd told her patients, she said without preamble, 'I am not pregnant.'

'Ah, a lover's spat.' He sighed and fell silent.

'Father!' It took her a minute to be able to speak rationally, rage and humiliation warred so strongly within her. 'Trent is no lover of mine, not that I should even have to explain myself.'

'Are you really not pregnant?'

The hopeful joy in his voice destroyed her, not to mention melted any residual anger, and she sank down into the closest chair. Molly, as always on her heels, sat as well, waiting patiently.

Joy. Pride. How could she use those things against him? Yet how could she let him believe her pregnant, even if only to buy herself time? 'To hear you so happy makes this all the more difficult,' she started. 'I don't want to hurt you. But I can't live my life for you, I just can't. Please understand, there's nothing between Trent and me.'

'He says differently.'

'He doesn't know what he's talking about.'

'It is a lover's spat,' he said as if she hadn't spoken. 'I understand these things, Hope, though you might not believe that. But I'm not so old that I can't remember what it's like. Your mother – '

'I know, Father,' she said with a sigh of her own, absently petting Molly when she plopped her heavy head into Hope's lap. 'You two had a volatile relationship.'

'But we loved each other. Very much.' The sadness crept into his voice. 'We were very different. Yet in one thing, we agreed. It was her place to stay home and raise you. No baby should be without her mother at home.'

'When I have a child,' she assured him, 'I will never put anything before the proper care of that child. You should know that. But I have an important job here – '

'A job someone else can do. You work too hard. You've never taken time off to enjoy yourself, not once.'

'The clinic stays busy. It's not easy to take off, and the work I do here is important to me.'

'What's important,' he told her earnestly, 'is life. Hope, please. Think about this.'

She didn't want to. Oh, how she didn't. But a little voice whispered that her father was right, even if just a little bit. She didn't take time for herself, she never had.

'Trent wants to take care of you.'

I don't want to be taken care of,' she said slowly, wondering how such an old-fashioned man made it in the modern world. 'The man – '

'Cares about you. It would give me great pleasure, Hope, if you'd consider him. That's all I'm asking.'

'You're asking me to give up everything I've ever wanted.'

'I'm just asking you to consider it.'

'No, it's more than that,' Hope insisted, her fingers lifting from Molly to run over the notice she'd received in the mail. 'You've said you'll take this place from me. I got a notice to vacate.'

'I just want to see it used for what it was meant for. *Babies.*'

She made a sound she recognized as desperate frustration. They couldn't solve this, not this way. Not without hurting each other.

'You and Trent will work out this silliness,' he said. 'He's important to me, Hope. So are you.'

She'd heard it before. Her father wasn't getting any younger and he wanted an heir. 'This is the late twentieth century! What you're expecting of me is barbaric.'

He laughed, almost as if he'd just been baiting her. 'Just hurry it up, Hope.'

She hung up on him as gently as she could, then fretted.

Give up, she told herself. *Call his bluff, and if you have to, just give up the property and go somewhere else to practise.* Seattle. San Francisco. Portland. Anywhere. It shouldn't matter so much.

But it did. She'd grown up here and she loved it. This

house felt right. In it, she caught her mother's spirit. It gave her joy and hope, and she didn't want to leave it.

Besides, she loved the freedom of her small practice, and she loved the variety the clinic afforded her. She wanted to stay.

She stiffened as the hair rose on her neck. She wasn't alone.

'Hope? Are you sure you're all right?'

Turning from the wall and the telephone, she faced Kelly, who had come silently into the room. Hope pasted a smile on her face and wondered how long Kelly had been standing there. 'I'm fine. Why?'

'That telephone conversation seemed to upset you.'

Hope didn't answer immediately, trying to remember exactly what she and her father had said, and how much Kelly could have overheard.

'That conversation seemed to upset you,' Kelly said again, more slowly. Exasperated, Hope said, 'I did hear you, Kelly. If I'm looking at you, I hear – or see – almost everything you say, believe it or not.'

'I'm sorry,' Kelly said, looking genuinely so. 'I just thought – I mean, I know you can't always – Oh, hell!' She offered a little smile, the first Hope could remember seeing. 'I didn't mean to insult you.'

'It's all right, but I really hear better than you must think.'

'You do?'

'Normally, yes. It's only when I'm tired or upset I start to miss things, and then I read lips. So unless you turn away, I'll still understand.'

'Oh.' She looked horrified, probably remembering all

the times she'd slowly and methodically spoken to Hope as if she were a half wit.

'And while we're on the subject, I hear that buzzer the first time. It's made with a special tone. I can't miss it.'

Kelly bit her lip. 'So when I ring you fifteen times, it must get a little annoying.'

'A little.' But she smiled. 'It's all right, I should have explained sooner. Don't worry about it.'

'I'm really very sorry,' the nurse said again, still looking mortified.

Hope didn't want that, it was no way to build a trusting work relationship, and in their business, they had to trust each other. Implicitly. 'Don't be.' Hope forced a smile. 'Let's make a deal. If I don't hear you, I'll ask you to repeat it. Okay?'

'Good idea.' And for the first time in the week they'd known each other, Kelly smiled, genuinely, at her.

In that moment some of the tension between them dissolved, and Hope found herself offering a true smile back. It felt good, and in light of the unsettling conversation she'd just had with her father, it relaxed her.

'Are you really feeling okay?' Kelly asked. 'Because you look . . . kind of pale.' Just for an instant, her gaze lowered to Hope's belly.

Before Hope could say a word – which was just as well, since she had no idea what she would have said – Kelly asked, 'Did you ever return Trent's calls? He rang several times for you today.'

'Uh . . . no.'

'He seemed worried. He says you work too hard, and

that he's going to have to make sure you don't do this to yourself for much longer.'

A threat? Hope made a sound that must have passed for a reply.

'It was sweet, especially when he said he plans on taking care of you since you won't do it yourself,' Kelly said, stretching her back and wincing, not noticing Hope losing five shades of color. 'And if he knew how hard we worked today, he probably would have had a coronary. Between Tommy's crayon and that pregnant woman eating an entire jar of pickles, then thinking she'd gone into labor . . . Whew, we were busy. I think he worries. Trent, that is.'

A shiver raced up her spine. Another strangled sound appeased her nurse.

'How nice that must be, Dr Broderick. To have a man like that care so much.'

A man like that. A not so welcome reminder of how much Trent was known and liked.

She managed a last weak reply and excused herself.

Long after Kelly left, and well after she'd fed herself, Clay, and her flock of animals, Hope walked the house, restless. She should sleep, she desperately needed it, but she couldn't.

All day she'd been doing what she loved, even while fighting off feelings of dread and fear over her future. And all day, in the back of her mind, had been her house guest.

There was no doubt in her mind what she wanted to do now – she wanted to see Clay. *Needed to see Clay*.

Somehow, some way, he soothed her, even when he did nothing but lay there and smile at her.

In less than a minute, she stood in the doorway, fumbling for an excuse to be there.

He was fast asleep.

The best thing, she told herself, even as she'd spared a few minutes to watch him, telling herself she did it to make sure he was okay. Telling herself it had nothing to do with how absolutely appealing he looked, his bruised face softened in sleep. His sandy hair fell over his forehead, making him look young, and so vulnerable she had to touch. Gently, she pushed back the wayward lock of hair. Though he didn't awaken, the tense lines around his eyes and mouth eased.

She realized that for nearly three days she'd thought of little else but him and wondered why. But looking at him made her feel good so she looked her fill.

His lashes were dark and long, his nose straight. And his lips . . . they were impossibly sexy, even with the cut.

He was something, she thought, and her pulse fluttered a little wildly. Tough, rugged features were the only thing that kept him from being too pretty. That, and his lingering bruises.

He was undoubtedly one of the most attractive men she'd ever seen.

One that deserved more than he'd gotten from her.

She had justified waiting until now to tell him the truth. After all, she would need more than a five minute break to tell him. He deserved that much. And he'd looked so bad, seemed so tired, she hadn't wanted to wake him.

But she would now.

She wouldn't be able to sleep until she did.

First, just one more minute of looking. Unable to resist, she reached out to touch his lightly stubbled and bruised cheek.

What was it about him that made him seem more than just a patient? That made it all seem . . . as though he really could be her lover?

He was warm, resilient, and she wanted to touch more. She did, running her fingers down over his throat to his collarbone, just for the simple pleasure of feeling him. As her fingers wandered over the hard planes and ungiving muscle of his chest, her gaze lifted to his face . . . and she froze.

He'd awakened.

She would damn her poor hearing, but it had been her own libido that made her lose her concentration, nothing more. No mistake about it. Both his eyes were open and leveled right on her. Deep, forest green, filled with secrets.

'Hi,' she said stupidly. Then yanked her hand back, embarrassed to have been caught fondling him in his sleep.

But he reached out and took her hand, pulling it back towards him. 'Don't.' His voice was rough from sleep.

'Don't what?'

He settled her hand against his chest, where beneath the light smattering of hair she could feel the solid beat of his heart. 'Don't not touch me. I like it.'

'Oh.' How could she do this? she wondered wildly. How could she tell him the truth, when he was so impossibly, gorgeously . . . hers?

'Clay – '

'Tell me about us,' he urged, closing his eyes, still holding her hand against him. 'Something other than our crazy menagerie of pets.'

She could feel his bone-deep weariness, and for a flash, before he'd closed his eyes, it had happened again. She'd seen, no *sensed*, something much deeper, something much more disturbing. She'd gotten the feeling that all this was supposed to happen, that this was meant. It unnerved her into stunned silence.

She had to be wrong. When this was all over, he'd walk away, right out of her life.

'That hard, huh?' He sighed. 'You know, Hope, I get the uncomfortable feeling you're keeping things from me.'

'You do?' she asked, startled.

'Yeah, like maybe I was a jerk before. It drives me crazy. I really wish I could remember that I treated you right.'

He spoke quietly, mumbling a little. She had to rely on reading his cracked lips. 'Why wouldn't you have treated me right?' she whispered.

'You tell me.' He hesitated while his free hand touched her arm. Through the material of her blouse her skin sizzled. 'But if I was rotten, would you consider giving me another chance? Especially since I can't remember being that way?'

Guilt swamped her. Guilt and an overwhelming sense of awe that he cared so much for her. 'You . . . weren't rotten, Clay.' Somehow, she knew that. 'And your memory will come back, I promise.'

'I like the way you do that,' he said, squeezing her arm

softly before dropping his hand from her, letting it fall limply back to the bed. 'The way you read my mind and offer comfort, sometimes before I even realize I need it.'

He liked that she sensed his feelings . . . if it were true, he was the first one to ever say so.

'Thanks for the food today,' he whispered, his words coming slow and thick, as if he were so tired he could hardly keep awake. 'I know . . . how busy you were.'

'I like my work.'

'But you work too hard. Are you feeling okay?'

She started to answer glibly, intending to tease him about *him* being the patient, not her. But she went still as she remembered.

Just like everyone else, he thought her pregnant. Because she'd told him it was so.

Her throat thickened at the unmistakable tenderness in his sleepy voice, and for a minute, she closed her eyes and let herself believe. It'd be so wonderful to have someone really care, really want to know about *her*, for a change.

But as tempting and novel as all that was, it just wasn't possible, she'd sealed that fate the moment she'd lied to him. 'I'm fine,' she said more briskly than she intended. 'You're feeling better?'

'Hmmm.'

He fell silent. Hope struggled with the words she needed, not easy to do with the heat of him seeping through her hand and into her body.

'You were great today. Was I proud of you?'

He mumbled, and his mouth hardly moved. She missed every word. 'What?'

'Your work. Tommy and his crayon, which,' he said with a gruff little laugh, 'I have to admit, was a very creative way to get to see you. I'd have tried it myself, if I thought it'd get more of your attention – and if I didn't hurt so damn much already.'

That startled a laugh out of her.

'The way you handled that other little boy terrified from his fall, and then that teenage girl.'

He'd heard, she realized, staring at the wall of the room she had him in, the one that connected with her office. She tried to remember everything she'd said, if she'd given herself away in any way. 'Those were privileged conversations, Clay.'

'She was afraid because she'd had sex,' he said slowly, his eyes closed.

She watched him closely as he spoke, since when he was tired like this, she couldn't always understand.

He shook his head, his eyes still shut. 'She thought God was going to strike her dead in her tracks. Poor thing.'

It was pathetically sad, but true, all thanks to the girl's idiotic religiously-fanatic aunt. Hope had spent the better part of two hours convincing the girl God wasn't going to punish her with a deadly bolt of lightning. But the next shock had come when Hope realized that she hadn't known a thing about birth control and AIDS, much less self-respect. She'd spent a long time on that last thing, since it was so very important, especially to a girl that age.

Had she done any good today? She prayed she had, and it had been a small reminder of how important, and diverse, her job was.

'You were so good with her, Hope. Was I proud of you, before?'

'We never really talked about it.'

He didn't say anything, but a spasm of pain crossed his face.

She sighed and sat at the edge of the bed. His hand had loosened on hers, so she played with his covers, busying her hands with making sure he was tucked in. It was time.

She took a deep breath. 'Clay . . . I need to talk to you . . . and I'm not sure where to start.' A nervous laugh tickled her throat. 'It's actually almost funny. You're my patient, but you're not. And it leaves me . . . well, I'm not sure how to treat you.'

She paused, hoping he'd say something, anything, to end her nervous rambling, but he didn't. 'That night I found you,' she continued quickly before she lost her nerve, 'I wasn't myself. I'd just – ' She bit her lip, knowing she had to tread carefully. She didn't want to say anything too jarring, because while she wanted him to remember, desperately, she knew it had to come naturally.

It'd be hard for him if she made him remember before he was ready 'I – I'd just found out s – something upsetting,' she said, stuttering slightly as nerves jumbled up in her stomach. She stared down at her hands, hands that had helped so many people, but were capable of helping so many more.

Just tell him!

'And I knew it would change my life. So I was really off-balance. Not that it excuses anything, but – '

Just tell him!

'– Well, here it is –' She broke off abruptly at the soft, deep breath. She lifted her head. 'Clay?'

A soft snore was her answer.

She let out a little laugh of disbelief. Nice to know she hadn't lost her touch. She still bored every man that came across her path – except for Trent. With a helpless sigh, she stared at Clay.

She'd wanted to tell him the truth so badly.

Oh, well, what was one more night? Only hours without sleep, she told herself wryly.

Gently as she could, she tucked him in and turned off the light. 'Sleep well, Clay,' she whispered, and left the room.

She hadn't gotten to her bedroom before her home phone line rang. Late as it was, she knew it could be only one person.

Trent.

She let it ring.

But Trent was persistent, and the phone rang on and on. She stared at it. No. She wouldn't get it.

But the fear that Clay might pick up the other extension had her changing her mind, and diving for the phone on the seventh ring.

'Hope. I was waiting.'

The deep exaggerated voice had her sinking weakly to her bed. There weren't many people who made her feel this way, small and scared. But Trent did, and she didn't understand why.

'You've been a busy little bee,' he said in a voice most would consider charming. To Hope, it seemed slightly threatening. 'Are you ignoring me, Hope?'

'As you said, I've been busy.'

'You know I couldn't get Kelly to put you on the line once today.'

Thank God for Kelly, as strained as their relationship remained. 'We had patients all day.' She glanced at her watch. 'And I'm really tired, Trent.'

It was too much to hope he'd take the hint. 'Nice woman, your new nurse,' he said casually.

Inspiration struck. 'Why don't you ask her out?'

He laughed. 'Beautiful as she may be, Hope, it's you I want. You know that.'

Shivers ran up her spine at just his voice. 'You've been talking about me. Telling lies.'

He sighed, a small breath of sound Hope barely caught. But the mock patience in it snapped her temper.

'I'm not pregnant,' she snapped. 'And you know it. I want you to stop saying so.'

'We've known each other so long, Hope. We belong together.'

'I'm sorry,' she said, then grimaced, annoyed at herself. Why should she say she was sorry?

'You don't want to be with me.'

His voice had thickened, as if he'd gripped the telephone harder and brought it too close to his mouth. 'It's nothing personal,' she said as kindly as she could, even now, after all he'd put her through, not able to bring herself to hurt him. 'I just don't want to be with anyone.'

Big lie. There was a man laying in her spare bedroom that she wanted to be with. Only she'd blown that. 'Do you understand?' she asked Trent.

'Yes.'

She couldn't feel relieved because she didn't believe him. 'Do you? Do you really?'

'You think I'm not good enough for you.'

'No, I – '

'I'm somebody, Hope. And I'm on the fast track to higher aspirations than you could ever understand. Do you hear me?'

His voice had risen so she couldn't miss a single word. 'Yes, but – '

'And you're going to be mine. You have to be.'

Yet another chill raced along her spine as he became openly hostile. 'I don't have to do anything I don't want to, Trent. And I don't want you to call me any more.'

'What?'

The shocked, angry surprise in his voice made her cringe. 'And please, leave my father out of this. Just stop talking about me.'

'Okay, Hope,' he said quietly. 'I can see I'm not going to get anywhere with the nice guy routine. So let's try this: *don't mess with me*. I have your father on my side about this, and he believes in me. He thinks we've had a little lover's spat, and it's the truth. If you want to keep that practice of yours, you'll go with what I say.'

'I won't.'

'Oh, yes you will. You're pregnant with my child – You are,' he repeated when she made a sound of protest. 'And we will marry. Soon.'

He hung up.

She stared at the phone and laughed in disbelief,

though she really wanted to cry. Just who did he think he was?

And was there really cause for this unreasonable fear inside her?

Brushing off her unease, she started down the dark hallway. Halfway down, Molly, who'd been walking beside her protectively, went rigid. The dog lifted her head, sniffed, then growled low in her throat. The black hair rose on Molly's chest and tail.

Hope hesitated. Molly never growled unless she had a good reason. That she did so now had the hair on the back of her own neck rising. But, frustratingly, she could hear nothing out of the ordinary, no matter how she concentrated.

'Molly?' she whispered, touching the dog for her own comfort more than anything else. 'What is it?'

The dog sniffed again, turned to Hope and whined softly. Warningly. Hope's heart leaped in her chest.

The front room was dark, just as she'd left it when she'd gone to Clay.

But from outside, where there was nothing but dense woods, came a beam of light. Then another.

Someone was out there, in the dark, searching for something.

CHAPTER 6

Hope's breath backed up in her throat as she sidled up to the wall, watching the flickering light. From where she looked out into the dark night, she could see little.

Molly growled again.

The deep, thick woods surrounding her house were private, without another neighboring house for at least two miles, maybe more. No one should be on her property at night without her permission. No one.

Unless, . . . *oh, no*!

Unless they were looking for the body they'd abandoned the other night. The body that wasn't a dead body at all, but her Clay.

It couldn't be the police. First of all, they didn't show him as missing – Hope had checked twice today alone through her friend and his computer. No one was looking for him at all, and he wasn't wanted by the police.

With or without a record, Clayton Slater was not a criminal. Which left her only one bleak thought. Whoever looked for him most likely was.

What if they found him?

Would they finish off the job they'd started?

And what if she told Clay the truth about what she'd done? How she'd lied, how she'd used him to get herself out of a scrape?

The first thing any reasonable person would do would be to leave – angrily – no matter what pathetic excuses she might offer.

He'd leave, and walk directly into their hands. She couldn't tell him, she just couldn't.

Hope stood there, nervously flattened against the wall in the darkened hallway, long after the lights disappeared.

The next morning, Clay came to slowly. Dreamland had been pleasant, no pain. He knew better than to hope being awake could be as good. Carefully he tried to open his eyes. They both opened easily.

Things were improving.

Still, nearly four days and no memory, just a nagging sense that he'd forgotten something. Too bad that something included his entire life.

Cautiously, he sat up. His vision swam, his ribs screamed, but he didn't feel as if he were going to throw up at the slight movement. A good sign.

Today was the day, he promised himself. He'd not only stay in a sitting position, but he'd stand up. He was tired of viewing the world from flat on his back. Although he couldn't remember, he knew he wasn't a man used to idleness. It drove him crazy.

If only he could remember what he *was* used to. It was the first thing he intended to ask Hope.

But he could at least find out what he looked like, if he

could just get out of the bed and across the room to the mirror. A quick peek under the covers assured him he was still quite nude.

Beside his bed was a neatly folded t-shirt and a pair of scrubs. *Thank you, Hope.* So she thought of him as often as he thought of her. Before he could hold his lip, he smiled, neatly splitting it open again.

'Dammit!'

'You okay?'

He lifted his head and found Hope standing in the doorway, wearing her doctor's coat and a worried frown.

'I can't remember,' he said.

She frowned and he risked a laugh, holding his ribs with one hand, his lip with the other. 'I'm kidding.'

'Oh.' But she gazed at him worriedly.

'Really,' he said, still smiling, feeling ridiculously cheered by just the sight of her. 'I'm . . . better.'

'Okay.' She didn't look convinced and her gaze remained fixed on his lips.

But he couldn't dwell on that suddenly, not with a new question burning in his mind. 'Why am I in a spare bedroom, not in our bedroom?'

It had only just occurred to him, and his only excuse for not once thinking about it sooner was his incredible pain and exhaustion.

'What?'

Patiently he repeated his question, wondering why she always seemed to have such trouble hearing him. Did he speak funny with his lip cut?

Hope paled at the repeated question. 'Well. You *are*

feeling better,' she said in that low, unusual voice, moving into the room. 'Still no memory?'

'We had broken up, hadn't we?' It was the only explanation he could think of. Why else would she nearly leap out of her skin every time he touched her? Why else wouldn't he be sharing a blanket with that delectable body of hers?

She sighed as she came up to his bed and leaned a hip on it. 'Oh, Clay. It's so darned tangled up now.'

'What happened, Hope?' he asked quietly, disturbed by the distress in her face. Had he really been a jerk, then?

Her shoulders sagged in what he would have sworn was relief. 'It's the baby,' she whispered hoarsely, still watching his mouth. 'I'm not really – It's not what – '

'You don't want it,' he said flatly, stunned. It hadn't been him that had broken them up, but her.

'No, it's not that,' she said quickly, sinking the rest of the way to the bed, her hip brushing his. She put her hands to her temple and rubbed. 'It's really so complicated, Clay.'

'Complicated.' He let out a harsh laugh, then nearly cried out at the unbelievable shaft of pain that shot through his ribs, or would have cried out, if he had been able to take a breath past his searing lungs.

But he couldn't breathe or cry out, he could only open his mouth and fight for the air that wouldn't fill his lungs.

Instantly, Hope was there, hovering over him, holding his shoulders with her hands. 'Clay, breathe. Slowly, that's it, just go real slow. Real slow, I'm right here. You just knocked the wind right out of you, that's all. Those ribs are going to give you this trouble for a while. Come on, that's it. Breathe again, real slow.'

Aware of her voice through the fog of agony, he went with it, breathing like she said. 'Hell,' he managed on a gasp, wrapping his arms around his middle and hunching over. It didn't help, but he couldn't have unwound himself for anything. 'I feel like I've got a knife deep inside me, twisting.'

Her lips tightened, her eyes filled with compassion, worry. Her palms ran up and down his arms, squeezing gently at the knots of tension in his shoulders. 'Those ribs are going to take a while to heal, you've got to take it easy on them.'

In her eyes was something new, something he might have missed if she hadn't been practically in his lap, with her hands on him, her soft breath brushing his face.

Fear.

Of him? No, he was weak as a baby, completely harmless, and she knew it. So what was she afraid of? That what had happened to him would happen to her? Was she afraid, as he was, that he would bring his crazy world to her?

'What do I do for a living?'

She blinked at the suddenness of the question, her gaze straight on his lips. 'You run your own business. In Seattle.'

'What kind?'

'I stayed out of it.'

Not good enough, and he had to know more. Had to know if whoever had gotten to him was satisfied, or if they'd come back for more, and next time, maybe hurt Hope as well. 'There's more, a lot more,' he said, watching her drag her teeth over her lower lip. His dread increased, as did his fear for her. 'Are you trying to protect me from something?'

Her gaze dropped, telling him she was hiding something, and he wasn't going to like it. 'Hope,' he said urgently, leaning close. 'Why was I outside in the storm that night? And who would want me dead?'

'What?'

His damn lip! It must be making him mumble. Making a conscious effort to form his words better, he repeated his questions.

'I don't know.'

'Then how did you know where to find me?'

'Molly found you.' She swallowed hard, clearly troubled. 'Thank goodness, Clay. What if she hadn't? What if I'd ignored her – '

'Don't.' But he reached for her hand and squeezed it thankfully. 'I'm here now, and getting better. My thousand questions should tell you that.'

She gave him a little worried smile, her dark, full eyes on his face.

'Are you ever going to answer some of them?'

'Yes. When you're much better.'

That was difficult to accept, and if it hadn't been for her stricken expression, he would have pushed. He managed to give a half smile without splitting his lip further. 'Know what? I don't even know what I look like.'

She looked at him doubtfully.

'Come on, it can't be that bad.'

She twisted her fingers together and said nothing.

'What's the matter?' he asked with a careful laugh. 'I can't be that ugly.'

Now she laughed, and it was a wonderful sound. 'You'll break my mirror, no doubt.'

'That bad, huh?'

She nodded, her lips still curved.

Now he knew he wasn't a vain man, or at least he liked to think he wasn't. But he suddenly found he wanted her to think him handsome.

'I'm kidding,' she said softly, reading his mind with startling clarity. 'I think you're beautiful.'

Ego and embarrassment warred. 'Not pretty?' he teased to hide it. 'Just beautiful?'

'Both,' she declared.

He sobered. 'Then talk to me.'

'You're not better.'

'I am,' he insisted.

Silently, she leaned back, pulled down the sheet, exposing his chest. Above and below the wrapping on his ribs were deep, vicious, colorful bruises. Staring down at him, her lip quivered. Her eyes filled. 'Oh, Clay,' she whispered, bringing her trembling fingers to her mouth.

Watching her, he had no doubt how she felt about him. Separated or broken up they may be, but she still cared. Deeply. It stirred him, right down to the heart inside his chest that he knew nothing about.

'I don't know what happened to us,' he told her, 'or what would have happened between us if I hadn't lost my memory. But I do know one thing.'

'What?' she whispered with a sniff.

'I don't want to lose you.' He slipped a hand past the white doctor's coat to her middle, holding her tummy possessively. 'Or the baby. Promise me I won't. That you'll give us another chance.'

She swallowed, hard. Then lifted dark, drenched eyes to his. 'You mean that, don't you?'

'With all my heart.'

'But you know nothing about me.'

She sounded awed, a little overwhelmed. *Good. It would make her think twice about giving up on them.* 'I know you are the kindest, sweetest woman there is. Also the strongest. And when I think about what you're doing out here, caring for people who might not otherwise get care –'

'I'm not a hero,' she said flatly, withdrawing. 'I'll get it.'

'Get what –'

A red light flashed over the phone, and she took advantage, leaping up, avoiding his narrowed gaze. 'I've got to go,' she said quickly, turning away.

The light flashed again, bringing his attention to the large, awkward looking receiver that he'd wondered about. But before he could ask about it, or how she always knew the phone was going to ring before it did, she said quickly, 'Kelly's paging me. I've probably got a patient.'

'How do you know who it is?'

She squirmed. 'Lucky guess. I've got to run. Don't get up yet, Clay. Give it another day.'

He said nothing, just watched her as she moved quickly to the door.

She turned back to him. 'Are you going to stay put?'

'Will you promise to come back and discuss this with me later?'

She sighed. 'Yes. If you stay still.'

His overwhelming exhaustion would see to that. 'I'm not going anywhere.'

She gave him a long look, then nodded slowly. 'Rest now.'

Unbelievably, despite his mile long list of questions, he did.

'Dr Broderick?' Kelly stuck her head in Hope's small office that afternoon. 'Agatha Kilner's on line one. Again.'

Hope stifled her groan and glanced at her nurse. 'Don't tell me, she's thinking about getting married again.'

'Yep.'

'This makes number seven, you know.'

'Yep.'

'Tell her congratulations for me.'

'Nice try,' Kelly said dryly. 'But she wants to talk to you.'

'She wants to know – again – what I think of having pre-marital relations, though we've had this discussion six other times in so many years.'

Kelly, who'd clearly heard it all before, didn't blink. 'Not this time, Doctor. She was hoping you'd tell her raspberry root will increase her boyfriend's sexual drive.'

Hope set down her pen and laughed. 'He's ninety.

She's eighty-five if she's a day. The only thing that's going to increase that poor man's sex drive is a good dream – '

'You're the doctor,' Kelly broke in. 'It should definitely come from you.' At Hope's long look, she smiled innocently. 'I shouldn't be handing out medical advice.'

'Chicken,' Hope mumbled and picked up the phone. 'No, Agatha, raspberry root won't – '

'Are you sure, dear?' Agatha broke in. 'Because I've been putting a tad in Albert's tea, and I think it might be working. You should see how he's responding. His manhood – '

'Uh . . . Agatha,' Hope interrupted quickly before she could get an anatomy lesson she didn't want, 'We've discussed this. I'm a medical doctor. What you're suggesting is folklore. A myth.'

'I realize how you new fangled doctors do things,' Agatha said, her voice shaking with either age or excitement. 'Drugs, drugs, drugs. But I'm telling you, this works! And as the direct descendant from a Russian gypsy, you of all people should believe me.'

This wasn't the city. This was the deep backwoods, where tradition and culture meant far more than money and education. Hope knew, perhaps better than most, the meaning of mind over matter. It was what had allowed her to prevail and become a doctor in spite of her handicap. Who was she to tell this woman that adding a harmless raspberry root to tea wouldn't work?

'Okay, Agatha,' she said gently. 'But not more than one dose a day for a week. All right?'

'Oh, thank you, Doctor! Thank you so much!' She

giggled. 'You've given me a shot at husband number seven!'

Hope hung up the phone, laughing at herself. But the amusement faded soon enough. Truth. Trust. Powerful emotions indeed. Her patients gave her both without fail. Clay had as well, and she'd dishonored them both by not telling him the truth this morning.

For truth was her life, and trust was everything. Having to twist the first and give up on the second hurt more than she could have possibly guessed.

Only pure and simple desperation kept her from telling Clay the truth now. She didn't want him to try to leave, not when someone was clearly looking for him.

She refused to admit it had anything to do with how she was beginning to feel for him.

Hope had only one patient left when Kelly stopped her in the doorway of her office. With unusual candor and kindness, the nurse put a hand on Hope's arm.

'Doctor? You feeling okay?'

Did she look that awful? She was tired, true, and maybe a little stressed over Trent's disturbing behavior, but beneath it all lived her usual joy and excitement for life. And added to that was a new awareness for the man asleep in her spare bedroom. 'I'm . . . fine.'

'You worked hard today.'

'Kelly, I'm not pregnant.'

Kelly looked at her, obviously torn, and who could blame her? Hope knew Trent called several times a day, and always spent time talking to Kelly. He'd apparently told Kelly different, and the poor nurse now had no idea who to believe.

'And,' Hope said, making the rash decision to trust the woman. 'I'm not involved with Trent.'

Kelly smiled knowingly. 'He told me you're shy about letting people know. It's all right, Dr Broderick. You don't have to mention it. I'm not going to repeat it to anyone.'

'I mean it, Kelly. We're not together. Never will be.'

Her nurse looked at her for a long moment as Molly trotted into the room and leaned against Hope.

'You mean that,' Kelly said.

'I most certainly do.' For comfort, she leaned back into Molly, the two of them holding each other up.

'That's why you never take his calls.'

'Yes.'

Kelly stared at her, then a spasm of regret crossed her features. 'I'm sorry, Doctor. He's just so friendly, so charming. So open. It's so easy to get drawn into a conversation with him.'

'I understand, believe me.' Any female in the entire county would have understood.

'I just assumed – '

'Please, don't assume anything about me,' Hope said, having had enough of that for a lifetime. She softened her tone when Kelly's face went taut. 'In the future, Kelly, I'd appreciate it if you'd not discuss me with Trent.'

'Of course.' Kelly said, a little stiffly.

Hope could only sigh. Back to formalities.

Molly nudged her. For the first time, Hope looked down at the dog, then felt her eyes widen in surprise. In

Molly's mouth was a floral paper plate, the one she'd brought Clay his lunch on. Empty of food except for a smear of what might have been catsup, the words *Thinking of you* had been printed in large block letters, followed by a heart.

Hope snatched the plate out of Molly's mouth with a quick glance at Kelly. Her nurse was staring at her own hands. Hope folded the plate in half, covering the writing. Then nearly laughed at the words scrawled on the back.

Think of me back. Please?

Hope rolled the plate up quickly, heart thundering. Her face split into a ridiculous grin she couldn't control. She felt like a teenager. Molly panted and seemed to grin back at her, as if they shared a secret, which of course, they did.

Unbelievably, Hope felt a bubble of laughter tickle her throat.

'You're . . . sure you're okay?' Kelly asked, glancing at her strangely.

'Fine,' Hope said, her heart still racing as she gripped the plate behind her back. She bit back the giggle with some trouble. Eighty-five-year-old Agatha wasn't the only one with sex on the brain.

Think of me.

As if she could do anything else! But there was no denying the spark of joy that came from knowing Clay lay close, thinking of her.

Kelly went back to work, obviously still a little uncomfortable. Hope went back to work as well, unable to wipe the smile off her face.

* * *

That evening, after their patients had all gone, Kelly paused in the doorway to wave goodbye to Hope.

It was the gesture she made at the end of each work day, usually with a tense expression.

Today there'd been no tenseness at all, just a surprisingly honest, open look of camaraderie. It had made Hope smile, expecting nothing in return. What she got back was an honest smile from the heart, and it meant the world to Hope.

The front door of the clinic closed behind the nurse a minute later and Hope let out a deep breath, feeling optimistic. Would they settle into a more comfortable routine now?

She could only hope.

Flipping out the lights of the clinic, Hope let out a whining Molly, then studied the darkened rooms. She loved it here beyond reason. Would she still be here this time next year?

No time for moping, she decided. She had to feed the animals. And then check on her patient, the one with the amazing, kind, laughing eyes. The one that could fluster her with just one look. She couldn't stop thinking of him.

It was the only excuse she had for not reacting quicker, that plus the fact that he moved so sly and fast, she couldn't hear him coming.

As she shifted, someone grabbed her, hauled her against a hard, ungiving body. It startled a scream from her before a hand slapped over her mouth. Struggling, she pulled frantically at the arm clamped around her, desperate for air.

The hand didn't give, and right there in the dark,

unable to hear anything but the roar of her own blood, she panicked with fear.

From the other side of the door came violent scratching and the sound of Molly's nervous whine. Then frantic barking.

There was no one to help her.

The hand over her mouth lifted and she screamed again.

CHAPTER 7

Clay jerked awake, then lay there trying to figure out what had woken him.

Then he heard it again, Hope's scream.

Wrenching himself upright, he gasped in pain. The room swam before his eyes as he wasted precious time waiting for the nausea to pass. When it did, he shoved off the covers, planted his feet on the floor and tried to get up.

A scuffling noise came from down the hallway, and all sorts of tortuous thoughts went through his mind. What was wrong? Was someone attacking her?

The same someone who had attacked him?

No! Please, no.

He had to help her.

He got to the door, shaking and already sweating, before he remembered he was still buck naked. Swearing to himself, he stepped back into the hospital scrubs he'd just recently kicked off because they were too stiff and prickly over bruised legs. He yanked them up, then bolted for the door, ignoring the pain in his ribs.

Another muffled scratching noise came to him, renewing his terror. But when he managed to get to the door and crack it open, everything in the hallway sounded ominously silent, except for Molly's now frantic barking and whining, coming from the back.

Molly locked out meant one exceptionally terrifying thing – Hope was completely alone.

Fear spurred him on. Glancing back at his bed, he saw the telephone on the table there, and wondered if he should call for help. But the thought brought more panic, and he felt certain that if this was trouble he'd brought on Hope, the police couldn't help.

He just couldn't remember why.

In the hallway, all was dark and silent. Quietly, he crept down the hall, his vision swimming, his head drumming out an angry beat that matched his heart rate. Two steps and he was holding his on-fire ribs for dear life.

He was going to pass out.

A fat lot of good he was going to do Hope if he did, but he had to stop to slump against the wall for a minute until he could see clearly again. Dammit! He was wasting precious time.

His muscles had started to shake and sweat trickled down his back, but he straightened and moved resolutely forward.

Then, without warning, he passed out.

Hard, glittering eyes stared down at Hope. 'You've seen all your patients, Hope. Now it's my turn.'

'Trent,' she gasped, her heart in her throat. 'You scared me to death.'

Though she struggled, he didn't release her. 'Did I?' he murmured, running his hands down her back with alarming familiarity. 'Ready to marry me yet?'

'Of course not,' she snapped, anger replacing fear. 'Let me go.'

'You feel good.'

He wasn't going to release her, and panic flared again. She knew how he looked at her, and it made her feel a little sick. Why did her father like this man so much? 'What are you doing here?' she asked him, pushing at the immovable wall that was his chest.

'Wanted to see how much you missed me.' One of his hands banded around her back, the other drifted low, pressing her to him.

'Don't,' she gasped, shoving hard, so that when he released her, she staggered back so fast she hit the wall. He advanced slowly, steadily, while she wondered whether she should scream or run.

'I'm not alone,' she said bravely, lifting her chin. Molly was barking loud enough to wake the dead. God help her if Clay heard the commotion and tried to get up and come to her aid. In his condition, he would be no match for Trent.

'You are alone,' Trent said. 'I saw Kelly driving off as I pulled in. It's just you and me, babe.' He smiled, an evil one that gave her the shudders.

At least he didn't know about Clay. Hope had never seen Trent like this, so confident, so terrifyingly intimate. Actually, she'd rarely seen him alone. In the presence of her father or others, he was . . . different. Charming, elegant, cool.

Nothing about him was charming now, including the startling amount of hungry desperation in his gaze. Dressed in black from head to toe, he looked exceptionally tall, exceptionally disturbing. And far too powerful.

Then he smiled again, though his eyes remained dark and intent. Her unease grew. 'I haven't seen you all week,' he said with mild censure. 'People are going to think that we've had a fight if we don't get together more often.'

'I don't care what people think,' she said in a surprisingly even voice. 'What do you want, Trent? I'm rather busy.'

One last step, and he'd blocked her in, caged her against the wall. He leaned in until his chest brushed hers, and when she tried to cower back, she came up against the cold wall behind her. 'Don't,' she managed.

He pushed closer, his eyes darkening when her breasts were smashed against his chest. 'Don't what?'

'Don't . . . do whatever it is you're planning to do.'

That grin gave her the shudders. 'At least we're thinking along the same lines.'

Strange to know someone for so long, and still be so afraid of him. 'Trent – Please.'

'You must be tired. Your voice turns ugly when you're not careful to pronounce each syllable. Funny, I never noticed that before.'

Heat flooded her face at the cruel reminder of her deafness, and how it made her voice low and unappealing. 'Get out, Trent.' But her voice wobbled, making the threat laughable.

His hands bracketed her head, his body pressed closer still, sandwiching her between him and the wall. One hard tug, and he had the doctor's coat off her shoulders and caught at her elbows, leaving her unable to struggle, helplessly vulnerable.

His eyes ran over the modest dress she wore beneath. 'I've tried to convince you nicely,' he rasped, 'but I don't feel like being nice any more.' Another tug, and the scooped neck of her dress stretched to bare a shoulder, ripping at the seam. Renewing her struggles, she managed to butt heads with him when he dipped down to press his lips to her skin.

'Ouch, dammit,' he grated, squeezing her tighter to him. Bending his head again, he nipped painfully at her shoulder with his teeth, making her cry out.

'Listen carefully.' He gripped her tight until she met his gaze. 'As far as everyone is concerned, you are pregnant with my child, Hope,' he grated, shaking her with each word. 'We'll marry and then I'll give your father that grandchild he wants so badly. If he lives that long.'

'We've never even slept together!' she hissed, squirming desperately.

'Your father will be so pleased,' Trent continued as if she hadn't spoken, 'an added bonus, of course. It'll look so good in all the press photos. One big happy family.'

'Press photos?'

He blinked as if he'd forgotten where he was. 'Never mind. Just know this. We're going to be together.'

'I don't understand – '

'You don't need to understand,' he said, his voice turning deep and harsh, his fingers digging into her skin. 'You just need to do as I say.' His dark brows lifted. 'Now, about that little detail you just mentioned, about us not sleeping together – ' Dipping his head, he buried his face in her neck, touching her skin with his lips. 'Let's take care of that right now – '

His breath ended on a whoosh as Hope jerked up her knee hard, jamming it into his groin. With a moan, he fell back, his eyes glazed.

Hope didn't hesitate, but tore through the living room to the kitchen, her doctor's coat flailing about her. She freed one arm and ran like hell, grabbing the first thing she could find – a broom.

She whirled, just as Trent came on her, and they both crashed to the hard tile floor.

'Shouldn't have done that, baby,' Trent wheezed, covering her body with his. 'I would have been gentle.'

Knowing he wouldn't had her scrambling all the more desperately to escape.

Clay!

For an instant she froze. Hope didn't question the feeling that told her Clay was on his way, she just reacted by fighting all the harder, panicked Clay would get hurt.

A thud from the hallway gave her the opening she needed. When Trent lifted his head in distraction, she turned hard and squeezed out from beneath him. Scrambling to her feet, she gathered all her strength and whacked him over the head with the broom.

'Get up,' she panted, knowing her voice was slurred

and low, but unable to help it. Terror did that to her, and there was no way she could concentrate on her speech. 'Get up and get out or I'll call the cops.'

Wiping at the corner of his mouth where a drop of blood appeared, probably from where he bit his tongue, Trent stared at her in surprise. 'I'm going to make you sorry for that. Very sorry, Hope.'

'I don't think so.' She waved the broom again, threatening, despite the fact that she'd lost one shoe, her coat hung askance off one arm and her other shoulder was still bared. Her hair hung in her face and she couldn't seem to catch her breath to save her life.

At the pathetic threat, Trent shook his head and laughed, pulling himself to his feet. 'I can see you're not in a mood to listen to reason.'

'Reason?' she sputtered. 'Why, you – '

'Ah, that Russian temper. I love it,' he rasped. 'But I don't feel like fighting you right now.' His scorching gaze traveled the length of her. 'No,' he said in an intimate, husky voice that gave her the shivers, 'I want you willing. Willing and begging. And believe me, you'll come begging soon enough.'

'Never!' But some of her resolve faded. *Why was he so sure*? What did he know that she didn't?

Moving toward the back door, Trent rubbed the back of his head where she'd gotten him with the broom. 'This isn't over, Hope.'

'Oh, yes it is.'

'No.' At the door, he turned to look at her, temper and heat simmering in his eyes. 'I'll ruin you, you know.

Your business will die away. It'd be so much easier to give in.'

'Get out,' she whispered harshly. Fumbling over her own clumsy feet, she backed to the phone and put her hand on it, even though she knew calling the sheriff would do her little or no good. First of all, he was friends with Trent, as just about everyone within a hundred miles was. Second of all, the sheriff was at least forty minutes away.

Forty minutes alone with this man, and one of them would end up dead.

'I know this clinic means everything to you.' His cocky, confident voice sounded as if he were discussing breakfast rather than her hopes and dreams. 'And I don't want you to be unhappy.'

'Then go away.'

'I'd hate to have to destroy it,' he said so softly she had to read his lips. 'But I will, if you won't give me what I want.'

It was her greatest fear, for she loved this place, loved what she did. The product of a truly sheltered upbringing, she didn't know which was greater, her fear, or her overwhelming shock that someone wanted to hurt her. 'The people need a doctor.' She quelled her alarm. 'They won't stop coming because of you, or anything you do.'

He actually smiled.

'They won't,' she repeated stubbornly.

'Won't they? This may be the twentieth century, but out here in the Washington backwoods, they're fifty years behind the times in mentality. You've seen that over and over again, Hope. You know that I'm right. And you know as well as I do, if they think you're a loose woman, you're as good as buried.'

It was true, she thought with rising panic. And he'd set the ball in motion already with his rumors of her pregnancy. 'They need a doctor.'

'I'll bring another one in,' he said simply, and by the tight set of his jaw and the determination shimmering from him, she knew he meant it. And he had the power and the wealth to do it. What she didn't understand was why she meant so much to him.

'Why?' she whispered, letting the broom sag to the floor. 'Why, Trent?'

He shrugged and gave her an evil smile. 'Because I want you, Hope. I always get what I want. Want to give in yet?'

'My father – '

'Your father is going to help me. He thinks he's protecting you by taking this place back.' His eyes burned. 'And we all know, no lender will give you the money you need for another. You're female, young and handicapped.'

Again, that hot blush burned her face at his reminder of her failings. She backed to the wall and hugged it behind her. 'I'll find a place to work no matter what you do.'

'No, you won't. Once I let it out that you're refusing to do the right thing by that baby, you're ruined.' He laughed. 'Wait until you don't start showing – they'll think you aborted. You'll be shunned.'

She was afraid, so very afraid, he was right. 'Why me?'

she demanded. 'Why are you doing this to me? It can't be just because you want me.'

His smile was slow, his perusal of her body insulting. 'But it is. And I will have you. *You're mine*. Remember that. Change your mind now and I won't make you beg when you finally give in.'

'Never!'

His lips tightened. 'One way or the other, you will be mine. I promise you.' He opened the door and Molly, who'd obviously raced around the house to scratch at the back door, pounded in, skidding to a halt before Hope.

Hope put her hand on the dog's head, unbelievably comforted when Molly turned her wet, warm nose into her hand.

'You'll change your mind,' Trent warned. 'You'll have to.'

Molly lifted her head and growled low in her throat. Moving smoothly, Trent left without another word.

The minute the back door shut on him, Hope's legs started to tremble, and it spread throughout her body until she had to sink to the floor.

Molly whined and licked her face.

'I can't believe it,' she whispered. 'He tried to . . . he wanted to hurt me.' She gulped in air and tried to calm herself. What else could he do to her?

Ruin the business. His own words had told her that.

Her shoulders slumped and she dropped her head into her hands. Molly nudged Hope's shoulder with her nose, obviously worried, but Hope couldn't rouse herself enough to reassure the poor animal.

He'd tried to hurt her. If Clay had heard, and if he'd tried to intervene – Her head jerked up as she remembered – *Clay*.

With a worried sound, she leaped up, then collided with the well-meaning, but nervous dog. They both lost their balance and toppled to the floor.

Molly, in her happiness to have Hope with her, pinned her down and licked her face, trembling. Hope let out a shaky laugh and hugged Molly tight. When her face was nice and soaked, she tried to pull back, but the dog, relieved beyond belief, wouldn't give up.

'Molly, please.'

Molly didn't budge.

'Sweetie, a ninety pound dog is not a lap dog!'

In answer, Molly whined and placed her very wet nose in Hope's ear.

Freeing herself with a soft exclamation and a verbal vow to never get any more pets, especially large, useless dogs that drool, Hope stood. Gently pushing Molly out of her way, she ran out of the kitchen and through the living room, where she hesitated for another second in the dark.

Molly, following close on her heels, plowed directly into the back of her with a soft *oomph*.

Hope didn't feel the impact, not when she was staring at the very spot where Trent had slammed her into the wall. What could have happened to her right here in this room . . . a cold seized her veins, until she shivered with it. She wrapped her arms around herself for warmth and comfort, but it didn't help much.

Clay.

She wanted him more than she could ever remember wanting another person in her life. Moving quickly, she stepped into the even darker hallway, where she tripped over a large bulk that moaned.

She went sprawling on her face.

CHAPTER 8

Clay heard Hope coming, and called out a warning to her, but she still barreled right into him, catching him directly in his broken ribs with her foot.

Agony speared ruthlessly through him, and then he could do nothing but curl up tight and moan. He felt the sweat pool at the base of his spine, felt the nausea rise, and for a minute, he thought he was going to die.

Then he gradually became aware of something other than his own pain. Beside him, Hope dragged herself up on her hands and knees. Her eyes were wild, her hair tousled. And her clothes –

'Clay,' she gasped on a rough sob, then launched herself at him.

By some miracle, he managed to catch her, but as he was flat on his back, there was nothing he could do but wrap his arms around her and hold tight. 'Hope, what the hell happened?'

She started babbling crazily, speaking before he'd even finished the question, as if she couldn't even hear him. 'It's nothing, really. I'm being silly, just a little jumpy. Molly, stop barking! I'm sorry if you got worried – '

'*Worried?*' With great difficulty, he grabbed her shoulders and pulled her back so he could see her face. '*Worried?* I was going out of my mind! I heard you scream, then couldn't get my damned body working fast enough to get to you.'

He paled at his next thought, and grabbed her close, slipping a hand over her still flat belly. 'The baby,' he whispered roughly. Panic such as he'd never known pummeled him like a fist. 'Did you hurt yourself when you fell? Hope, tell me!'

'What?'

'Are you hurt, dammit?'

'No,' she gasped, her face reddening.

He relaxed a fraction. He may not remember a single thing about himself, including if he had cared about this woman and the baby she carried. But he did now, to a degree that was beginning to terrify him. All he had to do was get her to feel the same way. But her disheveled state kept the fear bubbling at the surface. 'What happened? Are you sure you're not hurt?' he pressed.

'Yes, I'm . . . fine. I didn't fall that way.'

'What the hell is going on? Why were you screaming?'

'It was just a . . . friend of my father's,' she said quickly, her eyes wild and glazed as she stared at his lips. 'He came unexpectedly, and I didn't hear him. Kelly had just left so I thought I was alone. I haven't seen him in a week or so, not since I went to visit my father last. He runs this huge logging business, you know. My father, that is. Trent's worried, he works for my father. And the company's had problems . . . we had a . . . disagreement. That's all. I heard a crash in the hallway.'

'I must have passed out,' he admitted tightly. 'But I called out to you after, and just now when you came running in here. Why didn't you answer me?'

Her mouth opened, then closed. Her eyes remained directly on his lips. Not so strange when he was imagining she wanted him to kiss her, but now, it seemed quite out of the ordinary. He tucked his chin to take another breath, trying to block out the pain in his ribs. 'Why didn't you answer me?'

'What?'

He lifted his head and stared at her as something horrifying occurred to him. If he wasn't looking right at her when he spoke, or if she wasn't looking at him, she responded by asking him to repeat his words.

Strange. Unless . . . *Oh, no*! Unless she couldn't understand him without watching his lips.

His stomach clenched.

'Hope,' he said carefully, slowly. 'I heard you scream.'

'He . . . startled me.'

'Hope.' There was a wealth of emotion in his tone, in his face, he could feel it, and knew she could too. He lifted a hand to cup her face and she flinched.

Rage flowed through him.

With an air of calm he didn't come close to feeling, he smoothed her hair, caressed her cheek. Then took a shallow breath – his aching ribs wouldn't allow anything more than that. 'He hurt you.'

'No,' she whispered, then closed her eyes.

'Hope, please.'

Nothing. No reaction. *Because her eyes were closed.* Anger and fear tightened each and every muscle in his body. Slowly, so as to not startle her, he skimmed his hand down from her face to her shoulder, where her jacket hung askance off one arm. Gently he removed it the rest of the way from her.

Immediately, she raised her arms to cover her chest. The gesture tore at him. With an equally gentle, tender movement, he reached out to straighten her dress, which had been torn off one shoulder.

It was then he saw the clear bite mark on her precious, white skin. *Teeth marks.* Never in his life – that he knew of – had he felt so dangerously close to murder. 'He more than startled you.'

He got no response to that, and he swore luridly at his own damn helplessness. If only he hadn't given in to his pain and passed out, if only . . . 'Please, sweetheart, tell me the truth,' he said hoarsely. He made himself ask the question that had fear lodged like a wad of cotton in his throat. 'Did he – Where else are you hurt?'

Her eyes were still closed, and as she sat there, swaying lightly, he got absolutely no reaction. *She hadn't heard him.*

Heartsick, he pulled her dress up over her bared, injured shoulder and cupped her face in his hands.

Her eyes flew open.

'Hope, it's all right now. Do you understand me? It's over.'

She blinked, then swallowed hard.

'How . . .' He could barely form the words around the

questions he needed to ask her. The images that swam through his head struck terror in his heart. 'How badly did he hurt you?' he asked in a voice gruff with fear and emotion.

'He . . . didn't. Not really. I heard you, it must have been when you fell. We were wrestling . . .'

Wrestling? She was pregnant, in the early, delicate stage where so many things could go wrong, and she'd had to wrestle a man for her safety? Without thinking, his hand slid to her stomach again, holding it possessively. 'Hope!'

'We heard a noise. He looked up and . . . I hit him with my broom.'

'Good girl.' Thank God, Clay thought. The jerk hadn't raped her, no thanks to him. Disgust filled him at his helplessness. 'I'm so sorry, Hope. So damned sorry I didn't come sooner.'

Her eyes filled. 'You would have come if you could.'

It wasn't a statement, but more of a question. He realized she was awed, struck dumb by the thought he'd wanted to help. That he would have, if he could.

What was the matter with her? Had so few people in her life wanted to be there for her? Had he, in the past, never made her feel safe? Told her that he would protect her with his life? If he hadn't, then what the hell was the matter with him?

'Of course I would have come. I nearly killed myself trying,' he joked, but it backfired.

The tears swimming in her eyes ran over, streaming down her cheeks. She made a choked sound that tore at him.

Without a second thought, he folded her into his arms, sucked his breath in against the pain, and very carefully leaned back against the wall, cradling her against him. 'Oh, Hope,' he whispered, knowing he'd get no response since his chin was resting on her head.

She couldn't see him, therefore she couldn't hear him.

Sobs wracked her slender frame. Hope didn't cry gracefully, or even quietly, but as he was beginning to suspect, she didn't even realize it.

'Hope,' he whispered again, willing his mind past the agony in his body. 'Sweetheart . . .' He trailed off, sick to the very depth of his soul, but it had nothing to do with his own hurt now.

The beautiful, independent, competent woman in his arms wasn't responding to him because she didn't hear him.

In that moment, if he hadn't already, he lost his heart to her.

He had no idea how long they sat there, in the darkened hallway, holding each other. Molly pressed close as well, and between the shaking woman and the damn dog, his ribs were jarred so much that he felt weak with the jabbing pain.

But it didn't matter, he would take it and much more, if only to continue holding Hope in his arms. She felt tiny, warm and so vulnerable he wanted to protect her forever. He had so many questions, he was ready to burst, but he had to wait.

Wait. It just might kill him to do so, and he instinctively knew he wasn't a patient man. Seems he'd have to learn that as well.

The pants he'd put on chafed at his bruised legs. A thought leaped to the surface for the first time, even in the midst of his fear – he'd never worn these pants before yesterday. *Never*.

Which led to the obvious next thought – where were his clothes? Not the ones he wore that night he'd been attacked, those were ruined, but the ones he would have at Hope's house. Because this was his house as well, right?

There hadn't been much time to ask, but now he wanted to know. Then he realized another thing, she'd never answered his question the other night, and he'd been sleeping ever since.

Why didn't they sleep in the same room? Would she ever tell him? Would he ever remember?

When the silent beauty in his arms hiccupped and lifted her tear ravaged face, he gave her a soft smile, touched her face gently and skimmed his lips over hers once.

The kiss electrified him to his toes, but he forced himself to raise his head and look at her. 'Hope, we should call the police.'

She shook her head.

'He broke into your house, threatened you.' His jaw clenched as he grated out the words that produced more fury. 'He hurt you, Hope. He should be punished.'

She didn't answer.

He couldn't help but see her in a new light. For the first time, he realized how much she depended on watching him speak, how low and hesitant her voice was. Her air of confidence and strength came from the way she held herself, not from how she spoke.

Gently, he turned her to face him. 'You're a woman of incredible integrity,' he said, wondering at her wince. 'You'd never, under any circumstances, let a man get away with hurting one of your patients the way he hurt you.'

'You don't understand.'

'Damn right I don't,' he said roughly, angry at his helplessness, at hers. 'Explain it to me.'

How could she, Hope wondered, especially when she was still reeling from their first kiss? It should have shocked her, should have made her sick, after what had just nearly happened to her in her own kitchen, but it hadn't. It had the opposite effect, had warmed her where nothing else could have.

'Please,' he added hoarsely. 'Tell me.'

Would he really understand the predicament she found herself in? Would he forgive her the deception? She was afraid not, and was more than a little surprised to realize how much it would hurt when he turned from her in anger, in disgust.

When she didn't answer immediately, he tucked her closer, ran his palms up and down her arms in a soothing gesture that made her want to cry again. For just a minute, a very weak minute, she allowed herself to remain snuggled close in his arms, her face pressed to his bare, fuzzy chest . . . His bare, fuzzy, *black and blue* chest. Yes, he was hard and lean, his belly flat, and so taut and rippled with muscle she ached to touch, but he was also covered in angry, vicious welts and contusions that reminded her of what he was doing here in the first place.

She must be hurting him, badly. In fact she could feel him tremble slightly against her, but it felt so incredible to be held tight against his hard, warm frame. To be comforted instead of the one doing the comforting. How long had it been since she'd been held like this?

She'd never been held like this, and again, her throat tightened, thickened.

With as much grace as she could, Hope lifted herself off him. He sat on the floor, his back and broad shoulders to the wall, his long legs spread. She was kneeling between them, and suddenly, it hit her . . . he wore only a pair of hospital scrub bottoms that were slung low on his hips, nothing more.

'You're . . . not dressed.'

'You noticed.' His laugh was harsh. 'When you screamed, I just started running. I didn't realize until I reached the door of the bedroom that I was still bare-ass naked.'

'Oh!'

He touched her hair, regret in his eyes. 'Yeah. Oh. I decided to stop to don these and it almost cost you big. I don't think I'll easily forgive myself for that.'

'You mean you could be here on the floor . . . naked?'

'Isn't that a picture?' he said dryly.

Now that she was calmer, she could concentrate on his words, and she missed nothing – especially his attitude. But Hope had never been a person to take things at surface value. Eyes narrowed, she studied him and saw the tell-tale signs; the tight, grim mouth that was still cut so badly, the stress lines around his eyes, the light sheen of sweat on his brow . . . the man was hurting, badly.

'You're not feeling well,' she said softly.

'Hope,' he said tersely. 'I want to know why you'd let that man get away with nearly raping you, father's lackey or not.'

His breathing was shallow, his color completely gone. And she couldn't face his questions, not yet. Not until she got a semblance of her control back, which she couldn't possibly do until he either put on a shirt or got under his covers again. 'You need to get back in bed.'

'Dammit, stop playing my doctor!' He lowered his voice. 'Please, tell me what's going on.'

'It's not easy to explain,' she said quietly.

With a grimace, he came up on his knees and took her shoulders. They kneeled there on the floor, facing each other. She'd already realized how powerfully built he was, but seeing him upright, having him this close, brought it home. In spite of the torture someone had put him through, his sinewy strength was unmistakable and she wondered exactly how many men it had taken to do this to him.

'I know I can't remember a damned thing,' he grated, 'but I'm not an idiot. There's a lot you're not telling me, and I've got to know. Please, talk to me.'

His eyes had darkened to a deep forest green, glittering with anger, fear and a hundred other things she couldn't think about. 'You're upset,' she said with a calm she didn't feel. 'Because you think you should have come racing to my rescue. But I didn't need to be rescued, Clay. I'm a big girl, and I can take care of myself.'

He rolled his eyes at her ridiculous statement. 'Yeah!

And that broom was real effective I bet. Did you at least hit him in the –'

'Head.'

He shook his, then winced and swore luridly. 'You should have aimed lower, sweetheart.'

Right there, in the middle of the most upsetting time of her life, still shaking over what Trent had done, Hope got the giggles. Dropping her forehead to his chest, she started laughing with genuine mirth, and forgot to try to do it quietly, gracefully.

She galvanized Clay. 'Oh . . . sweetheart, don't cry, please don't cry. I'm sorry. Please, just don't – '

Lifting her head, she gaped at him as tears of amusement rolled down her face.

His expression darkened. 'You're—' He bent, peered into her face. 'You're laughing!'

'I'm sorry,' she managed, then continued to laugh helplessly.

That handsome face tightened into a scowl. 'What the hell is so funny?'

She'd just figured it out, understood why this big, competent man was acting like a baby. 'You're sulking. It's sweet.'

He stared at her for so long she thought maybe she'd pushed him too far. Then he smiled too, a wide, sexy, heart-stopping smile that had her breath catching – and his lip splitting. Holding it, eyeing her closely, he continued to grin while he asked, 'You think I'm sweet?'

She'd never been knocked senseless by a smile before. 'Uh, maybe. A little.'

He snagged her hips and pulled her closer, careful to

avoid his ribs. 'I'd rather see you smile like that, even if it means you're laughing at me, than see you cry any day.'

'I'll remember that.'

He looked down at her with a mixture of tenderness and exasperation. 'Why were we yelling at each other?'

'Fear,' she whispered. 'It makes me talk loud.' *Because she forgot to control her voice.* 'And I'm so sorry, Clay.'

'No.' He placed a finger against her lips and shook his head slowly, his eyes solemn now. 'No apologies. You're safe. That's all that matters to me.'

She could feel how rigid he held himself, how his hands trembled. 'You're hurting,' she whispered. 'Let me get you back to bed.'

His eyes went opaque, smoldering with a heat she couldn't miss. 'Take me to bed?'

With a nervous little laugh, she added, 'To get some sleep.'

His face fell. 'I guess that wasn't the invitation I've been waiting for.'

Which reminded her. In all the craziness, she'd forgotten. 'I got your note.'

'Yeah?' He looked pleased. 'Molly came through for me.' His gaze held hers. 'So, did you?'

'Did I what?' she asked, wincing at the breathless quality of her voice.

'Did you miss me?'

'No,' she said, smiling when he frowned. 'Well, maybe . . . just a little.'

He grinned now, cockily. 'More than a little, I bet.'

While he sounded fine, she wasn't fooled. His color was ghastly. And she suspected he was too weak to stand by himself, that he was holding on by a thread and sheer self-control.

'Come on, Clay.'

'Are you sure you're all right?'

'I'll be fine.' He let her pull him gently to his feet, and when he swayed slightly, she carefully wrapped her arms around his middle and steadied him. 'You shouldn't have gotten up at all,' she chided lightly as they walked toward his bedroom.

But he remained silent, and she suspected he felt even worse than he let on. When she backed him to the bed, he sank wordlessly down, with obvious relief.

For a long moment, she sat on the very edge of the bed, watching him as he lay there. His breathing seemed too rapid, he was far too silent. Gradually, his breathing evened out, and still she watched, wanting to make certain he hadn't made himself worse.

Who are you, Clayton Slater?

Not that she'd ever get a chance to find out. Because as soon as he was well enough to take care of himself, she would tell him the truth. He'd leave then, most likely furious.

Because she couldn't help herself, she fussed over him, pulling the sheet over his body, tucking it carefully along his sides. Her fingers brushed over the skin of his chest and it shot heat directly through her.

He was the first man to have her dealing with this incredible hunger. Okay, she didn't have much in the way of comparisons. But Clay Slater had no comparisons – he was one in a million.

Her stomach fluttered strangely. Arousal, she realized

with some surprise. This man did something to her insides, something almost deliciously . . . wicked.

Because she couldn't resist, she let her hand linger, sweeping it across his chest gently. Beneath the resilient, soft skin, he felt hard as steel. Her fingers itched for more. She couldn't help but wonder . . . what would it really be like to be with this man?

To have him make love to her.

To be carrying his baby.

Her hand moved over him, her fingers curled lightly over his shoulder, admiring the taut, amazing strength of him. She smiled, remembering how he'd sulked because he hadn't been her white knight –

He grabbed her hand with lightning speed, then in complete contrast to the quickness of the move, he leisurely, lightly, ran his lips over her knuckles.

All thoughts flew out of her head.

He chuckled, bringing her back to earth.

'You're not asleep,' she said, breathless.

'And you're hiding things from me, Hope.' His eyes opened, dark with swirling emotions. 'Aren't you?'

CHAPTER 9

'What?' gasped the wide-eyed Hope sitting hip to hip with Clay on the bed. Her dress, the one that had been ripped in her fight with Trent earlier, had again slipped off her shoulder, revealing the growing bruise marring her white skin.

His gut churned. 'I said, you've been hiding things from me.'

Clearly flustered, she fidgeted. 'I don't know what you mean.'

'Let me spell it out for you,' he said quietly, but when she tilted her head and narrowed her eyes questioningly, his agitation drained immediately. In his distress, his frustration, he'd spoken too fast, mumbled his words, and she hadn't caught it all. But the prideful woman wouldn't ask him to repeat it. Not when she was worried he'd guess her little secret.

'Hope,' he said carefully, clearly, biting back his own pain to reach for her hand. 'We have to talk.'

'You're not well.'

'I'll get well faster if you'd just humor me. Just for a minute. I have a question.'

She crossed her arms, a childish gesture that would have made him smile if this wasn't so desperately serious.

'Just one question, Hope.'

'I'm the one in charge here,' she said.

'You weren't in charge at all earlier,' he pointed out, tugging to keep her hand in his when she would have pulled it away. Being close to him made her nervous and he wanted to know why. He liked her, very much, but he wasn't sure he could say she felt the same. She held part of herself back, and he wanted that part for himself.

'Clay, please.'

Her voice was soft, an appeal. Normally, it would have melted him to butter, but he couldn't afford to let her get away with this.

'I want to know why you won't call the cops on this Trent, and I want to know why he feels he could harass you in the first place. Doesn't he know about me?'

She sighed. 'No.'

That dealt a surprisingly painful blow, one he hadn't expected. 'I want to know if he's the one that attacked me, or had me attacked.'

'No.'

Nothing else. Just no. Her eyes filled with stubbornness that he knew spelled trouble – a stubborn Hope meant a silent Hope. 'I want to know why when I put these pants on I knew I'd never worn them before. Where are my clothes, Hope? Where are all my things?'

Now she paled, bit her lip.

He pressed on. 'You have yet to tell me why we don't share a bedroom. And what the hell did I do before I made a career out of lounging in bed?' Before she could rise, he slipped his free hand around her waist. 'And why aren't you happy about being pregnant?'

Her deep breath was shaky, far from controlled. 'I'm not unhappy . . .' But she trailed off.

Her dark eyes clouded with nerves, and he couldn't blame her. But he wasn't finished. 'And most of all, Hope,' he said as desperately as he felt, 'why don't you trust me?'

'I do,' she whispered in a low voice. 'I trust you, Clay.'

'Do you really?' How he wanted to believe that.

Her hand, in his, relaxed. Her shoulders sagged. 'Yes,' she breathed, as if she didn't like the idea. 'I really do.' She looked a little surprised. Actually, stunned was a better word.

'Why don't you want to?' This had been bugging him. 'I hate the way that makes me feel. As if I wasn't trustworthy before.'

She sighed. 'This is difficult. More difficult than you can imagine.'

He wondered now why he'd never noticed how different her voice was. How low and husky. Had he been that out of it for the past four days? Yes, he admitted, he had. 'Did I know, Hope? Did I know before . . .'

'Know what?'

'That you're deaf, or the closest thing to it?'

Her gaze jerked from his. Her body stiffened.

'You . . . know?'

His heart clenched. His stomach turned. 'Are you telling me I didn't notice before? That I was that indifferent?'

'You said you had one question,' she said with dismay. 'One. Not twenty.'

'I lied.'

She closed her eyes.

'Hope.' Gently, he squeezed her waist, waiting until she opened her eyes. 'Please, sweetheart, I need some answers here. I need your help.'

'But you're still so sick,' she protested. 'You can hardly even stand.'

He really hated that, the weakness he still felt. 'It could be weeks before I'm fully recovered,' he said bitterly. 'I can't wait that long for answers, Hope. I'll lose it.'

'You . . . still remember nothing?'

She sounded suspicious and he searched her features. 'You doubt that?'

'Of course not. I'd just hoped that there were at least flashes of memories, something to go on.'

The only flashes he'd had were strange, erotic dreams about this angel who'd rescued him. The brown-eyed, long-haired lovely angel he didn't want to be without. But he had to face facts. It didn't seem as if he'd been worthy of her.

It terrified him that he would remember who he was and not like that person.

'We don't know each other very well,' she whispered.

The way she said that brought him up short. Maybe they'd been a one-night stand. It would explain his not having clothes here, why while he loved her place, it didn't feel like it had been his home. Had he slept with her just once and gotten her pregnant? 'Or for very long?' he guessed.

She flushed and shook her head, and he instinctively knew that if it had been a one-night stand, it had been her first. She wasn't a woman to take such things lightly, which only made him feel more protective, more possessive.

'We can fix that,' he told her, meaning it. 'We've got all the time in the world to get to know each other better.' He had no idea if he'd been the kind of man to want that before, but he wanted that now.

'How do you know how long we have?' she asked, uncannily reading his mind the way she tended to do. 'We may only have until you get your memory back and discover you don't feel the way you think you do.'

He slipped his hand to her belly. 'I'm not going anywhere, Hope, if that's what you're worried about.'

'You're talking about the baby.'

'Yes, of course. But you, too. I'm not going anywhere because of the both of you.'

Something flickered in her eyes. Relief? Sorrow? Hard to tell, and she was so damned closed mouthed. So much to learn. 'What about your hearing, sweetheart?'

'We . . . never discussed it.'

He ran a finger over her cheek. 'I'm sorry, it's hard for you to talk about.' She flushed and he shook his head. 'No, don't do that. Don't be ashamed of it, it's just a part of you, that's all.'

Her gaze flew from his mouth to his eyes, as if searching for honesty. 'Some people find it annoying,' she said slowly. 'And my voice . . . it's coarse. Flat. Ugly.'

'No. Whoever told you that is an idiot.'

'It'll drive you crazy in no time.'

She'd turned her head away, and he brought it back, waiting with patience until she looked at him. He stroked her full lower lip with his thumb, and when her lips parted, he nearly groaned at the unbelievable need he had to lose himself in that mouth. 'I didn't bring it up to make you feel self-conscious. I just wanted to be sure I wasn't a complete ass before. It doesn't matter to me one whit if you can hear fully, except that I hate to think of you suffering. How bad is it?'

'Just my left ear.' But she still blushed. 'My right ear is fifty percent operational.'

'So you hear a quarter of what the rest of us hear?'

'It's not as bad as it sounds, really. I hear fine, unless I'm upset or nervous. It seems to fade then.'

'How can you practise medicine?'

'I have special equipment. Even my phones are rigged. It hardly affects my life except . . .'

She didn't have to finish, he knew. Except when she needed to protect herself and couldn't. 'Must have been rough, growing up.'

She shrugged, giving him far more of an answer than she had intended. A young girl without a mother, living with her nearly obsessively over-protective father, isolated from any sort of social life. He ached for her. 'Talk to me, Hope.'

'I've had it easy compared to most. School wasn't as difficult as it might have been because I learned quick. The people around here have always been kind. Even when – ' She stopped abruptly, bit her lip.

'When what?'

She lifted her gaze heavenward, as if seeking assistance. None came.

'Hope?'

'I sometimes see things, all right? I feel things,' she mumbled. 'No big deal, really.'

'What do you mean, you feel things? As in you know who's calling before they do?'

He had noticed. 'Sometimes.'

He smiled. 'So you're a true gypsy, huh?'

She looked at him, a shadow of a smile playing over her lips. 'Yeah. Afraid?'

'Why? Gonna cast a spell on me?'

'Not if you're good.'

'Oh, I'm good, sweetheart. Try me.'

She let out a little nervous laugh and shook her head. 'I'll trust you on that one.'

'Are you my destiny, Hope?'

She paled. 'What?' But before he could repeat the words, she said urgently, 'What made you ask me that, Clay?'

He narrowed his eyes at her sudden tenseness. 'Just a question. Dammit, Hope, I can feel it. You're hiding something else. What is it?'

She bit her lip, hesitating before saying, 'That night I found you, you looked up at me . . .'

He blinked, suddenly transported back to that night, laying there in the mud, bleeding, hurting beyond belief. Thinking he was going to die without knowing who he was. Then Hope had come and he hadn't felt alone since. 'I remember,' he said. 'I thought you were an angel.'

'And I – Oh, never mind,' she said quickly.

But he knew . . . she'd thought the same. She'd thought he was her destiny. 'Why can't you say it?' he wondered aloud. 'We're where we're supposed to be, Hope. Together. We're each other's destiny.'

Her eyes widened even more, if that were possible. 'We make our own destiny, Clay. And my destiny is here, caring for my patients.' She said this firmly, as if hoping to convince herself.

'I see,' he said quietly, stung. He touched her face until she looked at him. 'And there's no room in your life for anything else.'

'No,' she said firmly, and he could feel the resistance in her taut jaw, knew how badly she wanted to look away. Yet she couldn't, not and risk missing his words. His heart squeezed a little for her.

'But you're right,' she said. 'I do owe you a few answers about tonight.' She inhaled deeply. 'Trent is very popular here in Green County.'

Clay sighed for the lost closeness, but accepted it for now because he needed answers so desperately. 'Why?'

'He's charming, rich, attractive. Single. Helps my father run one of the largest logging companies in the west. Every Momma within two hundred miles is parading her daughter around in hopes of snagging him.'

'So charming, so single that he has to attack his employer's daughter?'

'For some time, he's been trying to . . . court me, I guess you'd call it. The word "no" seems to irritate him.'

'I'll say,' he muttered, looking at her torn dress. Anger surged again. 'Is your father going to leave Trent everything if something happens to him?'

'No,' she said slowly. 'But I'm an only child, so I guess if he dies . . .'

'Whoever you're going to marry has a lot to gain.' Hope nodded grimly and he knew she understood this could be what Trent was counting on.

'But Trent's rich in his own right. It makes no sense.'

'This is a logging business, right?'

She nodded. 'But why would Trent need me when he already works there and practically runs the place for my father?'

'I don't know, but we'll find out. Why are you protecting him?'

'I'm not,' she protested. 'But the sheriff's useless, trust me.'

'Not useless, if you're going to get raped, dammit!' He couldn't begin to clamp down on his worry, his fear, that next time, he wouldn't be around to help her. 'Doesn't your father know you're pregnant? That you're with me?'

'Um . . .' She bit her lip, gave him a guilty, nervous glance. 'I haven't told him about you. He thinks that Trent and I are just having a sort of quarrel.'

'Why doesn't Trent know about me?' he demanded.

'It's complicated,' she whispered. 'All I know is that he's told the entire town that I'm pregnant with his child, and people seem to believe that.' Clay made a noise, but she rushed on. 'Even my nurse Kelly looks at me with these questions swimming in her eyes, it drives me crazy. It's why my business has slacked off a little.'

'Your business has slacked off? You've been busy as hell! You can't get any busier without killing yourself.

And what do you mean,' he said slowly, dangerously close to shouting, 'that everyone thinks that my baby –' he pointed to her stomach with a care that belied the temper in his gaze '– *is his*?'

'It's a lie, of course,' she said quickly. 'But he's hoping to force my hand because he knows how much this clinic means to me.' She covered her face with her hands. 'And there's no way,' she said, her voice muffled, 'that he was the one to hurt you because he doesn't know about you.'

He tipped her face up, caressed her tight jaw. Her gaze met his and he spoke again. 'Well, that will have to change,' he said grimly. 'And soon. Which brings me to the next question, Hope.'

She went utterly still, looking young, dejected and so completely exhausted, all the fight went out of him.

She'd been physically attacked, and he was doing the same, just verbally. He was taking his fear out on her. It brought him a pain such as he'd never known. Gently, slowly, he reached out with his other hand and touched her arm. 'I'm sorry,' he said, never meaning those words more. 'Hope, I'm so sorry.'

'For what?' She looked at him warily, through narrowed, distrusting eyes, and he couldn't blame her one bit.

Because it hurt to move more than an inch at a time, he let go of her, slowly held out his arm, scooting over a bit on the bed. He wanted her right next to him. 'Come here.'

She stared at the space he'd made, then lifted her gaze to him, slowly running that misty look over the length of his body. He sucked his breath in, feeling as though she had caressed him . . . and the way she was soaking in the sight of him made his stomach muscles quiver. It created other interesting reactions lower down too, and if she didn't stop, she'd soon discover there were parts of him that had completely recovered and were raring to go.

He'd never been so completely aware of his own near nudity before, for the surgical pants he wore were thin and insubstantial enough that if she looked close, she'd see whatever she wanted and then some. He was male enough to soak in the appreciation in her eyes, confident enough to know that his body was more than decent and appealing – except for the bruises – and just human enough to want to squirm.

Finally, her gaze met his. Her eyes sparkled like black diamonds, filled with a heat he couldn't miss. A heat and a shimmer of something he almost did miss – a sweet innocence.

'I won't grill you any more tonight,' he promised in a raspy voice he recognized as pure arousal. 'You deserve far better from me.'

She took a deep breath and visibly brushed off the heavy-lidded air of sensuality. 'You're frustrated, and with good reason,' she told him, her eyes serious. She still didn't move. 'You don't have to be sorry.'

'I am. I'm scared to death, too,' he said seriously. 'Hold me?'

For another long moment, she didn't move, and he almost exhaled in defeat. Then she sidled up to him carefully, fitting herself in the crook of his arm, stretching out her legs next to his.

'You're cold,' he said with a disparaging sound,

covering them both with the blanket and snuggling her small body close to his. They lay there like that, silent, for a long time. Degree by degree, she relaxed against him, having no idea how sweet a torture it was for him to feel her lush body against his and not be able to do a thing about it.

By the uncomfortable stirring in his pants, he had the feeling he hadn't been a slouch in the sexual relations department before. This patience was new . . . and not easy.

Eventually, she sighed against his chest, an exhausted sound. 'I know you're unhappy,' she said finally, not looking at him.

With his free hand, he turned her face up to his so that she could see him as he spoke. 'Not true,' he said firmly. 'I hurt and I have a lot of questions that I need answers for, but I'm happy, Hope.'

Unexpectedly, her eyes filled. 'You deserve answers,' she said in a small, choked voice. 'But, I don't know – '

'Shhh.' As much as he could without killing himself, he hugged her close. Now their bodies lay facing each other on his bed, their legs entwined. They shared a pillow. Sweet pleasure mixed with pain and he cursed the fate that had certain parts of his anatomy working overtime, and other parts refusing to work at all.

'When Trent came tonight, I thought I could handle him,' she said suddenly, softly. 'I thought that if I screamed, you'd try to come help and he'd hurt you.' Her words ran together as they tended to do when she was upset. 'I didn't want you two to confront each other until – '

His mouth met hers, silencing her. The soft, velvety texture of her lips felt so good, so right beneath his that he angled his head and went to deepen the kiss . . . and nearly swore right into her mouth.

'What?' she gasped, pulling back. Then she gasped again and sat up. 'Oh, Clay, I made you bleed again!' Leaning over him, she reached for a tissue on the bed stand . . . and inadvertently jiggled the two most perfect breasts he'd ever seen right in his face. That they were covered by her dress didn't matter, he seemed to have X-ray vision when it came to her. Or at least his imagination did.

'Here,' she said, pressing it to the corner of his mouth. 'Does it hurt?'

His eyebrows lifted, his mouth twisted wryly. 'Yes, but not where you think.'

She looked at him blankly and he had to laugh, even when it hurt his mouth more. 'You're sweet,' he said. And innocent, he thought. Though he knew that couldn't be, she continually struck him as guilelessly naive. Oh, she had a body to die for, and a sensual way of carrying it, but it was all so artless, so uncontrived.

He imagined she turned all that sweet coolness into a raging fire when they made love, and wished with all his heart he could remember it.

She was leaning over him, watching his mouth . . . waiting for his next words?

'You kissed me,' she said in a wondrous, dreamy sort of voice.

She wanted him to do it again, he realized, and nearly laughed again. Would he ever be able to read this woman straight? He moved in close, ready to oblige her when Molly leaped up on the bed, delicately stepped over Hope's legs and plopped herself down on his middle.

Spots swam before his eyes and he sucked in a sharp breath of pain, but couldn't release it. Not when a thousand points of agony were dancing in his head.

Vaguely, he heard Hope's worried voice calling to Molly to get down, felt her hands on his shoulders, but it was a long moment before he could blink her into focus.

'Hope,' he gasped in a throaty, thick voice, his arms around his on-fire ribs. 'I've got to tell you, sweetheart . . . I don't think I like dogs.'

She smoothed back his hair, made sympathetic noises in her throat. To his dismay, she backed off the bed and pressed her fingers into his wrist, checking his pulse. Since he still couldn't move, he lay there complacently enough, pain slashing through him, but when she reached for the bandages on his ribs, he stopped her.

'I'm fine.'

But the doctor was back. Cool eyes, professional demeanor, impersonal but caring hands . . . he wanted his hot gypsy back.

'I'm sorry, Clay,' she said. 'Molly's not usually in the house, but she's over-excited because of what happened earlier. It won't happen again, I promise.'

'It's all right, Hope.'

But it wasn't, he could see that clearly. The moment was gone, and so was her softness, the awareness in her eyes. It'd been replaced by that independent, competent woman that preferred to be alone against the world.

And that woman wouldn't find it easy to let him in. He

understood independence, or he thought he did. The main difference between them now – he was growing used to understanding that they were meant for each other.

While she was not.

'You're running a fever,' she said, frowning as she felt his forehead.

Yeah, he was running a fever all right, but it wasn't in his head. 'I'll be fine, Hope.'

'As soon as you take this Tylenol,' she agreed, her voice low, controlled . . . distant. She took a deep breath, and beneath her blouse, her breasts shifted enticingly.

Oh good, because he hadn't been nearly hard enough. He wondered if she had noticed his problem.

'You need more sleep,' she said. Her voice had chilled several degrees.

Yeah, she'd noticed.

Hope had withdrawn – again. Self-defense, he knew, but it was as irritating as anything he'd known. Or could remember knowing.

She handed him two pills and the cup of water by his bed, careful not to touch him, or to let him accidentally touch her.

Her gaze didn't meet his.

It didn't discourage him, but rather the opposite. If she didn't care so much, she wouldn't be fighting him at all.

Nope, she wouldn't take to this together thing easily, not at all, but he could work on that. With one finger, he stroked her bared shoulder, lightly touching her bruise. Her breath stammered and she frowned. She yanked at the dress, pulling it into place. The pulse at the base of her neck leaped frantically.

She might be cool on the outside. But on the inside, she was all fire and passion, and as acutely aware of him as he was of her.

Carefully, minding his lip, he smiled and leaned back, letting her doctor him all she wanted.

What the hell. He was a very patient man and he had all the time in the world.

CHAPTER 10

Trent stared at his computer and sighed. The locals polls showed he would be a favorite. The time was right.

He would run for city council, and he'd win. It would be just the start of a most brilliant career. He'd work his way all the way to the top – to the Presidency.

He'd do it by playing the good guy, by giving up his solid, hugely successful logging career for the good of America's forests. For the future of their environment.

He'd be a hero.

Only one glitch – he couldn't give up the logging company as a sacrifice until he actually owned it. He was working on that. It wouldn't be a problem.

The only problem he did have remained Hope. He wanted her. Even more after their little tryst the night before. She'd felt so good in his arms, struggling and squirming – he'd almost taken her right then and there. But then he'd seen the disgust and fear in her eyes, and it'd shocked him to the core.

She'd been turned off by him.

All affection and warmth for her had vanished, replaced by a bitter hurt he felt down to his bones. Oh, he still was going to have her, no doubt about that. But there'd be no tenderness, no consideration for her. No one hurt him and got away with it, not even his beautiful, wild Hope.

She'd give in, or he'd make her.

Trent called every morning for the next two days. Each time, Hope avoided the call with Kelly's help. Normally, it wouldn't have been difficult to plead that she was too busy to talk, but she no longer had that excuse.

Business had dropped off sharply, leaving her plenty of free time.

On the second day, with no patients waiting for the first time in the clinic's history, Kelly and Hope sat restlessly behind the check-in desk.

It was only ten a.m.

Hope wondered what was happening to her business. Kelly filed her already perfect nails and remained characteristically silent. 'Would you like to go home early?' Hope asked, knowing she couldn't afford to pay the woman to sit and look pretty.

'You don't think this is just an unusual lull?'

She wanted to, oh how she wanted to. 'It seems strange.'

The phone rang and both women jumped at the unexpected noise. 'Don't get it,' Hope said, knowing it would be Trent, again.

Kelly gave her a long look. 'Don't get it? Aren't we in the business of helping –'

With a growl of frustration, Hope snatched the phone off the receiver. Her greeting sounded curt and ungrateful, but it was the best she could manage with her nerves frayed.

'Enjoying your day?' Trent asked in an annoyingly knowing voice.

He was ruining her. He'd promised, and now somehow he was making good on the threat. Without a word, she set the phone down.

Kelly glanced at her. 'Wrong number?'

'Uh . . . yeah.'

'I heard what you told Mrs Contey this morning.'

'That she wouldn't get those fainting spells if she stopped wearing her girdle so tight?'

'No, although if Mr Contey would glance at her once in a while, she wouldn't try so hard to gain the attention of every man within three hundred miles. I heard you tell her that a man has to be far more than just handsome to make you look twice.'

'That's true.'

'Well Trent is gorgeous and rich enough to make even a saint forget about anything else,' Kelly said casually, carefully inspecting a fingernail.

'I meant what I said. It takes far more than pretty brawn to impress me.'

'Hmm. But it does help.'

'What helps is something solid upstairs in the brain department.' Hope sighed, thinking of Clay. 'An intelligent man is an attractive one.'

Kelly laughed, and nodded as if she agreed. After that rather intimate conversation, things seemed easier somehow. At least between the two women.

They still didn't have any patients.

Kelly stopped checking with Hope each time Trent called, taking it on her own initiative that Hope would not come to the phone. It lightened the load between them even more, as if they had a mutual mission. Kelly also stopped talking so ridiculously loud to Hope, another good sign.

And once, in the late afternoon, when Hope couldn't hear Kelly, and had to ask 'what' three times, Kelly actually teased Hope by saying, 'But you can hear everything I say, right?'

Both women laughed, then egged on by the stress of work, they caught the giggles. Every time they caught sight of one another after that, they would start laughing again, utterly incapable of stopping.

For Hope, it was the stuff that the magical word friendship was made of, and it was wonderful. Things went blessedly smoothly. Clay recuperated and Hope treated the few patients that trickled in, with no one the wiser to her guest.

Things would have been perfect, except for one major thing – she and Kelly saw eight patients that day, only six the next.

'We were incredibly slow today,' Kelly commented as she left. 'Should I be looking for another job?'

'No,' Hope assured her. 'We'll be fine.'

Kelly gave her a long, appraising look, but it wasn't unkind. 'Dr Broderick – '

'Hope,' she corrected gently.

Kelly smiled, relieving her. 'Hope.'

'You look worried.'

'I am,' the pretty nurse said frankly. 'I need the work.'

The bad feeling inside Hope grew, not because of anything Kelly was doing, but because of Trent and what he'd done. 'You have work.'

'For how long?'

'As long as . . .' She broke off frustrated, knowing she was unable to make any rash promises with her own finances so weak. 'Gossip,' Hope said with a frown, shaking her head. 'I can't believe how vicious it can be in a town this size.'

'Gossip most of it may be,' Kelly pointed out sadly, 'but it's working. You earned nothing today.'

'That's not true. Mr Garner paid me.'

'Yeah, in turnips.'

The women looked at each other . . . and nearly caught the giggles again. 'Just try paying me in turnips, Hope,' Kelly laughed. 'And I'll – ' A teasing light came into her eyes. 'I'll make you talk to Trent the next time he calls.'

'No, anything but that.' But Hope smiled, or tried to. 'I'm sorry you're worried, Kelly. We'll get through this.'

'I hope so. I really need the paycheck.'

The woman was too polite to ask, but Hope felt she needed to say it regardless. 'The rumors are mere speculation, Kelly. And pretty mean to boot.'

'Well, then, we'll just have to ride them out, won't we?' Kelly's cool face warmed several degrees, and she reached out and squeezed Hope's hand. 'I know how you feel about this clinic, and believe me, I want it to work out.'

'It will,' Hope said with bunches more confidence than she felt. Kelly nodded and opened the front door.

They both stared in dismay at the For Sale sign someone had posted at the top of the driveway.

'The plot thickens,' Kelly muttered, then sighed. As if to mock Hope's troubles, it started to rain. 'Damn. I was just beginning to really like this job.'

'Good,' Hope said firmly. 'Because it isn't over yet. I'll fix this, Kelly.'

Kelly turned to her. 'You know what? I believe you will.' She slipped on her sweater. 'Anything I can do, let me know. You can count me in, Dr Hope.'

'Thanks, Kelly.'

Hope watched her, and the minute Kelly's car turned down the drive, she allowed the worry to cloud her face.

Remaining optimistic was not only draining, but getting more difficult daily, made all the harder by the fact that she had a feeling it was going to get far worse.

Obviously, Trent was not just getting to the population of Green County, but her father as well. If he sold the house from beneath her, what would she do?

But her greatest concern was her reduced patient flow. Were the people not seeking help when they should, simply because of whatever damage Trent was wreaking with the rumors? But they had no other place to go, except Seattle.

Was she through?

It hurt to think it, but it might be so and she'd have to face it. She'd decided days ago she couldn't use Clay, that as soon as he was well enough to defend himself against whatever it was he'd gotten himself into, she'd tell him the truth.

He'd leave and she'd be forced to deal with Trent, alone.

Feeling unusually down, she slipped into a chair in the kitchen, relieved her day was over. Groaning, she dropped her head into her arms, and it felt so good to rest there, she didn't move.

She wished she could hear more of the soothing sound of the pouring rain, but the scent of the storm helped. Fric and Frac sat in a cage in the corner, as they always did when it rained, whistling and cajoling her, begging for attention as usual, but she couldn't give it. Not with her heart in her throat and her nerves shot.

Suddenly, she sensed him. Jerking her head up, she caught her breath. Clay.

'Hope.'

At the achingly familiar male voice, she leaped up out of the chair, as though caught guiltily doing something she shouldn't have.

'I didn't mean to startle you,' he said.

'What are you doing up –?' Her words broke off in her throat as she lifted her gaze.

He stood in the doorway, wearing a fresh pair of surgical scrubs and a t-shirt, which stretched tightly over his broad shoulders. In his other life, the one that didn't involve her, he must be an athlete, he was certainly built like one. Broad chest tapered to a lean waist, made even leaner by the bandages that she knew still bound his ribs beneath his shirt. Long legs that even through the material of the scrubs looked hard and powerful. His face, that rugged, lived-in, beard-roughened face, the one that had become unbearably, disturbingly dear, seemed taut with tension.

Though she'd realized it before, she felt awed at the sheer size of him, at how big he really was, how tall, how . . . latently male.

And how hopelessly attracted she'd become.

He frowned at the noisy birds. 'They make enough commotion to wake the dead.'

'I know. But it's raining. They get nervous.'

They whistled and hooted at him and he just stared. Then he turned his attention to Hope, and her heart caught at the heat in his gaze.

'You're pale,' she said inanely, taking a step back as he took one forward. 'I think you should be in bed – '

'I've had enough of bed,' he grumbled. 'Five days and I still feel like death warmed over.' He took another step towards her, and again she backed up.

'I miss you,' he said in a not-very-gentle voice. 'I wanted to see you.'

'Miss you,' one of the birds parroted in a sing-song voice.

Clay glared at it. 'They talk.'

That voice she'd begun to count on to accelerate her pulse wasn't going to fail her. It raced uncontrollably, and he'd hardly spoken. Then she realized what he'd just said.

He'd missed her.

Dear God, that shouldn't affect her heart so.

Then another thought occurred to her, and it erased her fuzzy, warm feeling. He was up. In another minute, he might have sought her out in the clinic.

She hadn't told anyone about him for fear of stirring up more controversy. What would Kelly say when she saw this gorgeous man padding about her house? Probably not much, knowing her quiet nurse, but her eyes would bug right out of her head.

'You're just bored,' she said, afraid to believe he spoke the truth, that he had really missed her. Afraid and thrilled.

'No, not bored.' His gaze glimmered. 'You know that's not it. I can see it in your eyes.'

She bumped into the sink and reached behind her to grab onto it, needing the support for her ridiculously weak legs. 'I guess you really are feeling a little better. I'll just make you some . . . soup.'

His brows came together in a sharp line. His frown tripped up her heart rate another notch, and he made a noise that might have been a growl.

'Yeah, that's it,' she said quickly, thankful for something to do with her hands. 'Soup.'

But he came close before she could move, bracketing her hips with his large hands, caging her in, towering over her. 'No soup, Hope.'

'No soup, Hope,' came the taunting birds, repeating the words that Hope hadn't caught. 'No soup, Hope. No soup.'

'Damn birds,' Clay muttered, then pressed himself closer, until he was a mere fraction from her, eyes blaring with temper.

Suddenly there wasn't enough air in her lungs. 'A sandwich then.'

'Stop it. I'm not hungry.'

'What?' she squeaked.

He gave her a knowing glance as he repeated his words.

'I'm not hungry for food, Hope. Ask me what I am hungry for.'

The birds whistled.

Hope's heart did a slow roll in her chest.

His nearness suffocated her. Yet . . . she felt the insane urge to have that hard body pressed against hers. 'Okay, so you're not hungry,' she said quickly, nervously. 'I'll get you another pain-killer. Let me just – '

'I don't want the doctor routine,' he said unevenly, giving her a hard look from beneath lashes long enough to make any woman jealous. 'Nor the hovering mother.'

So he still sulked, just because she'd refused to sleep with him, or let him sleep with her. But, God looking at that tough, still badly bruised body, she knew she'd done the right thing. That, added to the fact he still could hardly stand – this was the first time she'd actually seen him do it by himself – and she had one fine-looking, heavily pouting male on her hands. Which almost amused her.

Almost.

If he hadn't looked so temperamental, so dangerous . . . so gorgeous. 'Okay, so you don't want me to doctor you.'

'Or mother me,' he reminded her, giving her a look so blatantly sexual, so outrageously suggestive, her mouth went dry.

'You want – '

'You,' he said huskily. 'I want you.' Leaning in, he planted his open, wet mouth against her neck, sucked a patch of her skin against his teeth and gently tugged.

She felt it down to her toes.

'Oh my,' she whispered, reaching out to grip his arms to keep her balance in a world that had just tipped on its axis. She heard her own soft moan when he did it again.

'Oh my,' claimed a bird in falsetto.

Hope whispered it again, unable to help herself.

Against her skin, she felt him smile. He lifted his head briefly enough to tease her. 'So profound, Dr Broderick.' He let out a slow, deep, warm breath into her ear.

Goose bumps raised her flesh, her stomach fluttered. Then his hands lifted from the tile and slipped around her waist. His eyes moved over her slowly, thoroughly, and in her simple doctor's coat, layered over an equally simple and modest dress, she felt startlingly plain and unsophisticated.

But his gaze didn't express any distaste, only approval and need. 'You're beautiful,' he said simply. 'But you're wearing too many clothes.' With that shocking statement, he unbuttoned her white overcoat and slipped it off her shoulders, letting it fall to the floor.

One of the birds whistled, low and slow. An equally slow and mysterious smile played about Clay's lips. 'Remind me to put a towel over their cage when we make love.'

'A towel – ' His meaning, as well as the rest of the sentence finally registered on her. 'Oh!'

He smiled. 'Yeah, oh.'

Dazed, she stared down at her feet, and at the puddle of white material there. Her heart was drumming so loud now she could hear nothing but the echo of it. 'I guess you're feeling even better than I thought,' she murmured, a little bewildered by the emotions he caused, and he laughed softly.

She felt the chuckle vibrate in his chest and it went a long way toward calming her. This was the gentle, easy-going man she'd taken care of for the past week, and he looked so happy and confident she couldn't help but smile back.

'That's it,' he told her, cupping her face so that she gazed directly into the deepest green eyes she'd ever seen. 'I love it when you do that . . . You know, I am feeling much better today. Want me to show you exactly how much, Hope?'

He was asking permission. For what, to kiss her? To continue removing her clothes? She wasn't sure, but coming on the heels of her abuse at the hands of Trent, it touched as well as terrified her. 'I don't know,' she answered as honestly as she could.

His hands again slipped around her waist, holding her loosely, without restraint. 'Think about it,' he suggested with a sweet, beguiling smile.

He wouldn't push. At that knowledge, she felt almost giddy with relief. Until she felt him tremble slightly, heard his shallow breath. When he shifted his weight against her, putting out a hand to the tile to bear most of it, she knew the truth.

Arousal had taken a back seat to pain.

'Clay,' she said, knowing she had to be careful or bruise his already bruised and abused ego, 'Let's sit down.'

'I'm fine.'

'I'm fine, I'm fine, I'm fine,' one of the birds mocked.

'Really, I am,' Clay said weakly.

'Don't be stubborn. You need to sit, I can feel you shaking.'

'I'm not,' he insisted quietly, taking his other hand from her waist and putting it on the tile behind her. Then he grimaced and rubbed his forehead to hers. 'Dammit,' he whispered. 'I'm fine . . . really.'

'Hmmm.' Carefully she encircled his waist with her arms, trying to bear his weight. That he allowed it spoke volumes. 'You're fine. You're tough. You could probably run a race now, right?'

'Or something else equally physical,' he assured her, nudging his hips to hers with a wicked, hot look.

But beads of sweat had popped out on his forehead, and his skin had turned pasty. He needed to sit, and she'd have to bully him into it. 'Want to bet?' she asked sweetly.

'Yeah, if you're the prize.'

Oh, he was something all right. One hundred and eighty pounds of aroused male and nowhere to take it. 'Fine.' She added an innocent smile. 'All you have to do is take this bowl – ' She handed him the cat's bowl of dry food that had been on the counter. 'And take it outside. Leave it on the bottom step for Huey, Dewey and Louie.'

At the mention of the cats' names, the birds started to squawk and chatter, and Clay stared at her in disbelief. 'Huey, Dewey and Louie?'

She bit her lip to keep back her nervous laugh.

'You've got to be kidding me.'

He was one fine looking man, even bruised and

speechless. She held out the bowl and raised her eyebrows. 'Can't do it, huh?'

'The bottom step?' He laughed confidently, even as his color faded another shade. 'No problem, sweetheart. Then you're mine.'

'You're mine sweetheart,' sang Fric and Frac.

'That's right,' she said with a guileless smile, watching him walk carefully, slowly, deliberately to the back door.

He made it down the first two steps before he grabbed for the railing, and Hope started to perspire just watching him, it was so painful. The doctor in her itched to grab him and toss him back in his bed with a stern verbal lashing for pushing himself this way.

The woman in her yearned to throw her arms around him and beg him to stop.

She did neither, just bit her lip and watched him hesitate on the third step, in obvious agony.

'Hope?' he spoke hoarsely, his back to her. 'I hope to God you can hear me.'

She ran to him and relieved him of the bowl. Slipping her shoulder under his arm, she helped him back inside. 'I can hear you, you silly fool,' she chastened as he winced and clamped his jaw tight on the very last step.

She didn't stop in the kitchen, but passed the whistling Fric and Frac and took Clay back to his room, lowering him gently down on his bed.

'Winning suits you,' he grumbled when she couldn't swallow her reluctant smile. He moaned dramatically when he shifted for comfort.

When she didn't respond, he groaned again, then

peeked at her expectantly. In spite of her sympathy for his pain and discomfort, her smile spread.

'Yeah, winning suits you all right,' he said with disgust. 'But that cocky grin of yours kinda spoils it.'

She bit her lip to hold back the unaccustomed laughter at his grumpy tone. 'If you had won, Clayton Slater, you'd be bragging from here to tomorrow, and you know it. So don't you dare take this moment from me.'

He laughed, then held his sides and sucked in his breath. 'I wouldn't dream of it.'

Their eyes met . . . and good humor filled the moment. So did companionship and genuine camaraderie. Hope's despair faded away. 'So you're admitting I won?' she asked.

Still holding his sides, Clay chuckled again. 'Oh, you win, all right. I'm all yours.' He reached for her.

'Oh, no,' she said, laughing and jumping off the bed. 'I never told you what I'd claim if I won.'

'True enough,' he said in a suddenly low, husky voice that made her insides hum. 'But I could suggest something if you're short on ideas.'

CHAPTER 11

It was hard to believe, Hope thought, that a man so obviously in pain, so completely colorful with bruises, could be so heartstoppingly sensual.

So impossibly irresistible.

'I bet you could suggest several things for my winning.' She studied Clay with a little smile. 'But I think about now, you're all talk and no go.'

Groaning, he leaned back. 'As much as it kills me to admit it, you're right. I'll have to settle for companionship tonight.'

But his face had grown unusually serious, and he studied her intently. So intently she squirmed. 'I think,' she said a little shakily, 'that you have more on your mind than mere companionship.'

He tapped the bed by his side, his gaze still quiet, probing. 'Sit a minute?'

'I – I can't,' she said, stuttering a bit. 'I'm really . . . busy.'

'You're always busy. It's not good for you to push yourself this way.' His gaze dropped to her stomach. 'Are you feeling all right?'

'I'm fine.'

'You didn't look fine when I first came into the kitchen. You looked sad. And alone.'

'I'm not alone now.'

'No, you're not.' His gaze intensified. 'Do you like it?'

'I'm not sure.' Awareness coursed through her when he looked at her like that; like he wanted to devour her, care for her . . . touch her.

'Please come here?'

'You'll . . . kiss me again.' There. She'd said it.

'I might,' he said seriously, tipping his head to study her. 'Are you going to tell me you didn't like it?'

'It was . . . just a kiss.'

'No.'

'A simple little kiss.'

'If you say that again,' he warned, sitting straight up. 'I'll –'

'You'll what?' She crossed her arms and looked at him in amusement.

'I'll – I'll kiss you again until you're completely senseless.'

Having never been kissed like that, and being certain it was impossible, she burst out laughing.

He fumed, looking positively insulted. 'Come over here, Hope. And let me prove you wrong.'

She actually had to fight from jumping onto the bed with him. She, the disciplined, uptight, frigid Hope, wanted to leap against him and beg him to do what he'd just promised. 'How do you even know you can kiss me like that? I thought you couldn't remember anything.'

'It's like getting back on a bicycle,' he promised, holding out his arms. 'Come here.'

It would be a big mistake, she told herself. Major. Because even though she was convinced she could resist him, she didn't need to stroke that ego of his any further. Besides, he should be resting and she should be . . . Her feet took her to the bed before she could blink. The mattress bumped her knees.

Tugging her down beside him, he grinned cockily into her face as he leaned over her. 'Be kind,' he whispered, 'I'm a very weak man.'

She rolled her eyes and opened her mouth to retort, but his mouth came down on hers. Still connected to her, he moved again, this time bracketing her shoulders with his elbows, which he used to prop himself over her. One of his long legs slid between hers, his thigh lying warmly and heavily against the heat he found there.

He held her face between his large hands as his mouth took her with violent tenderness, forcing her to respond, then pushing her harder until she was moaning in his arms and his hands were sinking into her hair to hold her even closer.

Reflexively, her arms went around his shoulders, gripping the taut skin with fisted hands. At her touch, he let out a low, wordless sound of arousal and shifted his leg between hers suggestively. She gasped into his mouth and pressed against that leg, shamelessly riding it.

Heat spiraled through her.

He lifted his head slightly, holding his mouth a breath from hers. Breathing harshly, he whispered, 'Hope?'

But she didn't want the kiss to be over. She grabbed

fistfuls of hair and tugged his mouth back to hers. He gave her what she wanted; a hot, wet, slow, thorough kiss. She explored his bruised face with her hands. He caught the tip of one of her fingers between his teeth and nipped it, then sucked the ball of it into his soft, damp mouth, his impossibly dark gaze never leaving hers.

She threw her head back, whimpered and ground herself against his leg helplessly.

'Hope?' He kissed his way down her neck, slipping her dress off her shoulder with his mouth. His tongue slipped beneath the material, flirted with her collarbone. 'Sweetheart?'

She wanted another kiss, and she told him so, loudly.

With a secret smile, he bent his head and complied, sliding more tightly to her, gently rocking them together so that she could feel every inch of his lower body. Every thrust brought them even more aligned, closer, letting her feel exactly how excited he was.

She moaned helplessly.

'Hope,' he said, smiling tenderly down into her face so that she could see his words. 'You – '

'No. Kiss me again, Clay.'

He tried to resist, but she wouldn't have it. She didn't want to talk. She wanted that mind-blowing sensation of his lips on hers. She wanted to lose herself, as she'd never done before. Again, she tried to tug him back to her, but this time he managed to hold her off, smiling down at her with what looked suspiciously like humor instead of arousal.

'Hope, I – '

'Clay!'

'I just wanted to tell you –'

'Kiss me!' Was the man dense? Could he not see that he'd offered her something she'd never thought to feel?

'You're sweet,' he said on a laughing moan. 'Especially like this.' With a wicked smile, he leaned close and she sighed with relief. But instead of kissing her, he merely whispered her name, his lips so close to hers she could feel his heat – but she was so far gone she couldn't hear a thing, could only read her name as it left his mouth.

She shook her head, not wanting to listen, but he just said her name again, waiting with that sexy little smile, but for what she couldn't imagine.

'What?' she gasped finally, wondering why he wasn't kissing her. And why was he smiling at a time like this? Couldn't he see what she so desperately needed?

His thumbs played with her tingling lower lip, his fingers caressed her jaw. His lower body snuggled close, intimately flush with hers, though he'd been careful to hold his torso, and his hurt ribs, away.

'*What?*' she repeated, becoming annoyed. What was the matter with him?

'I win, baby.' Those emerald eyes sparkled. 'You're as senseless as you can get.'

Clay felt better the next morning. Grinning, he remembered the absolutely flabbergasted look on Hope's face when he'd told her he'd won their little bet. Still grinning, he managed to get out of bed without groaning.

He took a long, hot shower and didn't feel like crying when the spray hit his ribs.

And he pulled on his pants without wincing in pain – too badly.

But he stared at the stranger in the mirror and his euphoria died. Dark green solemn eyes stared back at him. His unsmiling mouth went grim and he plowed his hands through hair that didn't so much as feel familiar.

Who the hell was he?

He didn't understand the urgency, but knew it was real. He had to find out and soon, but he didn't know why. It infuriated him.

It terrified him.

Would he bring whatever danger he was in to Hope? He hoped not. The woman meant . . . what? What the hell did she mean to him? He couldn't speak for the past, but he had an uneasy feeling that women in general hadn't meant much.

They did now, or at least one did.

Wait a minute.

He stared at himself in the mirror. Had he just made a conscious decision that she belonged in his life – permanently?

He backed away from the thought and the mirror.

As he had every morning since he could stand, he lifted the wallet that Hope had found on him. Empty of whatever cash he might have been carrying, and void of a driver's license as well, it was completely empty.

His fingers played with the expensive brown leather where the name Clayton Slater had been monogrammed on the front.

Much as he'd looked at it, pored over each and every

little crease the past few days, it still looked completely unfamiliar. It meant nothing. Nothing.

He fingered the soft, supple material, concentrating, hoping, and suddenly . . . voices filled his head.

'Here, darling,' said a laughing, female voice.

Her voice seemed to echo loudly, gratingly, in Clay's head, making it pound painfully.

She handed him the wallet, brand new. 'Merry Christmas to the hardest man in the world to shop for,' she added huskily, tossing her long blonde hair over her shoulder.

He had smiled. 'I'm not that hard.'

Her light brows lifted. Her red lips curved as she moved her sensuous body toward him. 'Aren't you?' she murmured, reaching for the zipper of his pants. 'Allow me to fix that.'

Clay tossed the wallet over his shoulder to a tall dresser and sucked his breath in sharply as the smiling woman 'fixed' the situation.

She laughed low in her throat when she touched him and shot him a look of victory.

He'd tossed her to the bed . . .

'Clay?'

But she didn't have dark eyes that saw clear through to his soul and he stared down at her.

'Clay?'

He jerked from the hazy dream-like state back to reality and blinked in confusion.

'Clay? Are you all right?'

It wasn't the tall leggy blonde at all, but Hope.

CHAPTER 12

Clay snapped out of it and turned to the low, hesitant voice. She might not be tall, blonde, or even gorgeous, not by a model's standards. But Hope, with her luscious, thick hair, huge, wide eyes and small, hourglass figure, was the most beautiful woman he'd ever seen.

'Are you all right?' she asked with a worried frown, coming into his room. 'You're pale.'

Had he just had his first real flashback? And what did it mean? 'Hope, I – ' He couldn't think clearly. That other woman had meant nothing, he realized. Nothing compared to this woman looking at him with her heart in her shining eyes.

'Sit,' she said firmly, swallowing her fear at the look on his face and pushing him gently to the bed. 'You're shaking, Clay.'

'Am I?'

He wasn't wearing a shirt again, she thought, as her hands touched bare skin. Pleasure at the great view he afforded her mixed with pain – his torso was still hopelessly bruised, and his ribs – 'Where is your binding?'

she demanded when he sat on the bed. 'You'll hurt yourself if you don't keep your ribs bound.'

'I showered.'

Oh, yes, he had. His slightly too long hair was damp and combed back from his face. His shoulders gleamed. And he smelled so good, so fresh . . . so absolutely, positively male. 'I can see that,' she said primly. 'Hold still.'

She fell silent while she set herself to the task of rewrapping his ribs, though it was hard to keep her composure – and her distance – while she kneeled at the floor between his spread legs. She opened a fresh bandage for his ribs.

Placing her hands on his middle made it worse, so did the small smile that crossed his lips.

She sent him a frown, just to be sure he knew she meant business.

With an innocent look, he lifted his arms out to give her room. 'I'll be good,' he said in a voice that suggested the opposite.

'Hmm. That's what I'm afraid of.'

He laughed, a low, incredibly sexy laugh that just about undid her. With as much care as she could when her heart thundered against her ribs and her hands shook, she leaned forward and reached behind him to run the bandage around his body. Her breath fanned his belly. She saw the muscles there tighten. Her own repeated the motion. She felt more than actually heard the soft, strangled noise he made in his throat.

'Am I hurting you?' she asked quickly, looking up.

Big mistake. Real big mistake. Those green, fathomless eyes were on her, filled with such hunger, such passion, it stole her breath. Slowly, he closed his thighs a little, so the insides of them touched her sides. He completely surrounded her with rock solid muscle and warm skin.

The feeling was heady indeed.

'Clay?' she asked hesitantly, poised with her arms around him, the bandage behind his back. Because of her sixth sense, she felt his pain as her own, only this pain was different than that other more physical pain. She didn't understand it, until he spoke.

'You're killing me,' he whispered, sinking his fingers into her hair. 'But don't stop.'

She pulled the bandage around to the front of him, adjusted it and wrapped it around that magnificent torso, again and again. Each time she did, her face moved close to his bare skin. If she opened her mouth, she could taste him, and oh, how she wanted to. Her knees wobbled at the thought. Beneath her arms, his strong, powerful legs provided support. Against her stomach, she felt the unmistakable, rigid bulge of his arousal.

It leaped every time she brushed against it.

'Oh, my,' she whispered, completely bowled over by the strange and new feelings that swam through her body every time she came near him. 'Clay . . .'

'Shhh.' He took the end of the bandage from her fingers and finished it off himself, then put his hands on her shoulders. 'I'm trying not to rush you, Hope. But it's getting harder each day.' He paused when her eyes widened. 'No pun intended,' he added with a wry grimace.

She dropped her gaze from his and encountered his lap. She realized she was staring, her mouth hanging open when he let out a small, helpless laugh.

Slamming her eyes shut in mortification, she felt her cheeks flame, and he laughed again. 'Hope, it's nothing new. You walk into the room, I get hard. You speak, I get hard. You look at me, I get – '

'I get the picture,' she said weakly. And what a picture, she thought.

His fingers ran over her shoulder. 'Are you still bruised here?'

Before she could answer, he slipped the v-neck t-shirt she wore off her shoulder, skimming his thumb lightly over the mark Trent had left. 'You are.' He tensed, though he smoothed the marred skin with light, gentle fingers, his gaze watching the movements.

Unable to speak, unable to move, she remained where she was, in the undeniably erotic position of kneeling between his legs as he sat over her on the bed. So overwhelmed by that, she missed his next words. 'What?' she asked, lifting her gaze to his.

One of the things she'd discovered she liked most about Clay was that he never seemed to resent repeating things. She knew how annoying it could be. Yet he never showed anything but a certain enraged tenderness that let her know he hated her deafness for her, while letting her know it didn't bother him.

It had allowed her to lose most of her self-consciousness about the handicap, and as a direct result, she had begun to feel more comfortable in his presence than she had with anyone else – which in turn terrified her.

'Has Trent bothered you?'

'No.' Her voice came hoarse, unsteady, so she licked her lips and said it again. 'No.' Then she managed to stand by locking her knees together, but didn't – couldn't – move from between his legs.

That gaze she couldn't resist moved slowly up her body until it met hers. 'You'd tell me, wouldn't you?'

She couldn't miss the heat in his gaze or the demand behind the polite question. 'Yes, Clay, I'd tell you.'

'But he has tried to call you.'

He'd been busy. And his ears worked a hell of a lot better than hers. 'I've avoided him.'

'He needs to be faced. I'd like to do that.' His gaze hardened.

Her stomach leaped. 'Clay. You're still not well.'

He ran his hand down her arm, past her elbow, to her hand, linking her fingers with his. Then he brought their joined hands to his chest, and pressed it there so she could feel the steady, heavy beat of his heart. 'I don't want anything to happen to you,' he said.

'It . . . won't.' But further speech was impossible, because he left her hand on his chest to move his up the center of her body, over her shirt, until it covered her heart, which beat wildly.

'I know you're a woman used to being on her own, Hope,' he said slowly, lifting his gaze from his hand on her chest to her face. 'You don't have a lot of people you've let be close to you.'

'I have people close to me every day.' Was that her voice, that faraway, wispy, shaky female whisper?

'You don't have people that you've let into your life,'

he corrected, his hand still on her. 'Patients don't count, Hope.'

'They count to me.'

'That's not what I mean,' he admonished gently, his eyes filled with warm understanding.

'It's – ' She could hardly think with him so close, could hardly breathe with his hand over the center of her chest, his fingers brushing the inner sides of her breasts. 'I'm . . . not an easy person to know.'

'You're plenty easy to know, dammit, and I want to be a part of your life. I want to be with you. Please, Hope, let me in.'

He leaned forward and placed his lips to her heart. Then he nuzzled her breasts, rubbing his cheeks against them. 'I like the way your heart sounds when I'm near,' he announced huskily, his voice as affected as hers.

'It's going to leap right out of my chest,' she murmured, hardly able to form the words with his hand on her and his face moving from one side of her body to the other.

He looked up at her. 'I like you, Hope.'

'I like you too.' She knew he could feel how her heart raced, could hear the harsh, choppy way she dragged air through her lungs.

'No. I mean I *really* like you. Enough that it just about scares me to death.'

She felt herself pale at his words, knowing she knew exactly how he felt. 'I really like you, too, Clay.'

'It means a lot to hear you say that.' He smiled, a slow, lazy smile. 'Especially when you don't really want to feel that way.'

She didn't get much by him, that was certain. 'I'm not used to this,' she admitted, but stopped short of admitting the rest. How could she explain that she had never let a man into her life? That she'd locked herself away, first in her studies, now in her practice? He thought she carried his child, but wouldn't he be shocked to find out his pregnant 'lover' was a virgin.

A very inexperienced virgin at that.

But then his hand rose up, touching her throat gently. Leaning forward, his lips touched the bare skin above the open neckline of her shirt. She whimpered. *Whimpered*. For just a flash, his lips hovered there, across her cleavage. Heat suffused her and she could feel her muscles straining, as though they were waiting for more.

Gradually, with the care of a man still in some pain, he kissed his way up her chest and neck as he came off the bed. Standing, he gently pulled her to him, smoothing his hands up her spine until she shivered.

'Cold?' he asked.

'No.'

'So it's me you're trembling for?'

She gasped at his words, at the unbelievable confidence she heard behind them. At the way he made her blood surge uncontrollably. 'You're . . . not well,' she said lamely.

One blond brow quirked. 'Well enough, sweetheart. Just try me.'

She had to laugh. 'How am I supposed to take you seriously with lines like that?'

Carefully, with one finger to his cut lip, he grinned. 'Thought it was worth a try.'

She backed from him and he sighed for the lost moment. But a quick tumble in the sack wasn't what he was after with Hope. No, he wanted something much more long-term, and he'd discovered he could wait for it rather than blow what he had with one foolish move.

The flashback he'd just had before she'd come into the room suggested to him that maybe he wasn't used to thinking that way, and that bothered him a great deal.

Was that part of the reason behind her hesitancy to let him into her heart? Had he hurt her? Maybe with other women? Or had she just not known him well enough? He could change that.

That he wanted to no longer shocked him. 'I remembered something before,' he said slowly, and she whipped her head up to stare at him, almost . . . fearfully?

'What?'

'I remembered something.'

'I heard you,' she said with a ghost of a smile. 'For once. I meant, what did you remember?'

His eyes narrowed and he came closer to her, lifted her chin with one finger. 'Why doesn't my remembering something please you?'

'It does, of course it does,' she said quickly, giving him a smile he knew damn well was forced. 'What did you remember?'

'Nothing important.' Important would have been how he'd come to be lying half dead in her woods, and how he could avoid a repeat performance.

'Clay, what did you remember?'

'How I got that wallet,' he said dryly, remembering

the buxom blonde clearly. No name with that face, though he knew she'd been just that to him then, too. Just a face.

'The rest will come,' she said with a regret he couldn't miss.

'Hey,' he said softly, cupping her shoulders in his hands and peering down into her face with concern. 'You can't be worried about that, worried that I'll just leave. I already told you I wouldn't.'

Under his hands she shrugged, but he caught the truth in her eyes. 'You didn't believe me.' Sweeping his hands down her arms, he grasped her hands and brought them to his mouth. Over their joined fingers, he watched her. 'Hope, you're a part of me. You're my future.' He believed that with all his heart. Knew by the fear in her eyes that she did too, whether she wanted to admit it or not.

Now he let go of her hands to slide a hand over her belly, knowing the gesture was ridiculously possessive, but unable to help it. 'You and that kid you're carrying in there for me are my future. How could you think I'd leave all that, just walk away and leave you alone?'

'I don't want to be your obligation.'

'You're more than that, and I think you know it.' He narrowed his eyes on her, seeing far more than she would have liked. 'I think that scares you. A whole great big bunch.'

'This isn't about me,' she said, backing up so that his hands fell to his sides. 'It's about you, and getting your memory back.' She crossed her arms over her chest. 'I have to get ready for my patients.'

She'd made it to the door before he spoke, and at his words, she froze.

'I heard you on the phone with your father last night,' he said casually to her back, loudly enough that she wouldn't have missed a single word.

She didn't, given the sudden tenseness in her shoulders. Slowly, she turned to face him, her expression giving away her every thought. 'I'm sorry if I spoke too loud and woke you up.'

He hated how self-conscious she felt, and wished he could change that. He *would* change that, he vowed. 'You didn't speak too loudly, Hope. I was listening.'

The roll of emotions she showed fascinated him.

'I thought you were sleeping when I made that call,' she said stiffly.

Defensive, he thought, with his own burst of emotion. And so damned alone he wanted to go wrap his arms around her and never let go. 'Nope.'

She continued to look at him, everything she felt shining in her eyes; the fear, the resentment . . . the hopeless attraction, all bubbling to the surface.

'If you go see him this afternoon as you promised,' he said evenly, suppressing the urge to hug her tight, 'I'm coming with you.'

'That was a personal call, Clay.'

'I'm coming with you,' he repeated patiently. 'Because you know as well as I do, you could run into Trent what's-his-name.'

'Blockwell.'

'*Blockhead*. No way am I going to let you face that alone.'

She just stared at him, and he wasn't sure whether it was dismay or a guarded relief she felt.

'It's time he found out you're not alone,' he said firmly, his hands on his hips. 'And I want to see the face of the man who tried to hurt you. I want him to see mine.'

She made a face, shifted uncomfortably on her feet. She uncrossed, then recrossed her arms over her chest in a comical attempt to act casual. 'You sound like a . . . Like a . . .'

'Like a what?' he asked, coming closer, keeping his gaze directly on hers so that he could be sure she heard his every word. 'Like a worried man who cares about you very much? Like a man who wants to make sure the woman in his life isn't hurt again?'

'I'm not yours,' she whispered, shaking her head, gripping the door behind her. 'I don't belong to anyone but me.'

'Of course you don't.' He went close enough to tug her hair playfully. 'But I'm still coming with you.'

She made a noise of disgust, which hardly masked the relief he could see so clearly in her eyes. 'My father won't be expecting you.'

'Tough.'

'I don't want to cause a scene.'

'Neither do I.'

She licked her lips, drawing his attention to her very kissable mouth. 'It's a long drive. Hours. Bumpy roads. It'll hurt your ribs.'

'I'll be fine.'

'I'm just going to ask my father to consider taking this

place off the market. That's all. Then I'm coming right back.'

He touched her shoulder, ran a finger down her arm, just for the contact. 'Will he listen?'

'I doubt it.'

'Sounds like a real nice guy, Hope.'

'He is,' she insisted. 'He's just . . .'

'Just?'

She gave him a little smile. 'Possessive. Over-protective. Sound like anyone else you know?'

Ah, that was it. She fought him so hard because her father had always pushed her, and now Clay was as well. He immediately changed tactics.

'Then why bother to ask him?' he asked. 'Why not just contact the bank and make arrangements to buy it?'

She fell silent. Then, in a voice that told him exactly how much it had cost her pride to answer, she said, 'I don't have the money to buy it. I was hoping to just buy some more time while I look for another place.'

She was a doctor, a damned busy one. Or at least, had been until Trent had pulled his latest stunt. Why wouldn't she have money? Yet he knew she didn't. Her office might be up to date, with the latest modern medical equipment, but her house was in a state of disrepair. Clay wanted, badly, to offer to help her. But he had no idea if he had money or not. 'I want to go with you. Please?'

She nodded curtly and started to leave, but he stopped her with a hand on her arm. 'Just one last thing,' he said, then touched his lips to hers, slowly, lightly, running them back and forth over her silkiness.

She went still and he did it again. Then again, until

she'd melted against him with a sexy little sound in the back of her throat.

Then, with a last gentle squeeze he backed off, letting go of her. He wanted more, wanted that badly, but he had to know she wanted it, too.

She brought her fingers up to the lips he'd just kissed, and stared at him. 'Wow!'

'Yeah. Wow.' The heck with waiting, he thought, and reached for her again.

'I've . . . got to go,' she whispered, avoiding his touch, then she dashed out of the room.

He watched her retreat with a little smile. The look she'd given him had held more than a little bafflement, and a whole lot of arousal.

Oh, yeah, he was getting to her. Getting to her real good.

Before long, he'd finish cracking that wall she seemed so fond of, the one she'd built so tightly around her heart.

Then he planned on tearing it down, one brick at a time, until she let him in.

Oh, things were good. Real good. Grinning from ear to ear, Trent reflected on his excellent fortune.

First, he'd managed to stir up yet another ecologist group about the unnecessary waste the logging company had each year – the waste he'd managed to multiply by messing with the cut orders and rerouting memos.

By stepping up front and center, and admitting that maybe the company had gotten greedy, he'd brought attention to his thoroughness and eagerness to work with the public.

Soon, very soon, he'd force Hope's father out and use the company as a sacrifice to jump-start his own political career. All the ecological groups would be on his side because of what he'd done for them.

Still grinning, Trent backed away from his computer. He'd been busy, given what delicious havoc he'd also been wreaking on Hope's life. Oh, he bet she was sorry now, and his only regret was that he couldn't see her face.

One more quick phone call told him the rest of what he needed to know. Hope had seen three patients all day, and she'd only gotten those because there were still people he hadn't been able to contact, favors he hadn't yet called in.

He knew from his snooping that her bank account was hurting, near desperation time. It'd been a stroke of genius that her father had finally added to the pressure with the notices from his property management firm.

There'd been a time he'd wanted the best for Hope as well as for him, but that had passed when she'd continued to scorn him. He still wanted her, oh, how he still wanted her. But he no longer cared about what she wanted. He wanted her to hurt and suffer, just as he had.

He'd bet she was hurting now.

Soon she'd come crawling back to him, begging him to take her.

And he would . . . after making her grovel.

Rain drummed against the house with a pleasant hum. Feeling better, Clay wandered around while Hope worked. It was the idleness that bothered him the most now, he decided, and set about to fix that.

Everywhere he went, the big black dog tailed him happily, her tongue lolling, her eyes sparkling. He kept tripping over her. 'Why don't you go outside?' he grumbled finally, after nearly killing both of them on the slick kitchen tile.

Molly glanced at the window, where rain ran down the glass in rivers and seemed to shudder in distaste.

'I thought you're supposed to help Hope,' Clay muttered, opening a cupboard for a glass. 'Go. Go help her.'

'Go. Go,' mimicked Fric and Frac suddenly and sharply from their corner. Clay jumped in surprise, then hit his head on the cupboard.

Molly barked and seemed to smile when Clay hopped around, swearing and holding his head.

Fric and Frac cackled.

'I thought you were going to help Hope,' Clay snapped at the dog. He wished *he* could, but she wouldn't let him into the wing of the house she used as the clinic.

He suspected it was to keep him from hearing the vicious rumors that went on in her waiting room. Or to keep the curious and petty eyes of the gossips off him.

He was going to put a stop to the madness, one way or another. Though they hadn't discussed it – she'd refused – he knew how much it bothered Hope that her business seemed to be dying, and how much she worried about Green County not having medical care available.

Clay had Trent to thank for putting that fear in her, and he would take care of that too. Slowly, he sank to a chair and sighed. Maybe he wasn't quite as well as he thought. His hands shook as he shoved his fingers into his hair.

Molly went to the back door and whined. Groaning, he rose and let her out, then stood in shock as three black cats bee-lined their way past him into the kitchen.

'Wait!' he yelped as the last brushed his ankle with cold, wet fur.

All three ignored him and proceeded to prowl the kitchen, black tails switching back and forth, yellow-green eyes staring at him. 'Okay,' he said firmly, hands on hips. 'Everyone out.'

No one moved.

'Out!' he commanded to no avail.

Fric and Frac scrambled around their cages, squawking and crying, obviously frightened of the cats. With good reason, given the hooded look the cats had taken on. One of them licked its chops, its eyes darkening with sharp awareness.

'Huey, Dewey and Louie, I presume,' Clay said dryly. 'Which is which?'

The cats swished their tails and glared.

Fric and Frac screamed.

Okay, he needed a new tactic. 'Look, you're not allowed in here,' he said as diplomatically as he could over the racket, tempted to open the bird cage himself and let the cats have lunch. 'So get out.'

Not one of them moved, except for their eyes which hungrily followed the birds' every move. Rain splattered Clay's face, igniting a temper he knew would do no good. Sighing, he tried to bend and scoop one of the cats up, but his ribs protested.

So did the cat. Loudly.

Then Molly started barking and howling over the screeching of Fric and Frac.

'Quiet!' he yelled to no one. The noise continued.

In less than a minute, a frazzled looking Hope dashed into the kitchen. 'What's going on?' she demanded. 'There's enough noise to – '

'Wait a minute,' Clay said, feeling more than a little frazzled himself. 'You're half deaf. You can't hear me when I try to talk to you about something serious, yet you can hear the cats?'

'They have a certain pitch that seems to get through.' She lifted her chin in that endearing defensive gesture she had. 'Did you hurt one of them?'

'Cats, cats, cats,' screamed Fric and Frac, hopping in their cage.

'What?' yelled Clay to Hope.

'Cats, cats, cats,' screamed Fric and Frac, louder, just as Hope repeated her question.

Clay swore ripely and turned round in the insanely busy kitchen. Animals were everywhere. 'I didn't catch a damned word you just said.'

'Now who can't hear?'

He whirled to her, but there was no mistake. She was laughing at him. He sighed, and pinched the bridge of his nose, waiting for patience. It didn't come, so he gave up. 'Listen – '

But she wasn't, and didn't. With a loving, affectionate smile not meant for him, she picked up first one, then another of the black cats, crooning to them softly and she headed back to the door.

'Come on, girls,' she sang sweetly. 'You know you're not supposed to come inside.'

'Girls?' he asked amazed, watching as the cats rubbed against Hope with affection, their yellow-green eyes half slitted in pleasure. 'You named three girl cats Huey, Dewey and Louie?'

She ignored him. 'I know, I know, it's raining,' she murmured as she shooed them out and went back for the third. 'But the garage is open. Go get warm in there. I'll bring food soon, I promise.' With a last caress, she shut the door and turned on Clay.

Fric and Frac fell blessedly silent. Molly plopped down in the corner.

'How do you tell those cats apart?' Clay wanted to know. 'They're all black with yellow eyes.'

'They're not all the same,' she said, turning on him with a stern eye. 'Don't let them in again. My patients might be allergic.'

He could only stare at her. 'This is crazy, you know that? A dog, two parrots and three cats?'

'We had this discussion. Are you starting to forget things that have happened after the accident, too?'

So she had a sense of humor. He knew that. He just hadn't realized it had such a wicked streak to it. But he couldn't concentrate on that now . . .

An image hit him, and hit him hard.

A little boy kneeling beside a make-shift grave. An older, kindly looking man standing beside him, his big, work-roughened hand resting on the boy's shoulder. The boy's bare hands were dirty and scraped from the rocks. Tears ran down his face as he sobbed over his dead dog, so cruelly run over by the speeding car that never bothered to stop and help.

'I'll never own another pet,' he promised the deceased dog, swiping at his face with his grimy shirt. 'Never.'

'Shh, son,' the man said kindly, softly. 'Things will change in time, you'll see.'

'No.' The boy shook his head. 'I won't.'

'Time heals everything,' the man said. 'I promise, son.'

'No.' Time wouldn't help him. He'd never get another animal, not if it meant experiencing this wrenching pain.

CHAPTER 13

'Never!'

'What?' Hope asked, glancing at him strangely.

He'd sworn to never have another pet. Clay could be positive of that much, at least, though he could remember little else. That bone-deep pain stabbed at him even now. He looked at Hope, who was watching him, nervously biting her lip.

As if she had something to hide.

'Huey, Dewey and Louie are our cats?' he asked, testing her.

'Uh . . . yes.'

But she'd hesitated, damn her, which meant only one thing that he could think of.

She'd lied.

She'd just claimed that these three hellion cats were *theirs*, but he knew different. He wasn't sure how he knew exactly, but he just did.

He'd not owned a pet since he'd been that grief-ridden little boy kneeling before a make-shift burial. The knowledge that Hope had purposely deceived him shocked him to the very core.

'You're sure?' he asked again, giving her a chance to explain, to come up with an explanation he could buy. He badly wanted her to do that.

She didn't answer, and he lifted her chin with a finger until their gazes met. 'Hope.'

'Yes. I'm sure.'

'That's interesting.' He felt ill.

'Why?'

'I just remembered I've never owned a cat,' he said flatly, crossing his arms and staring at her.

She flushed and said nothing.

'Well, am I wrong?' he asked her softly.

'Fine.' She crossed her arms over her chest. 'They're my cats, if you must know. Obviously, you have a thing against them,' Hope pointed out testily. 'Ignore them if you wish. I have to get back to work.' Her voice softened. 'You should be resting, Clay.'

He wasn't satisfied, probably wouldn't be until she felt as grumpy and fed up as he did. 'I'm tired of resting.'

She smiled at his petulant tone and patted his shoulder patronizingly. It was the last straw.

'I'm starting to remember,' he told her angrily. 'And these little pieces are driving me crazy!'

She went still. 'What else are you remembering?'

For the first time, he looked at her and saw a stranger, and it scared him. He wanted to trust her, dammit. Wanted some stability in this world that had gone mad. But could he? Could he really trust her now, knowing she was hiding something?

'Clay?'

A sudden memory of the night she'd rescued him

rendered him speechless. He'd been laying in the mud, watching the rain fall, semi-conscious as waves of agony rolled over him. She'd come to him like an angel in the night, and she'd gazed down at him from shocked, worried eyes.

Eyes that had registered no recognition.

He was her lover, and if nothing else, the father of the child she carried. Why hadn't she tossed her arms around him and wept for what he'd been through?

Because that wasn't Hope, he reminded himself. She'd been calm, efficient, in complete and utter control, as she liked to be at all times. The perfect doctor. Only her eyes had reflected her fear and concern.

And later, her hands had as well. He could vaguely remember her coaxing him, cajoling him, finally bullying him up the stairs because she couldn't carry him. Then she'd stripped him down and he'd wanted to make a joke about how eager she'd been to get him naked.

Instead, he'd passed out.

He closed his eyes, struggling to remember more. Nothing happened except his headache returned. He sighed when he would have preferred to throw something.

She said his name again, in question.

'Nothing,' he said shortly, turning from her.

When he turned back a minute later, she was gone.

He swore the room blue. Then Molly rose questioningly and he swore at her too. When the rain came down harder, echoing throughout his empty part of the house, he cursed it as well, just because he felt mean.

He glared at Fric and Frac. 'Say one word,' he told

them, 'and I'll serve you on a platter to Huey, Dewey and Louie.'

They remained mercifully silent.

Clay stalked through the house, restless, not stopping until he was in Hope's den, eyeing her desk.

Her computer.

It called to him. Fascinated, but not knowing why, he padded over to it and sat down.

Of their own accord, his fingers flew to the keyboard – and worked those keys as if he'd been made for them. Before he could so much as blink or draw a surprised breath, he'd bypassed her security system and was in.

'Wow,' he whispered, impressed. 'I'm good.'

So fast it took his breath, another image came to him.

He was at another desk, his desk. The room was small, clean, but quite untidy. Stacks of files and manuals littered the floor around him. Two computers sat blinking at him.

The phone rang, but he ignored it. He had to, he was on a deadline.

His fingers worked the keyboard of one of the computers – his computer – with blurry speed. The urgency had him working around the clock, switching from one keyboard to another. He had to fix the security system before it was too late . . .

At his elbow, Molly barked and Clay nearly fell out of Hope's chair.

What was it he'd just remembered? Why had he been rushing, and whose security system had he needed to fix? His?

Someone else's?

The someone who had tried to kill him, the someone who had damn near succeeded?

Clay sat there, locked in the frustrating task of filtering out real images from vague dreams. Mindlessly, he let his fingers play over the keyboard, and before he knew it, he'd entered Hope's accounts receivable.

Shocked, he stared down . . . and realized why Hope never had any money. It seemed she rarely accepted actual payment for her services. According to her haphazard notes, which would make any accountant groan, in the last week she'd collected only thirty dollars. The rest of the patients had paid in trade or IOUs.

It explained a lot of things. Such as why her computer was so old. She couldn't afford a new one. At least she had a modem, and the latest medical services through the internet, but that was all she had. Her software needed to be updated. So did her house for that matter. It looked as if it could fall over in the next big wind. Except for the clinic, that is. There, she'd obviously spent every penny she had, for she had the latest high tech equipment available.

Hope took the clinic very seriously, even when faced with seemingly insurmountable problems. Her father fighting her every step of the way. Her patients not being able to pay her. Trent doing his best to ruin her. Hope ran this clinic because she loved it, because helping others was her life. Clay's throat tightened at how amazing and unselfish she was.

His Hope would never give up fighting for what she believed in.

His fingers clicked on the keyboard again and he

stared in disbelief at Hope's receipts from the other day. A bag of turnips.

With tight emotion overflowing from his heart, he laughed out loud.

Turnips.

He loved her. And he wanted her to be a part of his life – whatever life that was – forever.

In the far back of his thoughts he wondered how he'd known to home in on the accounting system without even trying. Obviously, he'd found a hidden talent.

It should have thrilled him, this piece of his past. But all he could see was Hope's face, and the stirrings of panic when she'd realized he was beginning to remember.

Why, Hope? he wondered. *What are you hiding?*

And why doesn't it matter that I know you're hiding things from me? *Why do I want you regardless?*

Clay lay in wait until he heard Hope break for lunch, though he knew she would consider the term lunch pretty loose after the morning she'd had.

He doubted if she'd had two people sign in.

She entered the kitchen carrying three bottles of a locally distilled wine. Clay looked at her from where he'd been sitting at the table with Molly, waiting.

'Oh,' she exclaimed, stopping short. In her arms she shifted the bottles. Wide, wary eyes met his briefly before darting away. 'I didn't see you there.'

Damn her. She knew he was starting to remember more and more and she didn't know what to do about it. 'It's amazing how quiet one can be without cats and birds around.'

She flushed. 'They're outside, I take it.'

'Going to start drinking?'

'What?' She glanced down at the bottles. 'Oh. Uh . . . no.'

'Changing careers?' he asked politely.

An embarrassed smile curved her lips. 'Definitely not. I just . . .'

'You just what?' he asked softly. 'Just accepted that as payment instead of money? Even though you don't drink? Even though you need the cash?'

Her face reddened and his heart cracked a little. Purposely, he hardened it. 'I played on your computer this morning,' he said evenly.

'What?'

He swore at himself beneath his breath for his impatience, and rose. Facing her, he took the bottles and deposited them on the counter. Then he tipped up her face, and only when her nervous gaze met his did he speak again. 'Your hearing gets worse when you're nervous.'

Her gaze shuttered, and the thoughts he'd been able to see just a moment ago were lost to him. In a chilling manner, she backed away from him. 'So I've been told. I'm also aware that I have an ugly voice, which gets all the more disgusting the more agitated I am, so you can spare me that.'

His heart clenched. 'Is that what you think I'm saying? That you disgust me?'

She didn't answer.

He reached for her, but she evaded him, skirting around the table. Ignoring the shooting pain it caused in his ribs, he dodged around, tossed a chair out of his way and snagged her around the waist.

She struggled, but he gritted his teeth and pulled her to him. Only when she'd given up with a frustrated sound, obviously afraid to hurt him, did he speak. 'I like the way your voice sounds, Hope. It's low and sweet and it turns me on.'

Another sound left her lips and she tried again to escape him, but he wasn't having it. 'We've waited too long to discuss this, really we have. We'll do that now. And while we're at it, I like the way you get flustered around me, how I can trip you up with just a look.'

'That's ego!' she cried, smacking him high on his chest lightly.

'Maybe,' he conceded, grabbing her hand. 'But it's true. And I really like the way you dress all prim and proper, the way you keep your cool under any circumstance, yet when we kiss, you go up in flames in my arms.'

Her cheeks burned, and with a miserable moan, she dropped her forehead to his chest as if she'd never just hit it. 'Stop it. Please, just stop it.'

Patiently, he lifted her face so she could see his mouth. 'I can't. I like everything about you, Hope.'

She inhaled deeply, but he could see he'd charmed her – a little. Could see also, how her eyes flared with that unmistakable surprise every time he made sure she looked at him before he spoke.

Had that few people cared enough about her to help her communicate? It took little to no effort from him at all to make sure she heard him, and it was to his benefit as well.

'I have to go back to work now,' she said.

'Why? You're not going to get many more patients, Hope. Not until we confront Trent.'

'We?' she asked weakly. 'How did this get to be a we?'

'Ever since this,' he said, lifting her face and setting his mouth to hers. It was the barest of touches, the slightest connection of soft, giving lips. But less than a minute later, the kiss had turned dizzying and deep and felt as necessary as air to his lungs. The endless shattering kisses and ensuing arousing caresses built and built until Clay's legs shook. He heard her moan when he finally tore his mouth from hers for the last time and he rested his forehead on hers.

After a minute, he lifted his head and risked a smile. Touching her cheek softly, he said, 'You feel something for me, I can feel it.'

'And I can feel that I do something to you too,' she said, then bit her lip, looking horrified at what she'd said.

At first he was so stunned she'd made a joke, he just stared at her. Pressed up against him as she'd been, he knew she couldn't mistake feeling exactly what she did for him. He laughed. Then, at her obvious embarrassment, he laughed again.

'I'm going back to work now,' she said firmly, averting her gaze. 'Kelly's probably wondering what happened to me.'

'So she'll come find you when she needs you.'

She paled at the thought, and he asked the question that had been bothering him. 'Why do you hide me?'

'Hide you?' Her voice rose several octaves, clearing showing him her distress.

'Yeah. You purposely haven't introduced us. She doesn't know I exist. Why is that?'

She inhaled deeply. 'I really have to get back. We can discuss this when I'm done for the day –'

'Wait.' He took a deep breath, and decided to go with his gut instinct – that while he knew there were things she hadn't told him, he could, and would, trust her. 'I remembered more today.'

'You did?'

'At your computer – which, by the way, is a very antiquated system. Why is that?'

'Clay!' She made that frustrated sound that so amused him. 'Forget the computer. What did you remember?'

'You know, you're really kinda cute when you get all mad at me like that,' he said. He nudged her. 'Do it again.'

Her eyes smoldered with heat, but it was temper warming them. 'Clay,' she said slowly, obviously struggling for patience. '*What did you remember?*'

'That I'm good with computers. Better than good, actually. I think I work with them. Is that right, Hope? You said I have my own business. Is it with computers?'

She sucked in a deep breath and held it. 'I think I liked the questions about my antiquated system better.'

He reached for her hands, entwined their fingers and looked her right in the eyes. 'I'd get down on my knees and promise you the moon if you'd just answer a single one of my questions straight, no half-truths, no lies.'

She opened her mouth, then shut it again. For a long moment, she just looked at him, and he didn't think she would respond. Finally, she took another deep breath and said, 'I don't know what you do for a living, Clay. I'm sorry, I wish I did.'

It was a blow, but one he'd been expecting. 'We hardly knew each other at all, did we?'

'I already told you that.'

And he hadn't wanted to believe her.

She cocked her head. 'That's funny. I'm not expecting anyone.'

'What – ' A heartbeat later, the doorbell triggered a red signal light in her kitchen. She gave him a half-guilty glance and he let out a little laugh. 'You amaze me.'

Molly growled and barked, and Clay followed Hope through the living room to the door. She opened it to a huge bouquet of flowers and a disgruntled looking delivery boy.

'You're much further out than I expected,' he told her shortly as she signed and fumbled through her many pockets for a tip.

When she stared down at the huge vase of fragrant flowers in hesitant, amused surprise, Clay knew a real pang.

By the stunned look on her face it became obvious – painfully so – that she'd not had much romance in her life. That had to be her own doing, he thought, because she was so lovely and caring he couldn't imagine there hadn't been suitors clamoring for her attention all her life. But Hope didn't seem to easily let people in, preferring instead to care for others, rather than let herself be cared for.

'Who are they from?' he asked gently.

She still just stared at the flowers. Then she bent over them, inhaling and closing her eyes.

A sweet pang tugged at his chest. She was so beautiful, so absolutely unspoiled. He moved closer and touched her shoulder until she looked at him.

'Who are they from?' he asked again, smiling down into her blushing face.

She shrugged with an apologetic little smile and handed him the vase so she could reach through the stems to pull out the card. As her fingers touched it, she went utterly still.

He knew by the look on her face she'd guessed who they had come from, or had sensed it. Watching her experience those uncanny feelings often gave him the chills, and now was no exception.

She read the card in silence, then blanched.

'What is it?' he asked.

In a voice that shook, she said, 'Throw them out. Please, just throw them out.'

'Trent.' He swore, then set the flowers down on a small table in the hall. Coming back to her, he slipped an arm around her waist. 'What does the note say, Hope?'

Those wide eyes he was beginning to read so well lifted to his, filled with a thousand emotions he couldn't begin to name. But one came out clear as a bell.

Fear.

'Hope?' he asked gently. 'Tell me.'

For that moment, she couldn't speak, not with her heart slamming into her chest.

'Hope, sweetheart, you're scaring me.'

She pulled away from him. He reached for her, but she

held him off, unable to think with his hands on her.

'Hope?'

She read aloud from the card, which had a newspaper clipping attached to it. It was from their small weekly local paper, one that announced the wedding intentions of one Trent Blockwell and Hope Broderick. 'The card attached says: We'll be married by this time next month. Get ready.'

He stared at her. 'What?'

She sighed. 'There you go again, losing your hearing in a stressful situation.'

It wasn't funny. 'He's crazy.'

'No doubt.'

'Whatever made him do such a thing?'

'It's not the first time he's suggested marriage, but it's the first time he's taken it this far.'

'Other than tell everyone in sight, you mean.'

'Yes.'

'He's already executed his threats. Look at your clinic. You have no patients waiting.'

Pain and worry filled those glorious eyes while rage filled Clay. He would fix this, he vowed. Even if he got to do nothing else for her, he would fix this.

She deserved that, at least. She deserved so much more.

'I don't know what to do,' she whispered, lifting her shoulders as she stared at the card. She seemed small and defenseless. 'For the first time in my life, I don't know what to do.'

'I do,' he muttered. He hadn't wanted it to be like this, had wanted more time to coax her, to get her used to the idea. He'd wanted to use romance to woo her, candlelit dinners, picnics, soft words of love.

But he didn't have the time for that now. 'Hope – '

'I can't believe he'd go this far, would just assume I would go for it,' she said in amazement, her eyes wide with shock. 'He just assumes I'm free.'

'Well, you're not,' he said with a lightness he didn't feel. Nerves coated his stomach.

'Not what?'

'Not free.'

'Clay,' she said with a little laugh. 'You're not making much sense here.'

'Sense? You want sense?' He grabbed the card out of her hand and tossed it over his shoulder, where it drifted harmlessly to the ground.

Tugging her close, he wrapped his arms loosely around her waist and waited until she looked up at his mouth. 'Marry me, Hope.'

CHAPTER 14

'*What?*' Hope's wide eyes settled on him.

'Marry me,' Clay repeated patiently. He could see her panic, could taste her fear. She hadn't taken a breath since he'd spoken.

'That bump on your head has gotten worse,' she whispered.

Clay smiled, his nerves gone as suddenly as they'd come. He'd never been so sure of anything in his life – or at least the life he could remember. 'I know it sounds like a crazy, hasty thing to do and – '

'Sounds like?' She let out a little laugh. 'It more than sounds like, Clay. It is a crazy idea.'

He smiled. 'Sounds less and less crazy every time I say it. Marry me, Hope.'

'You don't even know who you are.' She backed from him, her eyes huge in her face. 'You could be already engaged!'

He advanced on her slowly, without threat. 'I'm not. We both know that in our hearts.'

'Just because Trent scared me, it's no reason to get married.'

'You're right,' he agreed. 'Do it because I – '

'No!' She put her fingers to his lips, her heart in her throat. 'I don't want any false vows of love.'

Taking her wrist, he pulled her hand away from his face, smiling easily down into her troubled one. 'I think you know me better than to think I would give you false vows of anything, much less l – '

'Wait!' She did know that, but . . .

His steady, compassionate gaze on hers allowed for no half-truths, or even self-folly. 'If that L word scares you,' he said gently, 'we can avoid it for now.'

'It doesn't scare – '

Now he put his fingers to her lips. 'Please, Hope, don't complicate this with a lie.' She went still, her eyes round and huge on his, no doubt wondering how he could read her so well when all she wanted to do was hide.

It was because he so understood her. 'We belong together, Hope. You and me and our baby. Don't you think he or she deserves to have us together?'

'Every baby deserves two parents,' she said fiercely, eyes glittering with first-hand knowledge.

'I want this baby to have my name,' he said softly, reaching for her hands.

'You mean that,' she breathed.

'We're meant to be together, Hope. We've talked about this . . . being each other's destiny.'

'It's hard to believe it could be true, I don't want to believe it. But that first night, when I fished you out of the mud, I felt it so strongly.'

'One of your feelings? Or just a thought?'

'A feeling,' she whispered. 'The strongest one yet.'

He smiled triumphantly. 'Good.'

Wonder filled her eyes, a moment before it was squashed behind steely determination. 'It's too soon. And I've . . .'

He waited, but she never finished. Her eyes went dark, and sad.

'And you've kept things from me?' he guessed. By the resignation in her gaze he knew he'd hit it on the nail. 'I'm well aware of that, Hope. I'm also trying to prove to you that I can be trusted. That you can tell me anything.' Because he couldn't help himself, he slid his hand to her belly, loving the soft, yet firm feel of her. Loving the way he could picture his baby in there.

She went still. 'A baby would mean a lot to you,' she said, searching his gaze.

'Yes, everything. But you mean even more.'

She closed her eyes, but he'd seen the quick flash of regret just the same.

He cupped her cheek, waited until she looked at him. 'Hope? What's the matter?'

'Nothing.' She covered her face. 'Everything.'

He tipped up her chin. 'I guess that means you're not ready to answer my question.'

Again, she ducked her head, burrowing her face into his chest. 'No,' came her muffled reply. 'Oh, Clay.'

The tortured tone in her voice got to him and he moved close, wrapping an arm around her shoulders. 'It's all right for now, Hope. Just think about it.'

She leaned into him, warming his heart a little. 'You're the kindest man I've ever met, Clay. You deserve far more than this from – '

'Shh,' he told her, ignoring the pain in his ribs to pull her tighter to him. 'What I deserve, is you.'

Pressing her face into the crook of his neck, Hope remained silent. But the feel of her up against him, the perfect fit of her body to his buoyed his spirits.

They did belong together, he just knew it.

Yet there was little he could do until she chose to open up, or until he regained the rest of his memory, which he was certain would be soon now. 'Tomorrow is Sunday. No patients,' he said after he'd lifted her face from him so he could see into her troubled dark eyes. 'Let's go see your father.'

'I don't know.'

'It's time, sweetheart,' he said gently. 'It's time.'

Hope drove.

They stopped once, to buy Clay some clothes.

He had fun in K-Mart, teasing Hope until her face was fiery red. He held up a pack of cotton briefs, then a pack of boxers. With an innocent yet wicked grin he asked, 'Which one?'

Hope nearly choked, lost in the image of his hard, lean body wearing nothing but a tiny swatch of cotton.

At her silence, his grin spread and he tossed both packages aside. 'I guess I don't wear any,' he said casually, pushing the empty cart down the aisle.

Quickly, hastily, she grabbed several packages, a combination of both, and dumped them in the cart. She managed to avoid his laughing, knowing gaze for several aisles.

But she couldn't avoid the way her mind continuously

pictured him; gaze hot and hungry, body hard and ready. It left her in an unbelievably agitated state, so that every time they accidentally brushed up together – which was often, given Clay's way he had of being so near – she jerked in awareness.

She got the feeling by his glowing eyes and sexy smile that he both knew and liked how he affected her.

But once back in the car, he fell uncharacteristically silent.

Casting an occasional worried glance at the still and pale man beside her, Hope knew a real regret. She'd pushed him, and they still had quite a distance to travel. 'Clay, once we get into Seattle, I want you to get checked out at the hospital there.'

'Why? Don't you want to be my doctor any more?'

She couldn't return his teasing smile. 'You should be starting to remember by now. There's no skull fracture and your concussion is gone.'

'It'll come.'

And when it did, she'd promised herself to come clean with him. 'But – '

'It's already starting to come. Patience, doctor. Patience.'

When he discovered the truth about what she'd done, he would hate her. That would be the most painful thing she'd ever had to endure, because somewhere along the line, Clayton Slater had stolen a piece of her heart.

'You okay?' he asked suddenly, his voice almost unbearably familiar.

Hope looked at him, at his handsome, worried face, at his incredibly expressive eyes that held so much affection and warmth. *No,* she wanted to say. *I'm not okay, and once I tell you the truth, I'll never be okay again.* 'I'm fine. I was worried about you.'

'Don't be.' His eyes hardened. 'I'm going to enjoy this, believe me.'

'What?'

'There's no need to worry about me, Hope. This is exactly what I need,' he said, his voice terse. 'And what Trent needs.'

'It's Sunday, remember? I doubt we'll even see Trent.'

'Your father wanted to meet you at his office, right?' At Hope's nod, he said, 'If Trent got word of your arrival, he'll be there.'

Busy trying to catch his words, she nearly swerved off the road. 'I don't think this was a good idea,' she muttered.

'Pull over, Hope.'

'What?'

'Pull over. Please?'

'Why?' she asked worried, turning to study him. 'Is something wrong?'

'I want to talk to you and I want you to be able to see me do it without killing us. Please, pull over.'

The two-lane highway was empty. With a sigh, she studied the wide shoulder, the lush green, wet mountains. Then, without another word, she pulled over and looked at him. 'My father isn't the enemy, Clay.'

'No?' In the passenger seat, he turned to face her, grimacing at the movement. In the small space he looked huge, and surprisingly tough. Or maybe not so surprisingly, since he still sported bruises over his face which had now faded to a yellow-greenish color.

'Why did he put your place up for sale then?' he demanded. 'You love that house, and he must know it. If he's so damn wealthy, why would he do that to you?'

She didn't think he could understand. It had so much to do with the past, with what her father wanted for her. 'It's . . . rather complicated.'

He glanced at her balefully. 'Sweetheart, your entire life is rather complicated.'

She had to laugh. 'He just doesn't have the same beliefs I do,' she tried to explain. 'My mother died so young, and he loved her so much . . . that part of his life was cut off brutally young. Now he's having trouble with the business he loves so much. I think he suddenly sees himself as only mortal. I think it scares him.'

'Sad,' Clay conceded. 'But it's not your fault. He's being too over-bearing here. Was he always that way?'

For as long as she could remember, her father had been chasing away any few acquaintances she'd managed to make, saying no one was good enough. Now, suddenly, when she was more than capable of making those decisions for herself, he'd decided he wanted Trent for her.

A man she couldn't abide.

'Yes,' she said with a smile. 'He never liked anyone for me.' Until Trent.

'How awful for you.'

'No. He loved me. I was content.'

He studied her with narrowed eyes. 'There's so much you don't say every time you speak, you know that?'

'I was content.'

The noise he made held compassion, immeasurable sadness. 'Besides your father, you were alone,' he said. 'You still are, since you don't let anyone in. How can you be content like that?'

She lifted her chin. 'It doesn't take a man to make my life complete.'

'Of course not,' he said with a frustrated shake of his head. 'That's not what I meant, and I think you know it. Every time we get close to this conversation, you back away. Why is that, Hope? Does it make you nervous?'

Her palms went sweaty. Suddenly, she couldn't breathe. 'Of course not.'

'Then tell me why you retreat from everyone.'

She let out the air searing her lungs. 'We've discussed this. I'm . . . different.'

'Yeah, different as in terrific.'

'No, Clay.' But the compliment warmed. 'I'm . . . a little strange.'

'Stop that. You're too hard on yourself, dammit. Just because one of your ears doesn't work – '

'It's far more than that. I was always ahead of the people my age in school, years ahead. Everyone was nice, but . . . distant. And it didn't help that I don't easily make friends. To be thirteen in with a bunch of eighteen-year-olds – '

'It shouldn't have happened that way. They should have better prepared you.' His gaze met hers, and it was filled with anger for her. 'You were just a baby compared to those kids.'

'Yes, in some ways.' She managed a grin. 'But I aced them in grades.'

A reluctant grin tugged at his mouth. 'Good.'

'And I sometimes get . . . feelings.'

'You mean the thing that lets you know when someone's going to call you before they do? It's a pretty cool trick, Hope. Think you could teach me?'

That already he had begun to know her more than anyone else ever had terrified her. 'I've never tried before. Usually tends to run people off.'

'I'm not running.'

She ignored the sweet words that sent a pang directly to her heart and waited for his disgust to set in. But when she risked a peek at him, he looked the furthest thing from disgusted. He looked fascinated. 'So, sweetheart, what does that sixth sense tell you about me?'

She laughed nervously. *That I should keep you.* 'That you're too nosy for your own good.'

He laughed. 'That's true enough, but you've managed to change the subject. You're a doctor, a damn good one. What does your father have against that?'

'He wants me to stay home and give him grandbabies.'

Clay's eyes darkened to a deep, forest green. He took her hand, ran his fingers over the knuckles, which never failed to evoke a delicious sort of shiver down her spine. 'Mmm. Not a bad idea. And we've already started.'

She tugged her hand back. 'Clay!'

'I'm kidding. We don't have to have any more kids after this one.' He smiled widely. 'But we could just stay home and *practice* giving him grandbabies.'

The lecherous grin that accompanied that statement

made her laugh again. 'I can't believe this. I brought you along to back me up and you're going to go along with everything he says.'

'No,' Clay corrected, serious now. 'I came to make sure Trent stays away from you. And to tell your father exactly what I think of his so-called right hand man.' He reached across the car and tucked a loose hair behind her ear. 'I hate to see you unhappy, Hope. Just thinking about losing the clinic does that to you. I want him to know that too.'

'I can't tell him about Trent.'

'No?' His voice went steely. 'I can.'

'He's having a hard time himself,' she said, unintentionally turning her head from him as nerves bounced along in her stomach. 'And he's relying heavily on Trent at his work.'

He must have said something. She heard the deep baritone, but the nerves singing in her ears made her miss the words.

Gently, Clay slid his fingers around her chin to bring her face back to his. Instinctively she knew the temper in his eyes didn't come from the frustration of dealing with her deafness, it came from what she'd said. That he bothered at all to make sure she 'heard' him was sweet enough to have a lump forming in her throat.

'I'm sorry,' she whispered. 'I didn't hear you.'

'You're not going to tell him a damn thing, are you?'

The disbelief in his voice made her defensive. 'What would you have me tell him? That his beloved employee wants to marry the daughter he's dying to see married? Or that the daughter who has never wanted to be married in the first place has refused? Don't you think he knows both? That Trent hasn't told him a thousand times? And after what I've just told you about his past and his pain, don't you think he just might not see what's holding me up?'

'How about the fact that Trent is a bully? That he's been harassing you, threatening you, has even attacked you? That he damn near raped you just the other night and you have the bruise on your shoulder to prove it!'

For a long moment, they just stared at each other in the small confines of the car, stalemated.

'You don't understand,' Hope whispered finally, with a sigh. 'He'd never believe it. We can talk about Trent until we're blue in the face, I just don't think he'll believe it. I think it will sound like desperation talking, and he'll see right through it, right through me. All he'll see is that I haven't done what he wanted.'

'Then he doesn't deserve the title as your father, Hope. And I mean that with all my heart.'

She could see he did. Could see also that he seemed to know what he was talking about. 'I wonder what your father was like. Do you remember at all?'

Clay closed his eyes, rubbed his temple, and wished he could remember more than just a flash of an older, but loving man. 'I'm not sure,' he said with frustration. 'But it doesn't mean that I don't know what one should be like.' His gaze slid to her belly, and a pierce of longing shafted through him so hot he nearly couldn't breathe.

He wanted this woman and his baby more than he could have thought possible.

'My father loves me,' she said softly, the doubt

swimming in her gaze, leaving Clay wanting to shake the man.

'I'm sure he does, Hope.' His fingers sank into her hair at the nape, his thumb stroked her soft cheek. 'And since he does, your relationship with him will be able to bear this.' He hoped.

She nodded, her gaze darting away. 'When we get back – To the house . . .'

'Home,' he corrected.

Now her gaze flew to his. 'Home,' she said softly. Then she gave him a little nervous smile that he wondered at. 'When we get home, I need to talk to you.'

He had no idea why that made his stomach clench, but it did. 'All right,' he said easily. 'But it doesn't sound good. Are you about to kick me out on my bruised posterior?'

Her eyes closed and his stomach definitely did a slow roll in his belly. With a tone that sounded as if she'd be happier facing the death squad, she said, 'There are some things that I haven't told you because I didn't feel you were well enough.'

Definitely not good. 'And I'm well enough now?' he tried to joke. 'Have you taken a good look at me today? I look like someone took a set of marking pens to me.'

She cringed, as if she could feel his pain. 'You are feeling better, aren't you?'

'Hmm. A little. You are going to marry me, aren't you, Hope?'

Sorrow filled her eyes as panic filled his heart. 'I never expected you to like me,' she said.

Was that what this was about? 'Why not?' he asked. 'You're everything I ever wanted.'

'You don't know what you ever wanted,' she pointed out.

True, but . . . 'You're everything I want now. That's what matters most.'

'You might not think so when you remember.'

'I might never fully remember anything.'

'You will,' she said with certainty. 'It's already coming back a little.'

He looked at her, really looked at her, and tried to see her as a stranger would. A little distant. Slightly aloof, but only because of her handicap combined with eyes that clearly said, 'back off'. Unless she was with a patient, she tended to push people away. But he knew that was her defense against a world that hadn't fully accepted her. Smart and looks combined with that uncanny sixth sense and her loss of hearing made her seem unapproachable.

It didn't matter, in his heart and soul he knew the truth – they belonged together. 'Hope, when I get my memory back, it won't matter. I want to be with you. I want to be a part of your life, of my baby's life.'

She started as if he'd goosed her. 'I – It's such a shock when you say that. I still can't believe it.'

'Then you're not paying attention,' he chided gently, as he played with her hair. 'Come on, Hope, say you'll marry me.'

'Now I have two men badgering me.'

He stiffened. She was right, and he was an idiot for pushing her this way. Her wide-eyed look of confusion and bafflement made him want to pull her close, but suddenly he didn't dare.

He'd been no better than Trent. 'I beg your pardon,' he said seriously, after making sure she was looking at him. 'You couldn't be more right.' It horrified him. 'I promise, I won't push you again – '

'Clay – '

'No. I was wrong, and I'm sorry. When you want to discuss it, you bring it up.'

'Clay, I'm sorry – '

'No,' he said quickly, straightening up and away from her. 'Please, don't be. This was my fault, Hope.'

'It is different,' she said quietly. 'You asking me and Trent asking me.'

'How?' His self-disgust had deepened.

She touched his knee. 'You pushed nicely.'

She started the car with a small smile, then thrust it in gear. They were on the road for a full five minutes before she spoke again. 'You're so patient with me.'

'You'll come around,' he said loudly so she could hear him over the low drone of the engine. 'I'm irresistible.'

She laughed, and he smiled. 'Love that sound.'

'You make me laugh more than anyone else ever has,' she admitted.

'Good.'

She bit her lip and looked so troubled, his stomach hurt again. 'Maybe you should just tell me whatever it is now,' he joked. 'I know, let me guess. You're hiding another husband somewhere.'

She let out a choked sound that might have been a laugh, then fell silent. When they reached Seattle, she headed downtown and pulled into a parking structure next to a high-rise. She shut off the car and said quite suddenly, 'I don't deserve you in my life.'

'Of course you do. Why would you say such a thing?'

Her mouth opened, worked, but nothing came out.

Because of what she hadn't yet told him? 'Whatever it is, Hope, we'll work it out.'

Hope cleared her throat, grabbed her purse and opened the door.

'Wait,' he said, taking her arm and waiting until she looked at him. 'Tell me you believe that. That no matter what stands between us that I don't understand yet, you know I wouldn't leave you alone. I'd never do that to you.'

She tried to tug free. 'We've got to go.'

'What are you afraid of?'

'We can't talk about this here, now.' She gulped, blinked frantically, and he realized with some surprise she was near tears.

'Hey,' he said softly, reaching for her.

But she shook herself free and Clay had to bite back his body's groan of protest as he hurried to keep up with her. Always intuned, she slowed down immediately, then took his hand.

'I'm sorry.'

'I'm fine,' he said.

'No, I mean I'm sorry I'm dragging you into this.'

They entered the deserted building lobby and he stopped her. 'You didn't drag me into anything, Hope. I wanted to come and I'm glad I did. If you want to wait until afterwards to talk, then fine, we wait.

But it's hard, knowing that whatever it is doesn't make you very happy.'

'You don't understand,' she whispered.

'I want to.'

She nodded. 'Afterwards, then.'

Together they went to the elevator, ready to face her father.

CHAPTER 15

Clay waited outside the suite of Broderick's offices, after making sure Trent was nowhere to be seen. He'd wanted to go in, but the appeal on Hope's face couldn't be ignored.

He would have paced, but he hurt too badly for that. Yet the sitting and waiting was torture. When Hope finally came out, face white and pinched, he stood abruptly and took her hands. 'What is it?'

For a minute Hope just stared at him, her dark eyes huge in her pale face, filled with an immeasurable despair.

'Hope?'

But she only looked at him, so that he made a sound of frustration and set her in the chair he'd just vacated. 'I'm going in there,' he muttered, 'and tell him what I think of him upsetting you like this. Especially in your state. I'm – '

'No,' she said quickly, jumping up and grabbing his arm to block his way. 'I'm fine.'

'You're white as a sheet. Are you sick?'

'No.'

He didn't believe her. Touching her hand, he found her skin like ice. Swearing, he took both her hands in his, then realized how small she really was, how vulnerable. 'Hope, what's the matter? What's happened?'

She licked her lips, then took a deep breath. 'Clay, maybe you could . . . you know, ask me again.'

'Hope, just tell me,' he begged. 'What did he say to you in there?'

'Clay, please.' She clung to his arm, her gaze wide and nervous on his. 'Ask me.'

She was scaring him now, and it was all he could concentrate on. He took her hands in his. They shook violently. 'Ask you what?' he demanded.

She gave him a look that a woman reserves for a very stupid male, and in truth, he was beginning to feel like one.

'You know,' she said, biting her lip. 'Before . . . at my house, then in my car . . . remember what we talked about?'

He wracked his brain, going over the entire conversation they'd had about her father, but his fear over her reaction to her talk with her father swamped his thoughts. 'I'm sorry, sweetheart. We talked about a lot of things – '

'You've changed your mind,' she said dully, nodding her head in understanding as she pulled her hands free. 'No big deal. Let's go then.'

'What – ' He stopped, shocked, his stomach firmly lodged in his throat. 'Hope, you're really confusing me here.'

'I know. Just forget it.' She took his arm and tried to drag him away. 'It was ridiculous anyway.'

'Wait.' He took her arms in his hands, and found it took him a moment to get his words together when he looked down into the face he'd begun to cherish before all others. In her dark eyes were all the things he felt and more; fear, trepidation, nerves . . . and a hope he couldn't, wouldn't deny.

Ask me again, she'd said.

He was a very stupid male. It was difficult to speak around the emotion clogging his throat. 'Are you by any chance, Dr Broderick . . . asking me to marry you?'

Gladness and relief filled those dark eyes. 'Yes,' she whispered with a watery smile. 'I am.'

'Well, thank God,' he whispered back, hauling her against him.

Clay didn't want to think about what had happened in that office to make her change her mind, didn't want to think about the fact that she'd been pushed into this by something – or someone – he didn't understand. Knowing that both of those things were likely true didn't change his reaction of pure joy and undiluted relief.

Yes, she'd leaped into this, most likely out of fear, but he'd deal with that. He would, because in his heart of hearts, he knew this was the right thing for them.

The rest would come; the love, the easy affection, the warmth he wanted for them. It would come because they already had a head start on it. They'd make it work.

He realized she had pulled back and was staring at him, chewing on her cheek, waiting nervously for him to say something. He became aware of the noise around them, the muted voices from the few people in another office, a ringing phone, the swoosh of the elevator, and became aware too, that his beautiful Hope couldn't hear most of it. Ignoring their surroundings, he reached out to cup her cheek, then slid his fingers into her hair to hold her head. He pulled her to him gently, far too gently for what he wanted, which was to plunder that delicious mouth until they were both gasping. But she needed care, and he found now that everything was within his grasp, he could give it.

With a touch as soft as the spring rain outside, he kissed her. His hands moved to her waist, lifted her against him. Ignoring the ache in his ribs, he pulled her as close as he could and tasted her.

The wealth of emotions that swam through Hope made her dizzy. Just his touch did that to her. Then Clay's fingers traced her jaw and he pulled away to kiss her face tenderly.

'Does this mean that the offer still stands?' she asked shakily, giving an embarrassed look to a passing woman carrying a briefcase.

Clay lifted his head from where he'd been nibbling at her neck and she got a lazy smile for an answer. 'Oh, yeah,' he whispered, his voice rough with emotion. 'The offer still stands.'

Her knees shook with relief. The terror dissipated. 'Good.' She took her first deep breath. 'My father wants to meet the man I'm going to marry.'

Those light eyebrows of his disappeared into the hair that fell over his forehead. 'You told him?'

She'd had to. 'Is that a problem?'

He looked pleased and shocked. And touchingly nervous. 'No, of course not.' Without warning, his lips came down hard and possessive on hers. 'I'm so proud of you, Hope.'

The words stole through her, dissipating the chill that had settled around her bones. He would marry her, he was proud of her.

That she deserved neither would have to be dealt with.

Another kiss took her breath. Later, she thought on a shaky sigh. She'd deal with real life later. For now, she wanted the fantasy.

'Let's go,' he said with a gentle, tender smile.

Her heart constricted at what he offered her. 'Okay,' she said, offering her lips for another kiss.

He smiled, kissed her, then took her hand and led the way.

Hope said very little on the ride home. She couldn't, not with her mind on the unbelievable turn of events her life had taken on.

She'd committed to Clay, a man she'd lied to, and all for her own gain. All because her father had looked weak and older than she remembered. Because he had insisted on seeing her marry before he died.

Because she knew as long as she was alone, Trent would never leave her be. He'd left her a message that her father had been happy to deliver – 'Nothing will stand in the way of our marriage.'

A message that could be taken as sweetly romantic, or overwhelmingly threatening.

She'd guessed at the latter.

A quick glance at the man next to her slammed home the last and real reason she'd changed her mind.

The only reason that she would ever have allowed herself into this dilemma in the first place.

She wanted Clayton Slater.

Hope wanted to keep the fantasy alive, wrong as it was, and she wanted to pretend, just for a little while, she would get to marry the sweetest, most caring, sensitive man she'd ever met.

'Did you mean it?' he asked suddenly into the silent, tension-filled car.

She didn't have to ask, she knew immediately what he referred to. 'I rarely say things I don't mean, Clay.'

'Then marry me today.'

She laughed. She could do little else, except cry. Because once the rumors got out, once Trent got over the shock of being dumped, surely this man would get his memory back.

Then he'd leave her.

Her little fantasy would be over, but for now she held it dear to her heart.

Clay crossed his arms and frowned at her. 'Why is that funny?'

She'd insulted him. Pulling into her long driveway, she stopped the car and turned to the man who somewhere along the way had become the most important person in her life.

'We can't get married today, Clay.' *Or ever*, she added silently with an aching heart. 'It just isn't possible. We need a license – '

With a lightning move that had her gasping, he reached for her, unhooked her seat belt and dragged her across his lap. The gentle fingers that held her completely belied the strength it took to lift her over him. Before she could so much as finish her statement, he settled his lips firmly over hers.

His mouth ate tenderly at hers, nipping and sucking and stroking until she melted helplessly against him, unable to resist. Then he slid his tongue to hers, deepening the kiss possessively, masterfully. Kiss after kiss, and it got wetter, deeper, hotter. The tranquillity vanished, replaced by a hunger, a need such as she'd never known.

When it was over, and they'd pulled apart, she stared at him, her breath coming in short, aroused pants. Beneath her thighs, where she lay stretched over his lap, she felt him hard and hot beneath her.

'You . . . You did it again,' she whispered.

'Did what?' His voice was low, strained, grainy . . . and unbelievably sexy.

'Made me senseless.' She reached out and stroked his rough cheek, loving the feel of his strong, big body surrounding her. Loved, too, the feel of him so unmistakably aroused beneath her. 'I must be hurting you.'

'Another kiss like that and you'll kill me, but that's beside the point.'

'Oh, yeah,' she said quietly, remembering what they'd been discussing. 'The point.'

'Did you think I'd forget?'

'No.' She couldn't get so lucky. Unless. . . She stroked his face, loving the way his eyes darkened. 'Let's just kiss some more.'

He laughed, then grimaced. 'Much as I'd like that . . .' He shifted his hips to ensure she knew exactly how much he'd like that. 'We have things to discuss. Remember? You wanted to talk to me.'

She sighed.

'Hope?' he prompted, his gaze solemn and serious.

'Yes, I know. We can do that later.' She swallowed hard and met his gaze directly. 'You're probably wanting an answer to why we can't run off and get married right this minute.'

'I just want to know you're serious.'

'I'm serious.' It wasn't a lie, she promised herself. She meant every single word. 'I'm just not going to elope,' she said firmly.

'I thought you were in a hurry.'

'No one will push me into rushing this, especially my father. But...'

'But?'

'But I still want to marry you.'

He just looked at her.

'If you'll have me.'

His smile lit her day. 'Just name the day and time, sweetheart, I'll be there.'

She knew he meant it, for now.

It was late for a phone call, but... Hope whirled to stare at the light above her phone. Nothing. She was hearing things.

With a sigh she went back to tidying up the clinic.

Less than a minute later, the red light flashed, accompanied by the drone of the ringer.

Hope laughed at herself, but the amusement died immediately. *She wouldn't like this call.*

She thought of Clay, in the kitchen cooking a late dinner, and hoped he would let it ring as well. That same sense that had told her she didn't want to talk to whoever was calling told her letting Clay do so would be disastrous.

Ring, ring, ring.

Hope suddenly dove for it. 'Hello,' she gasped.

'Just me, darling.' Trent laughed softly. 'Good thing, too. The way you answered that telephone, all out of breath like that, well, I could hardly make out what you said.'

Humiliation burned, so did temper. 'It's late.'

'Not that late. What are you doing tonight, Hope?'

'None of your business. What it is you want, Trent?'

All pleasantness faded from his voice. 'I talked to your father today. He had some shocking news for me, news that you'd just given him.'

'Oh?' She feigned ignorance, but her heart started to pound, her palms went damp.

'Don't do it, Hope. Don't even think about marrying someone else to escape me. You can't.'

'Don't threaten me.'

'No?' he asked silkily. 'You don't like that? Then you won't like this. You're mine. No one else can have you. Especially him.'

Then the phone went dead, leaving her staring at the receiver in her hand. The man had gone insane.

A shiver ran up her spine.

CHAPTER 16

Very late that night, Hope sat in her office, ostensibly under the guise of doing her paperwork.

She had not made a single entry on the computer in over half an hour.

But to close her books and shut down her computer would be to admit her day was over, and she couldn't do that, not yet.

Not when the sexiest, most attractive man on earth was waiting for that very thing to happen so they could be together.

Together.

Just as that thought came, her body tingled in awareness, the same awareness that preceded one of her feelings.

She wasn't alone.

But no fear came with that thought, only a ... warmth. Sighing, she prepared herself to face Clay.

But she could never fully prepare herself for that beloved face, that incredible presence, and when she turned to look at him, her heart gave a little leap.

He waited until her gaze rose to his mouth to speak.

'You must be ready for a break,' came the husky voice she had come to know so well.

'No. I've got lots of work left.'

He moved into the room, but she turned away, knowing she'd melt if she continued to look at him. Keeping her eyes on her computer, she raced her fingers over the keyboard, having no recollection of what she was supposed to be doing.

His big hands appeared first, on either side of her keyboard, wide, strong and lined with blue-veined tendons. Then came his scent, that clean, very male scent that never failed to make her think of outdoors, of wild abandonment, of being kissed as if she were all that mattered. Leaning around her, surrounding her much smaller body with his, he lowered his face to hers... and smiled.

His eyes sparkled as if he knew a private joke, and she helplessly responded with her own smile.

'Will you be ready for bed soon?' he asked, his gaze roaming over her features.

Her fingers tripped on the keyboard, causing her to erase the small amount of work she had done. *Bed*. 'Uh... not quite yet.' Her voice sounded ridiculously high, even to her own pathetic ears.

'Hmmm,' he said, the sound echoing from his chest through her back. It was a very male sound and she wondered what it meant.

Oh, she was well aware of the fundamentals of a relationship. Knew that the usual custom for a couple living together was to share a bed. She just had no idea how to place herself in that situation.

She'd never done it before.

Clay swiveled her chair around to face him. She immediately studied the buttons on the new shirt he wore – until he lifted her chin with a finger, forcing her to meet his laughing gaze.

'Hope, are you by any chance avoiding me?'

She had to smile. 'I'm doing my best.'

'Why? So you don't have to talk to me about whatever it is that you mentioned before?'

'Uh . . .' With everything else, she'd almost forgotten she needed to tell him the truth about her not being pregnant. *Almost*.

'Or so you don't have to sleep with me?'

'Both?' she asked with a guilty smile.

Pulling up a chair, he turned it around and straddled it, leaning on the back with both elbows. Propping his chin on his hands, he studied her. 'We've slept together before.'

'You remember?' Oh, but she was skating a thin line here, digging herself in deeper and deeper, but unable to help herself.

'No.' His grin came slow, lazy and immeasurably sensual. 'But I have a good imagination. A real good imagination.'

At the smoldering look his heavy-lidded eyes had taken on, speaking was difficult. 'I bet you do,' she muttered, tingling from the inside out at just the thought.

'Since you're obviously not ready for me to put it to good use,' he said with a martyr-like sigh, 'we'll have to face the other.'

'The other?'

'This talk you're so nervous about.' With a small smile, he reached past her to the keyboard. With one click of his fingers, he brought the file she'd just neatly destroyed back to her screen.

She stared in amazement. 'You – How did you bring that back?'

He studied his hands with some surprise. 'I don't know, to tell you the truth. I seem to have this special talent with computers.'

'No kidding. Maybe you could help me – '

He ran his fingers up her arm, slid them over the skin of her throat. 'Talk to me, Hope.'

The air went right out of her sail. No more conversation changes, the moment was at hand. She'd put him off long enough, and he'd indulged her. But she suspected he wouldn't allow it to continue.

Yet how could she tell him?

Simple. Just come right out and say, *I'm not really pregnant*. Yes, he would be sad, and most definitely betrayed, but he had to know the truth.

It was one lie she simply couldn't continue, not when it obviously meant so much to him. Another surprise, for she truly had never believed he would fall so deeply for the baby she'd laid on him. 'This is difficult,' she started.

'Well, let me make whatever it is easier,' he said lightly, reaching for her hand. 'I love you, Hope.'

'Wh – *What*?'

With his gaze steady on hers, he repeated the words in that silky, thrilling voice of his, enunciating carefully without exaggerating. 'I love you.'

'Oh my.' She slid a hand to her heart and rubbed the

ache that settled there. 'And that was supposed to make this easier?'

He just smiled while her heart somersaulted in her chest like a crazy circus act.

'Earlier you tried to tell me something, and you couldn't,' he said. 'I could tell by the look on your face it was bad.' He shrugged. 'I thought it would help you to know how I felt about you, thought maybe you could use it to trust me with whatever's going on in that lovely, complicated brain of yours.'

'You – ' She had to gulp in air just to get her lungs functioning. Not since her mother had died had she heard those words. Not once. 'You . . . love me.'

'Yeah.' Standing, he pushed the chair out of his way, pulled her up from hers so that they stood, face to face, toe to toe. His strong fingers sank into her hair, tipped her face up to his. 'I do.'

'But . . . you haven't known me for very long.'

'Long enough.' His thumbs played over her lower lip until it tingled and yearned for more. Then his mouth replaced his fingers in a delicious kiss that she managed to enjoy without participating in for fear of losing herself completely in him.

He lifted his head and looked at her. 'You're holding back, Hope. In so many ways.'

'It's my only defense.'

He smiled solemnly and shook his head. 'Give in to it. Please, Hope, give in to this.'

Maybe it was the knowledge that this might be all they would have, but when he dipped his head again, meeting her lips in a deep, stirring kiss, it stole her breath, her thoughts. All resolve melted, and still he kissed her.

Hope tried to tell herself it wasn't defeat to give in to these wild feelings he caused, that there was no danger in kissing him back with all the pent-up passion he'd caused inside her.

No danger at all, she assured herself as her heart raced, her bones dissolved. Yielding to the coaxing insistence of his tongue, she slid her hands up over his hard chest and into his hair . . . and found out exactly how wrong she could be.

There was danger, a hot dangerous heat, and it came from within herself, not Clay. He fanned that fire by tightening his arms around her, opening his mouth over hers in a fierce, fulfilling kiss that made her clutch at him for balance.

Finally, he lifted his head and stared at her, his deep green eyes swirling with so much emotion it hurt to look. It humbled her to the very depth of her soul to see such honest feelings. It terrified her that she wanted them so badly, knowing she didn't deserve them.

'You're still thinking too much,' he said gruffly, his breath rasping unevenly. And he kissed her again.

This time she kissed him back, had to. He drew her tighter against the hard contours of his body, his arm angling over her hips to hold her snug to his rigid thighs. She slid her fingers over his jaw, around to his neck, holding on for dear life, while his hands moved slowly, thoroughly over her body, molding her to him.

Time slowed, then stopped as their shattering kisses and arousing caresses made them breathless. With a moan, he tore his mouth from hers and buried his face in her neck. She struggled for air and held him close, panting.

'That's very distracting, the way you do that,' she said into the silence when she could speak.

He drew a long, labored breath and tightened his arms on her. He lifted his head. 'Good.' Then he leaned toward her with the obvious intention of doing it again.

With a hand to his chest to steady them both, she backed her head away a fraction and murmured, 'I need to talk to you, remember?'

'Hmm.' He buried his face in her hair and inhaled deeply. 'I love the way you smell.'

'Clay?'

'Shhh,' he whispered, running his hands down her arms until their hands were linked.

'I – ' A moan escaped her instead when he opened his hot mouth on her throat. 'Clay . . .'

'Later, sweetheart, later.'

'But I – ' Any words she might have offered were swallowed by his mouth.

Still kissing her, Clay reached up, trailed his fingers over her cheek, caressed her jaw, tilting it up for better access. He couldn't get enough of her, and he knew, he'd never touched a woman quite this way before, with this much tenderness, with this much care. Her skin was soft, pale, and he ran his fingers over her features as if he could memorize them.

So fragile, he thought, so vulnerable, and a fear welled up so fast his throat closed up. When he got his memory back, would any of this change? Or would she fade away as his memories had? He hoped not.

His hands floated down, over her slim throat, past her shoulders to skim over her small, firm breasts. Brushing the tips lightly, he felt them react to his touch, just as he felt his own body's response.

'Clay,' she murmured, startled.

He just touched her again, cupping her breasts in his hands, holding them, lightly sliding his thumbs over the tight nipples until she gasped his name again, this time her voice filled with dreamy wonder, and a hunger that spurred his own.

She was wearing far too many clothes, he decided a little desperately, and he was already too far gone from just kissing her. Unbuttoning the sweater she wore, he slipped it from her shoulders.

Her head snapped up in surprise when he reached for the buttons on her blouse. 'What are you doing?' she whispered, panic in her voice.

'I want to feel you. Please . . . let me.' Then he bent his head to feast on the soft, white skin of her neck. She moaned, and dropped her forehead to his chest, her hands fisting and unfisting in the material of his shirt. 'Hope, sweetheart,' he whispered huskily as he trailed his mouth down to her creamy shoulder, knowing she probably couldn't hear him. 'You taste as good as you smell.'

Her shirt floated to her feet. He lifted his head to look at her and his mouth went dry at the sight of her slim, pale, perfect body. 'Hope!' Reaching out, he trailed his fingers over the soft swell of breast that escaped her white lace bra.

Pausing to whip his own shirt off over his head, he

pulled her to him, grimacing as she came in contact with his chest.

'Did I hurt you?' Her hands braced him as she tried to pull back.

He held her as close as he could, which would never be close enough. 'Stopping now would be the only way to hurt me,' he assured her, and bent his head to worship a breast through lace with his tongue.

She gasped. When he took her between his teeth, she cried out and clutched his shoulders, her breath coming in short, shocky pants. Her fingers wound through his hair, pulling him closer as she whispered his name.

The stunned panic in her voice should have given him pause. But it didn't, couldn't, not when he was tasting heaven. Lifting up, he flicked open the front fastener of her bra, his fingers brushing over her soft curves. Moving her arms to cover herself, she made a soft sound of embarrassment, but he took her wrists gently, spread her arms. 'You're so beautiful, Hope.'

She shook her head in denial, but when he bent again and took a nipple in his mouth, sucking deeply, she sobbed out his name, arching her back, offering herself to him. He took it, rubbing his face back and forth, licking, tasting, nipping until she was writhing in his arms and shifting her hips against his.

He knew that signal, he felt the urgency too. She lifted her wide-eyed gaze to his and his mouth captured hers, almost roughly, his tongue parting her lips and sinking into her mouth in a deep, erotic kiss that sent his blood pumping fiercely through his body. With a moan, she lifted her hands to his chest, and his skin leaped reflexively at her touch.

She jerked her hands back.

With a low, desperate laugh, he took her hands and set them back on them. 'Touch me,' he begged her. 'I like it.'

It occurred to him, in the deep recesses of his mind, that his wild, little Hope wasn't acting as someone who'd already made love with him should act. Her shyness, her hesitancy, her sweet fumblings, while all incredibly arousing, spoke of someone completely inexperienced.

What the hell kind of lover had he been before? Not a very good one, he was forced to admit. He became determined to change that. Biting back his own vicious needs, he found a tender patience, and set out to drive Hope wild. Scooping her up, he laid her gently on the couch, then kneeled at the floor next to her, splaying a protective hand possessively over her flat stomach.

At the contact, she jumped, slammed her hands down over his and looked at him, blinking glazed, passion-filled eyes at him in horror. 'Oh my God,' she whispered. 'I nearly forgot – Clay, wait – '

'No,' he murmured, leaning over her and halting her words with his mouth. 'No thinking, no talking.' He kissed her again until she relaxed. 'There'll be plenty of time for that later, much later.'

When she tentatively met his tongue with her own, passion erupted within him, refusing to be denied. Shaken by the strength of it, he swept his hands reverently down over her deliciously sweet body. When she lifted her hands to his shoulders, then ran them restlessly over his chest, touching him innocently, voluntarily, Clay lost control.

Sliding off the rest of her clothes, he stood to remove his, then went still, riveted by the way her gaze ran over his body, lingering in places that caused a very obvious reaction.

She moistened her lips and a groan escaped him. Propelled into movement, he lay down next to her, half covering her body with his. Shoving fingers in her hair to hold her captive, he took her mouth in a plundering kiss that rocked his world. He felt her hesitation, and struggled to stem the absolutely unbelievable ferocity of his passion. All he could do was kiss her until she kissed him back with an equal ardor, until her own hands and mouth rushed over his heated skin, consuming him with raging need.

Rubbing his rough jaw over first one nipple, then the other, his trembling fingers slipped low, over her ribs, her belly . . . into the slick heat of her. Her baffled whimper egging him on, he sank into that fire, stroked the swelling flesh.

Each soft sound she made fanned the flames, sent his blood roaring, as he led her from one level to the next higher one, whispering low, hoarse words of pleasure that he knew she couldn't hear. Beneath his hands, she writhed, arched, and when she finally cried out, coming in soft shudders, he moved, his body shifting over hers.

For a moment, he just looked down at the beautiful, flushed body spread out beneath him.

Her eyes fluttered open, her baffled gaze met his. 'Clay . . .' Her gorgeous eyes were damp. 'What are you doing to me?'

Dipping down, he kissed her softly. 'Right now I'm just looking at you. You're so lovely, Hope.'

Embarrassed, she dropped her gaze, but he tipped it up again. '*You are*,' he insisted.

No one had ever thought so before. That he did now only sent her spiraling back into that dark, sweet world where nothing existed but a sensuous, insistent need and Clay's eager hands and mouth. His lips, rough and tender, assaulted her neck and throat, then her own lips, until she heard herself moaning softly with a renewed sense of urgency. She could think of nothing but what he was doing to her, and her own body's shocking reaction.

Her entire body ached all over again, ached and yearned and . . . begged. And he responded, with his wonderful mouth at her breasts, his knowing fingers exploring and tormenting until she moved and wiggled against his hand.

'You like that,' he said with a very male, satisfied glitter in his emerald gaze. And he did it some more, until her hips moved greedily against his hand.

He leaned down and took her mouth in the same rhythm as his fingers.

Hope could only grab onto his biceps and ride out the pleasurable but torturous mounting tension. She was probably hurting him, but in that moment, she couldn't have let go of him to save her life. Quivering, on the edge again, she drew in a searing breath and prepared to plunge.

Then he stopped, just stopped, and she opened her eyes in hazy disbelief. 'Clay?'

His scorching gaze, glittering with need, intense and dark, held hers.

She reached for him, but he held off.

'I love you,' he said in that velvety voice she'd come to love.

She closed her eyes on the words that stabbed at her heart.

He loved her.

His mouth returned to hers, parting her lips as his thighs wedged between hers, parting her legs. Cradling her head in his large palms, he gave her one unbearably soft, sweet kiss.

Then he whispered huskily, 'Look at me, Hope.'

She could do little else.

Another velvety kiss brushed her lips. 'Look at me when I sink into you, when our bodies mesh, and know this was meant to be. That we are meant to be. Forever.'

She opened her mouth, suddenly, vibrantly, painfully aware of what she'd done, of how far she'd let this go. 'Clay – '

He rubbed his hot, hard length over the very core of her and she gasped in pleasure.

In response, he whispered her name thickly and did it again, slowly, his eyes deep and dark and full of fire.

Desperate now, she gripped the afghan draped over the couch in damp fists and moaned softly. 'Oh, please. . .'

Then he sank the tip of him into her, just a bit, teasing, and she lost herself, whimpering shamelessly for more, lifting her hips higher.

He gave her more, gave her all of him in one fluid movement, plunging into her full length.

Crying out into his mouth, she bucked up and into his chest, stiffening more from wondrous surprise than the fleeting burn of the intrusion.

Instantly, he froze, his eyes clenched shut, his mouth grim. His arms, taut with strain, quivered as he held himself rigid, still inside her.

In the ensuing, shocked silence, he swore.

'Why?' Clay demanded in a raw, hoarse whisper, lifting his gaze and piercing her with a betrayed, confused look that stabbed her soul.

That lie, the one she'd been meaning to tell him about, had exposed itself. 'Clay – '

'Why, dammit? Why?'

Beneath him, with his magnificent, bruised body poised over hers, she shivered at the hurt and anger in his voice.

He made to withdraw and she let out an involuntary wince that made him go positively still. Then he swore again. 'Why – How the hell are you a virgin?'

CHAPTER 17

Hope stared at him in dismay, her body still pulsing around him, and yearning unbearably. 'Please.' She clutched at him. 'Don't leave me.'

He spoke then, most likely a demand to know what was going on, something he deserved to know, certainly. But she couldn't speak, couldn't hear, couldn't do anything but try to pull him back down against her.

He resisted with the strength of a brick wall.

She panicked and gripped him tight enough to evoke a wince, but she couldn't stop it. All she knew was that the most incredible man in the world was about to withdraw from her, and she couldn't have it. Not when her hips were still rocking mindlessly against his, not when her breasts were still hard, aching points that needed his hot mouth back on them.

She knew he'd spoken again, but in the fog her brain had surrounded her with, she couldn't make sense out of the words. 'Clay, please,' she begged, biting her lip at the strange, hollowed sound of her own voice.

'No, Hope. Dammit,' he swore hoarsely, thickly,

when she wrapped her legs around his waist, opening herself up wider, holding him to her.

Eyes grim, he tried to dislodge her with his hands on her hips, but she snuggled closer. 'Please,' she said again, and in her wild, wide-eyed state she spoke too loudly, too jarringly. Heat flooded her face, forcibly reminding her how pathetic she was at this.

He would rear back in anger now, in disgust, she thought, closing her eyes. Waiting.

He didn't move away, but nor did he come closer. His gaze, when she dared a peek, wasn't filled with disgust at all, but sincere confusion — could she blame him? — and more regret than she could handle.

And an unfulfilled hunger she knew matched her own.

Though the grimness hadn't faded from his face, she could still feel him hard and throbbing within her.

'Clay,' she whispered, entreatingly.

He shook his head and gritted his teeth. 'No! The way I tore into you . . . you should have told me, dammit.'

He didn't want her. But a kind of desperate need won the war with humility and she reared up, settling her open mouth against his chest, flicking her tongue against his flat nipple, just as he had done to her earlier.

That accomplished what nothing else had, and he groaned.

With another short oath, he lowered himself to his elbows, sank his fingers back into her hair. At the slight movement, she braced for more burning between her thighs, but it never came.

His tortured, bewildered, and yes, angry, gaze met hers for one brief second before his lips met hers in a long, drawn out kiss designed to arouse. He kissed her until her fingers dug into the corded muscles on his back, until she was nearly mindless with this crazy need again.

Then he looked deep into her eyes, his own filled with that same shattering intensity. 'Are you all right?' he asked, his voice low and more than a little shaky. 'Am I hurting you in any way?'

She shook her head, but that he cared enough to find out touched her unbearably, and her eyes stung for this last sweet moment she would ever have with him.

Then, finally, with an exquisite tenderness, he began moving inside her, stroking her gently, slowly. It was unbearably, surprisingly good.

'More,' she begged, and he gave it.

Lowering himself down over her until they were torso to torso, he kissed her as he pulled almost completely out of her before plunging deep, again and again.

The passion, the hunger built inside her, built and built, until she strained against him. The intensity of it terrified her, or would have if he hadn't felt it along with her.

'It's all right,' he whispered. 'I'm right here.'

With just that soft, bittersweet reassurance, she exploded with pleasure. His kiss became fierce, urgent as she contracted around him. And as he thrust into her one last time, he clasped her tight, climaxing with her, moaning low and deep.

He rolled to his side instantly, taking her with him, his face taut and white. She knew, but didn't dare comment on, how much he must hurt. For long moments they lay there, tangled, damp, chests heaving.

It had been so much more than she'd ever dreamed, so perfect . . . she never would have guessed. Love, and the art of making it, had always eluded her. How ironic that now, with this man who would never want her again, she'd found both.

Hope was unaware of the tears rolling down her face until Clay gently wiped at one with his thumb and made a hoarse sound of regret. 'Oh, Hope,' he whispered agonizingly. 'I hurt you.'

'No,' she sniffed. 'No, it's not that.'

Sitting up with a groan and a hand to his ribs, he reached for the afghan and covered her.

Then he very carefully, still white as a sheet, sat up. She felt the heavy weight of his stare.

Taking the coward's way out, if only temporarily, she squeezed her eyes shut and wished for a giant hole to swallow her up.

No hole, but just a surprisingly gentle man's hands reaching for her, pulling her up next to him, cupping her face, waiting. With a sigh, she opened her eyes and faced the music.

'Do you have any idea?' he asked in a shaky, hoarse voice, 'how absolutely confused I am?'

'I think maybe I do.' The sensuous haze he'd surrounded her with in their love-making was gone, completely gone in the face of what she had to explain. Left in its path was only a bittersweet sense of loss and a sweet ache where they'd been joined.

Humiliation such as she'd never known overcame her. It was her only excuse for what she did next.

She ran.

She ran hard and fast, slamming the door behind her as she left the den, raced down the hall, nearly tripping over Molly in her haste to put what had just happened behind her.

Through the living room and down the other hall before she heard Clay calling her name. Actually, it was more like bellowing.

She ran faster.

Up the far stairs, to the wing where she slept, running, nearly losing the thin afghan that barely covered her, running, running, running.

As if she could outrun her mortification, her regret.

She'd just opened her bedroom door when she heard him shout frantically to her. But she just winced at the sound of his voice that even she couldn't miss, and shut the door behind her.

There was no lock.

Not that she could keep him out forever, she had to explain.

She'd dropped the afghan and jerked her hands into her own faded, rumpled bathrobe before her door crashed open.

Standing there in the doorway, completely, amazingly nude, was a panting Clay. He stood slightly bent at the waist, a hand pressed to his ribs, and his breath wheezed out.

It was a paradox, Hope decided. That beautiful, powerful, long body of Clay's covered in such horrific bruises. She shivered at the sight. The great irony was that she knew his skin would be so very warm, if only she could wrap herself up in it.

The fierce frown he wore discouraged her. Of course, it was all he wore.

The most insane urge to giggle overcame her. Instead, she covered her face with her hands.

'I never figured you for an ostrich,' he muttered loud enough for her to hear. 'But you bury your face enough to look like one.' In one shaky movement, he came into her room, yanked up the dropped blanket with a muffled moan and jerked it around his hips. Then he sank to her bed, ashen. 'You're going to be the death of me, Hope. You know that?'

'I almost forgot,' she whispered more to herself than him, dropping her hands to her sides and staring at him. 'What you did to me . . .' She gestured vaguely to the door and downstairs, where he'd changed her forever. 'I actually lost my mind and forgot . . .'

'Forgot? That you weren't really pregnant?'

Swallowing hard, she figured now wasn't the time to tell him that for the first time in her life, her sixth sense had failed her – she'd not seen what kissing him would lead to.

He quirked a brow, his voice sardonic. 'Or maybe you forgot you were a virgin?'

'I – Oh, Clay.'

'Or maybe you just forgot that you'd lied.'

'Yes,' she said sadly. 'Yes, to all those things.'

'Hope.' Clay let out a tense little breath and rubbed his middle where his ribs hurt beyond belief. Dammit, his head was spinning.

She'd been a virgin. He should have known. Yeah, she'd lied, but the signs had been there, if he'd been paying attention to anything other than his own need. Everything had been new to her; his deep, wild kisses, his hands on her soft skin – soft skin no other had ever touched. Yes, everything had been astonishingly, shockingly new to Hope; each caress, each aching, throat-tightening glance, how she'd climaxed in his arms with her breath caught in her throat, his name on her lips . . . it had all been a first for her.

It was hard, he found, to regret the most incredible experience of his life, even when he wanted to strangle the person who'd given it to him.

'I don't know where to start,' she whispered.

'Why don't you start at the part where you explain how you can be pregnant if you've never had sex. And while you're at it, how did you get to be as old as you are, look as incredible as you do, and still be a virgin?'

'I'm not that old.'

He stared at her for one incredulous moment, then let out a little laugh.

She let out a deep breath. 'Oh, Clay, I tried to tell you so many times. I'm not pregnant.'

'No kidding.'

'And we never slept together. Before tonight, I mean.'

'You're kidding me.'

'And – ' Her huge eyes lifted from his mouth to his wry gaze. 'You're laughing at me.'

'No, I'm not laughing. Laughing would hurt my ribs and they're already killing me.'

No, he wasn't laughing, but if he was, it would be at himself. He'd been taken for some kind of ride, and though he had no idea what the game was, it had knocked him for a hell of a loop.

'You're mad,' she said quietly in that low voice of hers. Color spotted her cheeks. 'With good reason. I lied to you, Clay. You'll want to leave now, of course.' She touched her flaming cheeks, averted her face. 'I understand completely. If you'll just give me a minute, I'll – '

'Dammit, you understand nothing. Nothing, if you can sit there and calmly discuss my leaving.'

Her head lifted and she frowned in concentration, her gaze on his mouth. 'What?'

He swore, but it only made him feel small when her lips trembled slightly. 'I'm not leaving,' he said carefully, clearly.

She just looked at him.

'Hope, I've got to know what's going on. You can understand that, can't you? You told me you were pregnant – with my baby.' His gaze slid over her, to where her delectable body was wrapped in that ridiculously old robe. It didn't matter. Her flat, perfect belly – and every other inch of her – had imprinted itself on his brain. 'Why, Hope? Call me an idiot, but I can't figure it out. Why did you lie to me?'

'I had a good reason at the time,' she said sincerely. 'Or at least, I thought I did. It's just that it sounds so . . . wrong now.'

Her voice sounded small, genuinely full of remorse. Bravely she met his gaze. 'There was a storm that night.'

'I remember.' He'd never forget. The searing pain, the cold, the fear of dying alone. 'You helped me.'

'Before I did, I was here, just thinking. Unable to sleep . . . Trent had just delivered his first threat.'

The way she said it, with her voice quaking slightly, abruptly drained any anger he might have managed to hold on to. Much as hated that she'd lied and purposely deceived him, he hated even more the fact she'd been afraid enough, desperate enough to do it in the first place.

'I shouldn't have panicked,' Hope said, not looking at him. That her words ran slightly together and were louder than usual told him how difficult she found this. 'I mean – ' She laughed a little, the sound harsh in the quiet room. 'What could he really do to me?'

Clay's entire body went tense at the thought of what Trent could really have done to her.

'I should have just – '

'No!'

'It wouldn't have hurt me to just – '

'Stop it,' he said gently, but she flinched anyway. Cursing himself, he bit back his temper. 'Hope – '

'I'm so sorry, Clay. Being afraid isn't a good enough reason for what I did.'

Clay sighed. 'Oh, Hope.' He didn't know what to say, he was so confused.

'I was sitting in my house that night,' she whispered. 'Thinking about my life, and how perfect it should have been. Me, here in the house I loved, running the clinic. I had my animals, my practice. I should have been happy. But I wasn't. I was afraid.'

He sighed again, feeling like the biggest jerk on earth. Why hadn't she felt she could go to him? Again, he fretted over the man he'd been. He patted the bed beside him. 'Come here, Hope.'

She hesitated and he patted the bed again. Fiddling with the belt on her robe, she came. Gingerly, her body stiff, her hands on either side of her hips, she sat.

He tucked a strand of her thick, glorious hair behind her ear. 'You were scared. I hate knowing that. I should have done something about that.'

She said nothing to that. 'I was desperate. Quite desperate.' She shook her head. 'But it was wrong, Clay, to involve you like I did. And I'm so very, very sorry. But Trent had already told my father that I was pregnant with his child, and my father believed it. I couldn't stand the thought of him thinking that I'd . . . That I'd . . . you know, with Trent.'

'That you'd done with him what you and I just did?'

'No!' she said vehemently with a shiver. 'I can't even think about it with him. Making love with Trent – '

'It wouldn't have been making love,' he assured her grimly. 'Not with that man.' Just the thought of Trent touching her had his hands fisting.

'But I was afraid that if I didn't come up with a baby – at least for a little while – my father would make me leave this place.' She stopped, looked around her with a wistful, nostalgic expression that dissolved any lingering anger he had. 'I can't imagine leaving.'

'You shouldn't have to.'

Her eyes filled with apology. 'Then Molly dragged me out into the storm. I thought she must have found another hurt animal for me to tend, but we found you instead. I was so shocked, so very worried about you.'

'Thank God you found me in that rain.' He shuddered, thinking about what would have happened to him if she hadn't come out at all, or if he'd been left further in the woods. Or if they'd finished the job properly.

'I saw you, right at the point of desperation,' she continued, watching his face, her eyes fixed and dreamy, and he knew she wasn't seeing him as he was now, but rather as she did that stormy night. 'Something deep inside told me what I wanted to do was so wrong, so very wrong.' Her lips curved slightly and she lifted a hand to her chest as if it ached. 'Just as something even deeper told me it would be all right, that I should do it anyway. That you were . . .'

'Your destiny?'

She blinked, focused those dark eyes and sighed. 'There's no excuse, Clay. I lied. You'll never be able to forgive me for that.'

'Would you stop telling me what I think, what I feel?'

'I'm sorry.'

'And stop apologizing.'

'I'm – ' She stopped herself short of doing it again, nervously playing with the tie on her robe. 'You must be going crazy, wondering about yourself. Where you came from, who you are. And all I can talk about is myself – '

'Hope.'

She looked at him.

Settling one of his hands over hers, he met her gaze. Yes, he wanted to know about himself. He had to know. But this needed to be first. 'Did I hurt you very much? Before, when we made love?'

She dropped her gaze to their joined hands, threading

her fingers through his. 'No.' She swallowed hard. 'No, you didn't hurt me at all.'

'Hope. The truth. Are you really all right? Did it hurt?'

'Just for a minute,' she admitted, her cheeks reddening. 'But before and after was . . . you didn't hurt me, Clay.'

He worried about that, fretted that he hadn't been gentle enough. But she'd been so hot, and he'd been so unbelievably out of control. 'Why did you let me make love to you?' They obviously hadn't progressed to that point in their relationship before. In fact, given her obvious inexperience, they hadn't progressed to much physically at all.

For a minute she didn't answer, and he wasn't sure she'd heard him, but then she whispered, 'I'm not sure I can put the words together to answer you. All I know is what happened between us tonight was amazing. I lost myself in you. Really lost myself. I never thought it was possible,' she said with some awe. 'I mean, you read about such things in books, but I never believed it could happen to me.'

'Why not?'

She shrugged. 'I'm not really the sort of woman that inspires that sort of passion from a man.'

'Yes,' he said with a little laugh, thinking of her warm, lush body. 'You are. You're incredible.'

She flushed again. 'Well, you're the first one to think so then.'

The ridiculous male ego boost that gave him didn't last. To be her first was indeed a fantasy, but it also meant something much more than that.

He'd been the first one she'd ever let past her considerable guard. It was that which gave him the most satisfaction, and touched him deeply.

'I really didn't think I could react like that,' she said in amazement.

He watched her, struggling with his own emotions. He wanted to be hurt, betrayed, angry, but it was difficult when he understood her so very well.

He only wished he understood himself so well. The questions that hounded him night and day surfaced now, and while she was feeling so willing to talk, he asked one of them. 'What else do you know about me?' he asked.

'You don't have a criminal record.'

'That's something. What else?'

'Your parents are on a two month cruise and must not know you're missing. You have no siblings and . . .'

He had a quick vision of older, but sweet and caring parents. Just a flash, nothing more. 'And?'

'You're not married.' She gave him a side-ways glance from beneath her lashes, hiding her thoughts. 'I guess that's a good thing.'

He agreed.

She studied her hands. 'You live in Seattle and work for yourself.'

'No wonder the damn animals didn't seem familiar.' He'd never lived with her. So much made sense now. They had hardly known each other at all. He rubbed his temples. 'No one reported me missing?'

She was carefully watching his every word. 'No,' she said quietly, after a hesitation. 'I keep checking.'

'Just as well,' he muttered. 'Whoever came after me didn't have any other targets.' Except now there was Hope.

He'd have to make sure she didn't get drawn into whatever he was involved in. He wouldn't, couldn't, stand it if she got hurt because of him.

Somewhere in the last few minutes he'd developed a splitting headache, not unlike the one he'd had for the first few days after his concussion. Nausea welled without warning, but he bit it back. His thoughts raced, and so suddenly, did his pulse.

'Hope,' he managed, holding his head. 'I've . . . got to lay down a minute.'

Her head snapped up, her eyes narrowed. Jumping off the bed, she immediately slipped into professional mode. 'Of course. I'll help you back to bed – '

'No,' he gasped, cringing against the wave of sudden and unbearable pain. He tipped over, winced at the contact as his head hit, even though it was just her soft pillow. 'Right here. I gotta lay . . . right here. Just for a sec.'

'Clay?'

He heard her, he just couldn't answer. Not with the angry voices shouting inside his head.

'Dump him here,' the rough, crude voice said in Clay's head, laughing. 'He'll drown in the river.'

'No he won't,' said the other man, the one who'd just kicked Clay viciously in the ribs until his vision had faded. 'He's already dead.' He squinted down through the driving rain into Clay's face. 'Quite dead.'

They laughed and roughly tossed him from the car.

Clay bit back his groan, wanting them to believe he was indeed dead, knowing his life depended on that.

'Now he won't find the security leak in the main system.

'Good.'

'The big guy should be happy and we'll get our money.'

'Finally.'

The voices faded in Clay's head, leaving in their place a throbbing ache that echoed throughout every nerve in his entire shaking body.

And he was cold, so damn cold.

He felt Hope pull up a blanket over him, but he couldn't stop shaking. Her hands ran up and down his arms, chafing, warming. He heard his own soft moan as a renewed shaft of pain shot through his head.

'I'm going to get you something for the headache, Clay, just hold on a minute,' she said, but he grabbed her hand, not wanting her to leave. He knew he'd just stretched over her entire bed, but he couldn't help himself. His vision started to fade.

'Hope?'

'I'm here, Clay.' Her hand brushed over his forehead, followed by her lips. Or he wanted to think so.

'They thought I was dead.'

'Shh,' she whispered. 'Just lay still.'

'I didn't want to be dead . . . but I hurt.'

'Oh, Clay.' She stroked his face with gentle, cool fingers. 'Keep your eyes closed, the dizziness will pass.'

'I just need . . . a sec.'

'Okay, take all the time you need. Just rest.'

That low, husky voice soothed him. The hard, pounding pain in his head sickened him. The warring emotions proved too much and he drifted off, dreaming about being beaten again.

Dreaming about being alone, without Hope.

CHAPTER 18

Clay jerked awake some time later to a pitch black room. Braced for the pain in his head that never came, he took a shallow breath, then another.

No headache.

The little radio clock glowing on the stand by the bed said midnight. He'd only been asleep an hour, though it felt like much more, given the lingering stiffness and soreness of his every muscle.

Tentatively, he stretched his feet . . . and encountered a set of warm, soft, smooth legs tangled with his.

He lay on a strange bed, his arms wrapped tight around an incredibly alluring female body. Dark, thick, flowing hair tickled his nose. It had the scent of a spring rain. The face he looked down into seemed angelic, aristocratically beautiful . . . so sweet he ached to bend to kiss those lips he knew would be pliant and giving.

Her huge, dark eyes opened slowly, unfocused. She didn't wake up quickly, or easily. Black fire, he thought, as he looked down into their depths.

A Russian gypsy's face.

She'd told him that once, he remembered. Told him also that she had the temperament to go with it; stubborn, single-minded, persevering.

He knew enough of her to know that was true.

A relative stranger, yet already he knew so much about her. Wanted to know so much more.

Her chest rose and fell softly beneath the tattered robe she still wore. Her dreams at least, had been peaceful. More so than her reality. Or his.

'Clay?' she murmured.

Hmmm. His name.

'Are . . . you feeling better?'

'My headache is gone.'

She looked relieved.

He stared at her for a minute longer, thinking she was the most lovely woman he'd ever known, inside and out. Stroking her cheek once he pulled away to sit up.

Then he had to laugh at himself. He was naked – again. 'Have you noticed? I seem to always be without clothes around you.'

Looking embarrassed, she pulled her own robe tighter around her body and struggled to sit up. The robe got caught beneath her, and as she pulled it, she exposed a long, trim thigh.

It shouldn't have moved him, just the quick flash of bare leg, but it did. Without meaning to, he conjured up the rest of that body in his mind, making it difficult to concentrate on the task at hand.

'We fell asleep.'

'Yes,' he said, still looking at her.

She squirmed a little, reminding him he'd been staring at her intently. He couldn't help it.

He must have muttered something because her eyes narrowed as her gaze dropped to his lips. 'What?'

Damn her. His heart tugged, even now, just from being with her.

'I didn't say anything,' he told her. 'I'm just looking at you.'

'You're looking at me as if you've never seen me before,' she said uneasily, holding the sheet to her chin. 'And I have a funny feeling . . . a strong one, but I don't understand it. What's the matter, Clay? Why do I feel this way?'

His heart did another little flop, this one painful. He didn't want to feel so much for her, but it was too late. 'It's complicated,' he said, lightly mocking her favorite avoidance line.

She chewed on her lip as he studied her.

'Hope Broderick,' he said, testing the name on his tongue. 'Dr Hope Broderick.'

But it was no use. He could repeat that name until he'd become blue in the face, it wouldn't change a thing.

He had his memory back.

All of it.

Everything was different, the way he felt, the way he saw Hope. *Everything*.

It all seemed different somehow, and that knowledge was as earth-shattering as losing his memory in the first place.

He must have realized earlier when they talked, that they had no past together. He just hadn't put it all together, not in the aftermath of the greatest sex he'd ever had.

No past.

He'd never laid eyes on her before the night of that storm, the night someone had worked him over good enough to almost kill him.

But because he'd had no other memories to go on, she had felt familiar.

She didn't now.

He licked his suddenly dry lips, rubbed a hand over the heart that ached so inexplicably. Even his head hurt again. His gut twisted as renewed betrayal and fear washed over him. Not fear for himself, at least not physically. But fear that this woman he'd fallen for had something to do with what had happened to him.

He looked at her and willed himself not to believe that, but she'd lied. Over and over.

No, he thought. *Please, don't let it be her. I won't be able to take it if it's Hope.*

Without warning, Molly bounded into the room, her tongue lolling out, a sparkle in her eyes that always made Clay think she was smiling.

'Molly, down,' Hope said quickly, but not quickly enough.

With a little grunt, Molly leaped up on the bed, and landed with all four huge paws in Clay's lap.

Stars crossed his eyes.

As the air whooshed out of him and he hunched over, getting a mouthful of fur, it occurred to him that he should be used to pain by now.

Molly scrambled for footing and found purchase – in his naked groin.

He heard a hiss and realized it was his own breath.

'Clay?' Hope said worriedly, pushing Molly from his lap.

'You okay?'

'I just remembered,' he said in an unnaturally high voice. 'I *really* don't like dogs. Or cats. Or damn birds that talk.' Clearing his throat, he held himself and breathed carefully. No damage. 'Not at all.'

There was a smile in her voice when she said, 'You already told me that. What you never told me is why.'

He glanced at Molly. He really wanted to dislike her, but then she licked his face once, twice. Wet slobber in the chilled air should have made him colder, but it didn't. She licked him again and he had to stop his hand from automatically lifting to stroke her back.

The warm, fuzzy feeling he got from her obvious affections couldn't be controlled.

Closing his eyes, he realized for the first time in a week how great an importance one's memories actually played in each individual life. His own memories came to him freely now, as if they'd never been missing.

He loved animals, always had. His dog had meant everything to him. Everything. And when he'd lost her, he hadn't the heart to get another. He never had.

One glance at Hope had that fear bubbling back to the surface. *She* meant everything to him. In such a short time, Hope had become his life.

And he was about to lose her.

'Clay?' she murmured again in that low, husky voice

she was so self-conscious of. 'You've remembered something else? What is it?'

How could he explain what he had only just begun to realize?

She waited, then said his name again. He heard the alarm in it, the distress, but he couldn't soothe her, not now when his heart was in his throat.

He looked at her. 'You're not part of my past at all, are you, Hope Broderick?'

CHAPTER 19

Hope paled, even as she stiffened. 'You remember everything?'

She dropped her gaze from his. Her pulse leaped wildly at the base of her neck. Her fingers twiddled together. She was hiding something else from him, he realized with shock, and not only that, but she was panicked about it. Watching this, Clayton Slater made a painful decision.

For now, at least until he could spend a few minutes putting his startling thoughts together, he would withhold the truth from her.

He lifted her chin with a finger to look into her eyes. He wanted her to hear every word. 'Not everything,' he said quite honestly. He couldn't remember why this perfect stranger would want to lie to him. For she had obviously lied.

They'd not known each other at all.

'Not everything?'

Damn her, but her voice wavered. Her dark eyes held relieved fear. Why? Was she afraid of him? The thought made him ache all the more as temper shot to the surface.

'No, my little Mrs Slater-to-be. I don't remember everything. I don't remember how, for instance, we knew each other before.'

Her brows came sharply together as she looked at him in genuine confusion. 'But . . . we already discussed this. We didn't know each other before.'

'Don't.' Dammit, she was going to be the death of him. Even as rage hit him over her deception and whatever part she'd played in trying to destroy his life, a small part of him still yearned, hungered for her. 'I lost my memories, not my marbles. You can't change your story now.'

'What?'

Swearing, he dragged his hands through his hair and turned back fully to her, making a conscious effort to make sure she could hear him. 'You told me we knew each other before, we just hadn't had sex.'

She winced. At his choice of words?

'But before you passed out, I told you the truth,' she said. 'I told you that I was sitting in my house that night thinking about my pathetic life – '

'You never said I'd not been in that life.'

'I told you I had my practice, my animals, and that was all.' Her words came fast, nearly jumbled, but by now he'd grown so used to her speech, he caught every word. 'I told you I found you that night for the first time,' she added.

'No,' he said, shaking his head. 'You never said for the first time.'

'Well I meant that.' She stared at him wide-eyed. 'I certainly never meant to deceive you . . . You're angry.'

He laughed shortly, in amazement. It was laugh or really lose it. 'Did you think I wouldn't be?'

'But . . . you said you weren't.'

'Look,' he said, trying to get a grip on the situation. 'I don't know what's going on here, but – '

'Do you remember?' she asked. She was watching him carefully, and he knew by the look in her eyes that she sensed he did. 'Do you remember who you are?'

Her face, the one that had lit up his life for so many days now, remained carefully blank. Her body brushed so close to his that strands of her hair clung to his shoulder. He could touch her by just leaning a fraction of an inch. He ached to do that, oh how he ached. What he would have given to see her wary eyes and tight mouth smile at him, that special, warm, affectionate smile he could worm out of her with just a look.

'Clay?'

He wanted to believe, wanted to trust. But he did remember, and he knew . . . his life was in danger. Very real danger. And since he remembered exactly who he was up against, he knew anything was possible. *Anything*. Even the most innocent looking, sweetest woman he'd ever known could be involved.

'Do you remember?' she asked again.

'No,' he said in a hoarse voice, lying – lying to the woman he wanted to crush to him and make love with again. He cleared his throat. 'No, I don't remember.'

She closed her eyes in defeat and leaned back against the pillows. *Oh, Clay*, she thought, *I'm so sorry*. Yet even as she thought that, relief snaked in past her guard. Then an overwhelming guilt.

If he didn't remember, he wouldn't leave her. Not yet. He would be hers, just for a little longer. Oh, she shouldn't have been thinking along those lines. Indeed, as his doctor, she should have been discussing how he felt, checking his vitals.

But what had started out as pretense, having him the father of her unborn baby, had turned into fantasy. A fantasy she didn't want to let go of. If only it were true . . . but how absurd that would be, a man like Clayton Slater, in love with her.

'I'm so sorry,' she whispered, not sure for which of her myriad sins against him was she apologizing.

Abruptly, he stood, then blanched and paled. Without hesitating, Hope leaped out of bed and ran to him, throwing her arms around his waist to try to keep him from falling.

They staggered together, then caught their balance.

Still holding him, her cheek to his bare, fuzzy chest, her body flush with his, Hope went absolutely still.

She'd forgotten something vitally important – he was stark naked. And most of that male nudity was pressed up to her, causing interesting reactions to the inside of her own body.

'Hope,' he said in a choked voice, putting his hands to her shoulders to try to push her away. 'Don't.'

Thinking he meant don't touch him, that he was disgusted by her hands on him, she pulled back an inch or so, but didn't let go. 'I can't, Clay. You'll fall.'

A sound escaped him. 'I'm fine, dammit.'

Unsure as to what this sudden, sharp change of mood was about, Hope let him go. She didn't want to, but she didn't have a choice. Her fingers left the warm, resilient skin of his back, trailed over his sides before falling to her sides.

Jaw tight, he yanked the afghan off the bed and wrapped himself up while she studied her toes.

She glanced at him, but at the drowning intensity of his gaze, she shifted her attention to the ceiling.

It needed to be painted.

But that would require money she didn't have.

Clay touched her face until she looked at him. 'Hope.'

She met his gaze, straight on. Could she do anything else? But she was startled by the mix of retribution and hunger in his incredible green eyes.

'I've far outstayed my welcome,' he said. 'It's time for me to go.'

Her heart dropped. Her stomach hurt. 'But you're not up to being on your own yet.'

'I've been on my own for a long time, Doctor,' he said with a formality that terrified her. 'I'll be fine.'

He didn't look fine, but pale and shaky.

'I'm tired,' he said bluntly. 'It's been quite a night. And as you can imagine, I'm kind of cold. I'm going to bed.'

And he didn't want to be with her any more. 'Oh.'

He turned and went to the door. Though she had no idea what she expected, it hadn't been that. 'You're going to sleep . . . downstairs?'

The smile that twisted his lips was not pleasant. 'Where else would I sleep?'

Good question. The answer she wanted to give was,

with me. But she didn't quite dare, not when he'd obviously changed his mind about her.

'Hope?' He waited, his distant smile speculative. 'You and I both know I don't belong up here, that I've never once slept here before. But if you want to tell me different, go ahead. I'll listen.'

She just looked at him, wondering how all of this had gotten so out of her control. He was going to leave and her heart was going to break. She'd known it, prepared for it, but still, the pain came far worse than she could have imagined.

'I'll get you some aspirin – '

'No. I'll be fine.'

And he then was gone.

She plopped back on her bed and once again studied her yellowing ceiling. As the tears tracked backwards into her hair she told herself this was for the best.

Definitely for the best.

If only she really believed it.

Clay shut the downstairs bedroom door and, for a minute, rested his forehead against the cold wood.

He hurt. And he wasn't thinking about the physical pain, though that had gotten bad too.

He was not a man who had been randomly mugged and left for dead. No, he thought with an ironic little laugh, he couldn't be so lucky.

He'd never been so lucky.

Officially, he programmed computer security systems sophisticated enough that governments from all over the world clamored for his help. He was paid big bucks to see if he could break into existing systems, then even bigger bucks to fix the leaks he found.

Unofficially, he was one of the most sought after computer hackers anywhere.

Up until very recently, his record hadn't been broken – he'd been given a job, he'd handled it. No glitches. He'd fixed entire countries' security leaks, secured famous museums' priceless and timeless art, had even had a stint in Hollywood, settling some very wealthy, and stalked, actors into their break-in proof castles.

Maybe he'd gotten cocky. After all, he knew how good he was, knew that no one could beat him at what he considered the greatest game in the world.

Wearily, he moved to the bed and sank into it, not bothering to don any clothes.

Yeah, he'd gotten a little cocky. Studying the chipped ceiling, Clay remembered the last job he'd taken. And then shot straight up to a sitting position on the bed, his heart in his throat.

The last job he'd taken ... Oh, hell! With some trouble, he forced his feet into a pair of freshly washed jeans Hope had bought him.

Wait. Think. Don't rush off half-cocked. Look at what it got you into last time.

The last job he'd taken had been for a logging company, one of the biggest in the Pacific Northwest – Hope's father's business. Entire shipments had started to disappear on a regular basis, then mysterious orders would show up in the field so that too much wood would be taken down. Then that wood would not make it to the processing plants. In response to this huge waste, both the Department of Forestry and certain ecological groups had made more than a few threats. Even Congress was getting into it.

Bottom line – the company was in for huge trouble.

Obviously, someone was trying to destroy the company's pristine reputation, and was doing a hell of a job.

Clay had been hired in-house by an assistant to the president – Hope's father's assistant, he knew now – to try to find how it was happening. What he'd stumbled upon was a complex computer loop that had convinced him the logging company's trouble was definitely generated from the inside.

And what he had learned that last night, when someone had dragged him from his car as he'd come home from work, gave him a clue as to who was involved.

He remembered, and winced as the events came slamming painfully back.

A kick to his cracked ribs had been followed by that evil, cackling voice saying, *'Now he won't find the security leak in the main system. The big guy will be happy and we'll get our money.'*

He'd been in too much pain to grasp the implications of that, and afterward, Clay hadn't remembered a thing. Until now.

The big guy didn't want Clay to find the security leak.

Hope's father and Trent ran the logging company that had hired him. Which of them had tried to kill him? The man who was desperate to keep his business intact, or the man who seemed desperate to take it over? Clay had signed a contract, but even so, he'd never met the senior Broderick, or Trent Blockwell, personally.

Until yesterday, when he'd been introduced to Hope's father as his daughter's fiancée.

Clay staggered into the bathroom and downed three aspirin. Staring into the mirror, he grimaced. He recognized the face – finally. The blond, neglected hair that did as it pleased. The dark green eyes that didn't easily show their true thoughts. His upbringing, he supposed. Though his parents had been sweet, loving and very attentive, they'd been much older, and quite detached from what had been their son's reality. Clay, superbly technically adept from a very young age, had always somewhat confused them. Especially when he continually took apart each and every kitchen appliance, reassembling them into robotics equipment or bombs.

The government had claimed him young, giving him training and more expertise. But after serving eight years, he'd tired of the restrictions, and had branched out on his own. He'd been extremely successful – until now.

He forced himself to keep staring in the mirror, to remember everything. His jaw was tight now – stress, he figured. Tall, thinner than he remembered being, he was still muscle-toned from his regular work-outs, which he knew he did as a way to relieve tension more than to keep his post-army athletic build.

The burning question as he stared at himself, was, of course, about Hope. Hope, his rescuer, his lovely temptress, his angel.

His love.

Was she involved in this mess with the logging company? And if so, which side? Was she on her father's side, trying to find the culprit who wanted to ruin a hundred years of reputation? Or was she on Trent's side, trying to gain control of a multi-million dollar corporation? And which one of them had tried to have him killed?

Had Hope faked every bit of emotion she'd shown him? No, he didn't want to believe that. She couldn't be involved, not Hope.

She'd only lied to him out of sheer desperation. A desperation he understood perfectly. He'd forgiven the lie easily. Hell, even he might have done the same thing in her position.

The smart thing would be to high tail it out of here, drop the job and go on to the next one. For that matter, he could just drop work period. He knew he had plenty of money stashed, he'd been working like a dog for years. He could take the vacation he kept promising himself and disappear.

Yeah. Just disappear.

Tempting. If only his brain hadn't just demanded justice. If only his damn heart didn't cringe at the thought.

Hope.

If she had nothing to do with what had happened to him – and he didn't want to believe she did, then there was a bigger problem.

She needed him.

Her terror after dealing with Trent alone in the house was real, she hadn't made that up. Nor had she made up Trent's threats. Clay had seen them for himself.

The only part she had made up was their relationship,

and she'd done that out of necessity. It hurt to think that everything she felt for Clay was pretense, but maybe, just maybe, he could change that.

No, he couldn't leave. Not until he knew what Hope was about. Oh, he was probably one hundred percent a love-struck fool, but he just couldn't go.

Not until he'd convinced himself she felt absolutely nothing for him. That this insane attraction he had for her was nothing more than pretense and lust.

Not until he knew she was safe and secure in this house she loved beyond reason.

There was one great big hitch in his plans – the lovely doctor didn't realize he had remembered. He couldn't tell her, not yet. Not until he tried to convince her that they could make this work.

As he stared at himself in the mirror, he wondered . . . How long would it take Hope to realize they had more than a simple chemical reaction?

Knowing the stubborn, fiercely independent woman, it could take a long time.

Her alarm didn't go off, and for the first time in her memory, Hope overslept.

Jerking on her clothes after the quickest shower in history, Hope knew her only excuse was that she hadn't actually fallen asleep until sometime near dawn.

Her fault, she chided. She'd made a huge mess of her life, and hadn't the foggiest idea how to fix it.

Clay would leave today.

She'd be back at square one in dealing with her father and Trent. That she could handle.

But she'd be alone, completely alone.

She'd never minded that before, but it seemed different now. Different because she could no longer imagine living here without Clay. Scary thought, very scary thought.

Ignoring the ache in her heart, she lifted her chin and determined that she would handle this.

Racing down the stairs, she headed directly for the clinic, wanting to greet Kelly before she came looking for Hope and discovered her tall, handsome secret.

Just what she needed, for her two worlds to collide.

But it was too late.

Skidding to a halt in the waiting room, Hope's stomach twisted. At the front counter, where patients usually stood in line to sign in, were Kelly and Clay, locked in what looked like a deep, chummy conversation.

She must have made a sound, though she wasn't aware of it. They both turned to her at the very same moment, Kelly's expression lit with genuine pleasure, no little amount of curiosity, and an avid speculation that had Hope groaning inwardly.

Clay's gaze held none of those things, only a dead-on intensity she'd only seen once before – just last night.

His charming smile, when it came, seemed in complete opposition to that darkness in his forest green eyes. So did the nonchalant way in which he held himself, his wide shoulders set easy in his t-shirt. His long legs were loose, his feet crossed at the ankles where he leaned against the counter. One hand rested low on his hip.

The stance spoke of a casualness that didn't fool her for one second.

Not with the absolute sense of tension shimmering from him like a beacon. When he straightened and moved toward her, she had to fight the urge to back up.

The way his lips tightened imperceptibly told her he'd noticed her nerves. Still, he came forward.

Out of the corner of her eye, she could see Kelly. Could see, too, how the nurse's ears pricked up with interest as she watched them.

Exactly what Hope had wanted to avoid – she and Clay would have an audience for round two.

Apparently without qualm or concern that their every move was being watched in utter fascination, Clay advanced.

Hope retreated.

Clay easily outdistanced her. In a move that startled a gasp from her, he slipped his hands possessively around her waist and gently squeezed, all while his heavy-lidded gaze held hers.

Hope couldn't have looked away to save her life.

As if their fight last night had never happened, Clay leaned close, smiling intimately down into her face. Then, right in front of her gaping employee, he gave her a quick, smacking kiss on the lips.

'Good morning, sweetheart,' he said in that thrilling, silky voice he somehow always managed to make sure she heard clearly.

CHAPTER 20

Confusion hit Hope first, then at the sharp glitter in Clay's gaze, suspicion quickly followed.

What was he up to?

Kelly sent her a guarded smile. 'Good morning, Hope.'

Hope managed a weak smile, not easy with Clay's hands on her. To gain a semblance of control, she backed up.

He let his hands fall from her with a knowing smile.

'I guess things make a lot more sense to me now,' Kelly said. Hope didn't miss the slightly injured tone, and knew the nurse was wondering why Hope had never mentioned Clay. Especially after the way Hope had been busy avoiding Trent like the plague, and recruiting Kelly for help in the process.

Hope flushed with embarrassment. What must the woman think? Actually, she couldn't follow that train of thought long, not when Clay stepped close again. He reached out and touched her hip with a familiarity that stirred her blood despite her racing emotions.

Her body still felt that strange, delicious soreness from

what they'd shared last night . . . and she needed to think. Shaking her head to clear it, she looked at him.

'Feeling okay?' he whispered huskily, making sure she looked at him before speaking. Shifting in front of her, he blocked her from view with his wide shoulders. His fingers shifted on her, caressing, moving alarmingly high on her ribs. A thumb brushed the sensitive underside of a breast.

Her breath caught and held. A shiver ran down her spine, even as she started to warm from the inside out.

The small, cocky smile that curved his lips told her he knew exactly what was happening to her, that he knew he was arousing her without even trying. That he liked it.

With a calm she certainly didn't feel, she again backed away from his touch and forced a smile at Kelly. 'This isn't what you might think – '

'Don't be shy, Hope,' Clay said smoothly, smiling down into her reddened face, sliding a finger over a hot cheek. 'I was just telling Kelly about us.'

She could feel Kelly's curious stare, but knew the woman was far too polite to verbalize what she must be dying to ask. 'That's . . .' That's what? Hope wondered a little wildly. She had no idea what Clay had told Kelly, but felt certain it was something interesting, given the avid speculation in her nurse's gaze. 'That's nice,' Hope finished lamely.

'You didn't tell me you were going to be married,' Kelly said, and Hope nearly fell over, would have if Clay hadn't supported her with his strong hands.

Hope stared at Clay, shocked, dismayed, *relieved*? Good Lord, she was confused. 'I – Well . . . Um.

Well, yes,' she said finally, while Clay just watched her with a steady gaze, letting her get completely flustered. His confident, all-seeing smile never faded.

'That's exciting news,' Kelly said. 'A wedding. That will certainly stir the town up, won't it?'

It would at that. But it was nothing compared to how her insides had been stirred.

'Nothing like a good old-fashioned wedding to perk up a town, is there?' Clay added, that insufferable smile firmly in place. His eyes still hadn't warmed, and Hope watched him with growing unease until he winked at her.

Only she didn't get the joke.

Oh, he was most definitely up to something, and she didn't need her sixth sense to tell her that.

'If you'll excuse me, Kelly,' Hope said, her eyes narrowing, 'I need to speak to Clay.'

'No problem,' her nurse said, turning to the counter and picking up the sign – in sheets. 'I'll set up.'

Clay just stood there, wearing a grin that Hope was dying to wipe right off. 'Speak away.'

'Alone,' she added stiffly, yanking his arm.

Kelly lifted her gaze to study them, obviously brimming over with questions, and Hope tugged harder.

'Ouch,' Clay complained as she dragged him down the hall into the kitchen. He tipped his head down until he looked into her face. 'Careful, sweetheart. I know how eager you must be to repeat last night's performance, but –' His words ended on a surprised grunt as she jerked herself free, and inadvertently shoved an elbow into his lower belly.

'Keep it up,' she threatened, 'and next time you'll really be sorry.'

His amusement drained instantly. 'Next, or again?'

'What?'

'Was that, *what* because you didn't hear me? Or was that, *what* you heard me, you just don't believe it?' he asked politely. 'Because if it was the first one, then I certainly don't mind repeating – '

'Stop it,' she cried. 'I heard you! I just don't understand. I don't understand anything! Not last night, not this morning, nothing.'

He just stared at her, those eyes she'd grown to count on still cool and distant.

And she had a terrible feeling, a bone-deep terrifying sense that things could get far worse.

'Clay, please, what's going on?'

'I figured you already knew.'

He'd turned slightly, raising his hands in front of his mouth to rake them through his hair. She missed his words, and in her distress, all she could hear was her own whirling thoughts. 'What?'

He dropped his hands, disgust evident on his face.

Heat flooded her own as humiliation kicked in. She'd gotten so used to his patience with her deafness, she'd forgotten to be careful. 'I'm sorry,' she whispered. 'Just – Never mind.' She'd no sooner turned away when his strong hands closed on her upper arms, turning her back to him.

'Don't do that,' he said, his mouth grim. 'Don't ever do that.'

'Do . . . what?'

'Be ashamed of what you can't hear. I'm the idiot. Not you.'

'I don't understand, Clay.'

'I've got to know,' he said tensely. 'The truth, Hope. Is there anything else you've not told me? Anything else you've hidden?'

'No!' Her shoulders sagged as she realized the truth. 'You think there's more. You think – ' She broke off, felt her color drain. Her hands covered her own mouth. She understood now, understood his barely suppressed fury, his coldness. And because she did, she felt sick. 'You think I had something to do with what happened to you.' Now her hands dropped from her mouth to her stomach, where bile had started churning and burning.

Pain slashed his features. So did regret and apology. His hands tightened on her shoulders. 'Are you okay?'

'No, I'd be sick over your shoes – if you were wearing any, and if I had eaten or drank anything this morning to throw up. Clay!'

Backing her to a chair, he managed to step on Molly's paw. The dog yipped loudly, and Clay swore colorfully as he pushed Hope to sit. 'Damn dog. What does a hearing dog do anyway?'

Hope managed to smile weakly as Clay sank to his knees between hers. 'Follow me around and worry a lot.' Clay's chest touched her legs and a jolt of pure longing shot through her. Yes, his chest was strong and wide and oh, so touchable. But her sense of need went far deeper than that. She wanted to be held, by him. Wanted to have that little nameless something that had always seemed to elude her in the past, something she had begun to suspect was more than simple companionship and comfort. More than lust.

He set his big hands on her thighs. Heat seeped through from his skin to hers. He was sandwiched between her legs, his face at a level with her tingling breasts. Thinking became difficult.

'What – What are you doing?' she stammered.

He took her hands in his, gave her a wry smile. 'I'm going to give an apology a whirl.'

'Why? For thinking I could actually hurt you, even though I saved your sorry hide?'

He winced.

'I realize my cooking isn't that great, but I promise you, I never once tried to poison you.'

His hands tightened on hers. 'Dammit, I'm trying to say I'm sorry here.'

'Try harder.'

'All right.' His eyes darkened with the challenge. His mouth relaxed, then smiled that killer smile as he kissed her knuckles. 'I already told you I was an idiot. I meant it.' Strong white teeth nipped at her thumb. 'I've watched you with your patients, I know how much their health means to you. I know how much it hurts you when someone you care for is sick, in need. Hell,' he grinned, 'I've seen you remove a spider from the house rather than kill it.' Now the grin faded, replaced by a seriousness that took her breath. 'I know you could never hurt me. That you couldn't even try. I'm just a little confused, Hope.'

Her heart slipped quietly and heavily to the floor when

he brought their joined hands to his cheek and rubbed them softly against his face.

'Say you know I am a jerk,' he begged softly. 'Say you forgive me, Hope.'

'You are a jerk,' she agreed readily, smiling when his head whipped up. 'But I'm one too. I do forgive you, Clay.'

'You're not a jerk,' he said fiercely, tightening his grip. 'I am really sorry, Hope.' His gaze, direct on hers, seemed to see into her soul. Her heart squeezed a little, and she wasn't sure she liked it.

He was the first man to make her feel, really feel. And yearn and ache. And burn.

He was her future.

Not this man, she thought with a quick glance heavenward. *Oh, please not this man, Not here, not now.*

'This whole situation has me on edge,' he said, taking a deep and trembly breath. 'I'm losing it, really losing it, Hope.'

'No. This is just difficult for you. It would be for anyone.' She unwound her hands from his and cupped his face. 'Really.'

Without warning, he leaned forward and gave her a soft kiss. 'You said you'd marry me.'

'But – Okay, now I'm the one who's really confused.' She took a deep breath, which promptly clogged in her throat when he tugged on her hair gently. She met his gaze and saw a flash of heat.

Then his gaze dipped low, ran over her slowly and thoroughly, causing her skin to tingle. 'Did you change your mind?' he teased.

'No.' Amazingly enough, her body responded to him, and he hadn't even touched her yet. Yearning sliced through her, yearning and an unbearable weighty sadness she couldn't dispel. 'But I thought you had.'

Regret crossed his features. 'I'm sorry if I gave you that impression.'

'You said you were going to leave this morning.' Just saying it hurt, but she had to have things out in the open. 'Is that because I lied to you? Because I let you think that we'd . . . shared a past?'

'I'm not going to leave,' he said quietly. 'Unless you want me to.' He watched her carefully. 'Do you want me to go, Hope?'

Last night, with an ease that had touched her, he had seemed to forgive her deception – then he'd turned on her quicker than she could blink. She hadn't understood it then, and she certainly didn't understand it now. 'Why do you want to stay?'

'I told you how I felt about you.'

'But that was before you found out I had deceived you. Then you seemed to feel the opposite.'

'I never hated you,' he said firmly. Lifting a strand of hair between his fingers, he studied it carefully while choosing his next words. His gaze lifted and gave her face the same intent inspection. 'It's hard to function when every single crumb of your past has been erased.'

It was hard to function with him looking at her like that. With his fingers playing in her hair. With him between her legs, his chest pressing against the inside of her thighs. It brought back other, more erotic images.

Clay had the same problem. His mouth, inches from

Hope's flesh, was watering. *Watering*. Then her fingers lifted and so very lightly, ran over his jaw.

'Your bruises are fading,' she whispered.

The simple gesture, the pleasure of her touching him, warmed him as nothing had since he'd gotten his memory back the night before. He had no idea what his brain had decided about Hope, whether or not he should trust her. At that moment, it didn't matter. Because his heart had made the rash decision that he could, that he wanted her – no matter what.

Reaching up, he held her hand to his face.

'You told Kelly about us,' she said, her voice a little stuttered, which told him that she was as affected as he was. 'To further the rumors?'

The statement brought him up cold. Straightening, he studied her . . . and realized the plain, hard, unbending truth – which should never have escaped him for so long.

It was the *pretense* of being in love, of getting married, of being with child that she needed – *not the reality*.

The joke was on him. 'With any luck,' he said with a lightness he didn't feel, 'When the new rumors spread about you getting married to me, your business will be back on track in no time. Maybe your father will even let up.'

She smiled. 'Thank you, Clay.'

Caught in his own trap, he could only stand and say, 'Well, I owed you one, didn't I? After all, you've been feeding me and taking care of me. I'll make sure to pay you back for the clothes.'

'You'd better not. But I'm glad you're staying.'

Well, he was glad she was glad, but he sure had hoped it had been for more personal reasons, like she'd fallen in love with him and wanted to marry him for real. He wouldn't give up on the hope he could change that.

'I did forget to tell you something,' she said hesitantly. 'Trent called last night, before you and I – Well . . . before.' She blushed. 'I hung up on him. I imagine he won't stay away for long, not after these new rumors hit.'

He heard the worry and watched her carefully.

She was looking at him, waiting. A million emotions shifted in her nearly black eyes, but one remained foremost.

'You look scared,' he said.

'I don't want him to hurt – '

'No one is going to hurt you,' he said firmly, tugging her up from her chair. He squeezed her hands as his chest squeezed his heart. '*No one*. I can promise you that, Hope.'

'That's quite a promise,' she said a little hesitantly.

'I mean it. What did he say to you?'

'I wasn't worried about me getting hurt,' she said, her gaze searching his. 'I was worried about you.'

He let out a little laugh as it hit him exactly what this woman thought of his physical attributes. But then again, he thought with a wry rub to his ribs, he hadn't given her much reason to think differently. 'You think Trent is going to hurt me?'

'He said he wouldn't let me marry someone else. That he'd stop me.'

Clay brought their joined hands to his chest, which brought her one step forward. The fear in her eyes had that strange sense of protectiveness surging through him. 'I'm not going to let anything happen to you.'

She looked at him doubtfully, and he was hard pressed to blame her. After all, Trent had nearly raped her while Clay lay helpless on her hall floor. 'I want you to believe that.'

'You're not afraid of him?' She bit her lip, lowered her gaze. 'That sounded demeaning,' she said quickly. 'I didn't mean it like that. I mean you're this huge guy . . . of course you're not afraid of him. I only meant that –'

'I know what you mean.' He doubted she did though. It meant she cared a whole lot more about him than she wanted to think. And it wasn't pretense that brought on her concern, it was a genuine emotion. 'Hope?'

She looked at him.

'I want you to promise me, you'll tell me when he calls you again. Can you do that?'

'Do you really still want to marry me?'

He grinned at the unexpected question. Her mind had certainly been busy. 'You bet.'

'Why?' she whispered, her dark eyes huge on his.

Touching her face softly, he said, 'You already know why. But I promised not to pressure you until you were ready.' His thumb outlined her lower lip and her mouth opened slightly, leaving him with the strongest urge to put his mouth to hers. 'Are you ready, Hope?'

He knew she wasn't, so he was relieved to hear her speak the truth.

'No,' she whispered. 'I don't think I am.' She drew a deep, shaky breath. 'Being with you throws me off, Clay. I can never quite catch my balance.'

He had to smile at her bemused and wary expression. 'I know the feeling,' he said.

She left him then, to go to the clinic. Still, he stood there smiling.

She was falling for him, and not even aware of it.

He grinned to himself for the rest of the morning.

Until, that is, he got onto Hope's computer. It wasn't curiosity that motivated him, or even that he wanted to gain information about Hope behind her back.

Now that he had his memory back, he had work to do.

He had his attempted murder to solve if he didn't want to upgrade it to his own pre-meditated murder.

Clay concentrated, but it was hardly necessary, as everything about the computer came as second nature. In a matter of seconds he'd accessed her father's business through the modem, which operated so slowly he had to grind his teeth until the urge to throw it across the room passed.

It wasn't long before he realized something pretty terrifying.

First of all, since his own supposed 'death', the security leak had gotten larger, probably because whoever was responsible thought him dead.

Secondly, someone had gone to a great amount of trouble to bring attention to the company's logging efforts. In doing so they'd lobbied all sorts of interesting congressional activists, had pooled an amazing amount of support.

For the good of the company?

Seemed unlikely, when most of that publicity had actually been negative. Now the company that had for years and years been of good standing, suddenly had a flailing reputation. It was poised on the edge of disaster, waiting for a final push.

Obviously someone wanted to hurt the logging company, and they were doing a fine job of it. Several warnings had come through, and several could end up in lawsuits.

Exactly what he'd been hired to stop.

But according to the memos, most of the damage had been done in Hope's father's name – the man who had Clay hired in the first place.

Why would he sabotage his own company, then hire Clay to figure that out?

It made no sense. Unless, of course, it had been to throw everyone off the track. Simple – except that Hope's father loved his logging business above all else, including his own daughter's happiness.

And the big question still had to be answered – who had taken Clay that night with the intention of killing him? Obviously, the someone who didn't want the security leak found.

Trent, of course.

All Clay had to do now was prove it.

CHAPTER 21

Hope stood outside the door of the clinic and grimaced. What would she say? How was she going to face Kelly?

Sucking up her embarrassment, Hope opened the door. Kelly was in the reception room, stacking magazines neatly. At the sight of Hope, she fumbled and sent her stack flying across the floor.

Hope smiled wryly and gave Kelly a sheepish glance. 'Clumsy . . . or nervous?'

'Both,' Kelly admitted, reddening.

Hope knew if they didn't work this out right here and now, she and Kelly would suffer a difficult relationship in the future. But how to straighten this out? After all, she could hardly explain this to herself.

Kelly continued to fuss about the reception room, avoiding Hope's gaze. The last few days had been difficult enough, Hope thought with a sigh. Hardly any patients, the unspoken stress of knowing both their jobs were on the line.

They'd barely talked, taking a huge step backwards in their growing friendship. On Saturday, as Kelly had left the office for the night, she'd smiled sadly and asked, 'Should I bother coming in on Monday?'

Hope had reassured Kelly the best she could, but obviously she hadn't done a great job of it.

'I'm sorry about this morning,' she said finally, clasping her hands and studying her short, unmanicured nails. 'I knew that someday I'd regret having the clinic where I live.'

Kelly shrugged and meticulously moved a magazine a fraction of an inch on a table, aligning it with the others. 'I guess working where you live can be . . . a little awkward. Not to mention inconvenient.'

'This is a business,' Hope said quietly. 'My personal life shouldn't interfere.'

Kelly straightened and sighed as she met her gaze. 'Of course your personal life is going to interfere. Everyone's does. You have nothing to be sorry for.'

Hope realized her personal life had never interfered before, because she'd never had a personal life. She didn't like the feeling that left inside her.

'I just thought – Oh, never mind.'

'No,' Hope said quickly. 'Tell me what you thought.'

Kelly looked at her. 'I thought we were becoming friends. But I guess that's not possible, not really. Not with you being the boss.'

'We are friends,' Hope said, her voice catching on the burst of pleasure Kelly's words had evoked. 'Oh, Kelly, I can't tell you how much it means to hear you say that. And it has nothing to do with who works for who. Nothing at all. We'd still be friends if you ran this place.'

'Really?'

'Yes.' Hope laughed. 'Maybe I should put the clinic in your name. You've got a whole lot controversy going on, it'd be good for business.'

Kelly smiled, but didn't look relaxed. 'I guess I just don't understand why you didn't tell me about Clay before. Especially with that business of Trent calling daily.'

'There hasn't really been time, not until the last few days.'

She didn't buy that. 'Still, it might have come up.'

'All right, that's true. I don't really know why I didn't say anything,' Hope admitted.

Kelly gave her a long look.

'Okay, okay, I was embarrassed.' She bit her lip. 'I'm really new at this, Kelly.'

Kelly's eyes remained serious, but her lips twitched. 'New at talking?'

Hope had to laugh. 'You know what I mean. This isn't exactly easy for me. I'm – ' Oh, what the hell. 'I have absolutely no idea what I'm doing, Kelly. No idea at all. I really hate that.'

Kelly just gave her an infuriating smile.

'What?'

'Do you know how refreshing it is to see the mighty, unflappable Dr Broderick not completely in charge for once?' Kelly laughed. 'You know, I just might never fear you again.'

'Fear me! Why would you ever fear me?'

Kelly shook her head, looking amused. 'Why? You're so good. So incredibly focused. It's hard to live up to that. It's even harder to work for someone like that.'

'I don't want you to feel that way,' Hope said, distressed over the image that projected. She certainly had never thought of herself as inflexible and regimented, as Kelly suggested. 'I'm far from perfect. I don't want you to ever think you have to live up to something that isn't true.'

'I'll remember that the next time our waiting room is overflowing and you're seeing three patients to my every one,' Kelly pointed out dryly. 'You always know exactly what you're doing.'

'That's just a job,' Hope said with a shrug. 'And working is my strong suit. Besides, you do most of the work in there, charting the patient up and prepping. I just come in and finish up. Believe me, I'd rather know more about living life than working.'

'You seem to be doing fine,' Kelly said with a kind smile. 'Just look at that man of yours.'

Oh, she'd looked at him. Plenty. 'But I really know nothing about what I'm doing.'

'Honey, no woman really knows what they're doing when it comes to dealing with men. We just wing it. Sometimes, if fate is on our side, we get lucky.' She shook her head. 'And boy, did you get lucky.'

'Lucky?'

Kelly gave her a long look. 'He's gorgeous, Hope. Really gorgeous, inside and out.'

Wasn't he just? Over six feet of pure masculine pride, stuffed between tough, lean muscle and a surprisingly gentle nature that never failed to tip her heart on its side. She could still feel him under her fingertips, taste his skin . . . could still picture him in that incredible moment of release, head tossed back, hot and deep emotions running across his beautiful face, bared for her to see.

Had anyone ever opened himself up to her that way, silently demanding she return the favor and give one hundred percent of herself back?

Had she ever given in?

Never, not once. Not until last night.

'No wonder you ditched Trent.'

'I didn't – ' This was how bad rumors spread, she reminded herself. Treading carefully, she said, 'I didn't ditch Trent. There was nothing between us to end. Ever.'

Kelly's gaze told Hope she wasn't sure if she believed that, and Hope sighed as she said, 'You don't really think I could just hop from one man to the next, do you?'

'Of course I do. They're both pretty fine, Hope. Who could blame you for not being able to make a decision? Tell you what,' she offered with a grin. 'You decide which one you don't want, and I'll take him. Just as a favor from employee to boss, you understand.'

They both laughed, but Hope knew a real unease. She didn't understand most of Trent's behavior, didn't understand why saying no to him wasn't enough. There was more going on there than she understood, and she had a bone deep fear that somehow Clay would get hurt.

She couldn't have it, he'd been hurt enough.

But Kelly liked Trent, Hope knew they were friends. What would Kelly tell him? And more importantly, how would Trent react?

'It looks like another slow day,' Kelly said carefully. Between the damage Trent had worked, combined with the huge For Sale sign out front, she'd be lucky if she ever saw another patient.

'I had a job offer in Seattle,' Kelly said suddenly. 'But I took this job instead.'

And now this one could disappear. 'Oh, Kelly. I'm so sorry – '

'Don't be,' Kelly interrupted softly. 'I took this one because this was where I wanted to be. You have a way with people, Hope, and it shows. I don't think you have any idea how well-respected you are around here.'

'So well-respected,' she said dryly, 'That we have no one waiting to be seen.'

'Those are circumstances beyond your control,' Kelly said grimly. 'And I think I'm beginning to understand some of those circumstances better now. She studied Hope a moment in silence. 'I'm also beginning to understand why you picked one man over the other. It's Trent that's ruining us, isn't it?'

Hope sighed. 'Yes.'

'Because you won't date him?'

'Because I won't marry him.'

Kelly's face hardened. 'Well then, we'll just have to outmaneuver him, won't we?'

'We?' Hope's heart hitched.

'Yeah, we.' Kelly smiled and reached for Hope's hand. 'You, me and Clay. Together.'

Together. How she liked the sound of that.

Some time later, wild red lights flashed. Without thinking, Clay picked up Hope's phone and was met with stoic silence.

'Hello?' he repeated, wondering if this line was Hope's business line, and if he should be answering with the name of the clinic.

'I know who you are,' a gravely voice said. 'It took me a while to place your name, but I finally figured it out.'

'Who is this?'

'Your father-in-law to be,' came the caustic reply. 'I want you to get the hell out of my house.'

'This is Hope's house,' Clay said calmly, leaning back in his chair. The adrenaline of confrontation zipped through his veins. 'Or at least, it will be, until you rip it out from beneath her.'

'You make me sound criminal. I'm not the one with a hidden agenda, you are.'

'I haven't the foggiest idea what you're talking about.'

'Look,' the older man said, his tone evening out with obvious effort. 'Just tell me what you want with her. We can work this out.'

'Can we?'

'How much to back off?'

'You don't have enough.'

'Listen, Slater, she's my daughter. I don't know what your game is, or what you think you can accomplish here, but I don't want you anywhere near her. Do you understand?'

'This is no game. I'm going to marry her.'

The exceptionally rude oath that crossed the line had Clay's eyebrows lifting high.

'No. Absolutely no way will I let her go through with this,' said Broderick. 'Not marriage. Not to you.'

Clay wanted to laugh. 'But you'll let her marry that slime Blockwell? That makes sense.'

'She's my daughter. I know what's best.'

'I'm afraid it's not up to you. It's between Hope and me. And soon as possible, I'm going to give her the money to buy this house from you so you'll leave her alone.'

The ensuing insult didn't bear repeating.

'Careful,' Clay admonished. 'You don't want to insult me if you want to come over for holidays with the grandkids.'

A disparaging sound came over the wire. Then a moment of stunned, hurt silence in which Clay almost felt a little sorry for the man who was going to lose the world's greatest woman because of his own stubbornness.

Then Broderick spoke again. 'You were hired by my assistant to help me! You were supposed to help me figure out who is sabotaging the company.'

'So you do know who I am. I was wondering,' Clay said. 'You know who I am and that I'm reliable. So what's the problem with me and your daughter?'

'When I saw you yesterday, I didn't place you because we've never met. But the name . . . it drove me crazy all night. I remember now, and I'll never forget again. You took my money for the job and just disappeared.'

Now Clay did laugh. 'Yeah, I disappeared all right.'

'You were supposed to find the leak,' Broderick said slowly, angrily. 'You were supposed to find out who is double crossing me.'

'Instead, I got double crossed.'

'What are you talking about?' Broderick demanded. His voice shook more now.

Clay couldn't worry about the age in the voice, or the fact that Hope would not thank him for upsetting her father. 'Someone took the money and beat the living daylight out of me. But you know nothing about that, right?'

'No!'

'Right.' But doubt crept through Clay. Always, he'd been an excellent judge of character. And his survival tactics had been honed sharp in the military. His instincts were sharp, incredibly so. Every one of them were screaming now.

He had a bad feeling this man was telling the truth.

'I can call the police, and I will,' Hope's father said. 'But first, I want to know what you're up to. I want to know why you're toying with my daughter.'

Clay played with the cord of the phone as his mind raced. Could Broderick provide Clay with the proof he needed to nail Trent? And even if he could, would he?

'Slater?' Now the voice shook even more. 'What do you want with Hope?'

To protect her. To care for her. To love her until the end of time. 'I want to marry her.'

'But why?'

'What do you care, as long as you get that grandkid you're driving her crazy for?'

'You don't understand,' Broderick said flatly. 'You couldn't.'

'Maybe not. But I'm going to see that she doesn't have kids before she damn well wants to. And that she doesn't lose this clinic. Which is more than I can say for you.'

'She works too hard,' the older man protested. 'Not that I need to explain myself to you, but I want her to slow down, to enjoy life. She can't do that and work as hard as she is.'

'She is enjoying life.' Clay would see to it. 'But to lose this clinic would kill her, and if you cared for her like she thinks you do, you would see that.'

'I do care for her. All I ever cared about was her. She—' Broderick fell quiet for a minute. His voice weakened with what sounded to Clay like despair, and more unwilling sympathy hounded him. 'She hasn't had it easy, my Hope.'

Clay instinctively knew that. He'd change it all if he could, but it wasn't possible. 'She has survived.'

'She's promised to Trent.'

'No one can make that promise but Hope,' Clay pointed out. 'And she's promised herself to me.' Thank God. No one had to know why she'd made that promise, or even that she didn't think she would keep it. All that mattered to Clay was that she had made it, and together they would make it work.

A shaky sigh came over the line. 'I called to speak to her, not you.'

'She's busy.'

'Now who's interfering with her life?'

A wry smile touched Clay's lips. Okay, so the old man had a little more spunk than he'd given him credit for. And deep down, Clay knew the man wasn't the bad guy. But someone close to him was. 'Are you going to back off taking this place from her, or not?' he asked.

'Why are you doing this?'

'I told you. She's going to be my wife.'

A long silence. 'You're doing this so I won't keep bugging her about Trent, aren't you? You and Hope schemed this up.'

'No.'

'Why else?'

'Is it so hard to believe that I want Hope for Hope?' Now anger did surface. 'You don't give her enough credit, Broderick. She's an amazing, intelligent woman, more than capable of making her own decisions.'

'You don't understand,' her father said again, wearily. 'You couldn't. Let me speak to her.'

'Clay?'

Clay tensed at the soft, hesitant voice behind him. When he turned to face Hope, still holding the phone to his ear, he saw that nothing about her manner seemed shy or hesitant now, just her voice.

Her face was pale, her lips tight. 'Who are you talking to? Who are you telling I'm going to be your wife?'

He forced a smile and held out the phone. 'Ah . . . it's for you. It's your father.'

The frown she sent him didn't discourage him, nor did the pointed look she sent him a second later as she brought the phone to her ear. Obviously, she expected him to be polite and leave. Unfortunately for her, manners were not high on his list.

He eavesdropped unabashedly.

'Yes,' she said into the phone, waving Clay away.

Clay didn't budge.

She shoved his crossed feet off her desk.

Clay straightened and grinned at her.

Hope pulled him up out of her chair, and he went willing, standing before her, wrapping an arm around her waist and burying his face in her long, glorious hair.

She smelled heavenly.

Then she pushed at his chest and gestured to the door.

Clay grinned again and shook his head, bending to taste her neck. *Mmmm, she tasted as heavenly as she smelled.*

Once again, she pushed him, more weakly now, and shot him a look that would have withered any other man.

He bent again, opening his lips and settling his hot tongue against her skin.

'I . . . can't discuss this now, Father,' Hope said a little breathlessly, her eyes closing.

Clay kept grinning, even as he tasted her, knowing that the satisfaction he gained from her wildly racing pulse was pure ego, but he couldn't help it.

'You know I can't,' she said into the phone, turning her back to Clay and stomping her foot for emphasis. 'I'm working . . . yes, I know . . . no, I won't consider giving Trent more time. I'm so sorry if that hurts your feelings.'

Clay snorted, then perked up his ears when Hope said, 'Actually, if you're going to push, you should know, I was just being polite. I think Trent isn't worthy of you or your business, and if you were smart, you'd kick him out.'

Clay wanted to see her expression. Needed to see her expression. Especially since she was standing tall and firm and making him so damn proud he wanted to kiss her. Gently, he settled his hands at her waist and turned her around.

She didn't look at him, just plucked at the fingers he'd wrapped high on her ribs.

He didn't budge them and she gave up. 'I have no idea what you or anyone else sees in him,' she said into the phone, avoiding Clay's gaze. 'I really don't.'

She listened for a minute, then paled. 'I realize you can take this place away from me, Father. You've made that very clear.'

Clay dropped his hands from her waist, unable to continue teasing her in the face of her silent despair. His amusement completely vanished. Hope's expression never changed, she didn't move a muscle, yet he knew . . . he could feel her restlessness, her growing panic.

He reached for her hand, enlightened when she squeezed his fingers.

'I'll find another place to practise,' she said with a sweet dignity that tugged at his heart. He fisted his free hand and struggled to remain silent. She would find another place. He'd help her.

'You met him yesterday, remember?' she said into the phone, glancing at Clay. 'We talked about this – '

Hope's unfocused gaze remained on Clay and narrowed. 'I see,' she said quietly. She dropped his hand, crossed her arms over her chest in a gesture he recognized as self-defense.

'Yes, I do see now,' she said. 'Clay said all that to you, did he?'

Clay squirmed under the intense look, but didn't back

down. He couldn't let her father talk her out of this. They were going to be married. And if he had to convince this lovely, very stubborn woman that they were meant to be together, than so be it.

He could do it.

He had to believe that.

But he'd underestimated her, he realized a second later when Hope took a deep breath and said, 'I'm sorry you're unhappy about this. But I've made my decision.' Staring directly into Clay's eyes, she said, 'I'm going to marry Clayton Slater.'

Clay knew at that moment she'd been backed to a corner, was simply scrambling to avoid her father's plans involving Trent, but it didn't matter.

How could he resent what had gotten him the woman of his dreams?

Then he realized she'd hung up.

They stared at each other.

'Why did you answer my phone?' she asked finally, trying unsuccessfully to harden herself to that devastating charm he exuded so easily.

He shrugged those wide shoulders and gave her a smile meant to apologize, but she wasn't fooled – Clayton Slater was not sorry.

'You upset him.'

'And he upset you.'

Hard to deny the truth, she thought, and took a deep breath. 'He's my father, Clay.'

His eyes went hard. 'Still doesn't have the right to hurt you. He won't again, if I have my way.'

'My hero?' Her heart gave a little treacherous lurch.

To have someone unquestionably on her side . . . it felt too good.

And she didn't trust it, or him.

'Well,' he drew out the word as he moved close, letting her feel his body heat. 'I'm missing the white horse, but I am at your service.' He reached out and swept her hair from her face, then cupped her cheek in his hand.

'I've never touched a woman like this,' he murmured. 'I've never wanted to. Before you.'

'How do you know?' she asked, moved despite herself. Damn her heart, it raced uncontrollably at his simple, sweet touch.

'I just do. You're so soft, so pale,' he said, trailing his fingers down her cheek and caressing her jaw, tilting her head up. 'So fragile – '

'I'm not fragile.'

'– Yet,' he continued patiently, 'you're the strongest woman I know.'

'I'm also the only woman you know.' With a wry smile, she pushed his hand from her. Immediately, she felt the loss.

A slow smile split his features and he slipped those magical hands in his pockets. 'True enough.'

That smile. It would be the end of her. 'I've got to go back to the clinic.'

'You need a break.'

He studied her as if he never planned to stop. He didn't move, and he certainly didn't tell her, but she felt the stress in him as if it were a part of her. The rigidness of his square jaw, the tension in his neck and shoulders, the secrets in his gaze, all confirmed it.

Something had changed. Suddenly the air crackled with tension, and she didn't understand it.

'What is it?' she asked, even as it came to her. She didn't need to see the raw hunger in his dark gaze to know . . . she could just feel it.

He wanted her.

She wanted him just as badly.

Silent, his hot gaze on hers, he sank to the closest chair, pulling her to him gently – far too gently for a man with such power. 'You already know what's wrong,' he breathed. One easy tug and she landed in his lap. 'I want you.'

She would speak, but she discovered one had to be able to breathe to talk, and breathing was completely out of the question with her bottom snuggled up to the hard, hot part of him she'd dreamed about all night long.

Settling her closer to him, he leaned forward and filled her mouth with his tongue and his hands with her flesh. He cupped her bottom and shifted her over him, over the heat between his legs, making her gasp.

Lifting his head, the fingers of one hand traced her jaw. 'That's what just being close to you does to me,' he told her in a voice gone gravely with need.

With a touch as hot as the charged air around them, he kissed her again. 'You want me back, I feel it,' he said.

Hard to deny that when his fingers grazed her nipples, finding them already tight and pebbly.

'Let me help you forget, Hope,' he whispered, staring deep into her eyes. His thumbs continued to deliver glancing, teasing blows to the tips of her breasts. Heat pooled between her legs, the legs that were draped over his long, hard ones.

'Forget?' With difficulty, she focused on his face. 'Forget my father, my past?'

'Yeah.'

'But it's your past that's been forgotten.'

'It's your past that should have been forgotten.' He kissed her. 'You're beautiful, Hope. The people around here will realize that sooner or later.'

His breath had gone raspy, labored, as he watched the movement of his fingers on her breasts. Her eyes drifted closed as the most incredibly erotic sensations washed over her.

Then he stopped and her eyes flew open. The minute she looked at him, he continued to touch her. 'Forget everything but me,' he said in that emotion-roughened voice. 'Forget everything but what I make you feel.'

It would be so easy, so very easy to give in to that deep, sexy voice, to give in to those talented, knowing fingers that even now were working her into a fevered pitch.

'I can't just forget,' she managed. 'It matters, my life matters.'

'Exactly.' Fastening his mouth on her neck, he nuzzled his way to her ear before focusing that hot gaze on hers. 'So you can't always hear. So you sometimes sense things others don't. You're still a person, Hope. A very lovely, very special person. If they don't see that, forget them. Besides, you have me, and I'll never turn from you. Never.'

His words, softly spoken, but underlined with a steely strength, shot straight through to the core of her. Her throat tightened, and she reached up to take hold of his hands. 'You really have forgiven me about . . . about lying to you?'

Those emerald eyes darkened to nearly black as he looked at her, and in that moment, she didn't even need the words – she just knew.

He had forgiven her.

'I love you,' he said in a velvety voice that thrilled. 'I'll always forgive you.' His eyes deepened, held hers. 'Could I say the same about you?'

Was he asking her if she loved him? Or did he mean he'd lied, too, and that he needed forgiveness?

'Never mind,' he said, touching her lips.

As he said that, Hope felt something, something that had been nagging at her all day. She just hadn't been able to put words to it. Her feelings worked that way sometimes, and it frustrated her.

Yet this one wouldn't go away, something was wrong. If not wrong exactly, then a little off. Was he hiding something? 'Clay, I really think you should get checked out by a neurologist.'

'No,' he said flatly.

'But your memory – '

'– Is coming back, slowly but surely.' He looked at her, but didn't quite meet her gaze. 'Time is all I need, Hope.'

He was hiding something from her, but what, she couldn't imagine. 'Clay?'

'I'll be fine. My memory isn't what I want to talk about.'

'What then?'

'You asked me if I forgive you. I want you to know I

do,' he said in a deep voice, bending his head to kiss her fingers. 'Unconditionally. I don't want you to worry about it any more. It's over.

Her strange sense of unease increased and she untangled herself from him, looking down at him.

Those eyes she loved met hers, but they flickered with secrets. 'Is there something wrong?' she asked.

'What would be wrong?'

She could think of a thousand things, and did as she backed to the door, determined not to give in to the crazy sensual haze that surrounded them. 'I don't know. Something. I feel it.' Behind her, she fumbled with the door handle.

He watched her movements with silence. 'No. Nothing is wrong,' he said finally.

But there was.

He was keeping something from her. She just couldn't imagine what.

CHAPTER 22

Though most of his elation had died, to be replaced by unaccustomed nerves, Trent dialed. While the phone rang in his ear, his fingers drummed impatiently against his desk. *Answer, dammit, answer*.

His Hope hadn't caved, though he knew she had to be desperate. Where was her strength coming from? That bastard that was sharing her bed? His fist curled.

'Answer the phone, Kelly,' he whispered harshly.

When she did, he sagged in relief. 'How many today?' he demanded, gripping the phone hard. He had to gain some control back, an impossible feat with so much on the line. 'Dammit, how many?'

'None.'

'Good.' Slowly he let out his breath. 'Okay. What I want you to do is quit. That'll show her she has no one. No one but me.'

'No.'

'No?' he asked in a dangerously soft voice. 'No one tells me no.'

'I just did,' said Kelly. 'I've answered your questions, Trent. And I took this job when you pointed it out to me, but I'm drawing the line here. No more information, and no more calls, or you'll be sorry.'

'You're giving me ultimatums?' He couldn't believe it.

'I'm just asking you to leave me alone. Leave Hope alone. She doesn't deserve this.'

'I'll decide what she deserves. You're finished, Kelly. You're as finished as she is.'

Kelly hung up the phone and closed her eyes, shaking a little in spite of her bravado. He wouldn't scare her off, she promised herself. She wouldn't allow it.

'Who was that?' Hope asked as she came into the room.

Kelly's heart leaped into her throat. She glanced up and decided Hope didn't need the extra stress. Kelly had screwed up, but she wouldn't again. She forced a smile. 'Wrong number.'

Restless in spite of the late hour, Clay walked. The woods were beautiful, even at night. Beautiful and dark and alive with haunting intensity. Like his Hope. He came to the edge of the clearing behind the huge house and stopped.

He could see Hope, sitting quietly on the back porch. Squinting in the dark, he tried to gauge her mood, and couldn't. But given the hard set of her shoulders and the impossibly straight spine, he didn't figure she was relaxed, or happy.

His fault, dammit. She'd sensed that he was hiding something from her, and he was.

He was hiding his memory. But the fear of telling her now, and having her back out of their agreement terrified him.

He needed more time with her, more time to prove there was room in her life for love. That he wanted to love her. For some reason, she thought no one could, but he did.

Helplessly.

Silently, he moved closer. The moon above glowed white, bathing the porch in a soft glow.

In and around Hope's lap sat three black cats, and he saw her stroke each one in turn. At her feet lay Molly. Slightly behind her, in their cage, were Fric and Frac. By some miracle, they were silent. Probably sleeping, he thought, because he didn't believe for one minute that they could be quiet by choice.

As he moved closer, his eyes were drawn to Hope, and her face. She seemed drawn and tight. Full of worry, fear . . . loneliness. It was that last that got to him.

She'd surrounded herself with comfort, and it hadn't been him.

Suddenly her head whipped up, her eyes staring unfocused into the dark night. An instant later, Molly stirred and lifted her head, looking right at him.

They sensed him.

'It's just me,' he said, stepping closer and stopping below Hope's feet. Squatting on the step below her, Clay looked right into her eyes. 'I can't stop thinking about you.'

Something flickered in that dark gaze, then was gone. She turned her head and studied the night. 'Since you have little else to think about, I'm not surprised.'

Stepping over Molly, he sat on the step next to her,

cupping her cheek until she looked at him. In the dark, she squinted to see his lips.

'It has nothing to do with not being able to remember anything,' he told her slowly, pausing while that sank in to her thick head. 'It's you.'

He knew by the look on her face that she didn't know whether to believe him or not. He felt the doubt like a blow to his chest and he found himself rubbing there to try to ease the ache.

Reaching for her hand, he looked into her eyes. 'This is very new to me,' he admitted, striving to make her understand this was the truth. 'Brand new.'

'What is?'

'Caring so much about someone.' He glanced at the animals that surrounded her. 'Wanting you so badly as to be willing to accept just about anything. Even six animals.'

She hesitated, soaking in the words. Then she smiled and it dazzled him. His heart stuttered.

'Seven,' she said, her dark eyes sparkling like black diamonds.

'What?'

'Seven animals, not six.' Lifting her arm, she pointed behind her and he craned his neck around, watching in stunned awe as a raccoon waddled onto the porch and stopped suddenly. He held something in his arms.

'Homer,' he whispered with a smile as the black-eyed bandit lifted his head and sniffed at the air. His entire body wiggled as his nose worked.

Huey, Dewey and Louie beat a hasty retreat. Fric and Frac flapped their wings noisily, but didn't speak, thank goodness. Molly growled low in her throat, lifting her head. Hope quickly put a hand on Molly's head and whispered, 'Stay.'

Homer had frozen at the small movements of the cats, but now he stared right at Hope, his nose working frantically. His huge eyes glowed with intelligence. Cradling his treasures, he moved closer to a bowl of water.

After another watchful minute, the raccoon dumped his armful at his feet. Snails rolled everywhere. Then he bent and held one up, holding it high in the pale moonlight. Inspecting the shell carefully with its tiny hands, Homer then dunked the snail into the water.

'Watch,' Hope whispered to Clay with a smile.

To see that smile again, Clay would have watched anything. Almost reluctantly, he turned to Homer. Meticulously, the raccoon scrubbed the snail in the water for several minutes before lifting it to his mouth and sucking the poor snail right out of its shell with a soft pop.

Clay shivered in distaste. Hope just watched, clearly fascinated, making him smile. A doctor through and through, he thought, knowing very little in the way of blood or guts disturbed her.

Chewing and swallowing, the raccoon carefully set the now empty shell down by his feet and lifted the next unsuspecting snail.

Not three minutes later, Homer set down the fifth empty shell in a perfect line. One rolled out of place and with a serious, intent look on his little furry face, Homer replaced it.

Clay could almost hear the animal's gratified sigh and wouldn't have been surprised to see Homer pat his belly in fulfilled contentment.

With an expectation Clay didn't understand, Homer turned to Hope, lifted his head and sniffed.

From her pocket, Hope drew something out and tossed it down to the raccoon.

Homer grabbed it, held it up to the moonlight.

A cube of sugar.

If raccoons could smile, this one did.

With greed, Homer turned and dipped the cube into his water bowl, prepared to wash it as meticulously as he had the snails. But in less than ten seconds, the raccoon lifted up his empty hands, looking perplexed. With a sound of disbelief that nearly had Clay laughing out loud, Homer picked up the bowl of water and looked under it.

Nothing.

Homer dipped his hands back into the water, searching. Still nothing.

The sugar had disintegrated.

In front of Clay, Hope made a sound. He looked at her in surprise, then nearly did a double take.

She had her hand over her mouth. Her shoulders shook as she giggled again. A rare sound indeed, and a precious one.

That glorious thick hair shimmered with the moon's glow, her eyes landed on his and for once, they were mercifully free of clouded trouble.

Light as a bird suddenly, Clay smiled back.

Homer turned to them and let out a stream of chatter,

then disappeared off the porch and into the night.

'That's a nasty trick,' Clay said with a laugh and a shake of his head. 'I can't believe you did that to him, Dr Broderick.'

'I'm just getting him back for wiping out my sunflowers.' Hope straightened, dragged a deep breath into her lungs when Clay turned to her.

His voice had been full of laughter, but his eyes were quite full of something else entirely. A hunger she knew matched her own, a deep yearning that went far deeper than the physical needs they shared.

'About before, Hope.'

When he said her name like that, she could almost believe she was the only woman for him. How she'd love to toss all pretenses aside and tell him she'd fallen for her own lies.

That she loved him.

But the sad truth of it was she'd fallen for a man who she'd tricked into thinking he loved her.

'We don't have to talk about it,' she said, taking the coward's way out.

'I think we should.'

She sighed and stared at the trees lining her property. She really had no idea why he'd agreed to marry her, but she was thankful, for as long as it could last. With Clay at her side, she felt safer somehow. As if she could handle just about anything that came her way, including the loss of her clinic.

But he would realize the truth soon enough – that he didn't really love her. He'd leave and her life would be . . . empty.

Completely empty.

She sneaked a peek at him and her breath caught. Profiled, with the silvery evening's light playing over his face, the smile playing about his lips made her ache. All the more when she realized he was smiling – *smiling* – down at Molly, and that the big dog had plopped her head right into his lap.

His big hand raised and stroked down the dog's back. Molly groaned and wiggled, begging for more. Clay gave it and Hope was lost.

He caught her watching him. 'What?'

'You've changed,' she whispered. 'You're touching Molly and not grumbling about her being under your feet.'

'Maybe because Fric and Frac aren't repeating my every word,' he said wryly. 'And I don't have to threaten to bar-b-que them to get them to be quiet.'

'You have changed,' she insisted.

His hand stilled on the dog. 'I know. Because of you.'

She denied that with a shake of her head.

'It's true,' he insisted. 'I wanted to talk to you – '

'It's not necessary,' she said quickly.

'It's not?' He looked puzzled. 'How do you know what I was going to say?'

'I didn't, I just – '

'Hope,' he said with a secret little smile. 'Let me finish. Please?'

She nodded and bit her tongue, mentally preparing herself for the blow of his leaving.

'Since we don't really have a history together – '

She winced, but didn't say a word. Yes, he was

leaving. But she'd survive. She'd been alone before. Without meaning to, she squeezed Molly until the poor dog grunted.

'It occurred to me,' he said, 'that I never really courted you.'

And just because she'd finally responded to a man didn't mean he had to be the one. After she found a way to get Trent off her back, she could find another. One that didn't have emerald green eyes that – '*Wait*. What did you say?' Her voice squeaked in a high pitch that made even Molly wince.

Clay didn't blink. Patiently he said again, 'I never courted you. Properly, that is.'

Courted – an old-fashioned out-dated word. A lovely word.

It was the last thing she expected him to say. 'Because of my lies.'

'However it came to be,' he said lightly, refusing to give in to her dark tone. 'We're engaged to be married after only knowing each other one week.'

Here it came. Her every muscle tensed. Without realizing it, she closed her eyes. She told her pounding heart it would recover. She wouldn't die of a broken heart, she just wouldn't.

She was a doctor, she knew these things.

Clay shifted closer, until their hips brushed together. Light fingers stroked her cheek, then cupped her face and she knew he was waiting for her to open her eyes, which she did reluctantly.

'I thought maybe we could fix that.' He smiled gently and she felt like crying.

'Okay,' she whispered. Maybe she could convince him to stay somehow, maybe –

'I want to take you out,' he said.

'What?'

'Out.' Another smile curved his lips. 'Like on a date. I've sorely neglected wooing you, Hope. What do you think? Dinner and a movie? Or is that too bland for you?'

'A . . . date.'

'Yeah.' His gaze searched her face. His grin faded. 'What did you think I wanted to tell you?'

She bit her lip. 'Uh . . .'

His fingers ran over her face lightly, gently. His eyes went somber. 'I can tell by the look on your face a date wasn't what you expected.'

'No,' she said with a choked laugh. 'It wasn't.'

'What did you expect, Hope?'

Leaping to her feet, she dislodged Molly, who grunted again, shot both humans a dirty look and stalked off.

'My phone's ringing,' Hope said as Clay surged to his feet beside her.

'No, it's not – ' He sighed and shook his head as the phone rang and a red light over the porch light went off.

She shot him a self-conscious smile.

'I'll never get used to that,' he muttered as she moved past him and into the kitchen.

By the time he'd followed her into the darkened kitchen, Clay thought Hope had already disappeared. Then his eyes adjusted, and he saw her, standing by the telephone.

'Hope?'

She just stared at him. He flipped on the light so she

could see him. As she blinked at the sudden flood of light, he said her name softly.

Flashing him a smile he knew was forced, she lifted her shoulders in a shrug. 'Wrong number.'

'Is that what they said?'

Silence.

'Hope?'

'No. They hung up. But of course that's what they meant, they were just embarrassed.'

He might have bought that, if she did. But she didn't and he knew it. 'Who was it, Hope?'

'I don't know.' She wrapped her arms around her middle and stared at the phone, her eyes wide as saucers.

'It's nearly midnight,' he pointed out, and stepped closer to her.

'Are you trying to scare me?' she asked shakily. 'Because you're doing a fine job of it.'

He placed his hands at her waist and pulled gently. That she came without hesitation had his heart skipping a beat.

So did the terror in her eyes.

'Trent?' he asked.

'Probably,' she whispered.

'He's not going to hurt you again.' His hands ran up her slim back and pulled her close.

Her hands slipped up his chest and around his neck. Clinging, she buried her face in his neck and inhaled sharply.

'He's not, Hope.'

'You sound so sure.'

'I am,' he said grimly, staring over her head and out the kitchen window into the black night. He'd put his life before hers.

He knew that he just might get that chance.

While Hope spent the next day in the clinic, seeing the few patients that trickled in, Clay worked fervently on her computer, putting himself to work on the job he couldn't get out of his mind – the last one.

The one which had almost cost him his life. The one that had given him the love of his life.

By lunch time, he'd made a disturbing discovery.

Over the past five years, Hope's father had made some very unstable investments. So unstable he'd borrowed repeatedly from no other than Trent Blockwell. According to the financials Clay accessed, Broderick was the closest thing to broke.

He'd lost nearly everything, and what little he had left, Blockwell owned the notes on.

Leaning back in his chair, Clay stared at the computer screen in shock. How had this happened?

Did Hope know?

No. She couldn't. The bastard hadn't told her.

Clay yanked up the phone, ignoring the shooting pain in his ribs from leaning too sharply too quickly. After asking information for the number, he waited in grim silence.

When Broderick came on the line, Clay didn't waste time. 'In sorry straits, aren't you?'

'What?'

'I've been checking,' Clay said softly, glancing at the

office door and wishing he'd shut it. He didn't want Hope to hear this.

What he heard was Broderick's slow whistle of surprised breath. 'Why am I surprised that a professional hacker checked me out?' he asked wearily.

'Why didn't you tell me when I took this job?' Clay asked. 'And how the hell did you pay me as much as you did? Not that I got to keep it.'

'Sticking to that story, are you?' Abruptly, the venom went out of Broderick's voice. 'I had you checked out, too. You're missing, you know that?'

'No kidding.' Clay let out a little laugh. 'Thanks to your goons. What I want to know is, why haven't you had them come for me here, now that you know where I am?'

'I've decided to believe you,' Broderick said quietly. 'I don't expect you to believe me, of course. But I believe you. I believe that someone attacked you, that someone wanted you out of the picture. I believe this,' he added, 'because of the mess I've gotten myself in.'

Clay tapped a pencil against the computer as his thoughts raced. 'Are you telling me that you had nothing to do with what happened to me?'

'Yes.'

'And that you're in as much trouble as I think you are?'

'Yes.'

Clay sighed. 'Why in the world do I believe this?'

'Because it's the truth,' the older man said. 'I know how bad it looks, with all the memos and press releases in my name. But as good as you are, surely you've discovered something to implicate someone else as well.'

'You're broke,' Clay pointed out. 'You could be desperate.'

'True. But it wasn't me.'

'Then why would you allow this?' Clay demanded. 'Why wouldn't you put a stop to it all with just your own word?'

Silence.

'You owe everything to Blockwell,' Clay said. 'Yet the business remains in your name. Why is that?'

More silence.

It hit Clay like a punch to the gut. 'Blackmail,' he whispered. He didn't need the following silence for confirmation.

'It's blackmail.'

'Slater – '

'Isn't it?'

'Yes,' he whispered brokenly. 'I was counting on you for proof.'

'I swear,' Clay broke in savagely, 'if you bring any of this to Hope, if she gets hurt in any way because of your stupidity, I'll – '

'Don't you realize I think of that every spare second of the day? I – ' The older man's voice broke.

At the sound, Clay had to lean back in his chair and shut his eyes hard. He rubbed them with his fingers while he waited for Hope's father to compose himself, but his gut churned at the pain and regret he heard in the man's voice.

'This won't touch her,' Broderick vowed. 'I won't let it.'

'You won't have a choice,' Clay said grimly, fingering

the bandage covering his ribs. 'You're playing with some pretty big boys. I've felt their revenge, remember?' He felt sick, thinking about Hope somehow getting caught up in this.

Trent.

She already was caught up in this.

'Tell me it's not Blockwell,' Clay begged.

No answer.

'Dammit.' Clay let out a shaky sigh. 'It is.' Then dark fury overcame him. 'You pushed that bastard on her, pushed her over and over, even knowing what he was capable of.' It made him so furious he nearly couldn't speak. 'You son-of-a – '

'– It was the only way to make sure she stayed away from him, given how badly he wanted her.'

'What?'

Broderick let out a shaky breath. 'I know my own daughter, Slater, despite what you think of me. And I knew that all I had to do was push Blockwell on her, hard, and she'd stay away from him like the plague. Hope hates to be pushed. Always did.'

Unbelievable. 'You took a hell of a chance,' Clay managed angrily.

'No,' he said flatly. 'Never again.'

'What does that mean?'

'It means I took a chance with her, once. And I'll never do it again. But that was a long time ago. When Blockwell demanded he have her, I knew the only way to keep her safe was to push her, and push her hard. It worked,' he said triumphantly. 'It was the only thing I could count on.'

'It's not over,' Clay said grimly. 'He hasn't given up yet.'

'I know,' he whispered desperately.

'Does Hope know you're broke? That you owe Trent everything, including most of the business?'

'No. She can't,' the old man said quickly. 'You can't tell her. She'll make herself sick with worry. She'll do anything for me, Slater. Anything. Even – '

'– Even sacrifice herself. I won't tell her,' Clay promised, knowing what her father said was true. If Hope thought her father needed her . . . This had gone from a bad dream to a living nightmare.

'I don't like you,' Broderick blurted out. 'But I have to trust you. I don't have a choice. Keep her safe. Promise me you will.'

'I'll keep her safe,' Clay snapped, his heart sinking like a lead weight. He would, but at what cost? By continuing to keep his memory a secret, he was betraying her.

'I didn't want to fail her. Not again.'

Every muscle tensed. 'What do you mean, "not again"?'

Hope's father was silent so long, Clay didn't think he would answer. Then, when he did, Clay almost wished he hadn't.

'Her mother died when she was only five,' Broderick said finally.

'I know. I'm . . . sorry.'

'I worked like a dog afterward. Had to. Work was everything. Everything,' he added bitterly. 'I used it to forget my own pain, and in the meantime, I forgot about my daughter's pain. Never thought about her needs other than to make sure she had daycare.'

Clay drew a deep breath. 'It must have been a difficult time.'

'I neglected her.'

No wonder she was do damned independent. 'She wouldn't see it that way.'

'To drown my own selfish pain, I worked. And worked. I ran this business twenty-four hours a day, it was all I allowed myself to think about.'

He didn't like where this was going. 'And Hope?'

'I left her in the care of others,' he said hoarsely.

'Others?'

'Yeah.'

Then Broderick went silent a moment, leaving Clay far too much time to think, to worry. At the thought of all that could have happened, a chill ran up his spine, yet sweat pooled at the base of it.

'The nannies kept quitting,' Broderick said. 'Too long hours, they complained. I'd just hire another one and forget about it. It was the easiest thing to do. If I thought too much, looked at her too long, it all came back to me, the pain, the sorrow. She looks just like her mother,' he whispered on a shaky sigh.

'What happened, Broderick?'

'For a while I just kept hiring every time one quit . . . I didn't always check the references.'

The raw pain came clearly over the telephone line, and transferred itself directly into Clay's heart. 'What happened to Hope?' he demanded.

'I hired someone over the telephone. Didn't even bother to meet her first.'

Self-disgust was evident, but Clay couldn't feel pity. Not with his heart in his throat. 'Tell me, dammit.'

'She hit Hope. Over and over. Boxed her ears,' Broderick choked out bitterly. 'It's why she can't hear. It's all my fault.'

CHAPTER 23

Clay had no idea how long he sat there after he hung up from Hope's father, staring blindly at the computer.

Hope had been hurt, badly, and there was nothing he could do but feel the pain of it.

A soft whine at his side stirred him. The warm, soft nose Molly pushed into his palm had him turning to the dog. Without hesitation, he opened his arms and the big black dog jumped into his lap. Ribs screaming, Clay wrapped his arms around her and hugged tight.

But the image of a young Hope, helpless against abuse, refused to leave him.

'Molly,' he whispered hoarsely. 'The way she suffered... I can't stand it.'

Molly whined softly and licked his face. Then, at the salty tracks she found there, she licked again and again. Clay closed his eyes and let her, for the first time in years turning to an animal for comfort, for love.

It felt good.

But he straightened and forced his aching bones into a stand.

Molly cocked her head and stared at him, her tongue hanging out the side of her mouth.

'I'm going to make it all better,' he reassured the dog. 'I can't take away the past, or her painful memories. But I can make her happy. I know I can.'

Molly barked her agreement.

Clay smiled. Yeah, he could make her happy.

He'd start slow, with that date he'd promised her. No more pushing. Hope had had a lifetime of that, and he intended to make sure it never happened again. No pushing, no cajoling.

No, she needed more care than that.

He was going to woo her right into the only safe place he could think of.

His arms.

While Hope worked, Clay walked. And walked. An incoming storm darkened the late afternoon sky, matching his mood.

As the sky churned and went black, Clay pushed himself, pushed and pushed until his mind went blank with exhaustion.

He had never suffered the indignity of having a parent who'd ignored him. His parents loved him wildly, they'd showered affection and attention on their only child with carefree abandon. He'd never doubted their love. Sure, they might have never fully understood him, or what he was capable of, but they'd never physically hurt him, or caused him to be hurt. He'd always been safe, as a child should be.

But Hope . . . Hope had suffered so much. Without

her mother, and with a father who had given himself up to work, she'd been truly alone.

And when the one person she should have been able to trust – her nanny – had hurt her, she'd had no one to tell. She'd been only five years old.

Practically a baby.

His hands fisted and he walked faster. The foliage along the creek crunched beneath his feet. The water crashed over rocks and plants. The sky above grew darker as the day came to an end.

Still he walked. He had to get rid of some of this anger, some of this terrible emotion swirling inside of him, before he faced Hope.

If he didn't, she'd take one look at him and know something was wrong.

He couldn't tell her about his memory, especially now.

He knew enough about her to know Broderick spoke the truth – she would go running to her father's side to help. She'd give herself to Trent.

And then Clay would have to kill him.

He sighed and stopped. Everything hurt, his legs, his ribs, his head. A big drop of rain splattered on his face. Then another. Then the sky let loose.

For a minute, he just stood there beneath the downpour, his mind locked on the image of Hope, and how she'd looked when she'd first admitted to him that she couldn't hear well.

She'd looked as if she expected him to scorn her, or at the very least, to desert her. He couldn't even imagine what she'd suffered in all these years.

He wanted, ridiculously, to race back to the house,

draw Hope in his arms and never let go. He wanted to protect her from any more hurt.

But she didn't need that. She'd resent that.

She'd learned long ago to rely on no one but herself, and she'd come so far, so very damned far. She'd succeeded, despite the huge obstacles in her way . . . and now she was a doctor, caring for others. She collected animals no one else wanted and loved them as her own. She gave room and board to a complete stranger who needed medical care and a place to stay.

His throat thickened at all she'd done.

In return, he'd doubted her, lied to her, and now, he'd hidden things from her. He could only hope she'd forgive him when the time came.

It took him half an hour to make his way back to the house, and by the time he did, he was drenched through to his soggy skin. Standing in the kitchen, dripping on the floor, he shivered.

'Wet!'

Clay jumped at the sharp, unexpected voice, then glared at Fric and Frac. 'No kidding.'

Molly padded into the room and came right up to him, lifting her face to be petted.

Absently, Clay rested his hand on the big head.

The house was unusually silent, except for the soft drone of water hitting the roof. He didn't like the feel of it, and before he changed, he decided he would just check and make sure Hope was okay.

The clinic was dark, empty, and a glance at his watch told Clay he'd been gone longer than he'd thought. When he'd left for his walk, Kelly had still been here.

She was gone now.

And he couldn't find Hope.

'Molly,' he said urgently to the dog following him through his search. 'Find Hope, girl. Please, help me find her.'

The dog barked and took off.

So did Clay's heart.

In the darkened clinic, Hope moved from room to room, running her fingers over her equipment.

She loved this place, loved what she had done.

Here, for the first time in her life, she felt important. She helped people, really helped them. And they let her.

Jumping up on the X-ray table in the dark lab, she leaned back against the machine, closed her eyes and sighed. Two patients today.

Trent had told her he would ruin her unless she gave in, and he meant to make good on that threat.

He hadn't called, but he would soon.

He'd want to know if she had changed her mind.

Suddenly, she jerked upright and opened her eyes.

Clay. He was looking for her. She felt his worry, could taste his fear.

For her.

'I'm here,' she called out into the dark room.

In seconds, the door crashed open, the overhead came on, making her squint. Before she'd adjusted her eyes to the light, she was yanked against a hard body.

A hard, wet, very cold body.

Clay. She sighed and relaxed, and he tightened his grip. She gave herself up to him, holding him as close as she could, not questioning what had brought him to her this way.

Plastered against him, his arms wrapped snugly around her, she could hear nothing. Nothing except the frantic pounding of his heart and the vibrations of his ragged breathing. She knew that most likely he was talking, but his hands tightened on her and she couldn't see his face.

Giving in to the wondrous sensations of being held by him, she burrowed in deeper, not minding the cold, the wet . . . until he shivered.

She struggled to pull back and he reluctantly let her go, only to immediately reach for her face and tip it up.

'Thank God,' he said hoarsely. 'I couldn't find you. I thought – ' He shuddered and yanked her back against him. Looking down at her, he kissed her. 'Never mind. You're safe.'

'I was right here the entire time.'

He looked at her with such softness, such heartbreaking tenderness, she felt stunned.

'You didn't hear me calling you,' he said gently. Something flickered in his gaze then was gone. Compassion? Understanding? She didn't know, but she felt . . . hugged.

'No, I didn't hear you. But I felt you.' She was doing that more and more, she realized. Feeling him, being intuned to his every move. 'Clay, why are you so wet?'

'I was walking by the creek and – '

'– You shouldn't have been out there!' Fear gripped her and she pulled him tight enough to evoke a wince from his handsome, drenched features. 'It's dangerous.'

'Hope, I was dumped there that night. Not attacked there.'

True enough, but . . . 'Did you fall in?'

He laughed, and the vibrations of that shimmied through her, bringing with it a warm, contented feeling. 'Your confidence in me needs work. No, I didn't fall into the creek. It's raining outside.'

'Oh.' She gave him a sheepish smile, but then he shivered again and her amusement fled. 'Take these clothes off.'

His grin came slow and wide. 'You got it.'

When she realized what he thought, she let out a startled little laugh. 'That's . . . not what I meant.' But his gaze was hot and settled on her mouth. Skittish, she jumped down from the table and backed to the door.

He followed her as he unbuttoned his shirt, his gaze never leaving hers as he peeled himself out of it. Slowly, he revealed the hard, wet planes of his chest, his flat, rippled abdomen, the light springy stripe of hair that disappeared into the waistband of his jeans.

Holding up a hand to ward him off, she said quickly, 'I'll . . . just go get you some dry clothes – '

The words dried up, as did her mouth when he took her waist in gentle but firm hands, backed her to the door, pressing her between wood and hard, male flesh. 'I want you.'

He did. She could feel it. 'Oh, my.'

He smiled.

Her heart leaped, missed a beat. If she lived forever, she'd never get used to this, having this man want her.

Her! Having him smile at her as if she were his entire life.

She struggled to remember this was simply pretend. It wouldn't last.

Then he backed up enough to drop his hands to the buttons on his wet jeans. 'These are wet too,' he muttered. 'Wet and far too tight.'

Hope's voice dropped to a shocked whisper. 'What?' she squeaked in sudden panic.

His fingers stilled as his gaze searched her face. 'I'm teasing you. I just want you to want me as much as I want you.'

She bit her lip. 'I do.'

He closed the distance between them. 'I want to make love to you, Hope.'

She inhaled sharply and held it.

Those strong, warm fingers ran up her arms lightly, lovingly. 'The real thing. No fake promises, no pretending . . . just you and me, lost in love.'

'Last time was real,' she said hoarsely. 'It was real for me.'

'Oh, it was,' he said, lifting a hand to her face, searching her gaze. 'But I was confused then, thinking we'd been together before, wondering why I couldn't remember something so right, so perfect.'

She felt the pale flush stain her cheeks. 'That was my fault.'

'It's over,' he said gently. 'But we're not. Let's try again, Hope.'

He held out his hand, and she stared down at it for a long, silent moment.

Slowly she tipped her head back and looked at him. His sun-kissed hair was slick with rainwater. A few drops ran down his temple, over his corded neck. His bare chest glistened, so did his jeans. Wet, they only served to outline his long, lean body. But more arresting to Hope were the swirling thoughts behind his dark green gaze. The thoughts he didn't try to hide from her. Her knees wobbled at the heart-stopping emotions, at the gut-wrenching fear.

He expected her to turn him down.

As if she could. She had no idea exactly how it had happened, but this man was part of her. No matter what the future held, she wanted to take this piece of heaven and keep it for herself. Oh, no, she wouldn't turn him down.

Taking his hand, she squeezed it, then gave him a shaky smile.

He returned it.

Wordlessly, she turned and led him from the room.

In her bedroom, she dropped his hand and turned the lamp by her bed on low. Then she stood there looking at him, her heart in her throat.

Wide and strong, his bare shoulders gleamed in the glow of the lamp. Reflected in his serious face was the need she felt so plainly on her own.

'I feel far more nervous this time,' she said, her smile suddenly gone, in its place an overwhelming amount of apprehension.

'Me too,' he admitted and went to her.

When he lifted a hand and touched her face, Hope sighed in relief. It would come now, she thought, the mindless passion, the pounding passion that would lift her up and away from reality. The incredible hunger and heat that only Clay could provoke.

She touched his arms, felt the muscles leap at her touch. She affected him. The knowledge gave her a surge of joy, of power. Of love.

She felt compelled to make him understand how much this meant to her. 'I was afraid you wouldn't want me ever again,' she admitted softly. 'Not after the lies.'

He put a finger to her lips. 'I've wanted you from that very first moment, Hope. When I looked up and saw an angel hovering over me. A dark-haired, black-eyed angel with everything she felt shimmering in her eyes.'

Hope stared at him, mesmerized, compelled, joyous . . . and doubtful. Then, cradling her face, he bent his head and brushed his lips over hers. The exquisite tenderness of the kiss, the way his fingers skimmed gently over her face, crumpled any remaining defenses she might have held on to.

He lifted his mouth long enough to murmur huskily, 'This is just the beginning. The very beginning . . .' His mouth slid over her cheek to her ear, sending shivers of anticipation down her spine. 'I'm going to love you, Hope,' he promised achingly, drawing her against his full length, shifting her back to the bed and following her down.

Hope knew it was wrong to lose herself this way, wrong to let him take off her blouse, slip off her skirt, wrong to watch with fascination as he shucked off his wet jeans, just as surely as it was wrong to trick herself into thinking this was real. 'Clay,' she managed to say weakly as his soft breath fanned her ear. 'I think we should make sure – '

He leaned over her, his arms bracketing her body. Their legs entwined. 'I am sure,' he said fiercely before his lips covered hers, parting them with familiar skill.

Clay knew the exact moment she gave herself up to him, felt some of her tension drain, felt her muscles relax enough that he could slip a thigh in between hers. The unexpected poignancy of the surrender undid him. So did the way her lips moved against his, sweetly at first, then with more confidence when she dragged a moan from deep in his throat.

Always, making love had been a pleasurable experience, but now, with Hope, it was so much more. Spellbinding, magical, exquisite . . . and for the first time in Clay's life, he felt at home within someone's arms. Hope's arms.

Badly, he wanted the future to be theirs, but he had jeopardized that. Before he could dwell on it, she entwined her fingers in his hair and pulled his head to her, as if she was afraid he'd escape. Only he had no intention of going anywhere, of doing anything other than showing her exactly how much he loved her. Using his mouth to tease and entice hers, he ran his hand down her side, over her narrow waist, past a curved hip, down her endless legs before retracing the route with tantalizing languor.

Hope moaned softly, and the sound had just enough baffled confusion he smiled and did it again. Shifting restlessly against his hands, she tried to move his hand inward.

Clay held off, not wanting to touch her there until she was mindless with need, wild for him. He wanted her as out of control as he felt every time he looked at her.

His thumb grazed the side of her breast and she whimpered. Her nipples were puckered, tight, and his mouth watered at the thought of tasting her, but he didn't. Not yet.

She tossed her head back and forth on the pillow, lost to what he was doing to her. He wanted to tell her he'd just begun, that he would drive her to the very edge of insanity before he was through, but he couldn't speak. Not with the sight of her glorious body spread out, waiting for him, yearning for him.

He rubbed the back of his knuckles lightly over her belly button.

Lifting her hips, she moaned.

The sound tugged at his slipping control, but he bit back his own needs, even as his heart thundered in his chest, as his body throbbed for her.

'Clay,' Hope gasped, reaching for his hand. 'Touch me. Please touch me.'

'I am.' To please himself, his fingers again brushed her silken thigh, coming within inches of the spot he knew by now had to be craving his touch. Her hips surged, lifted and she gasped again.

'Clay . . .'

He dragged his fingers up her other side, brushed over her hip bones. Her stomach tightened in anticipation and when he let just the pads of his fingers slide high on her ribcage, she moaned again.

'Please,' she cried, and when he didn't, she made a

frustrated sound and reached for him, curling her hand around the hot, heavy part of him dying for her. He jumped at the shock of the pleasure.

She stroked him, ran her hand down the rigid length of him until he groaned.

Freezing up, she yanked her hand back. 'I'm sorry,' she whispered, lifting her horrified gaze to his. 'Did that hurt?'

Letting out a choked laugh, he dropped his forehead to hers. 'Yes. Hurt me some more.' When she didn't relax, not even a fraction, he lifted his head, willing to beg. 'Please.'

Wide eyed, she slowly reached for him again. 'Touch me back,' she demanded, in a not very soft voice as she stroked him again.

Gently, he cupped her breast. Her breath caught in a lovely, strangled sound and she arched into him, digging her short nails into his shoulders when his fingers slowly slid over her hardened nipples.

He looked at her in awe. 'You're so lovely, Hope.' He drew one finger down the center of her. 'So incredibly lovely.' His fingers continued the trail down, down, past her flat belly . . . and into heaven.

Hope cried out and gripped him tighter. 'Clay . . .'

'I know, sweetheart,' he said, smiling tightly down into her huge eyes. Oh, how he knew. With a tantalizingly light touch, he ran a finger over the hot, damp bit of flesh that was her center, while dipping his head down and circling her nipple with his tongue.

Hope's head fell back. She panted and thrust her hips up, his name bursting from her lips.

She was going up in flames in his arms, and he was too, just from watching her. He kept touching her, just for the amazing pleasure of seeing what he could do to her. Again and again, he caressed her, sucked and teased her, until she strained desperately beneath him.

Waves of desire and affection hit him, yet even then he might have been able to continue moving slowly and steadily, driving her to the edge, if Hope hadn't chosen that moment to grab his head by the hair, drag him down to her, lift her hips and beg, 'Please, Clay. Now.'

The unbearable sweetness of her body wrapped around his, the sound of her voice, the heat in her eyes, all tore a silent groan from him.

Gone was his crazy notion he could hold back for her, that he could damp down his own needs until she caught up with him. He simply couldn't wait. All that mattered was being inside her, feeling her surround him with her velvet heat. He shifted over her, his arms trembling as he eased into her inch by inch, forcing himself to take it slow. His eyes closed as he sank full length into her, barely fighting the urge to plunge. Instead, he slowly devoured her with his body, his hands and mouth. Slowly, he stroked, once, twice, while she tossed back her head and lifted her hips.

'More,' she demanded.

He went still rather than explode.

She let out a soft moan.

Opening his eyes, he gazed down at the beautiful face that had become so much a part of him. Her dark, shiny hair spilled over them, her face was flushed with passion.

Her eyes stared up at him, nearly black with passion. And her body . . . her body.

His own body tightened, his muscles quivered with the effort to hold back. He had no idea how much longer he could, sheathed in her incredible heat. They were made for each other. This was the woman of his dreams, and some miracle had brought them here, together. Braced on his elbows, he cradled her head, touched her mouth with his. Whispering her name, he ran his lips over hers softly, overwhelmed and humbled by what she did to him.

His control slipped another notch when she sent him a watery smile and whispered, 'You feel so good filling me up. Please, Clay, love me.'

'I plan to.' He shifted within her, watched her eyes drift closed. 'Are you all right?'

'No.' She arched up, wrapped her legs around his waist.

With her opened up to him fully, his hips helplessly thrust forward. 'No?' he gasped, trying not to move, an impossible feat when he was gloved inside Hope.

But her eyes were closed.

'Dammit.' Was he hurting her? Kissing her eyelids, he waited until they fluttered open. 'You're not all right?' he grated out, the veins on his arms sticking out with the incredible effort to hold himself still.

'No. Help me, Clay,' she murmured, pulling at him. 'Please . . .'

He was lost. Just feeling her writhe and thrash beneath him and hearing her call his name were all it took. He plunged then, plunged into her, again and again, until they were both wild with wanting, needing, reaching together . . . He felt her convulse around him, shuddering, clutching him fiercely, gasping for breath. It became impossible to not respond in kind. His body exploded and he groaned, twisting his hips higher, pushing himself in deeper, shattering completely apart while she held him to her.

He knew his fingers were digging into her back, that he'd buried his face hard into her neck. Knew also that their hearts thundered out of control, that their limbs remained hopelessly tangled. But he couldn't budge, could hardly draw a breath in the aftermath of the most explosive moment of his life.

When his breathing had downgraded to outrageously labored, he shifted to his side, holding her close to him. Sliding a hand up and down her spine, he lay there, reveling in the luxury of holding her.

He smiled when he felt her lips nuzzling at his throat. Lifting a hand to her face, he pushed back her hair. What he saw shimmering in her eyes had his heart doing a slow, painful roll in his chest.

'I don't know a damn thing about you,' she whispered, staring at him. 'Not really. Nothing except your courage, your kindness, your inner strength, but maybe that's all that matters.'

He stroked a hand down her back and smiled. 'I love you, Hope.'

It would never fail to amaze her, that he was here, with her.

And he loved her.

She sighed and hugged him. The words melted her. So

did his face with those serious eyes. And that body . . . hard, long and tireless.

And all hers.

'But there's so much more than just this,' she murmured. 'Much more.'

He looked at her with laughing eyes and she was startled to realize she'd said it out loud.

She dropped her head and felt the heat flood her face.

He just grinned at her obvious embarrassment as he lifted her face, then nudged her, guiding her over so she sprawled on the top of him.

'You bet there's more,' he said.

Carefully, she braced herself high on his chest, avoiding his still bandaged ribs. She took a deep breath.

He was hard again, or still. He guided her hips. 'Lots more.'

'Clay . . .' She let out the air slowly. Her heart pounded. 'I meant, I love you.'

His hands tightened on her. Those deep emerald eyes filled with such joy it almost hurt to see, then that beloved face broke out into the sweetest most tender smile she'd ever seen.

'Thank you, God. Say it again,' he demanded, thrusting his hips up, probing and finding what he sought. He slipped into her.

Her breathless laugh ended on a moan. Dipping down until her hair fell around them in a curtain, she kissed him long and thoroughly.

'Hope,' he begged. 'Again.'

'I'm not sure what to do with all this love,' she admitted. 'But I do love you, Clay, hopelessly.'

Within her, he leaped and pulsed. Gathering her in his arms, he pulled her down on him, his eyes fierce, his smile soft. 'Let me show you what to do with it,' he whispered huskily.

CHAPTER 24

Hope sighed and plopped back in her bed, looking limp and sated and so incredibly beautiful Clay struggled to rouse enough energy to kiss her.

He stretched his pleasantly aching muscles first, then leaned over her, smiling, thinking he'd never felt so happy, so carefree.

'I'm hungry.'

Looking down at her, he let his grin widen suggestively. 'Yeah?' He dipped down and nipped at her chin.

'For food,' she squealed on a laugh, slapping her hands to his chest as he worked his way over her jaw to nibble at her lips. Her arms snaked around his neck for a quick hug that warmed his heart.

He could hold her like this forever, he decided, rolling and layering her over him, wrapping her tight in his arms.

'Feed me,' she demanded, her wild hair falling around them in a wave of dark silk.

He laughed, then sat up, watching with a mixture of pleasure and regret as she slipped on his t-shirt. 'It's a crime to cover that body up.'

For a minute, she just looked at him, embarrassment and joy mingling on her face. 'You need glasses,' she told him. 'I'm too skinny in most places and far too curvy in all the others.'

Yanking on sweat bottoms, he grabbed her waist and tugged her close. 'Everything is just right,' he assured her, rocking his hips to hers. 'And if you need a demonstration of that, I'd be happy to –'

'I believe you!'

He could tell by her lovely blush she did, so he led her down the stairs and into the kitchen where they dined on donuts dunked in milk as if it were the greatest gourmet feast.

Molly sat patiently on the floor between them, her gaze never leaving their plate. Clay tossed a bite to her and watched Hope stuff the last bite of a chocolate donut into her mouth.

Slowly, her eyes closed. 'Mmm,' she sighed, licking her lips and fingers.

Lust speared through Clay. 'Eating like that should be a sin,' he said thickly, standing and moving to her.

Laughing, she held up a hand and rose out of her chair, backing to the refrigerator as he stalked her. 'Clay,' she said around a giggle when she tripped over her own two feet.

He smiled at the sound of her laughter, and kept after her.

'We've ravaged each other for hours now. Hours!' Not that she was complaining. Far from it, she thought, as even now, a hot tug of yearning made her legs wobble.

Clay snagged her hips in his large hands and sandwiched her between the cool steel door and his own hot, solid body. 'And your point is?' he murmured, lowering his head.

'My point is . . .' she said, then moaned when his open mouth nuzzled up and down her neck and his hands streaked under the t-shirt to knead and squeeze her bottom. 'Oh, my!'

'The point?' he repeated, lifting his head with a challenging gaze. 'You had a point.'

'Yes, I did,' she said primly, then dissolved into helpless laughter when those amazing fingers of his snaked up and jabbed lightly at her ribs.

'Come on, Doctor,' he teased, tickling her mercilessly. 'Think.'

'Stop it!' she screamed with laughter.

He stilled. 'I love it when you do that,' he whispered.

'What?' Confused, smiling, she looked at his mouth, thinking it was the most sexy mouth she'd ever seen.

'I love it when you laugh.' His eyes darkened with an overwhelming intensity that stole her breath. 'I love everything about you. Remember that, Hope. Promise me you will.'

'Of course I will – '

In the next heartbeat he was kissing her as if he thought she'd disappear if he let go. Then what little clothing they'd put on came flying off, sailing in all directions in the kitchen.

Molly took one look at them and slunk out of the room.

Clay cleared the counter of the few dishes by shoving them into the sink with one swipe of his hand. Lifting her to the tile, he spread her thighs and came flush up to her body. 'I want you again,' he said, his expression fierce, his voice thick. 'Say you want me back.'

But his hands were on her and she couldn't think, much less speak.

'Say it,' he demanded, his fingers between her legs, teasing her until she arched up against him. 'Please, Hope, say it.'

'I – ' All she could do was moan helplessly when he dropped to his knees, threw her legs over his shoulders and replaced his hand with his mouth. She was on the edge, quivering helplessly, chanting his name mindlessly as she gripped the tile to keep from falling.

She had to have him inside her.

'Now,' she cried, grabbing his head by the hair and pulling him back up to her. 'Clay. Now!'

He thrust into her, making them both groan with pleasure, with unbearable need.

Then he stopped.

She knew what he waited for. 'I want you,' she sobbed, then grabbed onto his sleek, wide shoulders, buried her face into his neck and let him shatter her.

Afterwards, staggering with exhaustion, they tumbled into Hope's bed. Together.

As if they'd been doing it for years, Clay pulled her close, tucked her against him and wrapped his arms around her. The weight of his arm over her felt warm and securing, his long, powerful legs against the back of hers made Hope feel soft, feminine.

Wanted.

She'd never felt so cherished.

It felt so right it terrified her. And Clay felt so good, so safe and warm and hers, she wanted to wrap herself around him and never let go.

Maybe, just maybe . . . they could make this work. Maybe it didn't have to be a fantasy. She could love and be loved, for exactly who she was.

When the dark thoughts and doubts would have swamped her, she forced them back. Forced them back with the love that Clay had showered on her.

As she drifted off, he kissed her ear, hugged her tight and murmured softly. She felt the vibration of his chest in the dark room and she knew . . . He'd just told her he loved her.

She loved him too, more than she would have dreamed possible.

Nudged from sleep by a sound somewhere in the house, Clay came instantly awake. Grinning in anticipation, he reached for the woman who loved him. For Hope.

His hands came up empty.

She was gone, and by the coolness of the sheets, she'd been gone for some time.

Yanking off the covers, he stepped out of bed and onto Molly's head. She stared at him balefully while he swore, apologized and hopped into his jeans.

'Thanks for waking me when Hope got up,' he said sarcastically to the black dog, who just yawned and looked away.

Clay's gaze settled on the rumpled bed. 'It's early. Where is she?'

Bed was where he wanted her, for the rest of their

natural lives. Just thinking about the night before had him smiling with satisfaction.

Her words of love had been sweet indeed, but sweet didn't come close to describing what had transpired between them for the rest of the night.

Hot was the only word he could think of.

With any luck, he could coax her into repeating the entire thing.

The rain had let up, and pre-dawn light had the house glowing. In the kitchen, fresh muffins sat on the counter next to a coffee maker, filled with a steaming hot brew. Outside on the porch Fric and Frac flitted around in their cage. At his feet, Molly sat and looked up at him, her heart in her eyes.

Home. He felt so at home, so much more so than in his small, undecorated, cold apartment which he'd had no desire to go to.

Bending down, he gave in to the urge and pulled Molly close. She set her big head down on his shoulder and wagged her tail. Her entire body wiggled.

Clay laughed and admitted, 'All these years without a dog. Feels good, Molly, to hold one again. Real good.'

'Why have you gone so many years without a dog?'

Clay jerked at the sound of Hope's voice. Craning his head around, he saw her, standing in the doorway. She wore jeans and his shirt, which gave him such a dizzy rush of love he almost couldn't think.

She clutched a handful of wild flowers, and as she moved into the kitchen, their fresh scent reached him.

She'd gone out and picked flowers.

'Clay?'

Slowly, dreadfully, he rose and met her gaze.

'And how,' she asked carefully, crossing her arms over her middle and holding tightly, as if she felt sick, 'Can you remember that you've gone so many years without a dog if you don't have a memory?'

'Hope,' he said hoarsely, reaching for her even as she took a step back and shook her head. 'Wait.'

'No.' She still hugged herself, but now she threw the flowers down onto the counter with a choked sound that tore at him. 'No! You can remember.'

'Hope – '

'You can remember and you didn't tell me. Why?'

'Would you believe it's complicated?'

Her dark brown eyes filled, even as she ruthlessly blinked the tears back. 'I got up this morning, thinking how lucky I was. Thinking how much I loved you.'

His heart swelled until he felt as if it couldn't possibly fit in his chest. His dream, he thought. This had been his dream, and he'd shattered it. 'Hope, wait.'

'I couldn't sleep,' she said with a bittersweet smile. 'You know the cliché; couldn't eat, couldn't do anything but think of you. I picked you flowers.'

He could well imagine how betrayed she felt. 'You've got to listen to me, Hope. Give me a minute here.'

A sound escaped her, half laugh, half gulping sob. 'It's true, isn't it? You can remember.' She turned from him, covered her face. 'I knew you were hiding something from me. I just never believed . . .' Now she looked at him from eyes burning with pain. 'Why, damn you? Why?'

'I had to.'

'No,' she whispered. 'I'll never believe that.' She whirled and ran.

She didn't get to the door before he'd grabbed her arm and spun her around. She fought him. It took every ounce of energy he had to hold her. 'Hope, please,' he said, grappling with her flailing limbs. 'You don't understand.'

'I understand plenty,' she ground out, nearly slipping from his grasp. 'You let me think you couldn't remember. You made a fool of me.'

'Hope.' He sucked in air sharply when he moved too suddenly and jarred his ribs, but he didn't let her loose. 'Stop it.'

'Yes or no, dammit! Can you remember?'

'Yes,' he hissed, when an elbow snaked in under his guard. Wrapping his arms around her tightly, he bent slightly and wheezed. 'Hell, that hurt.'

'Don't you dare make me feel sorry for you.'

He tensed, holding her close, more for his own safety than anything else. But the beauty in his arms had stopped struggling. Stiff as a rock, she glared at him, hurt and disbelief swimming in her eyes.

He didn't expect the solid right punch to his gut.

Gasping, he dropped his hold on her and held his own middle. 'Don't go,' he managed, suddenly envisioning her taking the car and fleeing from him, only to run into the true danger – Trent Blockwell. 'Please, Hope, don't run.'

She sagged back against the counter, her eyes huge. 'I hit you,' she whispered in shock. 'I actually tried to hurt you.'

'I deserved it,' he assured her grimly, straightening gingerly.

'No. No one deserves it.' She covered her face.

Gently as he could, he took her wrist and held tight, trying to reassure himself that she wouldn't take off now, not until they'd talked.

'Please, don't touch me,' she said, trying to draw back. He went with the motion, coming in close contact with the only woman who'd ever stolen his heart and stirred his soul. 'And don't look at me like that,' she added shakily, closing her eyes.

With his free hand, he touched her face, and in that second it took her to open her eyes, he ran his gaze over her, trying to memorize every detail of her lovely features.

'I can't help but look at you like this,' he told her unevenly, his voice rough with emotion. 'I love you, Hope. I always will. Yes, I have my memory back.'

She made a sound and tried to jerk away, but he held firm, slipping a hand in at her nape and holding her head so she could see him talk.

'You told me you love me,' he said. 'I want to believe that, more than you'll ever know. But there's something I need to believe even more.' He waited a heartbeat. 'I need to know you trust me, Hope.' He nudged her body gently with his own when she remained silent, her huge gaze locked on his. 'Do you? Do you trust me?'

For the longest moment of his life, she stared at him. 'I've never had anyone to trust before.'

He hadn't thought he could feel such pain, just from

words. 'I know that, sweetheart. I know.' He inhaled and asked again. 'Could you try? With me?'

Her eyes, black with so much pain he wanted to cry, closed for a minute. Then she opened them and they were wet. 'I want to.'

'You can,' he assured her grimly. 'I swear, you can.'

The tears clinging to her lashes fell. 'Prove it. Tell me why you hid your memory. What are you hiding?'

With his thumb, he wiped at a teardrop, and wished he could tell her everything. 'I can't, Hope.'

She let out a disbelieving laugh, and her body, so close to his that he could feel her tremble, went taut with nerves. 'Why did you let me think you were hurting, so lost and alone? How could you let me worry like that? It was all I thought about, Clay. Every thought,' she said bitterly, 'every little one revolved around you, and how I could make you better.'

How he wanted to loosen the grip he had on her and run his hands over her shaking body. He could soothe her, he knew he could, but he was afraid. Deathly afraid she'd take off before he could make sure she understood the danger.

'What's the big secret, Clay?'

What could he say? How much could he tell her without giving away her father and his troubles? And when the entire truth came out, would she forgive him for not telling her? Would she understand he'd done it for her?

Her hands unfisted from between them and she touched his chest in silent appeal, only to jerk them back as they connected with his bare skin.

That little involuntary movement killed him. 'Already you can't stand to touch me.'

Her breath caught and she ran her gaze over him slowly. She took a deep breath as sadness filled her eyes. 'It's the opposite,' she said in that low, uncontrolled voice that told him exactly how difficult this was for her. 'The very opposite.' Moistening her lips, she turned her head from him. 'I don't trust myself, Clay. Not around you.'

'Hope.'

She didn't answer, and he turned her back to him. 'Hope – '

'Who are you, Clay? Why are you here? Why haven't you told me the truth before now?'

'So much for trust.'

'Does that mean you're not going to tell me?'

'I'm Clayton Slater. I'm single. I run my own business and I live in Seattle. Alone.'

She dropped her forehead to his chest, slumping against him.

They stood that way for a long moment.

Then she raised her head. 'More.'

'I can't,' he said, his eyes heavy with regret and a thousand other emotions she couldn't face.

'When can you tell me?'

He just looked at her and she wanted to shout in frustration. The worst part was not understanding.

Then something flickered in his eyes, and it told her what she didn't want to know.

He was worried, no terrified, for her.

This entire thing involved her. She knew that as

certainly as she knew her own name. Her muscles clenched.

'How long,' she asked suddenly, straightening so fast he jerked, probably thinking she was going to hit him again. 'How long have you known who you are?' she demanded.

His eyes closed. 'Clay!' she cried, grabbing his bare shoulders and shaking. 'Tell me something. Please, you've got to tell me something!'

'I've known since the night we first made love,' he whispered hoarsely.

She stared at him as that sank in.

'Afterwards, I got that headache, then fell asleep. And when I woke up . . .' He shrugged. 'I knew.'

She could only stare at him. Uncomfortably aware of his wide, sinewy flesh under her hands, she yanked them back.

Then she looked over her shoulder at the door, thinking she had to get out, had to be alone to think, to lick her wounds.

He snagged her waist and hauled him against her so fast her head spun. 'I didn't do this to hurt you,' he said in a voice so tortured, so full of regret and aching promise that fresh tears sprang to her eyes.

'Then why?'

He dropped his chin to his chest, and his words came so softly she couldn't hear them. Then she realized he was swearing, at himself. His shoulders rose with his deep breath, then he lifted his head, piercing her with eyes so clear and green she saw her own anguished reflection.

'I didn't tell you at first because I was afraid I'd lose you.'

He said this slowly, simply. Hope didn't want to think about why that little fact meant so much. Didn't want to think about a lot of things. How he always made sure she could hear him, the way he always talked loudly and clearly without making it obvious. Or making her feel like an idiot. He always did this, even when she didn't return the courtesy, even when she refused to look at him to read his lips.

She inhaled while her thoughts raced. Yes, she'd once thought this man was her destiny, but she must have been mistaken. Mistaken, she told herself firmly while every nerve protested that thought.

His hands at her waist squeezed gently, but didn't let go. For a minute, she just stared at him, at the chest still marred with bruises, at his ribs which were still wrapped. Then she looked into his face. 'I want to believe you,' she said unsteadily. 'I do want to believe you. But how could you possibly have thought you would lose me?'

His bittersweet smile twisted his lips. 'You were in a bind, Hope. You needed a husband, only temporarily. A convenient one, someone who would leave when he got his life together. I fitted that bill perfectly. You agreed to marry me only to get you out of that mess.'

She could feel herself redden.

His hands ran up her arms, closed gently around her face. His gaze went soft and tender. 'But it wasn't just convenience for me, Hope. I fell for you. Fell good and hard for the first time in my life.' His eyes hardened and he said fiercely, 'I would have done anything to have you fall for me the same way, but you didn't. So I took you however I could get you, even though you were only pretending to care for me.'

Pretending! He actually thought she could.

Clay's voice was raw and he dropped his gaze from hers. 'I thought just a little time, just more patience, more care . . . and I could make you love me. Really love me, not just pretend.'

'I never pretended,' she said and his head snapped up. 'Never,' she added in a whisper. When he leaned closer with the obvious intention of kissing her, she lifted her head. 'No.' Her hands fisted. 'This hurts.'

'Hope,' he whispered regretfully.

'Yes, dammit, I lied to you early on. But I told you why, and you said you forgave me.'

'I did.'

'But now you've lied and I don't understand the rest of it at all.'

'I know,' he said grimly.

She had to understand, and opened her mouth to tell him so.

The instant she did, his lips captured hers in a battle for her heart, her soul. His hand tightened in her hair, holding her head to his, while his other drifted low, angling over her back to press her against him.

At the first touch of his tongue to hers, Hope was nearly lost, but not quite.

Clay never stopped the assault, tenderly pulling her closer, closer, until they were locked from head to toe, until her mind and body gave everything she had. His hands took possession, streaking, caressing, cajoling an even stronger response from her, and he got it. Her fists relaxed, her palms spread over his sleek, muscled back, then around to run over his chest.

He groaned, low and deep, and her legs wobbled at the desperate, needy sound.

He was winning and all she could do was kiss him, helplessly. His mouth ran over hers with fierce, devouring hunger, and she tried to hold something back, knowing she was going down for the count.

In sheer panic she tore away. Breath heaving out of her chest, she ripped herself from his grasp.

He reached for her and she held him off with a hand to his chest. 'That was low,' she tossed out, backing off. 'Using . . . that to persuade me.'

'That?' he snapped back angrily, shoving hands through his hair as if it would help him think. 'That? Hope, you can't even say the word. We were making love – '

'No.'

'Yes.'

'It was just a kiss.'

'No way,' he said furiously, stepping towards her. 'That was not just a kiss – '

If she stayed, if she listened to him, or even looked into that achingly familiar face, she was going to give in and forgive something she didn't understand. If she didn't get out now, she'd break right in front of him.

Whirling, she ran through the kitchen door, slamming it behind her.

It didn't stop him for long, given the sound of the door

slamming back open, but she had a head start. It was all she needed to race to the front door, grab her keys and run like hell for her car.

Still, he would have caught her, if it hadn't been for the pebbled walk.

And his bare feet.

As she skidded out of the driveway in her car, his muffled curses vented the air.

CHAPTER 25

Hope got on the highway, heading toward Seattle without a thought for the long drive, or what Kelly would say when she arrived at work and found her gone. She had no idea why she did this, only knew she had to go there. Just as she had to suck air into her laboring lungs. Just as she had to stop at a red light. Just as she had to swipe at her streaming eyes with a tissue so she didn't get in a wreck.

Just as she had to stop loving Clay.

She needed to see her father.

The answers lay with him. She knew this, though she didn't like the thought.

Hours later, bursting unannounced into his office, she stalked grimly to his desk.

One look at her face and he said a curt farewell into the telephone he'd been holding and hung up. 'Hello, Hope.' He gave her a wary smile. 'You don't . . . look well.'

'I don't imagine I do,' she agreed, sitting in the chair by his desk. 'I've had quite a morning.'

'Then close up that damn clinic. Move far away and start a new life. A better one. Do something for yourself.'

She gaped at him in surprise. And sadness. 'You have no idea,' she breathed. 'No idea at all. Running that clinic is for myself.'

'Taking care of other people's health isn't doing something for yourself.'

'Yes, it is.' Why couldn't he understand? 'It gives me hope and joy. Those people come to me. To me, Father. They do this because they trust me. Because I can cure them. I can make a difference.'

'It's a job, Hope.'

'A darned important one! And besides that, it gives me satisfaction. Purpose.' She drew a deep breath. 'I'm sorry you don't understand that.'

'Hope – '

'No.' Now she stood, utterly unable to remain still. 'That clinic is everything to me – ' She broke off. It wasn't true.

Clay was everything.

She slumped back into the chair and stared at her father. 'I don't know why I came here. You don't understand me, not at all.'

'I do,' he said softly, his eyes luminous. 'Hope, listen to me. I do understand you, because we're a lot alike.' He laughed at her horrified expression. 'Just remember that. And . . . do what you have to do.'

'What?'

His gaze hard on hers, he repeated, 'Do what you must.'

Something passed through them, something strange and unaccustomed. Understanding, compassion, yes, but something even more. It stunned her. Hope stood, walked around the desk and reached for his hand. He squeezed it. 'I feel strange,' she whispered to him, leaning on the desk so that their faces were close.

'It's all right, Hope,' he said quietly.

'For the first time in years I feel like you're looking at me.'

Now his eyes misted over. 'I'm sorry. I'm so sorry.'

'You're trying to tell me something,' she said. 'I can feel that you are. Why can't you just say it?'

'You're so much like her, Hope. When I look at you . . .' He touched her hair and smiled sadly. 'I see your mother. So beautiful, so independent. So damned stubborn.'

Hope felt a smile bloom. 'It's the last that gets me into a bit of trouble.'

'Yes, it is.' Again he squeezed her hand. 'Hope, I'm sorry. I want you to know how sorry I've been all these years. What that nanny did to you – '

'It's done,' she said, shaking her head. 'It's over, long over.'

'But you've suffered so.'

'I'm happy now,' she whispered. 'I want you to believe that.'

'You're sure?'

'Yes. Father, are you all right?'

'I will be.' His eyes closed. 'Please. Stay true to yourself. Don't listen to me at all. I'll survive. No one can hurt me more than I've hurt myself.'

'What do you mean?'

He hesitated. 'I lost most of the money I made, Hope. Trent gave me more. Now I owe him everything. Everything!'

'You lost . . . it all? But . . . how?'

He opened his eyes. 'I'm sorry, Hope,' he whispered. 'So sorry. Move away, stay safe and forget me. It's for the best. Don't give in to Trent just to help me . . . I don't deserve it. Clay told me so.'

His secretary came in, smiling sweetly. 'The bank on line three.'

Hope stared at her father, heart drumming. What was happening? And what did Clay have to do with this?

'Father, please,' she begged quickly, as he reached for the phone. 'Can Trent hurt you?'

'I have to take this call,' he said in a low voice for her ears alone.

'Who is Clayton Slater really?' she begged, holding his arm from lifting up the phone.

'I hired him to help me.'

'Mr Broderick,' the secretary said kindly, 'They won't like to be kept holding.'

'Can Trent hurt you, Father?' Hope demanded. 'Can he?'

'Don't worry about me.' They struggled together for the phone.

'Tell me about Trent.'

'You don't have to marry him for me,' her father said with sudden urgency. 'I don't want you to. I just told you I did so you would get all stubborn and do the opposite.' A smile flashed briefly. 'I counted on that.'

She was part of a deal. Marry Trent and he'll leave her father alone. Was that it? And Clay. He'd been working for her father all along, damn his lying hide.

She held firm to the phone. 'What can Trent do to you, Father? Please, tell me.'

'Mr Broderick?' the secretary asked.

'Trent will take everything,' her father whispered to Hope quickly. 'He'll destroy it, then come out smelling like a rose.'

And he'll run for office. He'll win too, Hope thought desperately as her father took his call. He'll win and he'll win. He'll go to the top and no one will stop him.

Her father spoke quietly into the phone, didn't glance up when Hope moved to the door.

'I'll stop him,' she promised softly. 'Don't worry, Father. I'll stop him.'

Hope drove like a demon back home, determined to get some answers once and for all. Clay was going to give them to her, whether he liked it or not.

Clayton Slater. Her father's employee.

Unbelievable.

The drive had never seemed so long before, but it dragged and dragged now. Impatiently, she passed cars, revved through the few lights she came to. Twice, she had to force herself to slow down on the mountain passes.

A ticket now would just really top her day.

Some nerve, she thought shaken, Clay had some nerve. Telling her in that devastatingly husky voice how he'd fallen for her, how he didn't want her to marry him for pretenses. He wanted it to be for real.

He'd been lying the entire time, to help her father.

And if she thought she'd hurt before, it was nothing to this new knowledge. Everything he'd told her, every emotion he'd shown her was a lie.

Even worse, he'd done it to help her father. How was she supposed to stay mad at that? And how was she going to get over the fact that she'd fallen for it? Fallen for a man who'd pretended to love her, to keep her away from a monster.

Only halfway home, she slapped a hand down on her steering wheel and wished she could fly.

Afternoon hadn't completely given way to evening when she finally drove back up her driveway. The house was dark, but she'd expected that. Kelly would have left long ago, if she'd even showed.

If Clay was smart, he'd be laying low. No, Hope thought, that wasn't fair. He had wanted to talk to her, had wanted to explain.

She hadn't given him much of a chance.

Maybe he'd left. She ignored the pang her heart sent up at that and reminded herself that would be for the best. Letting herself in, she locked the front door behind her and stood in the darkened hallway.

She expected to find a sulking Clay, waiting impatiently.

What she got was a grinning Trent.

And a gleaming knife.

CHAPTER 26

Clay raced down the office hallway, more afraid than he'd ever been in his life. He'd better not be too late. If the damn taxi driver hadn't taken so long to come get him, if the jerk hadn't insisted on driving slower than a snail trying to make the speed limit . . . if Hope hadn't run off. So many ifs.

If only Clay knew that Hope was safe. But he couldn't shake the dreadful feeling she wasn't.

He charged into Broderick's office, hoping, praying – then sagged in defeat.

No Hope.

'Where is she?' Clay demanded as Broderick looked up at him. 'Where's Hope?'

'She just left.' Broderick looked down over his nose at Clay. 'What are you bellowing about? My employees will wonder.'

'I don't give a damn about your employees,' Clay grated, feeling his blood chill. He'd just missed Hope. A helplessness welled up within him. 'Where did she go?'

'I don't know,' her father admitted. 'But she was

upset. Why the hell aren't you with her anyway? You're supposed to be keeping her safe. Instead, she's alone, driving all over the state – '

'Upset?' His fault, dammit. But then Clay caught sight of something in Broderick's gaze, something that had him moving closer, leaning over the desk. 'Why was she upset?'

Broderick shut his mouth and looked away.

The dread increased until he could hardly breathe. 'What did you tell her?'

'Nothing I shouldn't have a long time ago.'

No. Dammit, no. 'You told her about Trent blackmailing you.' The ensuing silence told him everything he needed to know. 'Good job. Real good.' Ignoring Broderick's small wince at the sarcasm, Clay went on, mercilessly. 'Of course you told her that you didn't really want her to marry Trent as well.'

This was greeted with more silence.

Clay's anger doubled. *Tripled.* He could picture Hope taking the news, realizing that she'd become a pawn in this terribly dangerous game. Realizing that in order to save the father she loved in spite of everything, she would have to marry a man who scared her to death. He knew it was enough to make any woman panic, enough to provoke anyone past their limit. But Hope wasn't just any woman, she was amazingly strong, incredibly enduring. She wouldn't panic. He told himself this, but still, he hated knowing that at this moment, Hope was most likely helplessly alone.

'I had to,' Broderick said finally, a little defensively. 'I had to make her understand everything.'

'Of course you told her that you had lost everything to Trent, but that you kept it from her to protect her. Right?'

Broderick's eyes closed.

Clay swore softly, shoved agitated hands through his hair. 'No,' he hissed through his teeth. 'No.' He jerked his head up at his next thought. 'You didn't tell her I was working for you. Tell me you didn't.'

'I had to.'

So he could add betrayal to the list of what Hope had to be feeling. She would be believing the worst of him about now. 'How could you?' he demanded. 'How could you do this to her?'

'She came here knowing something was wrong, that I was hiding something. I thought she knew more than she did. You know how she is, always feeling things. She took one look at me and knew. I had to fill in the blanks.'

Clay whirled and kicked the chair, then kicked it again, despite the pain shooting up his leg. He turned on Broderick, furious. 'You've just shoved her right into Trent's waiting arms. Everything you feared is about to come true. Dammit!'

'I had to,' Broderick said quietly. 'I had to make my peace with her. Before I go.'

The anger drained abruptly from Clay. 'You're too stubborn to die.' At least, Clay hoped he was.

Broderick smiled and closed his eyes. 'I'm not going to die, you're right. I'm far too stubborn – and greedy – for that. I'm going to disappear, Slater. Take the nest egg I've hidden over the years and disappear.'

'So you're a quitter. At least it doesn't run in the family.'

'It's over for me here. I just want to be sure everything works out for Hope. She deserves that much at least.'

'Yes, she does.' Clay sighed. Why couldn't he hate this man? 'Where did she go?'

'Where she always goes,' Broderick said with a sigh of his own. 'Back to the clinic.'

'Don't you dare disappear until this is all over and you get a chance to say good-bye to your daughter. She'll never get over it if you don't.' Clay started to race for the door, then paused. She already had a head start on him. She'd be alone there, far too alone for comfort.

Abruptly changing direction, he yanked up the phone.

'What are you doing?' Broderick asked. 'Why aren't you going after her?'

'I am going to go after her, believe me,' he said grimly. 'Just as soon as I do one thing.'

'What's that?'

The impatience in the old man's voice assured Clay he did care what happened to his daughter, desperately. Clay was trying hard to remember that, despite his urge to strangle the man for putting Hope in even greater danger.

'Slater! What are you doing?'

'Taking out insurance.' He called information for Kelly's phone number and prayed the nurse would be home. For she was all the help Hope would get until Clay could get back to her.

Hope stared at Trent in disbelief. 'What are you doing here?'

'I've been waiting for you for hours, Hope. Actually, years.'

'I – I don't understand.'

'Sure you do. It didn't have to be like this, babe, really, it didn't. This is all your own doing, so I refuse to be sorry for how I have to treat you now.' He said this lightly, even kindly, and a chill ran up Hope's spine. Trent was not a light man, nor a kind one.

Where was Clay? Despite what had happened between them, Hope had never wanted him more than she did in that moment. 'The clinic is closed,' she said absurdly. She felt cold, so very cold. And scared.

He said something low and mumbled, but by the look of him, it wasn't casual banalities.

'What?' she asked, her heart hammering wildly in her throat.

He swore at her then, carefully and thoroughly, with a look of such disgust her stomach twisted. She actually opened her mouth to apologize for not hearing him, but managed to stop herself.

She would not be sorry for not hearing, not ever again.

If nothing else, she had learned this. Through patience and understanding, Clay had proven to her time and time again, her lack of hearing didn't make her abnormal.

'Listen better when I speak to you,' Trent said in a cruel, hard voice. Then he said something else as he ran a hand over his face and she lost those words as well.

More panic now, because he looked at her, obviously awaiting a response. 'I'm sor – I didn't hear you,' she admitted and almost before she'd finished speaking,

Trent struck out with his knife-free hand, slapping her hard across the mouth, spinning her nearly all the way around with its force.

A hard hand to her back shoved her face up against the door, and for one horrifying moment, she was trapped between door and hard, ungiving flesh.

Dizzy now, she shook her head, then realized Trent, pressed hard against her back, had spoken to her.

Dropping her forehead to the door, she bit back her fear, forced back the pain. 'Trent,' she whispered hoarsely, 'I can't hear you.'

Nausea joined the dizziness when he whipped her back around brutally fast, slamming her spine to the door. Gripping her arms in white-knuckled fists, he spoke quickly and through his teeth.

She missed every word to the roaring in her ears.

'Damn you,' he snapped, clearly, loudly, shaking her hard enough to rattle the teeth in her aching head. '*Listen-to-me-when-I-speak-to-you*!'

Blinking furiously, she bit her already bleeding lip and promised herself she wouldn't cry. 'I'm t – trying.'

'I refuse to repeat everything I say to you.'

He emphasized this with another shake, which brought her head in painful contact with the door, making her bite her lip again. She brought a hand up between them to touch her numb mouth, stunned. Almost instantly, the blessed numbness faded, a hot red streak of pain replacing it. Funny, she thought distractedly. She would have pegged herself for a woman who would turn cowardly with fear. Weepy. Pathetically hysterical.

Instead, she found courage, even as her veins iced over in terror. 'You might have to get used to repeating your words. Or at least saying them slower, more clearly. I'm more than half deaf, Trent. You can't ignore that, no matter how much you want to.'

His mouth tightened.

'I want you to leave,' she said in a little voice that she wished had come out bigger, stronger.

'Oh, I'm not leaving.' He shifted, moved closer, until she could feel his breath on her face. His body against hers made her feel ill. 'I'm not leaving until we have a little chat.' He leaned on her with all his weight, holding the knife up between them, close to her face. His belt buckle dug into her ribs. His free hand reached up and tightened in her hair, yanking hard enough to bring tears to her eyes.

'You're hurting me.'

'You've hurt me.'

'Trent, please.'

'No. You please,' he snapped. 'I've tried to do this nicely. For years I've waited.' His face hardened. 'I waited while you ignored me, laughed at me, scorned me.' He tugged on her hair harder, until her head had no choice but to tip up at a sharp angle. 'You played doctor. Pretended you didn't want a man in your life. Used sympathy in your favor to keep this clinic going.'

She wanted to deny that, but he had such a grip on her she was afraid to move.

'Then Clayton Slater comes along, glances at you and you give yourself to him without a second thought. I'm going to kill him for that.'

Her heart leaped. 'No!'

Something flickered in his eyes. 'All I needed was a show of support from you and your father. Neither of you could be bothered.'

'My father supported you.'

He raised the knife hand and she gasped, flinching, shrinking back against the ungiving door. Trent slammed it against the door, inches from her face. 'I never got support!' he said viciously. 'Never! I had to take everything I have.'

Her neck felt like it would snap right in half if he didn't let up on the brutal grip on her hair. The sight of the knife so close to her skin had her shaking.

He must have felt some of the terrible tension in her rigid body for he looked at her coldly, then thoughtfully. 'Things are starting to work for me now. I've a feeling my luck is about to change.' He nudged her with his full length. 'You're going to change it for me, Hope.'

'No.'

'Oh, yes,' he said slowly. Then he gave her a smile that sent shivers down to her trembling soul. 'Should have done this a long time ago,' he said, nodding his head.

'Done what?'

The hand that held the knife was on the door, inches from her face. His body pinned hers. The hand tangled in her hair lifted, freed her aching neck. His knuckles stroked her cheek until, with a choked sound, she turned her head away. But hard fingers gripped her jaw and brought her face back around.

'I own your father,' he said roughly. 'And that business he loves beyond reason. I have plans, Hope. Big plans. And you're a part of them.'

'No.' She cringed when his fingers tightened on her.

'You marry me, play the loving wife, and I'll let your father live when he misses his next payment to me – which he is going to do, believe me. He has no way to pay it.'

Horrified, she stared at him. 'What?'

His jaw tightened, his eyes went ugly with hate. 'I just told you to listen carefully. Already you can't follow directions. I'm going to have to do something about that,' he muttered to himself. 'Can't have the President's wife looking like an idiot.'

It was unbelievable. He'd completely lost his grip on reality. She squirmed, thinking if she could just get a hand free, or loosen her legs, she could fight him. Just the thought of the shining knife in her peripheral vision was enough to have her breaking out into a sweat, but she had to make a move.

Without warning, Trent pressed his body into her stomach, hard. The air whooshed out of her lungs. As she struggled and gasped for air, he slowly lifted his considerable weight from her middle and smiled evilly. 'Don't even think it again,' he whispered in her face. 'You're stuck here. With me.'

She could hardly breathe, much less respond.

'Now,' he said icily. 'Here's the deal. Say you'll be a nice little girl and you'll follow the rules. You'll marry me. Tonight.'

'Promise . . . you won't hurt him,' she wheezed, rubbing her stomach.

Disgust crossed his features. 'You have such an ugly

voice. I never really realized before. I wonder if we can fix that somehow?'

She went cold inside, absolutely cold.

'No matter,' he said suddenly. 'You'll talk very little.' He chuckled to himself, then ran his free hand down her body until she twisted, trying to escape his probing, hurtful fingers.

How could she do this? How could she go through with this and live? Having this man own her, dictate to her, treat her as if she were less than human? How could she handle him touching her?

The tears welled then, she couldn't help it. But all she could think about at the moment was how Clay had touched her, how he'd drawn from her responses she didn't know she had, emotions she didn't realize lived inside her.

No, he didn't really love her, but she loved him. She probably would forever.

Where was he now?

'Let's move it,' Trent said suddenly, his voice different, thicker, deeper. Grabbing her wrist in a grip of steel, he ruthlessly tugged her down the hallway. 'Where should we go?' he wondered out loud, yanking her despite her futile efforts to free her hand. 'The clinic?' he mused as they passed the hallway. 'Nah.' He stopped so suddenly she plowed into him.

He grinned down at her and if she hadn't frozen in horror before, she did right then.

'Here,' he said in the doorway of the room Clay had been sleeping in. 'Here is where I'll make you my wife in the biblical sense.'

She must have made a sound. His brows came together tightly, his grip on her wrist tightened so that she could no longer feel her fingers.

'What's the matter, Hope?' he asked, drawing her resisting form to him. He held up the knife as a reminder and she stilled. 'This room pose a problem for you?'

She could only stare at the gleaming steel he flashed in front of her face.

'I figured since you've been giving yourself freely to Slater, you'd have a particular fondness for this room.'

'Trent, please.'

'*Trent, please,*' he mimicked, then straightened. 'I like it when you beg.' With his superior strength, he easily drew her arms up over her head. 'Let's hear you say it again.'

Stubbornly, she tightened her mouth. He'd have a fight, she promised herself. She wouldn't give in without a fight.

Where was Clay?

She never saw the vicious blow coming, and it caught her on the side of the head. Pain exploded behind her eyes, yet she never fell.

Trent held her upright. His lips were moving, she saw, but for the life of her, she couldn't decide which of his four faces to concentrate on.

'Dammit,' she heard from the fog that surrounded her. 'Forget begging. I'll just take.'

It took a second to realize that she was falling and this time, it wasn't dizziness. Trent followed her down onto the bed and held her there. With one hard yank, he ripped open the shirt she wore. Buttons flew.

'Nice,' he murmured, nostrils flaring as he stared down at her. He shoved up her skirt.

Anger and humiliation ruled her. But before she could draw in a breath to scream, he encircled her throat and squeezed.

Choking, her hands automatically came up, clawing at him. He loosened his hold and glared down into her eyes. Slowly, he lifted the knife. 'It would be a shame to hurt you, Hope. After all, this is just the beginning. Now this is your last chance. Promise me you'll do what I say.'

Before she could so much as draw a breath, Trent stiffened, and loosened his grip on her. Then his eyes rolled back in his head and he fell full weight on her.

Above him appeared Kelly's white, pinched-looking face. She held up an empty syringe. 'How could I ever have thought he was as good looking as Clay?' she wondered aloud, her voice strained even as she tried to joke.

Hope immediately closed her eyes and concentrated on breathing. Breathing is a good thing, she told herself as Kelly shoved Trent's prone body off her and helped her up. A very good thing.

Trent slid bonelessly off the bed, onto his face. He didn't budge. Kelly kicked him, hard. 'Oops,' she said mildly. 'Got in my way there.' She glanced down into Trent's slack face for a long moment, as if to make sure he was really out. Then she shifted her concentration to Hope.

'How badly are you hurt?' she asked slowly and clearly.

Hope couldn't think of herself now, not yet. She held

her head gingerly and peered over the edge of the bed at the man that had so terrified her. 'He doesn't look quite so scary eating carpet, does he?'

'No, he doesn't,' Kelly said gently. She pulled a tissue from her pocket and came close. 'Let me help you, Hope.' Carefully she held it to Hope's swollen and bleeding lip. 'Where else are you hurt, honey? Tell me.'

Hope started to shake then and Kelly murmured in concern.

'No,' Hope said harshly when Kelly tried to stretch her out on the bed and wrap her in a blanket. 'I can't relax until he's taken care of.'

Kelly nodded, then disappeared. She was back in less than a minute holding up rope. 'I was a damn good Girl Scout,' she said in a cheery voice that shook. 'Got my knot-tying badge when I was thirteen.'

Hope let out a choked laugh. 'I knew there was another reason I hired you.'

'I've called the sheriff but you and I both know he'll have to finish his donuts first,' Kelly said when Trent had been thoroughly tied up on her floor, spread-eagled between her bed and desk. As a last-minute decision, she'd gagged him too. 'Nothing quite as attractive as a silent man.'

Hope could only stare down at him. Her head hurt and she was cold to her very bones.

'Hope.'

She jerked when Kelly touched her arm gently. When Hope turned to her, she realized by Kelly's expression she'd probably said her name more than once.

'Let me help you, please.' Gently, slowly, Kelly held

up Hope's own bathrobe. 'Let's put this on. It'll help get you warm.'

Hope looked down at herself and saw the shirt she wore – Clay's shirt – neatly ripped wide open, revealing her white cotton bra, her quivering stomach and brand new darkening bruises on the sensitive white skin. The full skirt she wore had slid back down somewhat, but still exposed her legs to high on her thighs. Hastily, she smoothed it down, making a little sound of fresh humiliation. Her throat hurt and she could imagine the bruises forming there as well.

'My head and mouth hurt,' she said in a hoarse voice, gingerly touching her neck. Then she lifted the shaking hand to her mouth. It came away bloody. 'Actually, I think everything hurts.'

'I know,' Kelly answered carefully. 'Hope, I'm sorry. I had no idea what he was capable of, how dangerously sick he is until it was far too late.' Her eyes shimmered with rage and fear.

Hope imagined Kelly's eyes reflected her own emotions. But Hope's anger was in the background, far behind the terror and nerves that still dictated her. She wanted to be held, comforted.

With a half-baked idea of finding Clay still somewhere in the house, she stood up. 'I want Clay,' she whispered brokenly, not realizing she spoke the words aloud.

Just as she spoke, Kelly turned towards the door, telling Hope without words that the nurse heard something, or someone.

Unreasonable panic overcame Hope and without thinking, she covered her face, unable to bear anything else. At the hard impact of the carpet on her knees, she realized she'd sunk to the floor.

When hands touched her shoulders, she jerked and screamed. Then lifted her head and stared into the most beloved, endearing set of dark green eyes she'd ever seen. 'Clay.'

CHAPTER 27

Just the sight of Clay had Hope relaxing in relief. The instant she did, her muscles took over, shaking violently.

Clay's jaw tightened, his eyes misted. The fingers on her shoulders tightened, then immediately gentled. He sent a quick questioning look over his shoulder to where Kelly hovered, still holding her robe.

'I haven't gotten to check her yet,' Kelly told him, her eyes wet. 'I don't know. Clay, hurry.'

'Hope, sweetheart,' Clay said in an unbearably tender voice when he turned back to her, yanking off his own long-sleeved t-shirt. 'I'm going to put this on you, you're cold. Arms in, there you go,' he said, drawing it over her head. It smelled like him and held his wonderful body heat.

She felt him turn his head to stare at the limp and still-tied Trent. The rumble of his chest told her he was speaking and she looked up to catch his last words to Kelly.

'. . . A knife! She fought him off and he was armed with a knife?'

Hope shivered.

His arms convulsed around her before he pulled away to run his hands and gaze over her quickly, his eyes grim. Kelly dropped down beside them, her face tense. Hope realized they were looking for a knife wound and she shivered again.

'He didn't cut me.'

'You're cold.' He drew her against him carefully, gently, as if she were the finest china. Then he surged to his feet and she grabbed at him dizzily. 'I've got you,' he told her, cradling her against his warm, solid, now bared chest. He shifted her with a slight wince, then he took her out of the room, down the hallway and up the stairs to her own room. He tried to set her on the bed, but she clung stubbornly, unable to let go.

'No,' she murmured, knowing she was being silly, that she had to let him go. That now the danger had passed, he couldn't want to hold her any more. She was probably hurting him.

But she couldn't force her fingers off him.

'I've got you,' he murmured over and over, hugging her to him. She could feel the slamming, frantic beat of his heart. 'I'm not going anywhere,' he assured her, bending over her to kiss her temple softly. 'I promise.' And he turned, backed onto the bed, still holding her close. Briefly, his gaze raised to Kelly's, who had followed them. He nodded at something she said and she hurried from the room.

'She saved me,' Hope murmured, snuggling close.

'I know,' he said hoarsely, ducking down to look into her cloudy eyes. 'I called her from your father's office.' Thank goodness he had, though he'd never forgive himself for arriving too late. Too damned late.

Clay hugged the trembling woman in his arms, ignoring whatever discomfort he felt in his ribs. 'Hope,' he whispered huskily. 'I'm sorry.' But her head was now tucked beneath his chin and she most likely missed every word he said. Pausing to rub his cheek over hers, he waited until she looked at him.

Her pupils were tiny pinpoints surrounded by a sea of deep brown fear and pain. Shock. He wanted to yell, wanted to swear, wanted to go smash something, but none of that would help her right now.

She continued to shake.

Enveloping her in his arms as tightly as he could, Clay kissed the top of her head and rocked her back and forth.

'I thought he had hurt you,' she said finally.

'He did hurt you,' he said, then had to grit his teeth hard as he lifted a hand and gently touched her bruised face. The image of her kneeling on the floor, eyes wild, hair tangled, her mouth bloody, the shirt ripped practically off her back . . . it would haunt him forever. His voice was thick with emotion when he asked, 'Was I too late, Hope?'

'I'm okay.' Her voice trembled, but her body had stopped being wracked by shudders.

'No, you're not.'

A muffled sound that might have been a groaning laugh escaped her. 'I'm a doctor, remember? I could use some Tylenol though. Extra strength.'

He closed his eyes a minute, relishing holding her in his arms, safe, sound . . . alive. But how long had she been with Trent? What had he done to her? What hurt that he couldn't see?

'Clay,' Hope said quietly, squirming a little.

He loosened his tight grip but didn't let go, couldn't bring himself to.

'I'm really okay,' she said, lifting an icy hand to his face. She shrugged, looking embarrassed. 'I just lost it there for a minute, that's all.'

'You're not okay,' he said through his teeth, pressing her hand to his face for a minute before kissing the palm. Lightly, he touched the bruises already forming at her throat. The urge to kill shocked him. 'Did he – '

'No,' she said quickly, hugging him again, shaking her head against his chest, tickling his nose with her hair. 'No, he didn't. I don't want to talk about him any more. Please, let's not.'

But she had to. They had to. 'I just missed you at your father's office.'

Hope froze. Her eyes, those wonderfully expressive eyes, shuttered. Right before his eyes, she withdrew into a shell. 'Funny how you do that to me,' she said. 'Make me forget everything that's going on.'

'I came after you as fast as I could.' A knot of tension clogged his throat.

'I should thank you for that,' Hope said stiffly. 'But then again, it's what you were paid to do, wasn't it?'

'What are you talking about?'

'Thank goodness it's all over. We've taken up so much of your time.'

His gut tightened at the finality of it. 'Hope – '

The brightness in her voice sounded loud, forced.

'You're free to go now,' she said with a brittle smile. 'Trent is caught. My father is safe. Your job is done here. What a relief that must be to you.'

She leaped up, then put a hand to her head as she swayed crazily. Swearing, Clay jerked upright and reached for her, but she backed away. 'Don't,' she choked. 'Please, don't. I can't bear it if you touch me now. Now that I know it's all been a farce.' She moved to the door, then turned back when he called her name.

'I don't want to see you again, Clay. I'm sorry, I know that sounds ungrateful, and I'm not. Believe me, I'm not. I just can't . . .' Her voice broke and so did his heart. 'I just can't see you again.'

She ran from the room.

Hope refused to speak to him alone again. The sheriff did finally show, and it was Kelly who stood by Hope's side as she gave her statement.

Clay stood by helplessly and listened as Hope described how he'd been terrorizing her and her father. Watched with a sinking heart as Hope tried to put it all behind her and pretend it didn't matter.

But it did matter. It mattered so much that he couldn't even think about letting it all go.

He bided his time, waiting until the house had cleared, until it was so late that it was almost early. Faint tinges of pink lined the eastern sky when he came into the kitchen and found her, surrounded by a sea of animals.

With a sad smile, he moved into her line of vision and looked at her.

She dropped her gaze to the black cat in her lap. 'I just

realized,' she said. 'You don't have a way into town. I could call – '

'I don't want to leave, Hope. Not without you.'

She stroked the cat with unsteady hands, then reached down for the other two who meowed for attention. Clay thought she hadn't heard him, and he moved closer, hunkering down before her.

Molly licked his face. Gently, he held her off and touched Hope's thigh.

'I don't want you to stay,' she said finally, quietly. 'I hate pity.'

'Is that what you think?' he asked roughly. 'That I pity you?'

'What else?'

'You know what else,' he said, reaching for her hand and bringing it to his chest where his heart beat out steady and strong. And terrifyingly fast. 'I love you, Hope.'

'You – ' Her voice cracked, speaking volumes about how much his words meant. 'You don't have to say that any more.' Those eyes he loved, were like twin pools of melting black ice. 'The job is over and I'm safe. The sheriff even said that with all the proof stacked against Trent, my father would likely gain back most of his capital in court. Certainly the money that was stolen from you that night.'

'I don't care about the money,' he started angrily, but she interrupted him.

'You'll get it. Then you'll leave. My father doesn't have to use reverse psychology on me any more with Trent going straight to jail. He doesn't have to worry I'll make any stupid mistakes.'

'Stupid mistakes – ' He cut off the angry retort and drew a deep breath, wincing only slightly at the fading ache in his ribs. 'Have you spoken to him again then?'

'Yes.' She met his gaze squarely, though her cheeks reddened. 'I realize now that I jumped to some conclusions, several of which aren't true.'

'Such as?' he asked gently, tucking back her hair to see her better.

'Such as you weren't really hired to keep me safe, as I'd thought.' Her blush deepened. 'This is very difficult for me, Clay. I hate being wrong.'

'Do you hate being stubborn, too?' he asked with a smile. 'Because you are the most stubborn woman I know.'

'Would you like to shift this conversation to personality faults?' she asked stiffly. 'Because then I could tell you, you're a bit – '

He laughed. 'No. I know exactly what I am, Hope. And it's hopelessly in love with you.'

Her heart swelled. A desperate yearning unraveled within her. A smidgen of hope flickered, but she ruthlessly stamped it down. It was impossible, no man had ever been able to see enough of the real Hope to feel that way. No man could.

'I am, Hope,' he promised in that silky voice. 'It will never change.'

'That's not true, it can't be,' she maintained steadily. 'You were hired to find the leak. To connect Trent to my father's financial troubles. That job is completed. You're going to leave.'

'No.'

She refused to think about that softly spoken denial. 'My father said he can now afford to pay you a bonus, for keeping me safe. You should have plenty of money – '

'I already have plenty of money.' Earnestly, he leaned forward, touching her face. 'I would never accept money to protect you, Hope. That was a job I wanted as my own, not because someone asked me.'

She tried not to think of how his velvety voice moved her as no other ever had. In her world, any sound was sacred, and the sound of his voice had become the most sacred of all. 'But you didn't tell me the truth. You could have. I would have believed you.'

The stroke of his finger over her cheek felt so good, so right, so unbearably sweet, she had to turn her face away. Gently, he turned her back to him, meeting her gaze square on with such heart-warming honesty it brought a lump to her throat.

'You say that now,' he told her softly. 'But would you really have believed me? Your guard was up, from the very beginning. I had to fight you every step of the way, for every bit of affection, for every single confidence. Every time our relationship took one step forward, you took us back three.'

'I was afraid of what you make me feel.'

His eyes looked at her solemnly. 'I know. You terrified me as well.'

For some reason that surprised her. 'You're not afraid of anything.'

Now he smiled, that slow, gorgeous smile that revved her pulse. 'I wasn't. Until you.' His face went serious as he looked at her. 'I wonder if you'll ever realize how much you mean to me? How much I want you in my life, for real. Forever.'

Her heart skipped a beat. 'It was all pretense, remember?'

'Not for me,' he said with a slow shake of his head. 'Never for me.'

'You . . . you're telling me that you didn't just pretend to fall in love with me so I wouldn't give in to Trent's blackmail and marry him?'

He laughed. *Laughed.*

'I don't see what's so funny,' she said primly.

'No, I can see you don't,' he said, not bothering to wipe the asinine grin off his face.

She crossed her arms. 'Care to enlighten me?'

That grin spread. 'I love it when you go all doctory on me, Hope. You know, when you talk in that uppity tone and look down your nose at me.'

'I'm so glad you find me amusing.'

With an obvious effort, he bit back his smile. 'I'm not all that sociable, Hope. I came from a small, quiet family, went directly into the military and have worked for myself ever since. There've not been a lot of people in my life to complicate it. I guess you could call me a loner.'

She felt her expression change, slip. 'I know so little about you,' she whispered.

'I know.' He brought her hand to his mouth, kissed her palm. 'I'm trying to fix that. For the first time in my life, I'm trying to let someone in. I'm not very good at that. That's why I laughed before, when you accused me of pretending to love you.'

'I don't understand.'

'Sweetheart, I wouldn't have pretended to fall in love to save my own sorry hide. I fell and I fell hard. Damn hard,' he said with a wry smile, tugging a strand of hair gently. 'You pack a wallop, Doctor. Got a cure?'

'You almost died because of us. How could you ever forgive that?'

'You almost died because of me,' he said carefully, but she saw the remembered emotion leap in his eyes. 'Because I didn't keep you safe, Trent almost got you. How can you ever forgive that?'

'It wasn't your fault!' she cried.

He just looked at her, all the love and patience, and warmth and affection there in his eyes, just waiting for her to take. Oh, she wanted to. How badly she wanted to just reach out and grab it. Self-doubt held her back.

'I'm not going to rush you,' he told her, gently scooping first one cat, then another out of her lap. 'Dewey, get,' he said with a smile, patting the affronted cat on his rear as it stalked away. 'It's my turn now, Louie.'

She looked at him in amazement. 'How did you tell them apart? You're always complaining – '

'You're not paying attention,' he chided lightly. 'I can tell them apart, I just didn't want to. Didn't want to risk my heart.' He gave her a look of such intensity, her knees wobbled. 'But I was fighting an uphill battle. I have risked my heart. It's all yours, Hope.' His smile revealed a touching amount of fear. 'Be kind.'

Then he reached for Huey, who had jumped into her recently cleared lap. 'Scram,' he said kindly. With her lap clear, he moved forward on his knees until he bumped hers, spreading them with light fingers. When their bodies were flush, he cupped her face, kissed her nose, her cheeks, each eye before settling his mouth to hers in a long, stirring kiss.

'You love me,' she breathed, lifting her head.

'Ridiculously.' He slipped a hand over her belly, the possessive, protective gesture warming her.

'I'm not pregnant,' she whispered a little breathlessly. 'You know that.'

'You weren't,' he corrected with a hot gaze that tripped her heart. 'But I didn't protect you because I thought there was no need. And after last night . . .'

'It couldn't happen that fast,' she said, shivering in delight when his fingers spread wide and slid upward to claim a breast.

'No?' He grinned wickedly. 'So we need to . . . practise?'

She laughed. 'I haven't said I've forgiven you yet.'

'You've forgiven me,' he said with an irksome amount of confidence. 'What you haven't done is decide to risk it.'

'Risk what?'

'Your heart.' He kissed her again, lingered over it until they both had a difficult time breathing evenly. 'Try it,' he whispered, nudging her. 'Reach for it. It'll be good, you'll see.'

She opened her mouth to answer but he put a finger to her lips. 'For some reason, you have a hard time believing that no one could love you for you. But I do, Hope. I love all seven of your animals, from every crazy cat to each insane bird. I love the way your voice sounds, all low and husky, especially after I've kissed you senseless. I love the way you feel things, the way you care so much for others. I love everything about you. Please, believe that. Accept it.'

'I do,' she whispered, suddenly vividly reminded of the night she'd found him. Of how somehow she'd known it would lead up to this. Carefully, she traced a lingering bruise on his strong jaw. 'I have to believe,' she said with a smile. 'Because you're my destiny, Clayton Slater.'

'Forever?'

The question in his voice told her he wasn't nearly as confident as he would have her believe. 'Forever – ' she started to say. But the word died in her throat as his lips came down on hers in a devastatingly soft, tender kiss that poured love from one heart to another.

'Clay?' she whispered a minute later, lifting her lips from his with effort. 'Uh . . . It's sort of nine animals,' she said a little sheepishly. 'You see, I found these two injured mice this morning in the pantry . . .'

Clay's shout of laughter echoed throughout the house.

EPILOGUE

Clay's fingers raced over the keyboard. He had a deadline to meet, a crucial one. Next to him, another set of fingers raced over a second keyboard. Concentration marred the small features.

'Sweetheart,' he said with a laugh. 'Are you working hard?'

'Just like you, Daddy,' Joy said seriously, nodding her head. 'I have deadlines, you know.'

'We couldn't miss a deadline,' he agreed with sham severity.

'Definitely not,' his prim little five-year-old told him. 'How is yours coming?'

Clay glanced down at the curriculum he was putting to disk for Joy's kindergarten class. 'I'll be finished.'

'Good.' Joy's dark brown eyes twinkled mischievously. 'Knew I could count on you, Daddy, no matter what Grandpa says. Momma says you're the fastest hacker – er, programmer – in the west. The best too.'

Ah, being the center of his daughter's universe was indeed a grand place.

'I'll get it,' Joy said calmly, still smiling at him.

'I didn't hear – ' He sighed. 'Go ahead, sweetheart. Get the phone.'

Joy laughed, a bright, happy sound. 'Silly Daddy. It isn't the phone that's going to ring. It's the – '

Intercom. It buzzed, accompanied by the red light. Returning his daughter's smug smile, Clay lifted the receiver. 'Sweetheart,' he said to Hope, 'do you suppose our next little Russian gypsy could simply be sweet and genius? I feel outnumbered here.'

Hope laughed. 'If you want to really feel outnumbered, come to the clinic. I've a full house.'

'Need help?'

'Sure.' Her voice came clearly over the line, low and husky as usual, yet full of joy and love. 'But I just wanted to tell you something.'

'You love me?' Clay guessed.

'How did you know?'

He laughed. 'Just a feeling.'

THE EXCITING NEW NAME IN WOMEN'S FICTION!

PLEASE HELP ME TO HELP YOU!

Dear *Scarlet* Reader,

Good news – thanks to your excellent response we are able to hold another super Prize Draw, which means that **you could win 6 months' worth of free *Scarlets*!** Just return your completed questionnaire to us **before 31 January 1998** and you will automatically be entered in the draw that takes place on that day. If you are lucky enough to be one of the first two names out of the hat we will send you four new *Scarlet* romances, every month for six months.

So don't delay – return your form straight away!*

Looking forward to hearing from you,

Sally Cooper

Editor-in-Chief, *Scarlet*

*Prize draw offer available only in the UK, USA or Canada. Draw is not open to employees of Robinson Publishing, or of their agents, families or households. Winners will be informed by post, and details of winners can be obtained after 31 January 1998, by sending a stamped addressed envelope to address given at end of questionnaire.

Note: further offers which might be of interest may be sent to you by other, carefully selected, companies. If you do not want to receive them, please write to Robinson Publishing Ltd, 7 Kensington Church Court, London W8 4SP, UK.

QUESTIONNAIRE

Please tick the appropriate boxes to indicate your answers

1 Where did you get this Scarlet title?
   Bought in supermarket ☐
   Bought at my local bookstore ☐ Bought at chain bookstore ☐
   Bought at book exchange or used bookstore ☐
   Borrowed from a friend ☐
   Other (please indicate) _____

2 Did you enjoy reading it?
   A lot ☐   A little ☐   Not at all ☐

3 What did you particularly like about this book?
   Believable characters ☐   Easy to read ☐
   Good value for money ☐   Enjoyable locations ☐
   Interesting story ☐   Modern setting ☐
   Other _____

4 What did you particularly dislike about this book?
   _____

5 Would you buy another Scarlet book?
   Yes ☐   No ☐

6 What other kinds of book do you enjoy reading?
   Horror ☐   Puzzle books ☐   Historical fiction ☐
   General fiction ☐   Crime/Detective ☐   Cookery ☐
   Other (please indicate) _____

7 Which magazines do you enjoy reading?
   1. _____
   2. _____
   3. _____

And now a little about you –

8 How old are you?
   Under 25 ☐   25–34 ☐   35–44 ☐
   45–54 ☐   55–64 ☐   over 65 ☐

cont.